THE SOUND OF SUMMER

THE SOUND OF SUMMER

MEAGAN WILLIAMSON

For my littlest love.

I'll always stay.

1

EVERETT

Every musician has a list of demands in their rider. From temperature-controlled spaces to private jets, Evian-branded water bottles to all-white roses, the sky is the limit. Weird Al once requested a new Hawaiian shirt for every venue he performed at. But me? I only asked for one.

"Twelve, thirteen, fourteen..." I whisper to four empty walls. My eyes are closed, shoulders pressed against the back of an overstuffed leather chair. Tight black cotton stretches over my biceps. I should feel the draft against my bare forearms as it twists around my dressing room, but I don't feel anything. I don't *hear* anything either.

"Fifteen, sixteen, seventeen..."

There's no more *Check, one, two,* or *Let's go over the look for tonight.* Not a *tick, tick, tick* from a clock on the wall, or the scuff of a hundred pairs of crew boots against amphitheater floors. Far into the recesses of my mind, I escape reality and float through time in a never-ending sea of my only request: *Silence.*

"Eighteen, nineteen, tw—"

A fist pounds, rattling the doorframe, and my eyes pop open.

The bottom of the door grates against the cement floor as Todd barges in.

"Five-minute warning, man," he says, checking off something on his clipboard and pressing the pad of his finger over the microphone in his ear. He doesn't even look up at me.

I release a breath and forgive him for not delivering his warning like we agreed upon—a soft tap on a closed door.

"I'll be right there."

My manager nods and slips from the room. I close my eyes, sink back against the seat, and continue counting.

"Twenty-three, twenty-four, twenty-five..."

My mind conjures up a performer—charismatic, talented, entertaining—everything a country music artist should be. The definition of what the world expects *me* to be. When I walk into a room, I'm praised for three top hits stacking several billboard charts on a forty-two-week streak. Recognized for my talent. Known for a strong voice and Southern charm, even if I come from the West Coast. In the streets of Nashville, on every stage I've ever performed, I've made a name for myself.

I know what I need to do to keep it that way, and I won't let anything jeopardize it.

"Twenty-six, twenty-seven, twenty—"

Bzz.

My eyes jolt open from the jarring vibration. I lunge forward, barely catching my phone before it sails off the counter. Every ounce of my carefully curated ritual dissipates as a bucket of ping-pong balls takes over my abdomen. I tumble out of the chair and stabilize my feet, preparing myself for the worst-case scenario.

There's only one person who could be calling me right now.

"Caroline? What is it? What happened?"

"Everett," she states in her calm, calculated tone—one of the few people in my life who still calls me by that name. "I need your insurance information."

I bolt across the room. It's more than five hundred square feet and not nearly big enough. I need double the number of strides to calm my erratic heart. A whirring sound funnels through my ears, and I clutch the phone tighter, attempting to eradicate it.

"What the hell is going on?" I press. She's being way too cryptic.

"It's not a big deal. Quinn tripped and bonked her head on the coffee table. Wade and I are taking her to urgent care."

Not a big deal? I picture a giant gaping wound lancing my toddler's forehead, blood dripping in a steady stream toward her eyes. Sure as hell sounds like a big deal to me. The kind that any kid would want their *parent* there for. To comfort them through. The thought rips my chest wide open.

I snatch the suede jacket from the sofa. "I'm on my way."

"No," she barks. "She's fine."

"She's *my* daughter," I snarl back.

I'm sure Quinn would rather have her mom there than me. I wasn't around much for the first couple years of her life, but I couldn't help it. I'm the property of Jonas Records, and they own my schedule. But I'm getting tired of my mother-in-law insinuating that I don't *want* to be there for my daughter when I'm doing the best I can.

"You know you can't do that," she adds, as if she can hear my internal debate.

"That's ironic, coming from you." The woman who hasn't supported my profession a day in her life. But she knows it would be career suicide if I left the stadium right now. She has the upper hand, and she's using it to her advantage, but I'll be damned if I don't bring attention to the fact that her sole purpose for pointing it out is to have more time with Quinn.

With zero inflection in her tone, she says, "Twenty-thousand people."

Yes, I'm aware of the number of fans who paid to hear me sing tonight. Does she think I don't know that?

No matter how much I want to go, unless it's an emergency I'm contractually obligated to stay. I may be the only parent Quinn has left, but that's exactly why I *need* this job.

"There's no bleeding or signs of concussion. We're just getting her checked out to be safe. She'll be fine," she reassures me.

I scrub a hand down my face. I wish this woman wasn't always right. Even more than that, I wish I wasn't backed into a corner with no other option.

"I'll text you a picture of the card," I tell her. "Keep me updated."

I don't know why I added that last part—it won't matter. Once I leave this room, there will be no checking my messages for at least three hours.

She hangs up before I can say anything else and suddenly, I feel it. The thrumming of opening chords that signals my stage entrance. My five minutes are up.

A knot the size of a grapefruit tightens in my stomach.

There's no more counting. No more silence.

I'm out of time, and I've never been this unprepared before.

I ditch my phone and jacket on the god-awful green velvet sofa across the room. Despite my distaste for the woman, Quinn is in capable hands with Caroline until I'm done here. I press my palms into the countertop in front of me, challenging my own reflection in the mirror. My cowboy hat tips forward, just enough to cover my forehead but not hide the glow around my dark irises.

In a blunt exhale, I remind myself of the one fact I choose to never lose sight of: "You're Rhett *fucking* Dawson. That's all they need to know."

I blow through my dressing door, leaving it gaping open. A dimly lit hall leads to a flight of stairs where Rex, a member of the sound crew, is waiting for me. He holds out a pair of IEMs in his hand. I loop the cables over my ears one at a time and wedge the custom-molded monitors into place, effectively sealing out the noise around me. He secures a cable clip to my undershirt and pins the wire against my body.

Todd is waiting next. I duck my head, and he fits my guitar strap across my shoulder.

When we finally make eye contact, his voice blares through the ear monitor. "Everything okay?"

"Why wouldn't it be," is the last thing I say to him before I take the stage, greeting an arena full of fans with a fake smile and a wave as they scream my name.

2
EVERETT

Six weeks later...

From record deal sound to hometown bound, Rhett Dawson's life crashed like—

I crumple the article and press the tip of a lighter against the edge. Orange embers lick at the metaphor and eat away the rest of that sentence. A small hand tugs at the thigh of my jeans, and I drop what hasn't disintegrated to ash in the sink, snuffing out the flames with the faucet.

With the way my back is angled to her, I hope she missed what I just did.

I turn around and squat. A clump of dark curls hides Quinn's face from me. I part them with both hands, tucking the loose strands behind her ears.

"What is it, sweetheart?"

Wide, glassy eyes study my face. It's clear I'm doing a terrible job of concealing my very adult problems from my very intuitive toddler.

Before she responds, my phone buzzes in my pocket. I pull it out, checking the caller ID. *Jane Dawson*—my mother and worrier of the family. I know she'll see right through how this little setup she arranged is going if I don't comfort Quinn before I answer.

I brush the backs of my fingertips down her cheek and offer her a smile—it worked the morning I had to tell her that her mom wasn't coming home again. To my relief, it works now too. Her eyes brighten, and she scoots in closer so she can see the screen. Then she swipes her finger across it.

"Everett?"

The moment I hear their unified voices, I regret answering. I've managed to dodge interactions when I need space or slap on a smile when I can't avoid people. Today, unfortunately, is the latter, and I need a minute more to get there. I tilt the camera toward Quinn.

"Damma?" Quinn's face lights up as two floating heads launch into an off-key rendition of "Happy Birthday." She bounds around the kitchen in a series of skips and twirls. Not much I do these days makes her happy, so the sight elevates my mood. Add it to the long list of reasons why I'm grateful for my parents.

They finish with their disappointment over missing her party and reveal where they left her present. Quinn flees my side for the storage ottoman in the living room as I flip the camera and stand.

"You two want to throw this party? You're already better at it."

My parents are the only people I reserve honesty for. With unconditional love at the heart of our relationship, there's no reason to keep anything from them. But only at this moment do I wish I would have held back from verbalizing it.

"Oh, stop. Let me see that cake you made," Mom demands. Her glasses magnify and her usual white button-up shirt with a belt around her waist disappears with her proximity to the camera.

Tin foil and frosting peel back at the same time I reveal my attempt at a *Bluey*-themed cake. It's more of a lopsided tower with a plastic character stuffed on top.

"It looks great, son!" Dad says.

Unconditional love right there. I cover it back up.

"How's the Amalfi Coast?"

The two of them left on a kick-off retirement trip to Europe last week. After raising two kids of their own and then stepping in to help take care of Quinn over the last six months, they deserve to be carefree, not countries away fretting over how their son is doing as a single father with a blown-up music career. My mother proves it was the right thing to ask when her mouth melts into a smile.

"Oh, it's dreamy. You should see your father. He got a massage yesterday." She giggles.

Just talking about Adam Dawson, my feet instinctively carry me to the den where he worked long hours as a financial advisor growing up. Years of monitoring the rollercoaster that is the stock market has to create some lasting muscle tension.

This room now feels stuffy and dark without his cardigan-wearing presence in it, offering me wise advice from his rolling desk chair.

"Wow, pops. Feeling relaxed?"

"Am I ever!" He winks at Mom, and I manage to crack a smile.

Leave it to my parents to make me think about sex. With everything going on around me, I've had very little time to consider how long it's been. But now that I am, I admit to myself that I miss it. Not just the stress relief, but the deep connection it creates with someone else. My world with El feels like a lifetime ago, and the one without her in it has left me detached from everything.

"How's the house?" Dad asks next.

I lift the flap on the office blinds to reveal the lurking shadow of my former life: reporters, everywhere I look. Privacy is not something a house on Harrison Boulevard affords you. With its long-standing history—named in honor of President Harrison after he signed Idaho's statehood act—and the decades it's hosted the city's most iconic Halloween experience, I've always known what living in this house meant.

But now the driveway is no longer the place I park my car as a teenager and make out with a pretty girl inside of it. The front steps are no longer safe to prop my guitar on my bent knee and write music. And the lamppost sign buried in the long boulevard median with mature trees sure as hell is not a place I'd even approach right now with a mob circling it.

No. "Boise's Historic District" is no longer home. It's the latest news headline for Rhett Dawson's fall from grace. And it's the last place I want to be.

"It's fine." I drop my hand, and the blinds slap closed.

The old oak floors groan beneath my footsteps as I clear the glass-pane pocket doors that lead from the study to the kitchen. I shuffle through the Albertson's sack on the countertop, taking inventory of everything I bought this morning—paper plates, napkins, forks.

"And how are *you*?" Mom asks.

"I'm fine too." I'm a little too tired to make it sound all that convincing.

"Our trip is still booked through the summer, but we can come—"

"We're here!" my least favorite voice trills from the foyer.

Of course my mother-in-law is the first person to arrive at this party.

"To-To!" I hear Quinn squeal, clomping in her glossy pink rain boots.

"Mom, Dad, I've gotta go. I'll call you in a few days."

My mom's back to that all-too-familiar look again. The pitying one I don't need right now.

"Okay, honey. Well, we love you. Give Quinny a squeeze for us."

"Will do. Love you too." I hang up and swipe a hand through my hair.

"My favorite girl," Caroline sings.

It would be endearing to hear her say that if she didn't *just* see her last night. I slap on my stage smile and round the corner. "Caroline!"

"Do you always let your four-year-old answer the door?"

"It's nice to see you too. I see you've let yourself in." I hold out my hands and she shoves a pan against my chest. Not the well-loved kind that's currently sitting on the counter with tinfoil crunched around the edges, but the silicone kind with the matching lid and fancy handle.

"Well," she huffs, shrugging off her fur-hooded parka into her husband's waiting arms, "you would have heard our knock if it weren't for all that racket. What on *earth* is going on out there? And don't even get me started on those reporters."

I roll my eyes at both comments. The reporters I can't help, but *that racket* is a four-man construction crew I hired to transform the garage loft into a music studio. It was my only selling point left to convince the record label not to drop me after having to move home. That's how this industry works. If you aren't ready now, you'll never be. I already compromised on Nashville, I think she can handle a few hammers and a table saw for the afternoon.

I ignore her question and circle back to her first comment. "I didn't think my daughter would be snatched from inside this house."

"Crazier things have happened." She skirts past me, holding Quinn's hand.

I kick the door shut and follow along with her offering clutched in my palms. I've memorized the back of this woman's head at this point—layers of dark curls bear resemblance to the two most important people in my life. It's the only reason I tolerate her.

"Coco, give the kid some credit," Wade says.

She clears her throat. "You're right. Congratulations on showing up to your daughter's birthday this year."

I grunt, even if I deserved that—I missed Quinn's third one. If it hadn't been for the video that went viral on social media last year, the trajectory of my life would be very different right now. I don't know whether to be grateful or devastated. I went from gigging at local coffee shop to being signed by one of the best labels in the country and offered a multi-state tour. Then became a widower at the age of thirty-three because of it. I wake up every damn day wondering if I hadn't pulled El from this place, maybe she'd still be with me.

"That small detail had slipped my mind. Thank you for the reminder."

"Well, Eliza's no longer here to do it, so..."

I grit my teeth. *What the hell is that supposed to mean?* This woman has had a chokehold on my life from the moment she entered it. Standing up to her had never come easy to El, and I'm sure there were times when she got walked all over by her mother while I was away. When she hounded El to call me and accuse me of being an absent parent. At least for the short time she still lived in Boise. But El never once did that because she was always supportive of my career. She was the one who uploaded that video in the first place.

I offload the couple dozen Pastry Perfection cupcakes onto the granite. Quinn stands on her tippy toes with her fingers clutching the edge of the countertop. She squeals when her eyes land on the frosted buttercream topped with bug rings.

Caroline takes off the see-through lid so Quinn can get a better look. "What do you think?"

"Waeybuts!" Quinn claps. Even with her back to me, I can imagine Caroline's smug expression.

I frown at the *Bluey* birthday banner suspended over the table and my pathetic attempt at dessert in the corner of the kitchen. Of all the ways in which Caroline drives me crazy, witnessing how much better she knows Quinn than me is at the top of that list.

"Ev, we're here!"

I don't register the addition of another voice in the room until she's gripping me by the shoulders from behind. I startle and turn around.

What is it with people not knocking anymore?

Emma may have lived here as long as I did—our bedrooms across the hall from one another's—but she certainly doesn't live here now. A detail I'm normally thrilled about. There's no one who celebrated the day my sister passed the bar more than me. If I share a similarity with her, it'd be our devout work ethic. But her freedom, because of it, grates at my jealous nerves now.

"How are you, big brother?"

"I hope you brought tequila," I whisper in her ear. At least she hasn't commented on the reporters out front.

She pulls back enough for me to read her lips as she mutters through clenched teeth, "Is that allowed at kids' parties?"

I don't get the chance to answer with her attention bouncing to the person next to me. "Hi, Caroline!"

"Emily." Caroline begrudgingly accepts her hug.

"It's—"

"Let's go watch for your guests, Quinny."

"—Emma," she whispers to the empty spot Caroline left behind for the front door.

"Big party day, huh?" My sister's boyfriend capitalizes on my attention as he slides a stack of gifts onto the kitchen table.

I count them—*one, two, three, four, five*—before turning to Emma.

I know it wasn't her decision, but I say it anyway. "You didn't have to do that."

"Of course we did. We're family," Nathan butts in, slapping me on the shoulder.

Not yet. Not ever, I hope.

I try not to recoil. Him in his plaid button-ups and aggressive gestures. I tolerate him. But I've always pictured my baby sister with someone... softer. Someone like—

"What is Will doing here?" The question gusts from Emma's lungs in a breathy whisper. Her eyes are glued to the back door.

I glance out the window as my childhood friend's backward hat and six-foot frame cross the backyard.

"Right now? Probably going to Delilah's for lunch. Before that? Building a music studio above the garage. He was going to come to the party but a guy on his crew called in sick. He's covering for him to get the project finished by tomorrow."

Will is a better person than I'll ever be, always taking care of his crew and checking up on his grandmother. She raised him in the house next door after his parents died in a car accident in high school. I never asked him many questions about it back then. I was always afraid it would be a give and take conversation.

A confused look transforms Emma's face. "You didn't tell me you were doing that?"

"It's... a new development."

Kind of like living here.

Four toddlers barge into the kitchen, chasing each other in a fit of squeals around the island. Caroline must have made a great first impression with their parents because they didn't stay to offer concern about the reporters or introduce themselves to me. After a week at a new school, followed by spring break, I don't have the faintest clue of their names yet.

"I'm gonna go see the progress," Emma says, drifting toward the back door. I catch a muscle in Nathan's jaw jump before he ignores her and turns to me.

"So, Rhett, you're really doing it... the whole domestic life thing?"

His use of my stage name irritates the hell out of me. Appearances have always been his priority over everything else. Hence the pile of gifts, the family connection to a famous music artist, and the way he uses my sister for her money.

Quinn launches herself at my legs. She grips my pants tight, hiding from a redheaded boy who was chasing her. She shrieks as he barrels into my side and reaches around to tickle her. I grip the counter to keep from losing my balance as two other kids come at me from the other side.

"Yep," I grunt.

Nathan wouldn't know a domestic life if it hit him in the face. Makes me question how committed he is to my sister. Over a decade on and off together and he still hasn't popped the question.

Nathan chuckles. "This is good birth control."

I'm not one to judge their situation. I didn't entertain a committed relationship until four years and nine months ago. There's nothing that makes you evaluate your life choices more than "Surprise! We're having a baby."

El and I had only been on two dates. The first hardly counted; I was playing a set at the country club where she worked as a waitress, and she offered me a glass of whiskey while I waited for the owner to cut a check for my performance. It was after hours, moodily lit, and only the two of us. She was the most gorgeous woman I'd ever laid eyes on, and it felt as close to a date as what I was used to having at the time.

I invited her out the next night. We went dancing at a club downtown. A few drinks and some grinding later, we woke up naked the next morning with very little recollection of how we ended up on the couch in my apartment.

She came from a well-to-do family and I, well, I was so focused on my music career I didn't have time for anything else. We parted ways until she showed up on my doorstep with that test in her hand and a terrified look in her eye. I hardly knew her and wasn't even sure if I could fall in love with someone. But we were having a child together, and I wasn't about to flake out on her.

The day they laid Quinn in her arms was the day I knew my answer to that question. Not only *could* I fall in love with her, I did. I snuck away while the two of them were sleeping to ask Wade for her hand in marriage and proposed that afternoon in the hospital room.

"He's doing a fine job." Wade squeezes my shoulder as he makes his way over to the cupboard where the glasses are kept. It shuts Nathan up.

I've always appreciated my father-in-law's support. Unlike his wife, I've had it as long as I've known him. He's a man of few words, but the ones he does say are always encouraging.

"Thanks," I tell him as Emma slips back inside at the same moment the next circuit of tag rushes through the kitchen, kicking up the volume another ten notches. Five kids and five adults all stuffed into one small space; I already feel my sanity slipping. At the first vibration of my phone, I pull it from my pocket. Todd's picture pops up on the screen.

"I've got to take this." I shake kids from my pant legs and dodge out of this hell hole. When I break into the hall, I answer. "Todd?"

Another child-like scream belts from the other room. I press my hand against the opposite ear to block the noise and march farther down the hallway. I stop once to look at the device and make sure the call is even connected. I can't hear anything, so I punch the volume button a few times. "Hello?"

"Rhett—I—Monday." His voice sounds like it's coming through a wood chopper.

Dammit. Not this again. It's been six weeks since it's happened and *years* before that.

"I can't hear you, man... Todd?"

The call disconnects and a text pops through seconds later.

> TODD: I'll call you Monday to discuss the details.

Well, that was helpful.

Even though I'm the one who told my label I needed a break, I didn't mean a month and a half and a move across state lines. They didn't either. I'd be lying if I didn't admit to the concern creeping in. I'm hoping *I'll call you Monday to discuss the details* means they've decided to reinstate my tour.

"Ev, where do you keep the crayons? They're not in the junk drawer like they used to be." Emma interrupts my thoughts.

"What?" I pull my eyes from the dark screen and look up at her.

She enunciates. "The crayons."

"Oh, uh... I don't know, Em. In the study, maybe?"

"*Really? Coloring? That's* the activity that was planned?" Caroline complains as I step back into the baboon exhibit known as the kitchen.

"Quinn likes coloring," I announce to the whole room, so she doesn't think it's directed at her.

Take that, Caroline. At least I got one of her interests right.

I shuffle through the Albertson's sack for the stack of *Bluey* coloring books.

Wade slides his palm across the counter, his forehead tipped low like I'll bark at him if he doesn't speak softly. "Quinn keeps saying something about bug pictures?"

That's the thing about toddlers. They change their minds every two seconds, and apparently, this is now a bug-themed party thanks to Caroline's damn cupcakes. I'm supposed to screw these coloring books. Got it.

"I'll go get them." I act like they're ready to go on the printer and make a break for the hallway.

Emma brushes by me. "Found the crayons in the hall closet."

"How could I forget," I grumble.

I type *bug coloring page* into the search engine and print the first collage it finds. The LaserJet printer spits out ten copies as a mob of children tackle me for a page. I give Quinn the one on top.

"To-To, woot! A waeybut! See?"

"That's a fly, honey." Caroline frowns. Quinn almost trips over a sneaker as she runs with her paper fluttering above her head. Caroline stalks after me as I collect the trail of hazardous shoes in a path to the front door.

"Everett, I think Quinn's behind," she says.

I look over my shoulder, expecting to find Quinn hiding in an unsafe crack of a door. She's perfectly content at the kitchen table.

"Behind what?"

"I took her to the library the other day and this little boy her age had a full-on conversation with her. I'm talking five-word sentences."

This has nothing to do with hiding.

"I think Quinn could use speech therapy," Caroline adds. "You need to get her tested."

The hair on my arms stands at attention. I quickly cover it with the gray sweatshirt I left draped over the dining room chair.

"Quinn's fine. She's barely four."

Every kid is different.

"She's a four-year-old who calls me *To-To*." She tries to make her point by emphasizing the Ts.

Ah. So, it's the *Wizard of Oz* nickname that's getting to her. She picked it. And it's not like *Coco* is an easy thing for a kid to say.

She presses in closer, lurking over my shoulder. "She calls you 'Da-eee.'"

"I like that she calls me that," I respond calmly, but I feel the tension rising. Blood pumps through my veins. She's acting like it was just yesterday she was a mother of a four-year-old. Frankly, it's been a long time. And also, it's not like Quinn isn't talking at all. She says plenty.

"Really?" she asks, as if it's a ridiculous notion.

I'm trying to remain a beacon of tranquility, but it feels impossible with her breathing down my neck all the damn time. She's been here every single day since my parents left. She shows up whenever she wants to. She demands to take Quinn for outings. Drops off groceries after her fit over the box of Fruit Loops she found in the cupboard. Folds laundry with my briefs in it. The woman has no boundaries, and I need to find a way to get some space from her or I'm going to end up saying something I regret.

She doesn't take the hint and closes in. "There are kids her age with a significantly larger vocabulary. You aren't paying attention."

I toss the handful of shoes in the basket next to the door and turn on her. "For fuck's sake, that's all I've been doing is paying attention! She doesn't need speech therapy!" I scream in her face at the exact same time a fist pounds at the front door.

"Watch your *language.*" Caroline scowls at me as I grip the handle and jerk it open. It swings wide and bounces off the wall, leaving a dent behind where a door stopper should have caught it.

"What the hell is it?" I say to the person on the other side.

A woman is crouched in front of a kid wearing a cowboy hat, patiently coaching him as his small fist hovers in midair.

"And that is why it's polite to knock softerrr—" She hangs on to the last letter when our eyes meet for the first time.

Her hair is tied back in a ponytail instead of a clip, and she's wearing a tank top and cut-off denim shorts instead of the T-shirt with my face on it the day we met.

She straightens. "Hi! I mean... hello?" Then she swivels her head from side to side until her eyes catch on the metal house numbers. "I'm... sorry, I—" She pulls her phone from her shorts pocket and stares at it. Then she chuckles awkwardly. "Funny story... we were looking for a birthday party, but I think we might have gotten the wrong address. I never expected—"

"You." I finish the sentence for her.

Impulsive. Smiley. Energetic. The ideal combination to get Caroline off my back. If there was ever a perfect moment for my path to cross with this woman again, it's now.

"Come in."

3

SUMMER

Six weeks ago...

"Tell me... why... this was a good... idea again?" my best friend pants.

I never notice our height difference until she's having to jog alongside my giraffe legs to keep up. The merch line already snakes past the concession booth, and I'm not compromising between the opening song of this concert and my new night-shirt. I drag her by the hand.

"Because we're thirty-one, single, and it's *Rhett Dawson*," I explain.

I have no idea what part of this spontaneous trip she's referring to, but knowing her, maybe the whole thing?

"What... is your... obsession... with this man?"

I stop dead in my tracks. It takes her rebounding off my body for her to realize it too. The ballerina bun that was once neatly wound into a tight knot at her crown now has four dozen flyways spiking in every direction.

"First of all, he's a hot musician from our hometown. How

often does someone from Boise, Idaho, become famous? But also… did you even *watch* those videos I sent you?"

It's a rhetorical question, really. If she did, she'd *know*. I open my phone camera, press our heads together, and say, "Smile."

One look at the photo has me pinching the bridge of my nose. Her expression is a mixture between an animal caught in headlights and a teenager asked to sit through a piano recital.

No, it's okay. She's been living under a rock. She doesn't have a clue about those Levi's that paint his thighs or how his voice drips like honey when he gets to the chorus or what a thrill it would be to wear his face.

It's not until she says, "Okay, that's creepy," that I realize I'm muttering out loud.

My eyes snap back to hers, and I continue closing in on the line. She returns to her marathon sprint.

"I'm just saying… this feels… like something… a twenty-year-old would do." She crashes into me a second time when I stop at the edge of the line and whip around.

"Jules, a country music concert?" I squint at her and then turn over my shoulder.

Standing on my tiptoes, I lean from side to side.

Dammit, she slowed me down. There's a gigantic line already, and now I'm going to be stuck justifying the next twenty-four hours to someone who spends Friday nights at home eating microwave popcorn for dinner. There's absolutely nothing wrong with getting a babysitter and going out in your thirties.

"You don't get out enough." She deserves this. And frankly, after the hellish week of divorce papers I've had to deal with, I do too.

She nods. "I'm aware. But what if Henry has one of his episodes at bedtime because Jake forgets to leave the hall light on? Or if he tries to make pizza for dinner instead of his peanut butter banana? Or—"

She's talking so fast I can hardly keep up, except for that last part.

"He'd eat a peanut butter banana over a piece of pizza?" Asking this question brings me back to *her* reality. This isn't just a night out. It's a plane ride away from her son. Even though I have no one to answer to anymore, I won't even begin to understand what it's like worrying about a child all the time. Not to mention, one with autism.

"Not helping, Sum."

"You're right, I'm sorry." I grab her by the arm and look into her eyes. "Did you leave a note for Jake?"

I expect it when she nods. The woman is more prepared than Santa Claus. She has to be.

"Okay, then it's fine. It's one night." I shrug to make my point, even if I still feel guilty at seeming so nonchalant. I care about the stress this is causing her.

Her eyebrows pinch together, and I give her arm a gentle squeeze, listing off all the things she already knows but may need to hear again.

"Jake is Henry's father. He's spent the night with him plenty of times before, and if he faces something unexpected, he'll figure it out. He gets to go out all the time. You deserve to have a little fun too!"

She chews on a fingernail for a second and then presses said finger into my sternum. "I'm sending you my therapy bill this month."

I grin. "Sounds like the perfect way to spend my divorce settlement."

She laughs.

I wrap an arm around her shoulder. "And you know how else I plan to spend it?"

"On popcor—"

"On a T-shirt with another man's face on it," I cut her off. "It's called self-care, babe." I kiss the top of her head.

"Aren't those two things in the same category?" she argues.

I twist her to face me. "For the next twenty-four hours, *everything* is self-care. Give me your phone."

She eyes me in the way only a person you've been best friends with for the better part of a decade would. She knows I'm going to turn it off before I even do.

I extend my arm toward her, palm flat, fingertips wriggling. "Give it."

She snatches it from her purse, taps at the keyboard, and powers it off before handing it over.

"Good girl. T-shirt, then popcorn." I take a step forward in line.

As the puppet I've made her, I twist her shoulders yet again to face the glorious display of pressed cotton tees with a danger-ously good-looking man in a cowboy hat on the front. The corner of my mouth kicks up.

Rhett Dawson, you're coming home with me tonight.

Forty-five minutes later we're stuffed into the upper-level tier of the Bridgestone Arena listening to a cover of "Save a Horse, Ride a Cowboy."

"Damn, he can sing!" Jules shouts, and knocks off the trucker hat she bought as a souvenir for Henry with her lasso arm. She's breathless as she bends over to pick it up and wedges it in her folded seat.

I don't even have to say it. Seeing her let loose is all the *I told you so* I need.

"Yes. He. Can." My eyes trace a path from his cowboy boots to that tight smolder he carries across his mouth. I know every other woman in this arena is probably doing the same thing, but deep down, it feels wrong to be gawking at someone who lost their fiancée six months ago. Ever since he walked out on this stage, I've found myself analyzing his every move because of it, the news report coming back to me...

Country music sensation, Rhett Dawson, loses the mother of his child in a fatal accident early Saturday morning. A fifty-five-year-old male driver operating a red sedan crossed the median and hit the female jogger at an intersection. According to authorities, the investigation determined that the driver suffered a medical emergency, lost consciousness at the wheel, and was pronounced dead at the scene. Emergency responders transported twenty-nine-year-old Eliza Blackwood to Nashville General Hospital with serious injuries. Medical professionals were unable to save her after less than twenty-four hours in the ICU. Both families are asking for privacy at this time as they grieve the loss of their loved ones.

The fact that he's up there at all is a testament to what a strong person he must be. Unlike me. It's taken twelve years to face the reality that I've been anything but strong when it comes to my husband. I knew the morning after we got married, when he said, "That's what you want to do with your life?" to something I'd been dreaming of, that I made a big mistake.

We'd known each other for six weeks. *Six weeks!* At nineteen, that felt like a lifetime. So, when he popped the question, I said yes—dove headfirst into a life-altering decision, just like I always do.

I frown.

"Do I make bad judgment calls?" It sounds like it's coming out of nowhere, but truthfully, it's been on my mind the entire flight here. I've just been pushing it away.

"What? No! I'm sorry I wasn't on board before but look at me now! I got my popcorn. You got your shirt. All is right in the world."

I don't believe her. "I do, don't I. It's okay, you can admit it. I won't be mad."

She stops dancing. "Who are you, and what have you done with my best friend?"

I stop dancing too, my mood nosediving. "I'm impulsive. That's always been my problem."

"Is *this* a bad judgment call?" Jules waves her arm, showcasing the massive stadium with glittering lights we're standing in.

"Not *this*. Brian. The steady stream of jobs." I drop into my chair, the weight of it all hitting me at once.

She maintains eye contact, worry sinking her eyebrows together as she feels around for the edge of her own seat and folds it open next to me.

"Okay... yeah. We can call Brian a mistake. He's an idiot who never deserved you. But the jobs? Sum, we wouldn't have met if you hadn't worked at the nursing home when my grammy got sick."

I cringe at the memory of sour-smelling bedpans. There wasn't a single second I loved about being a CNA. I didn't even give them notice. I just stopped showing up one day. She tugs on my arm when shame causes me to hide my face.

"And what about those priceless birth photos you took of Henry that I love so much? I wouldn't have them if you hadn't tried photography."

I chuckle. "*Tried* being the key term. It lasted six months."

Every client always wanted a posed photo. If I wanted to take pictures of statues I would have worked at a museum.

"No. It didn't," she argues, her voice slipping into a scolding tone. "You continued to use that talent with your blog and your

Etsy shop, even standing in that damn T-shirt line back there so you could document this night."

She's not wrong. That was one skill that transferred to several other creative outlets, none of which made all that much money though. *That* has always been the problem. Well, *Brian's* problem. He hated when I'd try new things and drop them if they didn't work the way I hoped they would. He's always called my life privileged, and he's right.

But now I'm no longer married to a spouse with a stable income. He's required to pay alimony for a while, but eventually, I'll need something, and I don't trust myself to choose what that is when I've clearly gotten it wrong every single time.

"I'm over here convincing you to go to a concert on a weeknight because I have no one to go home to, no real responsibilities. Let's face it, Jules, I'm terrible at calling the shots in my own life."

When she doesn't say anything it feels like a confirmation. My shoulders slump. I don't know where my confidence went.

"You should do it for me," I say.

"Yeah. Okay." She rolls her eyes at the same time mine grow three sizes.

"No, that's it!" I grab her by the shoulders. "Jules... there is no one in the world I trust more than you. You're the perfect combination of stable and brilliant. Maybe I just need some guidance for a while."

"You're asking for a single mother—a nursing student who lives off caffeine—to call the shots for you," she reminds me.

"Yes."

"Someone who will turn you down the next time you suggest, on a whim, to leave her kid for a country music concert."

"Yes?" I question what she's saying this time.

"I'm gonna go use the restroom and give you some time to

come back to your senses," she says, tucking her purse against her side and squeezing her way toward the aisle.

"I'll come with you," I offer, but she swipes her hand in the air.

"We'll call this a test. I'm making the decision. You stay and enjoy those stars in your eyes." She winks at me. "I'll be right back."

She disappears up the stairs, and I turn my attention back to the stage. Who wouldn't have stars in their eyes watching those hips sway, watching him tip his cowboy hat? I'm not sure god has given a better gift than that, to be honest.

It's several songs later when I'm wondering where she is that it hits me. *Her phone.* I shuffle through the contents of my purse. That minx! In the midst of my breakdown, she managed to snatch it back.

I check the stairs at the exact moment she happens to be hustling down them.

"Sum, I gotta go. It's Henry. He's being difficult for Jake, and he wants to FaceTime. It's too loud in here to do that."

She's clinging to her purse strap and gnawing on her bottom lip. I hate seeing her like this. I just wanted her to have one night of no worries, and the only way I can give her that now is by getting her back to the hotel where it's quiet. I scoot toward the aisle.

"You should stay. I'll Uber," she argues, but I shake my head.

"I got what I came for." I spread my arms wide, showcasing my merchandise.

She laughs and lets me follow her.

We take the stairs as the lights dim, and I glance over my shoulder one last time to catch that sexy cowboy picking up his guitar. He strums a single chord, and the hair on my arms stands at attention.

He's about to play my favorite song.

According to Julia, the only thing better than staying clear 'til the encore of a concert is leaving without the droves of people. Other than a few restrooms and concession stand lines, the hallways are completely empty. She seems more at ease.

Even with cement walls and steel doors in the way, I expected to hear the swell of music on our way out of the building. So far, nothing. The February breeze bites at my skin and tornadoes my long blonde hair in a scarf around my neck. I peel it away from my face and twist it up in a clip I find in the side pocket of my purse.

"I'm sorry I made you leave early," Julia says again.

"It's all right." I sigh for dramatic effect. "Maybe I'll roam the streets of Nashville. Find myself a hot cowboy who daylights as a veterinarian to take me out on a date."

"Why does *veterinarian* feel out of place in that sentence?"

"What? I like a guy who likes animals." I smirk because the only guy who has ever really been in my life definitely did not.

My attempt at humor doesn't make Julia feel any better, and I don't want her to torture herself anymore over this, so I shimmy and make a joke to get her to laugh. "You were just ready to sleep with me *and* Rhett Dawson tonight. No sense in being ashamed about it."

Hotels in downtown Nashville are not cheap. We opted for one on the outskirts of the city with a single queen bed to save on costs. The sleeping together part of that sentence is accurate, just not the sexual innuendo.

My joke works. She giggles, but then her eyes widen.

"Dang it. I forgot Henry's hat!"

I recall her stuffing it between her folded seat. It must have fallen through the crack and onto the floor when she sat during my come-apart. This is my fault.

I shuffle through gum wrappers, hair ties, several tubes of lip gloss, and crumbs before I pull out our rental car keys from the bottom of my purse. I toss them in the air, and she catches them.

"I'll go get it and meet you at the parking garage." I turn around before she can stop me and make a break for the window-covered building that looks like a UFO landed on top of it. The one—as I was about to discover—with the no re-entry policy.

4

EVERETT

A Nashville crowd knows how to do a country music concert right, and this one is no exception. Fans are on their feet, dancing and belting out the chorus. Eating up every lyric I throw out there. Normally it's a high I feed off of. I worked my ass off to become Rhett Dawson. There's no one I'd let down more than myself if I didn't put on a good show.

But tonight, in this arena, I'm going through the motions. Relying on the thrum of guitar strings, the pulse of a drumbeat, and the resonance of vocal cords to guide me. It's worked so far, until it doesn't.

Under a shower of applause and screams of excitement, I'm on the edge. I'm Elsa in cowboy boots. A voice chanting inside my head, *Don't let it show.*

How many songs have I made it through? *Five?*

Six... seven... eight...

I go back to counting. I always go back to counting when it's loud and I'm locked in a cage of static. One that's blocking out the band behind me.

I strum a chord. The one I know I'm supposed to play next.

"Your—Rhett—line." My music director's voice chops its way through my IEM.

Shit. I missed my entrance. That much is clear.

"Over—start." Steven's voice muffles. Jumbles. Causes immediate panic.

No.

"Doing—are—what y—?" I *think* that was Casey's voice—my drummer.

This is not happening. In all the songs I've sung, in all the stadiums I've performed, it's never happened on the stage before, and I don't know what to do. I make myself believe it's the speaker's fault as I press it closer to my ear. *Lie* to myself.

Deep down I know the truth.

A beam of light cuts a four-foot circle around my body, and I tug at the collar of my shirt.

"Rhett—up—come." Casey's words scramble again into an incoherent mess.

What is he saying? What does he want from me? I'm not sure of anything anymore.

Through the beam of light, I know there are thousands of eyes watching. Waiting. Listening.

You can't hide it this time, the voice in my head says, and something clatters to my feet, oblong and wooden.

The guitar. It lands on the drum. The crowd silences as the thump echoes through the microphone.

I stare at it. *Glare* at it.

If I pick it up I'll have to explain why I dropped it, and I can't do that. *I'll never do that.*

All that's left, I realize, is to run.

One, two, three, four, five, six, seven, eight, I make it off the stage. I'm down the steps. I'm through the hall. I'm at the back door. My hands slam into the metal bar and my shoulder takes the impact, knocking me back a step.

It fails to open.

Desperate, I try again. I keep my upper body out of it this time, crushing the bar over and over with my palms, begging it to break me free. By happy accident, it collapses with pressure near the locking mechanism. The door gives way, gifting me a gulp of cold night air.

"What—fu—doing—are y—?"

I rip off my hat and claw at the speakers wrapping around my ears. They drop into my palms. I ball the chords in a clenched fist and chuck the communication device along with my cowboy hat.

My boots eat up the length of the ramp until they're touching pavement, grinding against the cement with my pacing. I flatten my palms to the back of my head, elbows spread wide.

What the hell did I just do?

The last few minutes replay in my mind, amplifying my panic.

How am I ever going to explain this to my manager, my publicist, my fans, *the label?* I drag a hand down my face, before I turn and throw a punch into the side of my opening band's tour bus. It does more damage to my hand than the metal. My knuckle splits and bleeds, but I let it. The stark contrast of cold steel and sweat collide as my back drags down the side of the bus.

It's never gotten this bad before. I've had moments where stage presence overwhelmed me, especially in the beginning of my career. It's the reason for my rider request—a coping strategy for handling the intensity. It was working until that call about Quinn.

If I lost this career, what would that do for her? A twenty-five-thousand-dollar liability insurance pay-out from the at-fault driver who hit El will only go so far. I didn't need it to cover her medical and funeral expenses, but I'd rather invest it for Quinn's future than need it now.

My mind is consumed with an endless abyss of questions I don't have the answers to. I should have held it together.

A punch of metal rings through the air, and I look up as someone abandons the door farthest from me. They jog down a ramp, and I scoot back into the shadows to avoid them.

I try to make out any distinguishing features—hair, a logo, a face—that would give away who this person is. The dark is doing me no favors. Neither is being near-sighted.

It doesn't matter, I realize. Any member of my crew would know those doors are locked or have access to get back in. It's not one of them. Someone's trying to break into the building.

I've never had a break-in at one of my concerts before—I don't know the protocol. Tucked away in the shadows, they can't see me. I consider crawling over to the earpiece I abandoned and alerting security, but then I wouldn't just be turning this person in, *my* location would be compromised too. And truthfully, I'm not ready to rip off that Band-Aid yet. If they're determined enough to get in, who am I to stop them. And quite frankly, I'm interested to see if they can even pull this off. It's a concert arena with a large security detail.

I watch in fascination as they make their next move. They're closer now. Enough that I can make out the outline of their clothing. A body drowning in fabric at least three sizes too big.

My mind goes to the homeless population in downtown Nashville. There are a number of places you can sleep in an arena of this size, so it makes sense. It also makes me feel guilty for the privileged life I've led.

Even when I wasn't famous, money is not something I've ever had to worry about. Other than the purchase of a colonial-style house on Harrison Boulevard, my dad never touched his stock investments. Over time, they paid off.

Once you're well off, it's easy to stay that way with smart decisions, he told me once. But the vast number of people who never have the same opportunities is stark. And I hate knowing this person might be in that category.

As the oversized shirt stops swaying in front of the door I departed from—the one with the faulty handle—I hear the person say, "This is all your fault."

Emotion pours from a woman's voice. Not sadness, but frustration.

I don't have a clue what it is she wants inside. And maybe it's the desperation in her voice that's compelling, but the next time she tries with more force I decide to help her.

"You have to push on the left end."

Wish someone would have given me that tip before I barreled my shoulder into it.

"Shit!" She spins around and flattens her back against the door. It's still fairly dark, but not enough for me to miss her expression. I was expecting a wild look in her eye or a desperate plea on her face. I imagined her hair to look unkept or her clothes worn. Instead, her shirt still has fold lines from the shipment it came in and her hair, while messy from the wind, is tucked back in a clip. I think her lips part, but I can't be sure from here. I don't move from my position on the concrete. I figure she'll spot me if she really wants to.

I should apologize. I didn't mean to scare her, and I certainly don't need another PR nightmare on my hands. Just as I'm about to, though, her eyes widen.

"I bought a shirt with your face on it," she blurts.

My gaze drops to the obnoxious outline of my head on her chest. She's been inside the building before.

"Is that why you're breaking in? Revenge on the merch line?" I ask.

She doesn't say anything, so I continue talking. "I'd be upset too if they gave me a dress with a mediocre singer on it." I gesture to where the T-shirt drapes well below her belt line.

She takes a step closer and into the streetlight. I can finally see her smile bloom ever-so-slightly as she grabs the hem mid-thigh.

It's pretty, her smile. I don't know why, but I want to see more of it. She still hasn't owned up to a reason for trying to get in the building, so I take another stab at guessing.

"Wait, I know. You forgot your candied pecans, didn't you? That's what everyone comes to these things for."

It works. This time it's accompanied with a dimple and striking white teeth, making me forget everything I was worried about thirty seconds before I saw her face. She's beautiful, and that's saying something. A large percentage of fans that attend my concerts are the opposite sex. Ones who throw themselves at me with heart-covered signs and in-your-face cleavage—the opposite of what this woman is doing. Her XL shirt is drowning her entire figure. It's leaving everything up to the imagination, and I'm fighting not to let mine run wild as she steps closer to me. I haven't had sex with anyone since I lost my fiancée, and there's an embarrassing amount of pent-up pressure in a certain region.

"How did you know?" she asks.

I nod toward the door. "The way you worked over that metal bar. I can spot a feral nut lover when I see one."

She acknowledges my humor with a chuckle and takes another confident stride forward. And another. "And what's your excuse for being out here?"

I finally look at her again. Her attention is consuming—big blue eyes studying me with deep curiosity. She clearly missed my stage exit.

Perspiration beads on my palms—*when did that happen?*—and I rub them against the stiff denim on my thighs. I clear my throat. "They announced the supply shortage... yep—candied nuts, shirts, beer—it was ridiculous. I was just as pissed as you were."

She feeds me another laugh. It's flattering.

Her hands plant at her hips. They rubber-band her shirt to her narrow torso, leaving far less to the imagination than before. *Attraction*, that's all this is. I try to recall the last time I felt it. It's been a while. I always thought El was the most beautiful woman I'd ever seen. Dark curly hair, chocolate brown eyes, high cheekbones, and she liked a man in a cowboy hat. It worked in my favor. But our connection was never this *visceral*. I don't know what to do with my hands, my eyes, my *anything*.

"Well, what kind of crew are you running around here, Rhett Dawson? What did you do?" she teases.

Ran out on them. That's the truth. Hundreds of good, hard-working people who I couldn't do this production without. I let them all down tonight. It's why I feel so guilty.

A siren breaks the tension that's building between us with her unanswered question. We both let it capitalize our attention. The ambulance blazes down the street and then disappears.

"Do you mind?" she asks, gesturing to the spot beside me on the ground.

Even though I came out here to be alone, I'm not ready to watch her walk away yet. I want to hear what else she has to say, which is new for me. I happen to like being alone. I've made it so I never *need* anyone in my life. But then she came charging down that pavement and distracted me from an earth-shattering moment, and without even knowing it, defused the situation. Made me feel better. I owe her. The least I could do is let her sit.

"Sure."

Her shirt—my face—drapes over her bent knees when she tucks them against her chest.

"Was the door really going to work if I pushed on the left side?" she asks.

I stare at the metal rectangle—the only barrier between me and the mess I made. I'm *glad* she didn't get it open. Thankful she seems to have given up on her reason for trying in the first place.

"It looks like you'll never know."

She sighs at the door. "I guess not. Who needs a hat with a mediocre singer on it when I can buy a Chris Stapleton one online instead."

A smirk plays on her lips.

She's witty. I've always liked that in a woman. El appreciated my humor but rarely made *me* laugh. Which isn't a fair comparison given the mother she has. There was no room for joking around in the Blackwood household when everyone was always buried under a mountain of expectations. Comparisons are also why I haven't paid any attention to the opposite sex since El died. No one can hold a candle to the mother of my child.

But I suddenly have a strong urge to see what *this* woman looks like in *my* hat, even if she'll never know how much she saved me tonight. Call it my way of paying her back.

I scan the area until I spot it not far away. The large brim managed to ring itself around the tour bus's side mirror when I threw it. I push off the ground and unhook it, then squat down in front of her, caging her in with my forearm pressed to the bus behind her. I attempt to fit the cowboy hat on her head. It gets caught on the clip in her hair. She laughs and slides the prongs from her silky strands. They fan around her shoulders, and my nose fills with the scent of lemon as my hat sinks on her crown. She tips her chin back, the brim falling with it, and the moon reflects a milky orb in the deepest blue of her eyes.

"I take it back," she says as they fall to my mouth, sending an electric current flowing between us like two magnets trying their best to stay apart. My body is begging me to close the gap —toss off that hat just so I can kiss her. But then she finishes her thought. "I bet you run a great crew. They're lucky to have you."

The balloon around this suspended moment pops.

I wasn't expecting her to say that. I'm at a loss for words, actually. It's a compliment I don't deserve right now. Maybe ever, when I consider how many times I've lied to my crew over the years. Let them believe they're supporting a person who isn't entirely truthful about who they say they are. I have two names. They only know one of them.

I sit down next to her.

"I'm not sure I'll ever be enough."

That's more than I've admitted to anyone before. Maybe it's the fact that I know she tried breaking into the building. I have something to hold her accountable for if she tries to share this information with anyone else. Maybe the promise of me not seeing her again after tonight makes it feel easier to let my walls down. It's dangerous what I'm doing, choosing to open up to her, though. But it's what she says next that leads me to believe I made the right decision.

"I willingly gave up my decision-making power to my best friend tonight, if that says anything about me. I'm not sure I'm the person to be doling out advice."

"Why?" I ask.

With her gumption to get into a locked building, I didn't peg her as the indecisive type.

"Because I make commitments I can't keep. I eat leftovers after they've been sitting out all night on the counter. I drive my car until the red gas light comes on. I bring home stray cats from the foothills. I buy shirts with mediocre singers on them."

I snort. She's listing off all of these things as if they should be repulsive to me. They're not. At least she's honest about who she is.

"Well, I know a certain three-year-old who would be thrilled if I brought home a stray cat from the foothills."

She smiles. Somehow this conversation took a very personal turn and for the first time, I'm not mad about it.

"I wish I could say the same." Her smile falters, and I don't miss it. Don't miss the glint of gold around her ring finger either.

She's married?

I almost kissed her.

"Are you trying to get laid?"

My attention cuts to my manager descending the nearest ramp. He's stomping—rightfully so—and taking notes with his eyes on the woman sitting next to me. Gathering evidence in the event this is a crazed fan that needs to be turned in. It's happened before.

"You could have at least waited until after the show! That would have been really stupendous for me rather than the land-mine I'll be facing for the foreseeable future," Todd says.

She stumbles to her feet.

Is that what she thinks? That I was talking to her because I'm trying to sleep with her?

I stand too, turn toward her to defend myself, but she's already backing up. Rather quickly, I might add, and I try to stop her but her spine rams into the metal poll of the streetlamp.

"Are you okay?" I ask right away this time. Not because I'm worried about some lawsuit, but because I don't want her to think that's what this was. I was spiraling on my way out that door tonight, and for whatever reason, she was able to bring me back down to earth. I never thanked her for that.

"Yep. All good! See?" She swings her arms wide. One slaps against the side of another parked car. She clutches her crum-pled palm to her chest. "Okay. I'm gonna go now. Good night!"

she squeaks, taking off in a jog this time. I watch her disappear around the side of the arena. I never even asked her name.

"What happened out there?" Todd interrupts my staring.

I know by *out there* he means on the stage, but I'm still trying to figure out what happened *out here*, where my world tipped on its axis.

"Rhett."

I jerk my attention back to him. I've gotten so good at lying when it comes to this area of my life that I don't even have to think about it. It slips from my lips.

"It was Eliza. That next song on the set... I wrote it about her. I thought I was ready to play it, but I wasn't."

It's not a total lie, at least not the first part, and he believes it without a second thought.

"That's understandable, man." He steps off the ramp and closes the distance between us, placing a palm on my shoulder. "Listen, I know you've been through the ringer, and I'm sorry if you weren't ready for this. We've already sent everyone home, okay? We're issuing refunds. The label and the media might have a field day, but I'll figure it out."

"I'm sorry too," I say. But deep down, all I feel is relieved. Maybe there's a way of coming back from this after all.

He squeezes my shoulder and pulls me in for a hug. "Don't worry about it. This is what best friends are for."

But all I can think about is that we aren't best friends. How he'll *never* be my best friend. I can't have one of those. Because then I'd have to tell him why I really left that stage. And it has nothing to do with the last six months of my life and everything to do with the beginning of it.

5

SUMMER

Six weeks later...

I glance over my shoulder, convinced there's someone else behind me other than reporters hidden behind a hedge of boxwoods. There's no way Rhett Dawson would be inviting me —some random fan he met one time in the back alley of a concert venue—into his house.

Is this even his house?

"You live on Harrison Boulevard?" I ask, frozen on his covered porch. With all the media-fed facts I know about this man, how is it that I didn't know he lives *here*?

I mean, sure, I knew he moved home after the concert fall-out. The news said as much. And his presence does a better job of explaining the random reporters out front. I just didn't know home was five minutes from me.

If I hadn't seen him up close without his cowboy hat on, I might not have recognized him. His hair is ruffled, and dark circles frame his eyes. *Weathered* is how I'd describe his posture, with slumped shoulders and hands stuffed in the front pocket of a well-loved gray hoodie. He looks like he's lived a thousand lifetimes since I saw him all those weeks ago.

He blinks at me. "You have a kid?"

Maybe he meant it as a statement, a compliment about my age or something. But it sounds more like a surprised question to me, and it strikes a nerve. The topic of a growing family is the only thing anyone comments about my life these days. As a childless woman in her thirties, with a biological clock that's ticking, I don't need to be reminded of it every damn day. It's no one else's business. Not even Rhett Dawson's.

"This is Henry." I push him in front of me as if I can hide behind a five-year-old's spikey hair.

Rhett's eyes flit back and forth between our faces. Likely cataloging the one characteristic that we share: bleach blonde hair.

"Well... are you just going to stand in the doorway?"

His delivery is so blunt it would knock me back a stair if I wasn't curious about what lies beyond this grand entrance. I'm practically leaning into his foyer. This might be the only time I'm ever invited in, so sue me. I glance over my shoulder at all of the jealous reporters and cross the threshold, pulling Henry inside with me. I spin in a full circle, greeted by picture frame–covered walls and lamp-adorned surfaces. It's as cozy as a Nancy Meyers movie.

"Everett. I'm just saying—" A woman once hidden behind his tall frame squares her shoulders to him. The whole room fills with his deep exhale as she speaks. "She's too old now for the Infant Toddler Program. I checked. And you make too much money for Head Start."

He begins to turn back toward me when she jerks his arm. "Everett! She needs *something*. You could use some help."

The tension in the room is so thick I feel as if we've intruded on a private moment. This woman is half his height and yet he looks intimidated under her stare. I wonder if this is what he meant by *I'm not sure I'll ever be good enough.*

"This is not the time, Caroline. We have guests." His formal tone surprises me. In fact, everything about him is different from last time. Tense and serious and properly pissed.

"When would you suggest is a good time for doing what's best for your child, Everett?"

The way this woman continues to lay into him doesn't sit right with me. I can handle a condescending tone—got good at it with Brian—but talking down to someone just because they aren't fulfilling the expectations you set for them is a no for me now.

I thrust out my hand to the woman. "I'm Summer, Rhe—Everett's nanny."

Her eyes widen.

I don't dare look at Rhett Dawson to see what he thought of that lie.

The woman has the decency to shake my hand but doesn't offer anything about herself.

"And you are?" I press.

Her eyebrow lifts. "Caroline Blackwood. I'm Quinn's grandmother."

With the same last name as his fiancée, this must be Rhett Dawson's *almost* mother-in-law.

An adorable little girl in overalls turns the corner of the hallway. "To-To, come see!"

"Aw, what a cute nickname," I comment. "Is *The Wizard of Oz* her favorite movie?"

Caroline scowls at me. "It's *Coco*."

"Oh." I catch Rhett smirking out of the corner of my eye as I squat down so I'm eye level with Quinn. "You must be the birthday girl! I *love* your boots. Do they come in my size?"

She giggles and shakes her head.

I snap my fingers. "Darn it. I was hoping we could match."

"You asked a woman to be your nanny before she's ever even met Quinn?" Caroline accuses him.

Oops.

"When do we get cake?" Henry yells, and I've never been more thankful for one of his bold interruptions.

I pivot to face him, still on my haunches. "We wait patiently until they say it's time."

I can't imagine, after a couple of weeks, anyone in this family knows much about Henry. I stand to explain that he's on the spectrum, but I don't get the chance. A gentleman with a perfectly manicured beard and combed-over gray hair—Caroline's husband, I presume—waves us into the kitchen.

"I think it's the *perfect* time. Wadda ya say we dive into those cupcakes?" he says.

"Cupcakes?!" Henry drops my hand and pushes past Caroline.

She glares at him, and I have to bite my tongue not to tell her to have some patience. Despite working hard on them, social cues are not his strength.

They're not Rhett Dawson's either, given the way he abandons me in his entryway. I remind myself it was only ten minutes we spent together. Not nearly enough time to know much of anything about someone. It's unfair of me to consider his demeanor uncharacteristic in comparison.

"Henwee!" Quinn shouts, wrapping her small arms around his shoulders.

At least *she* knows who he is.

His hands remain clenched at his sides, and when she accidentally knocks into his glasses, he lifts a hand to straighten them.

"I'd like a cupcake," he tells her.

I lean forward and whisper in his ear. "Please."

"Please," Henry adds.

"Da-eee, tuptates?" Quinn runs to Rhett and jumps up and down.

He brushes a hand through her curls, and they bounce back into place. "Let's do it."

With Caroline already corralling the kids to the kitchen table, I need something to do. Standing off to the side as an observer is not my forte, so I sidle up next to Rhett and ask how I can help.

"I'm good, thanks," he says.

He's fishing through an Albertson's sack, and everyone but me misses it when he pauses. His eyes flash to Caroline as she divvies up the dessert. He pulls open a drawer in the kitchen island, rustling through tongs and spatulas.

"You sure I can't help with something?"

Either he didn't hear me or is lost in his own world. He doesn't respond.

Another drawer gives way with his frantic tug, sending measuring cups and silverware sloshing around it. He shoves the drawer closed and reaches for an upper cabinet. The deep wrinkle seated between his eyebrows is the definition of over-whelmed and stressed.

What is he looking for?

"Does everyone have one?" Caroline asks.

A guy in a flannel shirt—another adult in the room I haven't met yet—flags her for a cupcake.

"Wade, I need another plate," Caroline says, finally granting me the name of the bearded guy in the entryway. There haven't been many introductions since I walked through that front door, so I'm having to piece this family together one name at a time. So far, I know half of them.

Henry lifts his cupcake to his mouth, and Caroline reaches over and takes it from him.

"We have to sing first. Everett? We're ready for the candles."

He's looking for candles.

I can't bear to watch this poor guy receive another lecture. Even if it feels intrusive, he needs the help. I open the cabinet opposite from him, inspecting the shelves and find nothing but a hodge-podge of drinking glasses. I swing the door closed and catch it right before it smacks the frame. *Subtle.*

My hope wavers with one final Hail Mary cupboard between us. It opens to several spinning spice racks, sprinkle shakers, cookie cutters, and—*bingo!*—a mason jar filled with candles.

I pull it out and whirl around, the jar colliding with hard muscle. Impossible-to-read eyes bore into mine as Rhett looks from me to the object pressed to his chest.

Is he mad I went through his cupboards?

I don't know if I'm supposed to offer it to him or wait until he makes the next move. All of my nerves decide to wad up into a softball and squeeze their way down my esophagus as I swallow.

His hand, two sizes larger than mine, closes around the jar. Fingertips brush my skin when he pulls it from my grasp and pushes past me. It feels like the air has been punched from the room. I'm staring at his kitchen sink, wondering what in the hell just happened to me, before I finally get a grip on my surroundings.

People. Light. *Fire.*

Caroline has taken the candles from Rhett, pressed them into the frosting, and lit them. I get myself together and join everyone gathered around the table. The number of people I don't know is up to five at this point if you count the kids. This is a strange party.

I'm about to introduce myself to the dark-haired woman in an adorable tie-front linen vest next to me when Rhett starts singing.

I'm suddenly very aware that this isn't some arena view. I'm in his kitchen. He's five feet from me, and my eye contact could not be less discreet if I tried. I'm gaping at him. Lost in the way his voice expands the four walls of this room and carries us all to some otherworldly distant place.

Or maybe just me. *Definitely* just me. Everyone else is watching Quinn.

He looks more uncomfortable singing in his own house to his family than he did to a stadium of strangers. For the first time, I feel like Rhett Dawson and I might have something in common. I felt nothing *but* uneasy in my own skin under the roof I shared with Brian.

When the song ends, the woman next to me—who looks an awful lot like a female version of Rhett—says to Quinn, "Close your eyes and make a wish."

Quinn squints, sucks in a big breath, and blows out all four candles at once. Henry promptly takes a bite after she does. I make a mental note to praise him for that later, but right now, I need to call Julia privately, so I turn to the one person left with family resemblance.

"Hi! I'm Summer," I say to a woman with striking amber eyes and pronounced lines bracketing her smile. A small mole dots her cheek next to her nose, and her hair fans her collarbone. With naturally tinted lips and rounded shoulders, she's poised and effortlessly stunning.

"I'm Emma, Everett's sister."

I thought so. I love that she calls him Everett. It feels intimate, learning his real name.

"It's nice to meet you. I was hoping you could point me in the direction of the bathroom?"

"Of course! It's right down there." She gestures toward the nearest hallway.

I thank her, hoping it's far enough from the party to have this conversation.

A gallery wall of Rhett and Emma's school pictures guide me there. I shut the door, prop myself on the edge of a free-standing pink claw-foot tub, and dial Julia. She answers on the first ring.

"What the hell, Jules?"

I can still hear children giggling and adult chatter over my whisper-shout, so I flick on the switch to the bathroom fan and turn on the faucet.

She giggles. "How's Rhett Dawson?"

"You mean, *Everett* Dawson."

"Oh, the two of you are on a first name basis now? And I thought him gifting you his cowboy hat was intimate."

"This isn't funny. I was practically thrust into his house where he was being interrogated by his mother-in-law."

I pull open the top drawer of the vanity, needing something to do with my hands. Crest toothpaste and a Spiderman toothbrush stare back at me.

"Sounds intense. What's her issue?"

I swing the drawer shut, opening the next one.

"Him needing help with his daughter. You should see this poor guy, Jules. He looks so overwhelmed. He couldn't find candles in his own kitchen."

A clump of dark hair nests in the bristles of a glittery brush. I thumb the handle. A twinge of... *something* has me sailing the drawer shut.

"He sounds like me." She snorts.

I ignore her attempt at an overwhelmed-mom joke and continue rambling. "And so, what do I do, you ask? I say something stupid to his mother-in-law about being his nanny, and she—"

"Wait a minute... you said you were his nanny?" Julia interrupts.

"Yes! Keep up! And she *scoffed*. Drilled Ev—I mean, Rhett, about hiring some woman who's never met his daughter. Looked at me like I'd be terrible with children. She doesn't even know me, Julia!"

Now I'm sounding overly worked up about a job I made up.

"Maybe you should be thanking her. A single dad who loses his music career and moves into his childhood home, all in the span of six weeks? She's probably saving you from a messy situation."

"It's whatever," I grunt, opening the next drawer and shoving it closed without bothering to snoop. "I have no need to impress this woman. It's not like I'm going to see her again."

"Well, I wouldn't be too sure. You have a new job. She thinks you're her granddaughter's nanny. Your paths are bound to cross unless you fess up to the fact that you lied."

"Very funny."

"I didn't say you *should*. Now that I think about it, this could be good for you."

"What?" I freeze.

"Yeah. I think if he took you up on it, you'd make a great nanny. You're already helping with Henry. What's one more kid, ya know?"

I lean a palm on the countertop and squint at my reflection. "How much caffeine have you had today?"

"A questionable amount." She chuckles. "But the point is, wasn't this what you wanted? My advice in the decision-making department?"

Why the hell did I come up with that ridiculous idea? I can't even pretend I don't remember saying it because I was perfectly sober at the time.

"Well, he didn't offer me the job, so…"

"Some people have a hard time asking for help," she says.

I pause. That tracks, actually. It's not that he didn't *think* to ask for help… The way he jerked that jar from my hands, he clearly didn't *want* it.

"I'm not offering. The only thing I'm planning to do at this point is get a cupcake to go." I let out an exasperated breath.

"You might want to tell him that, not me. But I have to say… I'm kind of liking this fairy godmother thing I've got going on. I feel powerful," Julia gloats.

I hang up on her. I've got to get the hell out of here. I turn off the faucet and shove open the bathroom door, where it meets resistance partway.

"You have one speed," Rhett grunts.

"S-sorry."

His proximity pins me in the corner.

"What are you doing?"

"Uh—" We're trapped in a cramped hallway with his broad shoulders. There's nowhere else to look but right at him. "Using your bathroom?"

"I mean *here*. In my house. Telling Caroline you're my nanny."

I place a hand over my chest and tip my chin high. "If by *here* you mean Boise, then I live here. You were the one who invited me into your home. And I think what you mean to say is *thank you, Summer, for saving me*."

"I had everything under control." He tucks his hands in his pockets.

"Everett, we're opening presents now," Caroline calls from the living room, and a muscle tightens in his jaw.

"Yeah, no. I can see that. Control is the top priority here." I pat him on the shoulder. *Twice.*

His stare is so intense it's intoxicating. Eyes roam my face and down my neck—sweep my collarbone, and appreciate the tattoo he finds just below it. I feel heat creep into my cheeks. Panic follows it.

It's a heart tattoo with the word stay *in it, Summer. He wouldn't make the connection.*

I've spent an unhealthy amount of time thinking about our encounter at that concert, but I think this moment might top it.

He leans in closer, and my back meets the doorframe. My eyelids flutter and threaten to close as his breath ghosts across my skin. Not a single part of him is touching me, yet I feel him everywhere. My neck, my chest, my hands, a warmth that's spreading down my spine at his proximity. It spins up a tornado of butterflies that have lain dormant since the last time we spoke. I swallow down the embarrassing sound that fights its way up my windpipe, focusing instead on pulling an inhale into my lungs deep enough to ensure I won't faint when I finally let it go. He lifts a hand, and for a moment I think he's going to thread it through my hair. I anticipate his touch... *click.*

"You left the fan on," he grunts.

Then he's pulling away. Disappearing down the hall and leaving me breathless. And I ask myself, for the second time since I entered his home, *What the hell just happened to me?*

I take a few deep breaths. Gather myself before bolting down the hall. I whisk a cupcake from the counter and whisper *McDonald's* in Henry's ear. I know it's the only way I'll be able to get him out of here early without a scene.

Forget saying goodbye; most of the adults I didn't even meet, and the one I did is shooting daggers at me with her eagle eyes for interrupting Quinn's present-opening. She won't care that

I'm gone. And Quinn is four. In a week, she won't remember any of this.

My plan works. Henry runs willingly to the front door and slips on his light-up shoes. With a good tug on solid oak, we're home free. I stand on his front steps facing the reporters again, and the reality of the last thirty minutes sinks in.

I think I might be Rhett Dawson's nanny.

6

EVERETT

People like to warn you about the lack of sleep you get as a parent, but nothing prepares you for the seven a.m. alarm chanting for pancakes as you hit the best REM cycle of your life.

Nope. The next time you get sleep as a parent is when you're dead.

I shield my eyes with a forearm, blocking the aggressive rays that like to beat through my east-facing window. I miss the retractable roman shades of my Nashville house. Instead of a convenient remote, I'm left pawing the surface of a rickety nightstand, almost knocking a lamp to the floor before my fingertips close on the temple of my glasses. The once fuzzy edges of an ornate chest of drawers come into focus.

This house was furnished when my parents bought it—there are rules for living on this street. Agreeing to maintain the historical integrity of the outside of your home is one of them. The outdated clutter on the inside is not. They could have replaced everything and had the means to do so but appreciated its "antique charm." I glower at the dresser that's serving as a second reminder of how much my life has changed.

The mattress squeaks when I fling off the covers and swing my legs over the edge of the bed. An irritating stiffness made a home in my neck from sleeping on this ancient thing. I make a mental note to order a new one while my parents are gone. They'll never know the difference. But I have thirty minutes before Quinn starts school, which is not enough time to worry about it right now.

There are zero unread messages on my phone. I don't know why I even check it when the one guy I'm waiting to hear from isn't living with his own personal rooster. Todd's on East Coast time, and he's never productive before noon.

My feet fight the leg holes of a pair of jeans before I cross the hall to my sister's old room. It's the only space in this house that doesn't look like a mausoleum of my childhood. Mom insisted on fixing it up for Quinn before she left. Said she wanted it to feel more like home for her. I didn't have the heart to tell her a pink bedspread and dresser wouldn't matter much. The only part of *home* Quinn ever really cared about was having her mom in it.

With the door ajar, my daughter clomps right past me in last night's compromise—the rain boots and Spiderman underwear she insisted on sleeping in.

"Good morning to you too," I whisper to the empty room.

In a thousand ways, El was a better parent than me. Bedtime routines, good-night stories, and comforting kisses all came natural to her. The only thing I was ever good at was fun.

"Woah! What are you doing?"

In the thirty seconds it's taken for me to catch up to Quinn, she's pushed a chair up to the counter and is teetering on the edge for the cabinet door.

I plop her on her bottom and drag the wingback to the table where it belongs. She doesn't cry, but she doesn't squeal from the ride either. It's clear after the stress of the last couple of months, even the fun side of me has died.

I locate what Quinn was trying to reach, except it's a box of Kodiak Cakes instead of the bag of Krusteaz pancake mix I bought a few days ago. Caroline's doing, I'm sure. I find a bowl and a pair of scissors, cut the top off the bag, and pour the entire contents in it. Then I read the label.

Makes nine servings. Guess we'll have leftovers.

The directions seem simple enough: add water. But after a few cups and some strong-handed stirring, there's no way this gloppy substance will spread on the pan I've heated up. I hold the bowl under the faucet and guesstimate.

Pancake soup, that's what I make next.

Why couldn't she have asked for cereal? That's something I'm good at. Something that can't be messed up.

But now that I've used the whole bag, there's no starting over. I tip the bowl and hope for the best. Runny batter spills onto the pan and spreads into a paper-thin layer. Gravity has the last laugh when the pancake blackens upon contact with the hot surface.

Great. This is going well.

I flip it, give it five seconds on the other side, and toss it on a plate. Quinn grimaces when I slide it in front of her.

"Yeah, let's do cereal," I say.

I dump the hockey puck in the garbage and pour the rest of the batter down the drain. Caroline may have replaced the pancake mix, but she can't reach the cupboard above the fridge.

"Captain Crunch or Frosted Flakes?" I hold up both boxes for Quinn to pick from.

"Dis one." She points at the face of a giant tiger.

"Frosted Flakes it is." She sits up on her knees as I push her in tight and turn on *Spidey and His Amazing Friends*. I start a pot of coffee and check my phone, living on a naive notion that

Todd's called me in the last three minutes and I somehow didn't hear it.

No such luck. I *really* need the label to reconsider this tour.

While the coffee maker does its thing, I search Purple.com. Three clicks later and I have a queen-size mattress being delivered next Friday. This day is suddenly looking up.

"Nummy!" I hear Quinn say as I glance over at her. She's hanging her head over her bowl and lapping up the milk, sticky liquid dripping from her soaked curls.

"Oh, mess!" she complains as droplets fall onto her bare thighs.

"Quinn!"

I didn't account for a bath in our morning routine. No matter how fast I make this, our chances of being on time for school are slim. I scoop her off the chair and jog upstairs to the tub. She thinks it's a game, giggling and kicking off her boots as we go. I rest her feet on the bathmat and turn on the faucet. The temperature of the water is not cold, but it's not hot either, and I don't have the time to wait for it to heat up. I plunk her in.

"Mo ot," she whines.

I turn the dial higher. "I'm working on it."

She reaches for her *Paw Patrol* boat as I lather my hands with shampoo.

"Put the boat down. We have school."

She clutches on tighter. I give her another reminder before I'm forced to pry it from her hands. She cries as I shield her eyes like a visor and tip a cup of water over her head. I repeat the process with conditioner, making sure to get the front strands the most.

"No Miss Maimy," she says through a pouty lip.

I unplug the bath.

"You have fun at school with Miss Amy," I remind her.

At least I thought the week before spring break went well.

This is her first experience going to school. Maybe I should have had her start back in September, but preschool was the last thing on my mind when we lost El.

Her tiny body breaks out in goosebumps when I lift her out of the tub.

She stomps her foot. "No Miss Maimy."

I cover her head with a towel, rubbing circles against her scalp and muffling her voice.

Does she not like her teacher? When Caroline discovered Be the Brave had a preschool opening so late in the year, my whole family encouraged me to enroll Quinn. I agreed because I thought she could benefit socially from being around kids her own age. Her birthday party was evidence she's making friends here.

I flop the cat hood over her head and wrap her up, carrying her to her room. Her pink dresser drawer gives way with a one-handed pull. I pick the first shirt and pair of pants I can find. They're two different shades of purple. Probably a no if El were in charge, but it's all up to me now.

When I try to lay Quinn down, she thrashes against the carpet.

"Stop!" I bark. My patience is wearing thin, and I still need to get her dressed. I fight to get her head in the hole of her T-shirt. Underwear, pants, and socks are a wrestling match too. Air is gusting from my lungs by the time she's finally clothed.

I check the clock again. How did that take fifteen minutes? We're already late.

It's a sprint getting downstairs to brush her hair. I should have kept everything in the upstairs bathroom we share, but I moved it all down here the night before my parents left. Quinn wanted to stay up with them as long as possible, which included teeth brushing and hair combing in close proximity. It seemed like a reasonable compromise at the time. Now it's one I regret.

Along with not paying attention to how Eliza handled this situation.

Quinn screams when the bristles of the brush catch on a tangle. All of that running around at her party yesterday was no match for conditioner. I try again and get the same outcome.

"I'm sorry!" I say, stopping and holding her close.

Breakfast. The bath. Her hair? I'm terrible at this. I scrub at my face, and a bright yellow bottle flashes between my spread fingers. *Tubby Todd Detangler*, it reads. Thank god. After a generous spray, I'm able to comb through her hair with ease.

I gather her backpack, coat, water bottle, and lunchbox from the kitchen counter but I'm certain I'm forgetting something. Arms full, I flop her over my shoulder like a ragdoll and swipe the key fob next to my phone. I'm out of hands. Even worse, my phone starts to ring.

Of course it's Todd calling. The one day he manages to get out of bed, and it couldn't be a worse time for me.

Quinn's tears haven't let up. She's still recovering from the brush fiasco. If she's making a bunch of background noise, there's no way I'll be able to hear a word that he says, and I really don't want to call him back.

I swing her down to my hip. "How about some marshmallows?"

"Yep," she blubbers.

I've basically fed my child sugar for breakfast, and she's still upset.

"Okay, here's what we're going to do first... we'll grab you some marshmallows," I tell her, stuffing the handle of her lunchbox in my mouth so I can pour the bribe into her waiting palms. Several spill onto the floor and I kick them out of the way because I have about three more seconds before my manager hangs up. "And then we're going to get you in the car." I'm doing some sort of awkward gallop now as I exit the front door and shelter Quinn's face from the mob of flashing cameras that greets us.

The call rings for a fifth and final time, and I drop everything but Quinn to answer it.

"Todd?" I clutch the phone against my ear as I plop Quinn in her car seat. Once she's buckled, I'm chasing a rolling water bottle down my driveway. "Can you hear me?"

"Hey, man. How's it going?" he asks.

"Rhett Dawson, what's it like to be back at your childhood home?"

"When can your fans expect you to return to the stage?"

"Care to clear the air on what happened at the Nashville show?"

Reporters are feeding me question after question as I shove everything I dropped into the back seat and slam the door.

"Where... you?"

The middle of Todd's sentence gets lost when I turn the car on and my phone connects to the Bluetooth. The fact that he's still on the call is all I care about. I reach over the passenger seat to watch out the rear window as I back out of the driveway.

Several people rush to the sides of my car as soon as it touches the public sidewalk, knocking on the windows and pressing microphones to the glass. They have zero decency, clawing at the clear surface and shouting questions over each other. I'm always afraid it's going to scare Quinn, but all she does is blink at them as if strangers plastered against your car window is normal. I'm nervous one of these times they're going to stand behind my car and I won't be able to leave.

"Where are you?" Todd asks a second time.

"Trying to back the fuck out my driveway!" I holler, glaring at one of the paps.

"I'm sorry, man. I wish there was more I could do."

I don't need him to defend the situation. It's not something one thinks about before diving into this career, especially when a child's involved. But the truth is, if I was in Nashville it would be no different. This is part of the gig.

"Did you talk to the label? What did they say?" I change the subject.

"Do you want the good news or bad news first?"

"I want this guy to get the hell off the sidewalk."

"*Okaaay*, we're going with good. You sound like you need it."

"Just get to the point, Todd."

"Right."

The reporters take the hint, and I finally make it to the street when Todd lays it on me.

"The label is willing to renegotiate the tour."

A sigh and a brief hit of relief follow his announcement, until I remember there's bad news coming.

"And?"

"*If* you finish the album."

Shit, I mutter to myself. It's been months since I've written a single lyric. It's not for lack of trying. Every time I pick up a guitar there's a deep ache inside my chest that no amount of drive or motivation can push past. I don't know how to fix it.

"I already told them you'd agree to this because I believe in you," Todd says in the wake of my silence. "Is the new studio done?"

I peek out the front window at the two-car garage with the finished second story. A table saw and drill still sit in the yard from where Will and his crew worked until dusk last night. I haven't seen it yet because he told me he'd stop by later today to show me the finished product.

When I don't answer, he assumes it's a yes. "While your daughter is in school, use the time."

What *time*? He doesn't have any idea what it's like to be a single parent with no daycare. There *is* no time. Last week was spring break. She was home all the time. The week before that, I weeded the flower beds, cleaned the house, and grocery shopped. Every day was filled with something. A constant sprint. I barely had a moment to breathe let alone write. Creativity takes time and space. Two things I don't have.

"How long?" I ask him. I need to know the reality of their expectations before agreeing to anything. I'm better off renegotiating at this stage than signing on to something that's unachievable.

"Five weeks. They want the album we promised them finished the first Friday in May, and they'll pick up the second half of the US tour dates starting in Denver the following Saturday."

Pre-accident Rhett could have given that to them in a week, no problem. El was taking care of Quinn full time. I was writing music. Those were our roles. I sit in that for a moment, recognizing how selfish it sounds. Wondering if I told her enough how much I appreciated her for that. She sacrificed a lot for our family. Made this career possible for me. What the hell am I supposed to do now? I agreed to move back here for all the "help" I'd be surrounded with. I leaned into it the first couple weeks, but now it's a nightmare. My parents are gone, Emma's working all the time, and Caroline is already around more than I want.

I'll figure this out on my own. I will.

I have to.

"I'll do it," I say.

He cheers. "I knew you would! I'll have them draft up the new contract and get it emailed over to you by this afternoon."

I suddenly feel sick.

"'Kay. I gotta go. I'm at Quinn's school."

"See ya, Daddy Dawson." I hear him chuckle again before

hanging up. It sounds so lighthearted, and I kind of hate him for it. Other than managing my schedule, the guy is free as a bird. No expectations, no kids, just work.

I release a pent-up sigh. *What the hell did I just agree to?*

Five weeks to write three songs, that's what.

I'm pushing the twenty-miles-an-hour speed limit by ten over as I close in on the parent drop-off lane. Other than a crossing guard who's chatting with a guy in a suit, there's only one other car in front of me.

At least I'm not the only late parent. I slam into park behind it and shove against the door. Quinn is fisting her car seat straps by the time I get to the back.

"Come on, Quinn. We're late." I try to pry her fingers away, but she clenches on even tighter, her knuckles turning white.

"No!" she screams, slapping at my hands.

I try to press the button as she boxes at my arms. "Please, Quinn," I beg.

She's kicking her legs now. There are so many flailing limbs I can no longer get to the buckle on her chest.

"Quinn!" I pin her hands down. "We've got to go!"

She slackens enough that I can quickly release the chest buckle and feed her arms through the loose straps. We're making a total scene at this point as I sling her backpack over my shoulder and lift her by the underarms. She hangs like a limp noodle over my shoulder.

I'm two seconds away from having a total breakdown like the toddler in my arms. Nothing I'm doing is working. I need a different approach. I can't take her in like this, or she'll disrupt the entire school. So, I stop and kneel, setting her on my bent knee.

"It's going to be okay. We don't have to go in, okay?" I say in hushing tones. I've lost track of how many times I've used the word *okay*. I don't know what I'm even promising. I *need* her to go to school today. How people have more than one of these infuriating creatures is beyond me.

"Need any help? I'm great with children."

When I look up, a head is blocking the sun. Harsh shadows conceal most of his face. Based on his suit, it's the same guy I saw talking to the crossing guard.

I'm a little busy here, I want to tell him. "No, I'm good, thanks," I say instead.

I drop my attention back to Quinn. She's calmed down now that she's nestled against my neck. I gather her in my arms and stand.

"Listen, the school puts on a play the third Saturday in May. I was wondering if you'd be willing to help with the musical production part, being Rhett Dawson and all?"

He taps my shoulder as if I'm in on his joke. It's my least favorite part about being home. People feel like they can ask for favors here. Pretend they know me personally when they don't.

What is he... the drama teacher? Do they even have those in preschool? Well, I guess technically they also have a grade school. They very well could put on some type of play. I still feel the need to clarify with this guy that my tie to this institution is under the age of five.

"My daughter's in the preschool."

"It's open to all age groups. You'd be a big asset to the program."

By asset he means *you'll draw in a crowd that'll help fund this private school.* It's non-profit, but I know they offer tuition assistance to people who can't afford to pay to come here. If I wasn't late right now, I'd consider it for that reason alone.

"I really gotta get my daughter to class," I say.

"Just think about it."

I was too flustered with Quinn when he first approached to ask for this guy's name. Now it feels too late. I say, "Sure," just to get him off my back, and then I sprint. Ten yards ahead of me I run into the owner of the other car.

"Well, if it isn't the runaway nanny," I say to Summer, a bit out of breath.

It would be a lie if I didn't admit to the fact that I spent all last night wondering what I said that made her abandon Quinn's party without a goodbye. If I somehow crossed a boundary or made her feel uncomfortable when all I was trying to do was to figure out her angle. The hallway was the best place I could come up with that was out of Caroline's earshot.

I should have been floored to see her at my front door, but I wasn't anything but grateful. Appreciative of the fact that she did exactly what I hoped she would: she got my mother-in-law off my back for the afternoon. Because of Summer, Caroline spent the rest of the day focused on Quinn, under the assumption that her time with her granddaughter would soon be limited.

"I thought you didn't need a nanny?" Summer teases.

Says the woman who made up the fake title. Was I supposed to agree to it? And what kind of guy would let their beautiful wife nanny for a single man's kid? She's still wearing the ring.

"I don't," I'm quick to reply. The whole thing is a bad idea.

"Right." She laughs and nods. "You have everything under control. How could I forget?"

Hearing her throw my words back in my face annoys me. Everyone thinks I can't do this on my own, but they're wrong. I'm going to be fine.

I speed up my pace.

"In a hurry?" she quips.

"If you hadn't noticed, the tardy bell rang."

Summer and Henry are ambling toward the glass door that says Miss Amy on the outside.

"Did it?" She looks around.

"Hen-wee?" Quinn lifts her head from my chest. She *smiles* when she sees him, and it's the one thing that makes running into the two of them the best thing to happen to me this morning. She might not need another it's-going-to-be-okay pep talk with a friend by her side.

My best guess, Henry is slightly older than Quinn. A year at most if he's still in preschool. I'm grateful he's willing to be her friend despite the age gap. Having someone she recognizes seems to calm her.

Miss Amy greets us at the back door, and I set Quinn down, giving her a hug. She reaches for Henry's hand. He bats hers away.

"Look at how cute they are," Summer gushes to their teacher.

"Right?" she replies.

I'm too focused on hoping Quinn has a good day to join in on their conversation. She seems okay as she hangs her backpack up at her assigned cubby while I wait outside the door.

"See you after school, Quinn." I holler my goodbye, but she doesn't even look back at me.

"It's so wonderful when they're excited for school, isn't it?" Miss Amy says.

I wipe a drop of sweat that cascades from my hairline down the back of my neck.

"Yep." I force a closed-mouth smile like I didn't just survive a wrestling match with a rogue raccoon and turn to walk away.

"Uh, Mr. Dawson." Miss Amy stops me. "Are you available to meet on Friday at three thirty? I have something I'd like to discuss with you."

"Does this have to do with the school play? I already told another teacher I'd consider it."

"No, Mr. Dawson. This is about Quinn." Her expression

turns somber, and it sets off my nerves. Forces me to come up with an excuse to get out of this.

"We build a fort on Fridays for movie night," I say, hoping she'll appreciate a father trying to bond with his daughter.

"It's important," she pushes.

"I'm excellent at forts," Summer butts in. "Won a contest for it once at the county fair."

She's grinning at me with that smile that sets off a buzzing sensation beneath my skin. This is now the third time I've been in Summer's presence, and it still catches me off guard when I feel my body come alive like it is. I silently scold myself for being attracted to her at all.

"I got a free Pronto Pup for it," she adds when neither of us responds.

I'm sure, based on this story, that her son thinks she's the most fun mom, but I don't have time for this. In fact, my time-line is rapidly decreasing the longer I stand here with them. I have three songs that need to be written, and every minute I spend avoiding this meeting with Miss Amy is one more minute I'm losing in the studio.

"I'll figure it out. See you on Friday," I say to the teacher. "Summer." I acknowledge her with a nod and walk away.

What could Quinn's teacher possibly have to say? I'm not given the chance to ponder that question very long because the sound of flip-flops clomping behind me registers a moment later.

"Okay, no forts, heard you loud and clear back there. But I can give her a ride to or from school if you ever need it. I have to bring Henry anyway," Summer shouts.

The corner of my mouth lifts. "Says the woman who was late."

"We got donuts!" She could have sung it and it would have sounded the same. She's acting as if a donut run is a perfectly acceptable excuse for not being on time for her child's education.

She opens the front door of her white sedan and fiddles with something in the front seat as I keep walking toward my Bronco. I need to get out of here.

I climb in, start the ignition, and get a knock on my window. When I look up, she's holding a lime green box against the glass. I can't very well drive off with her standing this close.

She knocks again, forcing me to roll it down.

"I have work to do," I tell her, which is true. If I was a resourceful man, I'd take her up on her offer, let her drive Quinn home, and give myself that much more time in the studio. But that would mean I'd need to spend more time in her presence, and it's already proved to be nothing but a distraction.

"I know you clearly don't take handouts... but the sugar might do you some good." She leans her head in through the window, her hair falling across my chest, and sets the box on my cup holder. A draft of lemon wafts from her silky strands, and I do my best not to let it affect me. It's one of the many things I seem to have committed to memory about this woman. She smells like a bakery, and now I know why. She frequents them.

She doesn't wait for me to say anything more, just turns and heads for her car. So I peel out of the parking lot before someone else stops me.

I wait until I'm back in my driveway before I let myself look at the box again. It's my favorite kind of donut—a maple fritter—with her phone number scrawled across the cardboard.

7

EVERETT

"What do you think?"

I swivel the desk chair away from the turntable I've been staring at for several hours. Will's shoulder is tipped against the studio doorway, his arms folded across his chest. Same shaggy hair that curls at the tips, same worn jeans, same comforting smile. The only thing that's changed about my closest childhood friend is the smattering of dark hair across his face. Even if it's patchy in places, the beard suits him.

I don't know how to answer his question. I slipped into some kind of trance the moment I walked in here. There's a lot I'm still taking in about the space. Like the round wool rug in the center of the room that looks an awful lot like the one that once sat beneath his grandmother's kitchen table.

"She's into pawning everything she owns lately." He rolls his eyes when he catches me looking at it. "I think they'll take it if you schedule a garbage pick-up."

With the way his mouth bends down at the corner at the mention of Delilah donating their things, it's bothering him.

"You want to talk about it?"

His brow arches. Will and I don't do this sort of thing—talk about our feelings. Maybe it's my way of apologizing for always keeping everything inside when we were teenagers.

"I think she's sick," he blurts.

I stand. A reflex that has him straightening his posture too. I walk toward the couch, and he follows. "I'm sorry, man. Is there anything I can do?"

He shakes his head. "You know her." Stubborn is what he's implying. Even if he pressed her on it, she'd tell him, *I'm old, and old people are meant to die.*

"I just came over to say thanks."

I stare at him quizzically. "I should be the one thanking you."

His eyes map the acoustic foam paneling and the gallery wall of records above the sofa we're sitting on. They trail across an ergonomic desk and high-fidelity speakers. Land on the microphone and guitar. "This project has kept me busy."

When Will and I graduated high school, he did the opposite of me. He dove headfirst into a five-year college program. Graduated with a Master of Science from the University of Idaho in architecture, started his own company, and grew it to a four-guy crew before I ever signed with my record label. Based on that, I figured he was doing well. I don't love the forlorn look on his face that tells me he's not.

"You're incredibly talented, man. I wouldn't have wanted anyone else to do it but you."

He nudges my shoulder. "It's the fancy sound equipment. Makes any space look good."

I chuckle. "Well, they definitely know how to go overboard, that's for sure." The two dozen boxes on the back patio I need to break down for recycling day is evidence of that. "But Emma was right all those years ago. You're good with your hands."

The tips of his ears pinken at my mention of the comment she made about the front porch swing he built for Delilah when she lost her husband. Or maybe it's the compliment. The guy's never been great at accepting flattery from anyone.

"As Rhett Dawson's oldest friend, do I get to hear his latest hit?"

It's funny hearing him call me that when he's one of the few people who ever use my first name. Someone who knows more about Everett than Rhett.

I rub a thumb against my jaw. He opened up to me; I owe him one.

"There is no latest hit."

He studies me, waiting for an explanation.

"I've spent all morning in here. All of this pent-up stress, it's blocking me creatively, and I don't know how to get rid of it."

He lifts an eyebrow. "Sounds to me like you need to get laid, man."

I roll my eyes. "You sound like my manager."

It's definitely something Todd would say, but not Will. I haven't spent much time around him since I moved to Nashville, but I know he wasn't with anyone when I left. I think he should take some of his own advice.

"Well, I just wanted to stop by and make sure you liked the space, but I should get going. Delilah got the Halloween boxes down today, and she's hell-bent on going through them before I leave tomorrow."

I squint at him. "It's April."

"It's Harrison Boulevard. I know you've lived in Tennessee for a couple years now, but you couldn't have forgotten *that* much about this place."

Live bands, packed streets, king-sized candy bars, and an endless night of noise all come to mind. People plan and prepare early. A couple of years isn't long enough to forget what this place is like on Halloween night, or any other day of the year for that matter.

"Nope. Haven't forgotten."

Will makes his way to the door before looking over his shoulder.

"This was nice," he says. "Why didn't we ever do this growing up?"

Because I wasn't ever honest with you. His question is loaded with a million hidden moments that make up the latter part of my youth. He was there. We did everything together. We'd raft the Boise River. Ride mountain bikes in the foothills. Mess around with my guitar in this very loft. But we never shared our problems, and something tells me he's kept a few secrets of his own over the years.

But I want it to be different now. Hell, I wanted it to be different back then. *Different* has always been my problem, and I never planned on dragging him down with me. Will had a hard enough time being the nice guy who finishes last. I didn't need to add to that.

"You've always been my closest friend." I hope that's enough to convey that I've given more of myself to him than anyone else without having to admit that, even now, I still can't fully be myself around him. "Thanks again for doing all of this."

"Glad I could help." He opens the door. "I got a couple of small jobs out in Emmett the next few weeks. I was wondering if you could check on Delilah while I'm gone."

"Of course."

"Thanks, man. See ya."

He disappears down the stairs while I try to pinpoint the emotion buried behind his tone. Frustration? Sadness?

I never got the impression that Will wanted to stick around Harrison Boulevard any more than I did. But he's also the most loyal person I've ever known. He would lend a hand to anyone who needed it. If Delilah wanted to donate her things or go through her Halloween decor months early, it's not in his nature to withhold help.

I pick up the guitar leaning against the corner of the room and find a seat on the sofa. The gravity of a blank page pulls me under as I close my eyes and hope for my first melody.

8

SUMMER

"What is it?" Julia asks as I stare at the open Idaho Central app on my phone.

Seventeen hundred dollars I don't want.

"It's my first alimony payment," I tell her.

You'll get thirty percent of his salary for the next three years, my attorney explained after our uncontested divorce was finalized last week. It feels like an allowance from my ex, and I want nothing to do with it. But I don't really have a choice at this point. I still don't have a job, and after the apartments I looked into yesterday, seventeen hundred dollars is barely enough to cover rent for a studio in this city.

"Sum, you can stay here as long as you want—I told you that."

I could have moved back to California. As the hub of the entertainment industry, being an entrepreneur in Los Angeles is admired. Take my mother, Nina. She's spent her career as a freelance writer for *Vogue* magazine. I won best dressed in high school after patterning my wardrobe off her columns. Even my dad, George, understands the hustle of business. He's worked his way up the ladder at Vivint Smart Home and went from selling security systems to becoming the regional manager with multiple territories.

They've always supported everything I've wanted to do with my life, and that includes this. Respecting my decision that moving home would mean living with them for a while—something I haven't done since high school and that feels like an even bigger step back than the one I'm already taking. Not to mention the satisfaction it would have given Brian if I had to do that. My pride wouldn't let me stoop that low.

I stayed with my mom in a hotel through the heartbreak of the first couple weeks. We watched *Gilmore Girls* reruns and ate ice cream in our pajamas. But now they call and check in weekly, knowing I've built my life here. Even if Brian isn't in it anymore, that doesn't mean I want to leave Julia and Henry behind.

"I know. I appreciate you," I tell her.

When Julia offered me a room in exchange for dropping Henry off at school, I jumped at it. She doesn't know it yet, but I plan to give her half of my alimony check each month. It's not much, but it's something to put toward her mortgage, and I'll pay her back in full as soon as I'm on my own two feet.

"Something else is bothering you," she comments.

I sigh. "I know it's not a custody battle, but can you believe he's trying to keep Millie from me?" I chew on the end of a ballpoint pen, swiveling aggressively from side to side. It's been over a month since I moved out, but I've been to the house every single day looking for the stray kitten I rescued on a Table Rock hike last summer.

Despite having roamed the foothills for who knows how long, Millie didn't look worse for wear when I found her. I did my part—put up signs, checked the local animal shelter, waited a month before I considered her mine.

Brian hated that I didn't involve him in the decision.

What's the big deal about rescuing a cat who spends all of her time outside? I'd argued, and I stand by it. She was more of an asset to that mouse-ridden property than a burden to either of our wallets.

He'll never admit he didn't want to keep her until we became a him-and-me. Something else to hold over my head perhaps. It doesn't matter anyway. Night is the only time she ever comes home, and he's back from work by then. Now that the divorce is final, that would mean stepping on private property.

Other than missing Millie, I've gotten really comfortable at Julia's place. It's made the blow of trying and failing at finding a job easier, knowing I don't have a rent check due any day.

"He's doing it to get a rise out of you, and it's clearly working. You're about to rock the hinges off my barstool."

I freeze and drop my foot from where it was propped up on the seat. "Sorry."

It's not just the alimony check that has me on edge. It's been four days since my school run-in with Rhett Dawson where I leaned over his lap and delivered my phone number on his center console. Regret wouldn't even begin to describe how I feel about that gesture. Humiliated might be more accurate.

And maybe I'd feel different if I heard from him. But I'm not surprised I haven't. His screeching tires in a twenty-miles-per-hour school zone made it very clear he didn't want to spend another second in my sight.

Now it's Friday—the day he's supposed to have that meeting with Miss Amy—and I can't help but wonder if he asked Caroline for help. Bet she can't build a fort.

"Hello? Earth to Summer?"

"What?" I lift my gaze from the brown knot in the hardwood floor that was taking the brunt of my staring.

"What do you have planned for the day?" She crosses the kitchen and fills her to-go thermos with coffee.

Aside from dropping Henry off at school? Nothing.

Julia holds out the coffee pot, but I shoo her away. If my jittery fingertips are any indication, I think I've had my quota. She plunks it back in the coffee maker and collects a stack of ready-to-go belongings off the counter.

"Apply for a few more jobs like yesterday." I'm trying not to sound discouraged, but after going at this for a month with no leads to show for it, I am. I need the money.

"What about Kay's Flowers?"

I scrunch my nose. "No piercings or tattoos." Something tells me Kay won't appreciate when I show up for an interview with a diamond stud in my nose or a heart etched on my collarbone.

"Oh."

Ugh, it's all so overwhelming. I need a pick-me-up. I swipe out of the depressing bank app and open my camera roll. Millie's orange-and-white paw bats at the screen, and I giggle.

Arms full, Julia kisses me on top of the head. "He can't keep a cat he never cared for." Then she disappears to the living room to say goodbye to Henry before her med-surg rotation. I turn back to what might as well be my only child and wish Julia's words brought me some semblance of comfort. But I know Brian. Fighting fair is not in his wheelhouse.

I get Henry to preschool on time and spend the afternoon navigating the apps for local job listings. My list of credentials in my LinkedIn bio is unimpressive, so I stick to ones that claim no work experience is needed. I skip call centers and apply to be a waitress at Wingers, a receptionist at a dental practice, and a personal assistant at a law firm before I'm interrupted by a phone call from an unknown number.

Most people wouldn't answer, but most people don't have the kind of time on their hands that I do.

"Hello?"

"Summer? It's Everett."

His voice is a shock to my system. I sit up straighter and grin, deciding to play with him like I intended to do when I thought this was a solicitor.

"I'm sorry, have we met?"

He lets out an exasperated grunt. "Our kids go to school together."

I forgot I still haven't corrected him that Henry isn't my child.

"There are a lot of parents coming and going from that school."

"It's Rhett Dawson," he growls.

I love that I can smile and he can't see it. I also love that he called himself by his first name to me. Feels like we're making some sort of progress even if I still use his stage name. "Oh! Rhett! Hi! Are you running late for something? You sound rather breathless."

"This was a mistake."

"No! Wait! I'm kidding. What can I do for you?"

He sighs. "My sister was going to watch Quinn this afternoon, but she got caught up in a meeting."

"What about Caroline?"

"What about Caroline," he parrots. "Thanks to you, she thinks you're my nanny, remember? Are you going to help me out or not?"

"I'll have Henry with me. Will that be a problem?"

"I figured. Will you have a car seat for Quinn? I don't have time to bring you one."

I didn't think about that either. "Uh... I think Julia has an extra booster seat Henry can ride in. Quinn can use the one with the harness—she's younger."

"Julia?"

"My roommate."

"Do you remember where I live?"

"Something tells me the reporters on Harrison Boulevard will lure me there if I don't." I snort.

His silence tells me he doesn't appreciate my humor.

"There's a hidden key beneath the third solar lantern on the left side of the backyard. That'll unlock the French doors in the back."

"I do love a good treasure hunt!"

There's another long pause after I speak. I don't know why it's such a thrill to know I'm getting under his skin.

"It shouldn't be any more than an hour." He sounds even more annoyed than when we started this phone call.

"Take your time, cowboy. I've got it covered," I say.

"Do you? Because it doesn't sound like you're in your car. It's three fifteen."

Shit. I wasn't paying attention to the time. I slide off the down comforter, snatching the twin hair ties from my night-stand and twisting my hair up into haphazard space buns.

"Good luck at your meeting," I get out before I hang up. I jog to the backyard where I stashed the sidewalk chalk behind the garbage cans. After Henry realized how dirty it makes your hands, I know he won't appreciate it. Quinn might.

It's a ten-minute drive to the school from Julia's. I make it to the brick building with one minute to spare and spot Miss Amy's long auburn hair twisted in a braid over her shoulder. She's waiting outside the door with a handful of backpack-wearing toddlers. From a distance, Henry's towhead is hard to miss, but Quinn I don't see until I get closer. When she sees me she reaches for his hand, and he bats hers away again. *Poor girl.* Won't give up.

"Henry, your auntie's here!" Miss Amy points to me and waves as I hop onto the sidewalk.

"Hey, buddy! How was school?" I'm looking at his teacher as I ask my Julia-inspired question. She always wants a daily report. If I don't ask, I don't get much out of Henry to share.

"We're still working on eye contact, but he seems excited for his playdate with Quinn." She rubs her hand on Quinn's backpack.

Is she guessing or assuming? Henry doesn't get excited in the same way other kids do. Not in big smiles and a jumping up and down sort of way. He talks faster and louder. Right now, he's standing stock-still, not saying a word.

I squat down in front of Quinn. "Are you ready for our playdate?"

She gives me the reaction the teacher probably expected from Henry.

"Okay! Let's go."

Out of habit, I ask both of them if I can hold their hands to cross the street. Quinn accepts mine willingly; Henry tolerates me guiding him by the wrist. It's a good compromise. I pull open the passenger door, and Henry pushes past Quinn and climbs in first.

"Henry... Quinn's going to use your car seat, okay? You get to use that cool booster seat next to her!"

"This is my seat," he states matter-of-factly.

I didn't warn him. Henry does better when he's prepared. But this was last minute, and I couldn't do that. All I have to work with is making it sound as if it's the most exciting thing to happen to him today.

"I know it's your seat, buddy, but Quinn is smaller than you."

He has a few inches on her. Even if the seat belt hits Henry's chin, it will completely cover Quinn's face. "Can you use the booster seat just this one time? It'll be really fun! I promise!"

With a disgusted look on his face, he shakes his head. "I don't use that seat. I use this seat. This is the seat that I use. It's my seat. She can sit in the other seat."

I sigh. We might not need that key in Rhett's backyard after all. I don't think we're leaving this parking lot any time soon.

"I know. I know it's your seat. It's always been your seat. But just for *today*," I emphasize as if noting that it's temporary will be enough to change his mind. "We'll share it, okay?"

"No thank you."

I cover my mouth with my hand so he doesn't hear the laugh that slips from my lips. Julia's been working hard on teaching him to use manners, and I love that he chose to use them now with a *no* attached to it. I can't argue with that. He was polite. Now what am I going to do?

"Waeybut! Waeybut!" Quinn squats down to the pavement and presses the tip of her finger to its back leg. It springs into the air and lands on the car tire.

"That's a grasshopper," Henry corrects her. "They have ears on their belly and regrow their legs when they get hurt."

"Wow! That's interesting! Where did you learn that?" I ask him.

"Coyote Peterson."

I thought he might say that. Henry is obsessed with the YouTube show *Brave Wilderness*, where a guy in a cowboy hat travels the world for animal encounters.

Quinn scoots forward and touches its back leg again. "Aw-puh," she repeats. It springs so far in the air we lose track of it.

"Good job saying hopper."

Henry doesn't turn and look at her like I do. "You can ride in my seat."

My eyes widen. "Wow! That's really nice of you, Henry. Good job sharing!"

"Mom says if you do a good job, you should get a reward."

I realize now that's what he expects. The surprise bucket of chalk certainly isn't going to do the trick.

"How about we get an ice cream cone on the way home from school?"

"Yes. I want ice cream!" Henry yells.

I smile because he's happy. It means I did something right.

Ten minutes later, both kids are licking drippy ice cream cones in Rhett Dawson's backyard. It was a good thing I remembered which house was his because I was wrong about the reporters. They must have seen him leave and taken a break from their usual watch post.

It comes as no surprise to me that it looks like an English garden back here. What I don't know is if he hires a team of gardeners to keep it this way or does it himself. Rows of green hydrangea leaves preparing for their blooming season line the back fence. Clusters of bright yellow daffodils spot the garden beds. Black metal is almost entirely hidden by a wall of ivy. Even the spacious back patio catches my eye.

"I brought a surprise!" I pull out the bucket of chalk from behind my back. Quinn's face lights up. Henry cringes. Quinn stuffs the remaining third of her ice cream cone in her mouth all at once as I open the lid. She reaches inside and pulls out a green stick of chalk. Minutes later, squiggly lines frame her crossed legs.

"Those look like beautiful vines. Should we add some flowers to them?" I offer.

Quinn gives an enthusiastic nod, and I do my thing. Whoever said chalk is for children has never tried it as an adult. Maybe it's the kid in me, or more likely it's the chance to be creative without any set rules. I try to squash the voice in my head that tells me how immature I am for being someone who actively enjoys coloring outside of the lines.

After Quinn and I transform the cement into a mosaic of color, I say, "I heard they're doing *The Rainbow Fish* story for the play at your school this year. You get to dress up and sing and everything! That might be kind of fun, huh?"

Quinn claps. Henry shrugs.

"Not a big play guy?" I tease him.

"I don't know," he says.

When Rhett mentioned his invitation to Miss Amy, I didn't get a good read on whether he's considering participating, but I hope so based on his daughter's reaction. I bet she'd love it. Speaking of things she might love...

"What do you say we make a fort next?"

Technically, it was a milk bottle stacking contest I won at the fair, not the fort story I fed Rhett. But I thought it was sweet that he does that with his daughter, and I didn't want him to feel guilty for missing it.

Quinn squeals, "Yes!" at the same time Henry says, "No thanks."

"Come on, Henry. It will be fun!" I spot a heap of boxes in the corner. I have no idea if they're being saved for anything, but this could be an act-now-ask-for-forgiveness-later sort of situation.

After an hour, I've cut apart and taped together a dozen boxes. They dome at the top with a window on each side and a movable door. To finish it off, I scribble Query Lab across the front with a Sharpie I found in the kitchen.

"What's a Ca-ree lab?" Henry asks.

I snort. "Query Lab. Ya know, like Quinn and Henry put together. It's a science lab for your bugs."

Both of their faces brighten as I hoped they would.

"Can you take a picture to show Mom?" Henry asks.

Quinn pokes at the door. "Side?"

"Yes! You can go inside. How about I take a picture of you both through the window?"

Quinn reaches for his hand. This time he lets her take it. He helps her pull the cardboard door back, and it brushes through trimmed blades of grass as they disappear inside. When I peek through the window, they're pointing at the little counter and two box seats I made for them.

I snap a picture and then look up just as I hear Caroline say, "What's going on here?"

9
EVERETT

I tip my head back, taking in the towering red brick building before me. Be the Brave Elementary was not a place I ever planned to see again. At least, not up close. Yet here I am, with a daughter attending my very own alma mater. In the two weeks I've been dropping her off, I've managed to keep enough distance to avoid going inside the main building. Until today.

I cross the parking lot and follow the sidewalk that wraps the boxy exterior to the front entrance. Not much has changed about this place in the last two and half decades since I was a student here. Same clock tower and flagpole by the street corner. Same weathered playground equipment faded from the sun. Same pair of pine trees I'd spend recess under as a kid. And when I press the button to be let into the building and step through the front door, I'm reminded of why I avoided ever coming in here in the first place. It's not just the school that hasn't changed. I *feel* the same when I'm here trapped in a prison of memories I don't like being reminded of.

"Can I help you?" A woman who looks past retirement age greets me. She's pushed up to the wooden desk on the opposite side of the glass window.

"Uh... yes." I swivel my head around. I might remember the layout of the school, but room numbers not so much. "I have a meeting with Miss Amy?"

"Please sign the clipboard and take a visitor badge. She'll meet you in the conference room, which is down that hallway, third door on the right." She smiles at me in a polite way a stranger would, and I feel myself exhale. She doesn't recognize me. Even so, I choose to scribble my first name only on the badge I clip to the collar of my shirt.

"Thank you."

The farther I get from the office, the worse it smells—musty carpet mixed with hundred-year-old French fries. I could have spared myself the onslaught had I fought my family on this decision. It was a part of their homeward bound intervention plan the day after my concert exit. The five-to-one odds were not in my favor.

I pull out my phone on my way down the hall, checking the surveillance footage on the house. *Nothing.* Summer is still not there yet. *What's taking her so long?*

I swipe the app closed as I come upon the open conference room door. Miss Amy is already seated at the oval table in the center of the room. She stands when she sees me and gestures to the chair across from her.

"Mr. Dawson. Please, come in."

I stuff my phone in my pocket. "Thanks."

"Thank *you* for meeting with me."

My phone buzzes and I pull it out to check it again. A snapshot of Summer, Quinn, and Henry opening the side gate to the house fills the screen. It surprises me how much that fuzzy image calms my buzzing nerves.

A throat clearing interrupts my stare. "I'm sure you have places to be, so I'll get right to the point. Quinn is having a difficult time in class."

After the week I've had hauling her here kicking and screaming, this is not shocking news.

"As you know, Quinn lost her mom several months ago. And with my line of... work... she's not used to me being around much." I want to add that Quinn's been through more than anyone should at her age. She may not understand the feelings of grief or the purpose of death, but I know every night before bed when she says, "Mommy stay," she knows what it feels like to miss her.

"I'm not talking about Quinn's home life, Mr. Dawson."

"You can call me Everett."

She nods.

If it's not about the tantrums, then what is she getting at? Why am I here?

My phone buzzes again with another screenshot. I can tell it's the backyard based on the grill in the corner, but the people are farther away. I hold it closer to my face and see Summer turned toward the camera. She's holding out a bucket of something to Quinn. My heart does this brief stutter in my chest at the broad expanse of her smile. I don't like it, so I flip over the device and set it on the table.

"What I'm trying to say is, I think your daughter might need additional services I can't provide at this school."

A triggering onslaught of memories washes over me. Trapped in a small space, interrogated with concerns, pushing for answers. There's a chasm of doubt with my ability to be a capable father hovering over it. One gust of wind and it'll all fold like a house of cards. All that's keeping me upright at this point is determination. I'll tell this woman exactly what I told Caroline—Quinn is *fine*.

"She's four."

"I mean no disrespect." She freezes for a moment.

All of these thoughts and feelings are swirling around in my body. Being here in this building, having this conversation, it's all too much. I know what she's referring to, and I don't want her to say anything else.

"My own son struggled with a speech delay," she adds.

There it is. It was easier to ignore when Caroline was the one pushing. But Quinn's teacher?

She slides a card across the table. I pin my eyes on the wall instead of her face. I'm afraid she'll see the one emotion I hold tight to my chest: fear.

"There's a speech pathology clinic across town. They have a great working relationship with some of our students and accept most insurances. But, of course, you're welcome to see who else might be in-network if you prefer. They'll start with an evaluation and help her..."

Her words slip out of focus as I fixate on her pen.

Mrs. Dawson, your son needs help.

She clicks the tip, and it morphs into a pencil.

Tap. Tap. Tap.

I peer over my shoulder. The ghost of an eraser bounces off the surface of a desk, trapping my attention.

"Everett? Are you okay?" Miss Amy asks, but instead it's Mrs. Fuller's voice I hear.

Can you draw an oval for me, Everett?

Woosh. Woosh. Woosh.

I glance to the left. How long has the computer been making that sound?

Mrs. Fuller lifts the pencil and closes my hand around it.

Why is she squeezing so tightly? I can hold it myself.

I flex my hand.

"Are you okay? Can I get you some water or something?" Miss Amy asks.

Tick. Tick. Tick.

What is that? Where is it coming from? Why won't she let me find it?

You hold it like this. Here, let me help you.

There! It's the clock on the wall above her desk.

Cht. Cht. Cht.

Her shoes, my pants, the carpet. Why is everything so loud?

How do they not hear it too?

Mrs. Dawson, he struggles to focus.

Why can't I block out these sounds?

Why am I the only one?

"Everett!" Miss Amy shouts my name, snapping me back to the present.

The legs of my chair scrape against the carpet as I scoot away from the table. It's no longer just my seat that feels small. This whole room is suffocating me. I swipe the business card to appease her and stuff it in my pocket.

"We won't be needing the help but thank you for your time." Dismissing myself, I head for the door.

She stops me before I can exit. "Accepting help doesn't mean you've failed as Quinn's father. It means you're her biggest advocate."

I used to believe in help. As a kid, it was something I thought everyone needed. Learning to ride a bike, tie your shoes, make a waffle in the toaster. I expected it the first time I tried anything new. That everyone struggled once in a while, and it was normal.

Normal is exactly what I want for Quinn. It's what I want for *me.*

But that ended the day I was told I was different. The seemingly generic term—*help*—suddenly didn't seem so okay anymore. It felt ugly and wrong and embarrassing. As if a four-letter word had the power to destroy me. Even as an adult, help is filled with nothing but expectations and invisible strings. I don't want any part of it.

"As parents, we all have limitations. Something my therapist said to me after I found out Johnny needed speech therapy too." Miss Amy shrugs.

I appreciate what she's trying to do. Everyone wants to feel relatable. But being relatable is not how you survive in this world. It doesn't make you special or unique in the same way finding out what you're good at something and sticking with it does. We'll find Quinn's strengths and lean into them just like I did. Everyone will see.

"Thank you for meeting with me," I say, to be polite.

"If there's anything more I can do—"

But I'm out the door before she can finish that sentence. I know she's trying to do her job, but she could have kept her opinions to herself. She'll realize Quinn's not different. That she's not... *me.*

I take the drive back to the house slower than I ever have, replaying that kindergarten memory I shoved into a box a long time ago. I can't get rid of it. And maybe I wouldn't have found myself in this position, feeling triggered, had I taken my mom's advice. After running off the stage at my last show, she suggested therapy. But something about sitting in a stuffy room dredging up the past sounded like torture. I already know my demons. Talking about them won't make them go away.

Matters get worse when I see a black Range Rover parked in *my* spot on the driveway. I was already trying to prep myself to see bubbly Summer, but Caroline? If she knew I had a meeting with Quinn's teacher it would be the Spanish Inquisition for me. And I'm trying to shove it all back in the past. Memories Caroline, Summer, and the rest of the world need to know nothing about.

I pull the business card from my pocket and stuff it in the

glove box. Caroline is sitting at the table with Quinn, quizzing her with flashcards, when I get inside. Quinn doesn't run to me when she sees me like she used to do with her mom. I acknowledge it, but don't let it sting like it wants to.

"Where are Summer and Henry?" I glance out the sliding glass door to a map of color painting the patio and a couple dozen boxes taped together. The fact that Summer remembered Quinn likes to color... it's something a nanny would do. A thoughtful gesture that's hard to ignore.

"I sent her home," Caroline says without looking up at me.

"You what?" I shove my hands in my pocket as I approach the table in quick strides.

What is it going to take for her to get that she doesn't have custody over Quinn?

"This is an apple. Can you say, aaaa-ppple." Caroline enunciates the word and ignores my proximity as I tower over her.

Quinn climbs on her lap. "Appow."

"That wasn't your call to make," I interrupt.

She finally lasers in on my face. "You'd rather have your daughter spend time with some stranger than her grandmother?"

"She's not a stranger," I argue. In fact, as far as Caroline knows, Summer is the woman I hired to be Quinn's nanny. She can't just dismiss her when she wants to. That's my job. And after the day I had, I wasn't exactly ready for Summer to go home yet. For more reasons than simply not being in a great headspace to parent right now. Whether or not it's appropriate to be thinking about how much I liked seeing Summer in my home is an entirely different question.

"Are you sure about that? How much do you really know about this woman?"

She's acting like I'd trust my daughter with anyone. Summer's son goes to school with Quinn. And I can bet Quinn had a hell of a lot more fun drawing on the patio and playing in that impressive box creation than she is working through a stack of flashcards.

I don't like the look in Caroline's eyes. The Blackwoods are a highly connected family around here. They frequent country clubs and board meetings. It wouldn't be impossible for her to know something about Summer that I don't.

"I know plenty, thanks." I turn away from her, taking long strides toward the island, because now I'm questioning everything. A list of things I don't know about Summer unravels like a rogue roll of toilet paper in my mind. I don't know her last name or where she lives, other than with a friend. Which seems odd if she's married. I don't know where she works or who Henry's father is. And those aren't even things I'd find on a criminal record if she had one.

Does she have one? Would El have trusted Summer so quickly?

Being the only grandchild on both sides, we haven't needed to leave Quinn with so much as a babysitter. I convince myself this is simply new for everyone involved. And I owe Caroline some grace. She lost her daughter and is having to face watching her grandchild grow up without a mother. I get that it's hard on everyone.

It doesn't mean I'm a bad judge of character. Or that I should be taking the brunt of what she's working through. I'm a good parent. I show up if her teacher says she'd like to have a meeting with me. Something I'd use to prove myself to Caroline right now if I were okay with her knowing about it.

When I've determined how I feel on this subject, I turn to face her.

"I trust Summer."

Caroline raises an eyebrow. "Did you know Henry isn't her son?"

I hide my shock as a sick feeling stirs in my gut.

How did you find this out? I want to ask, but that would give me away. Because no, I did not know that information.

Even when the muscles in my jaw want to lock, I force myself to relax. No matter what, I'll get to the bottom of this.

"Quinn and I have plans this evening," I say.

It's a lie. The only plan I have is getting Caroline the hell out of my house and figuring out what I'm going to say to Summer.

Caroline gathers her flashcards into a pile but leaves them on the table. Her way of suggesting I use them after she's gone, I'm sure.

"I'll show myself to the door. Bye, Quinny." She wraps her in a hug and exits without another word.

The rest of the evening I try so hard to be present with Quinn. We watch *Inside Out* 2 but I miss most of the context of the movie. All I can relate to is the character Anxiety, and how it's taking over my own control center.

Summer had so many opportunities to tell me she isn't Henry's mother. Why didn't she?

Near the credits, Quinn falls asleep tucked against my arm. I carry her to bed, then head for the bathroom. I should be out in the studio, but after a day like today, it would be fruitless. Words won't come. The same way it's been this entire week.

I brush my teeth, use the bathroom, and strip down to my boxers. The relief I feel when the mattress that was delivered today molds to my body is the one bright spot I hold on to. Especially when the emptiness around me threatens to pull me under.

I have a love-hate relationship with nighttime. It's dark and quiet and lonely. I swipe a hand across the side of the bed El once occupied, missing the way she'd curl her leg over mine. She'd rest her head on my chest and tell me about her day. Now the only weight I feel there is the anxious ball that threatens to collapse my lungs at any given moment. The constant reminder that it's all up to me now.

I flick on the lamp, slide on my glasses, and pull out the journal I keep in the top drawer of my nightstand. I add a few necessary lines before tucking it back where it belongs. When that doesn't help me feel better, I pull up the empty text box that's been taking up way too much space in my head all night.

I consider myself a good judge of character. Todd, for example, wasn't the first manager who offered me representation. One guy who did is behind bars for three DUIs, and another is facing a lawsuit for selling the intellectual property of a fellow artist. I've never been wrong with who to trust before, and it's driving me crazy that I might have been too quick to trust this time. That I was acting in desperation and didn't know Summer as well as I thought I did. I'm basing my decision on *seems* instead of *knows*, but she *seems* too nice to find herself behind bars isn't enough. This is why I don't ask for help.

Summer deserves a thank-you for dropping everything last minute. More than one thanks, actually, in the ever-growing list of ways she's saved me. But, it seems, she's also been lying to me, and I'm still pissed about it. I war with myself.

When I finally hit send, the frustrated side of me wins.

10

SUMMER

"This show is so toxic." Julia stuffs a handful of buttered popcorn in her mouth.

I watch Stephen fabricate another half-truth to get his way with Lucy.

"That's why I love it. Makes me feel better about my life." I cross my cozy, sock-covered ankles and wrap an arm behind my head to look over at her. She's cringing at the TV screen before she inhales another bite.

"Isn't that the truth."

Tell Me Lies has become our Friday night routine ever since I moved in. I know what a sacrifice it is for her to watch this show with me, and I appreciate her for it. Evenings are her only time to recharge. I make myself scarce as much as possible, but having friends with busy lives and a bank account that's draining without a job, it's a lot smarter to stay in.

My phone vibrates against the couch cushion. I snatch it up, expecting it to be a recruiter for one of the jobs I applied for. I turned on my LinkedIn notifications earlier even though it's the weekend tomorrow. I'm desperate to hear back from someone.

It's not a recruiter. It's a text message from the same unknown number that called me earlier today.

> EVERETT: When were you going to tell me that Henry isn't your son?

I sit up with a start.

"What's wrong?" Julia presses pause on the remote.

"Rhett just found out I'm not Henry's mom." I cover my mouth with my hands.

"What do you mean *just* found out? How long have you been co-opting my kid?"

I look over at her with wide eyes.

"Wow," she says with an expression I can't read.

If it were from anyone else it would roll right off my back, but I admire Julia's opinion of me too much. She's better in every way, and it stings when the maturity gap between us feels a football field apart. I pivot my body so my feet touch the carpet.

I must look defensive because she adds, "I'm just surprised Henry didn't tell him already, that's all. You know his attention to detail."

Surprised. That's a better adjective than *disappointed* or *angry.*

The moment this afternoon when Henry corrected Quinn for calling a grasshopper a ladybug flashes through my mind. Julia's right. Henry's quick to tell it like it is. How did he not blurt this out at Quinn's birthday party?

I gasp.

"What now?"

"No, that's it! Henry asked me to take that picture of him in the box fort for you at the same moment Quinn's grandmother, Caroline, showed up. She must have overheard Henry and told Rhett."

"This Caroline gal sounds like a real meddler."

You have no idea. After she arrived, she told me I was *no longer needed today.* Like a maid she could dismiss as she pleased. I left without a scene because I didn't want to ruin my chance of spending more time with Quinn.

I know I made up the nanny job on the spot, and then questioned what I was thinking after it spilled out of my mouth, but today was the best day I've had in a long time. I think Julia might be right. I'd be a good fit as Quinn's nanny if Rhett ever offered me the job. But I'm pretty certain any potential in that scenario just launched into the sky and combusted upon atmospheric impact.

I perch on the edge of the couch, leaning on my knees and staring at the screen. "What do I say back?"

She tosses another handful of popcorn in her mouth. "The truth."

"Right." *It felt nice to pretend for a while* is honest. I type the reply and watch the bubbles appear and disappear and reappear again while chewing on my bottom lip.

What if he's mad?

I should have made a joke instead. That's the kind of relationship Rhett and I have. He dishes out blunt honesty, and I make light of the situation.

> EVERETT: Whose kid is it?

> SUMMER: My best friend, Julia's. The one I live with.

> EVERETT: Did you borrow her wedding ring too?

My eyes flare and then flash to the gold band on my finger.
I never took it off.

And he noticed it. How have *I* not noticed it?

It's been there since the day Brian put it on my hand. His BSU fraternity hosted a Halloween party off campus. I was invited to attend by a coworker I waited tables with. Some people might have been turned off by the last-minute notice or the costume dress code. I'd never been one to say no to a good time or a challenge. With scissors and a hot glue gun, I transformed a tea-length white dress, tulle skirt, and headband into a runaway bride situation. My outfit turned half a dozen heads at the party. It wasn't until Brian said *You're missing something,* that I paid attention. He unfastened a gold chain from around his neck and looped my finger with it several times.

Now you're taken, he said.

How often has that worked on a girl? I asked.

You tell me.

The way he looked at me... I felt like the only person in the room. I *wanted* to be the only person in every room he was in.

It didn't matter that it wound well past my knuckle and made it impossible to bend my finger. When you're young and infatuated with someone, you do stupid things. All that mattered was that he wanted me to have it. And that after six inseparable weeks, he had it melted down and asked me to wear it for the rest of my life.

Why, after everything he wanted in our divorce, did he never ask for it back?

"My ring is still on." My thumb and pointer finger remain touching it as I look up at Julia.

"I thought you'd take it off when you were ready." The sad look on her face is something I don't feel. I don't *let* myself feel it. My marriage is over. If Everett wants honesty, *that's* the truth. Forgetting a ring on my finger won't change that. I jerk it off and throw it across the room. It bounces off the stone fireplace, landing on the carpet.

I hate this gray cloud that looms over me whenever I think about Brian, so I go back to what feels comfortable.

> SUMMER: No need to borrow it from her when we're in a polyamorous relationship.

> EVERETT: Do you ever take anything seriously?

> SUMMER: I buy T-shirts with mediocre singers on them, remember?

Does he remember? It's the first reference I've made to that night. I really wish we were talking on the phone during this conversation and not over text when he doesn't reply. I don't know what he's thinking. But honesty was Julia's advice. So, I text him again.

> SUMMER: I'm kidding. I just went through a divorce.

If I wondered what he thought of me before that text, I'm desperate now. Once people know that information, they put me in one of two camps: I didn't try hard enough, or I should have never married him to begin with. Either way, both indicate failure in a relationship that meant a great deal to me, whether or not it was difficult to endure at times.

With parents who have been married several decades, I grew up believing in the sanctity of commitment. I may have rushed into a life with Brian, but I had no intention of abandoning our union when times felt hard. Something I believed we both had in common up until I was served papers.

> EVERETT: I'm sorry to hear that. And I'm sorry about Caroline.

His apology is appreciated. I should have anticipated it would change the subject from our night at the concert. I hate that I want him to remember it as much as I do. Feel the electricity that's only grown stronger for me since then. But he clearly doesn't want to talk about it, and I can't blame him when all this time he thought I was married.

> SUMMER: The bossy lady with the authority complex? She melted under my smile.

> EVERETT: I'm sure she did.

> EVERETT: Thank you for today.

> SUMMER: Anytime.

I stare at my phone screen for who knows how long after that before finally looking up. Julia has reclined her chair and twisted it toward me as if I'm the show.

"What?"

"You're blushing," she says.

I toss a throw pillow at her. She catches it before it flops in her face.

"Has he forgiven you?"

"I think so? He thanked me for helping him today, but—" I cringe. "If we're keeping to the honesty trend, I told him you and I are in a polyamorous relationship."

She tosses the pillow back at me. It knocks me square in the chest. "Summer!"

"What? He's too uptight." Didn't used to be, I want to add, but I don't tell her that part. I gave Julia vague details after I left him the night of the concert. I had to explain why I came back with a cowboy hat instead of a trucker one.

"I'm sure one flick of your wrist and he'll be unraveling in the palm of your hand."

"Jeez, Julia. He sounds like a yo-yo."

"I just meant, you're incredibly charming when you want to be. I'm sure he's already discovered that about you." She yawns and folds in the footrest of her recliner.

"We haven't finished the episode yet!"

"I have an exam on Monday and a five o'clock alarm set for the morning to study for it," she says.

"Fine. But we're finishing this tomorrow." I point a finger at her.

"Can't wait to see what train wreck Stephen has for me then."

I snort. "I'm gonna stay up for a while, but you can turn the light off."

She winks. "Sure thing. Good night."

"Good night," I say.

I lie awake waiting—*hoping*—for another text from Rhett as I replay our conversation. As much as I should have told him about Henry sooner, I don't regret it. My time spent with both him and Quinn might be the closest I ever come to feeling like a mom. For that reason alone, it was nice playing pretend for a while.

It's close to midnight when my phone light blocks the gray shadows of tree branches dancing across the living room wall. I get my hopes up for a second until I realize it's a message on LinkedIn: *Summer, I got your application. I know this is last minute, but would you be available for an interview at 8 a.m. tomorrow morning?*

I click on her picture. The app takes me to her profile page.

Emma Dawson, J.D., Senior Associate at Ford Law

I got the interview at the law practice, and the attorney is Rhett Dawson's sister.

11

SUMMER

The living room wall rattles with the *thwap* of the front door. I attempt to lift my head off the dilapidated hunk of cotton Jules considers a throw pillow and groan.

I should have never fallen asleep on this couch. The kink in my neck is evidence of that. So are yesterday's clothes as my braless chest comes face-to-face with Julia's ex in the entryway.

Jake's hands are planted on his hips as if he's commanding a room full of people. "Where is she?"

I snatch the ring from the carpet, fold my arms, and cross the room "Hello to you too. I'm going to wager she's where I find her every morning at this time of day."

It's a small dig that I know her schedule better than he does. A sizzle sparks from the kitchen, and his eyes dart in that direction.

"Thanks for the help." He follows the sound.

Jake's aware I'm not his biggest fan. To clarify, I like him as a person, but I don't appreciate his choices. The day he starts showing up for Henry and Julia, I'll happily give him a free pass.

I close the door to Julia's office—my room. We managed to

squeeze a twin bed in here, but I share it with a desk, Henry's bearded dragon, and a sewing table. Not to mention the pile of laundry belonging to me that litters the floor. It's a lot cozier than I'm used to, which is probably why I didn't give a second thought to sleeping on the couch. I toss my phone and ring on the desk and minutes later, when the paper-thin walls do nothing to mask their conversation, I give in and let myself eavesdrop.

"Did you think about it?" Jake asks.

I hear a clatter. A spatula maybe? Julia is the most even-keeled person until Jake comes around. He drives a motorcycle and has a sleeve of tattoos. Julia wears cardigans that button to her collarbone. They are the epitome of opposites attract.

"What are you doing here, Jake?" she demands.

"I can't come see my son?"

"That's not why you came. Your first question answered that."

"It's been over a month, and you still haven't answered me," he says.

Julia keeps her feelings for Jake pretty private. I know they're still there, but she's also a strong independent woman who doesn't need anyone. She'd rather be on her own and stuff away her feelings for him than let him weigh her down. I respect the hell out of her for that.

"I thought this was all too much for you," I hear her say back.

My stupid phone interrupts this intriguing conversation.

The interview! I replied before falling asleep and forgot to set an alarm. I read her message: *Great! See you soon!* before checking the time. Twenty minutes. That's all I have before I'm expected to be there.

I don't have time to shower, so I gather the only clean outfit I have left—a patterned pair of flowy pants and a hot-pink bodysuit. I've never worked in a high-profile setting before. I have no idea if it's dressy enough, but it will have to do.

With an armful of clothes, I sneak into Julia's room across the hall and grab a pair of nude heels from her closet. When Henry tolerates going, she attends church sometimes. The heels might be a tight squeeze, but I have small feet for my height. Hopefully she doesn't mind if I borrow them. It's not like I'm about to interrupt this intense conversation happening in the kitchen to ask her.

I slip into the guest bathroom, apply a swipe of deodorant, brush my teeth, and put on the outfit. I brush the tangles from my hair and twist it up in a clip before glancing at myself in the mirror one last time. Between the heels and the hair, it elevates an otherwise casual ensemble.

The hallway carpet muffles the clack of the pointy shoes. Jake and Julia don't hear me coming.

"You can't tell me you didn't feel something," he whispers.

My eyes shoot to the kitchen where he's covered her hand on the counter. His body language is screaming *kiss me now.*

I am a slot machine of questions. *What happened? Who felt what? Why didn't you tell me?* But it's *her* question directed at me that gets answered first as my heels meet the entryway's hardwood.

"Where are you going?"

I don't pause at the sound of her voice.

"Interview!" I shout over my shoulder.

"Good lu—" The front door cuts off the rest of that word.

I'll tell her thank-you later. Right about the time I ask her about Jake.

Any other morning it would be a twenty-minute commute to Ford Law, but on a Saturday, it's less than ten. Even set back from the main road, the five-story commercial office building covered in more windows than wall is not hard to spot.

I find a space right up front labeled *Visitor Parking* and catch a glance of the Boise River before slipping in the front door. The lobby is silent and empty. Black-and-white checkered flooring leads to an empty elevator bank. I'm certainly not taking the stairs after my ankles already threatened to collapse on foreign stilts while crossing the parking lot. I find my destination engraved in a gold plaque next to the elevator door. *Emma Dawson, fifth floor*, it reads.

The ride up is a lot faster than I'd like it to be. It's not enough time to think this through. I should have stopped and told Julia about it. See if she thought I was crazy. What makes me think this job will be any different from the last ten?

A *ding* and the doors open. I step into a hallway of plush burgundy carpet leading in two different directions. I completely skip over any wall signs and follow the sound of a female voice coming from the right.

When I turn the corner, a long desk with two receptionists greets me.

"Can I help you?" the closest one asks. Her cream-colored silk blouse is the only part of her outfit I can see over the shiny surface. Diamond studs sparkle through her shoulder-length haircut.

"Yes, hi. I'm here for an interview with Emma Dawson."

Her friend lifts a hand to her mouth. A stifled laugh supersedes her "She's on the left side of the building" directions. I gather *left* to mean *less than* with the way she emphasizes it. Her eye roll also suggests I should have read the signs and known that. Her attitude in general is a far cry from the politeness I expected in an office of this caliber.

I offer a thanks even if she doesn't deserve one. It's after I'm out of their line of vision but not earshot I hear the one who didn't talk whisper, "Did you see what she was wearing?"

I may not feel thirty in many ways, but the catty, mean-girl vibe they put off feels high school to me.

There's nothing about the opposite side of the building that's inferior. It's a mirror image of the right minus an occupied front desk. There's no one to check in with, so I knock on the only closed door.

"Come in," she calls from the other side.

I twist the gold handle, and a head of dark hair is visible over the top of a large monitor.

"Please have a seat, I'm just—" Her sentence ends abruptly when she lifts her head. "Oh! Hi! It's—"

"Emma," I fill in for her. "Good to see you again."

Her warm smile puts my nerves at ease.

"You too." She gestures to the two leather chairs facing her desk. I take the one on the left on purpose. There's no sense pretending I'm not *less than* in this place.

"I hope you found me okay."

I don't tell her it took a run-in with a pair of pompous receptionists to do it.

"I should have known it was you based on the application. It's not very often I run into someone with the name Summer. Can I get you anything to drink?"

"I'd love a water, please."

I regret accepting her offer the moment she stands and presses her palms down a navy-blue blazer and pencil skirt. By looks alone, Emma Dawson embodies every bit of poise I expected from this office. Thankfully, her eyes have never strayed from my face. She swings open the door of a black mini fridge to the side of her desk. Color-coded labels in neat rows line the shelves. She fists two glass bottles and swings the door shut, handing me one.

"Thank you," I say, taking it from her.

"Of course." She sits back down and rolls her desk chair to the side of her monitor. "Mind if I ask you a few questions?"

"Sure." I straighten and suck in a deep breath, puffing out my chest. *Is that what one does at these sorts of things? I'm so out of my element.*

She slides on a pair of glasses and thumbs through a stack of papers. "Oh, screw it!" She yanks the glasses off and tosses the paperwork in the air. It pinwheels a few times before scattering all over the small patch of carpet around her desk. "Since we've already met, I think we can skip the formalities, right?"

I hope she doesn't catch the bob of my throat when I swallow. Would I be reacting this way if this wasn't Rhett's sister? I'm second-guessing everything.

"I'm going to be blunt with you," she continues. "There are some people in this office who are... *difficult* to work with. They've driven away four perfectly capable assistants of mine, and I really need the help. Would you say you have thick skin, Summer?"

Does dealing with your grumpy brother count?

I don't say that. Instead, I return the level of honesty.

"I've had sixteen jobs in the last decade. My track record of sticking with something is not great. But I'm living with my best friend after going through a divorce, and I really need the money for a deposit on an apartment. I know my skill set may not transfer to this job, but I'm a quick learner. And if you're asking if I can handle those catty girls down the hall, the answer is a resounding *yes*." Of that I am confident. I unscrew the cap off the bottle of water and tip it toward my lips.

She grins at me. "You're hired."

I gulp down the liquid in a stiff bob of the throat. "Just like that?" A gust of surprise follows my question. I expected she'd need details. An even longer explanation of my work history. A trial run to make sure I make good on my word.

All the while, my heart is screaming *You already found the job you want!* while also being drowned out by the logical voice in my head that says *But it's something you can never have.*

"I can pay you thirty dollars an hour. Can you start today?" Emma's hands are folded in a pleading gesture.

All thoughts of being anyone's nanny vanish as I sputter and choke on another swig of water. "I'm sorry... Did you say *thirty dollars an hour?*"

She smiles. "I told you I needed help."

I calculate the math. That's... *sixty-two thousand dollars a year.* Ten grand shy of what Brian makes. I can't... I don't... *what?* I expected it to take me years—if ever—to work my way up to that kind of salary. I won't have to stare at Brian's court-deemed money in my account as soon as I can prove the income. There's no way I can turn this down.

A legal assistant wasn't the job I was hoping for, but I like Emma, and she's taking a chance on me. The thought of living on my own and supporting myself no longer feels as far away as it did. Right now, that's all that matters. And I remind myself that it doesn't have to be forever.

"Yes." I nod eagerly. "Yes, I can."

Eight hours of learning to manage Emma's calendar, maintain her case files, and handle incoming and outgoing emails and phone calls is how I spend my first day on the job. Despite my head swimming by the end of it, I've managed to keep it above water. Which is all that matters—it's all I promised her. It's obvious how backlogged her workload is and, like helping with Quinn, it feels nice to be needed.

I didn't consider how triggering and disheartening it would feel seeing the number of divorce cases that cross her desk though. I'm not surprised. I know the staggering statistics; I added to them. If there was any other way, I wouldn't have. It wasn't my choice. A memory of the ring on my finger and Julia's words from last night drift through my head.

I figured you'd take it off when you were ready.

I don't know what held me back. I don't like to think about it. Another reason why this job will be good for me. Gives me very little time to think at all.

I make it through a quarter of the stack before it's time to go home for the day.

"Thank you so much for taking this job. I'm glad my brother introduced us," Emma says as we walk to the elevator together.

"He's a good guy."

She eyes me with a smile but doesn't say anything as the other legal assistants step into the elevator with us.

"You're still here," one of them points out.

I wink at her. "First day."

They look at each other and share a smirk. "I'm Tara. This is Jasmine. You should come out with us to celebrate. Amsterdam Lounge. Have you heard of it?"

The first thing I notice is that they don't invite Emma.

"I have."

Their eyes brighten. The elevator dings and the doors open. They step out first, waiting for me on the other side.

"Sorry, I have plans. But just so you know, you'll need your fake IDs. They card at the door."

The two of them share a disgruntled look before scampering away. Once they're out of the building, Emma twists my shoulders to face her.

"That was amazing! *You're* amazing." She hugs me.

"So are you," I say.

When she pulls away, all I see are those familiar amber eyes.

It must be a Dawson thing.

12

EVERETT

After a rough Monday morning with Quinn, I'm treading dangerously close to a mental breakdown. I used to brush off her outbursts as toddler tantrums. They didn't faze me like they do now.

If it was my *only* problem, I could handle it. It's not. It's been almost a week in my new studio, and I haven't written anything but a basic melody.

I play a riff, adjust the tuning pegs until I get the perfect pitch, and then strum the first chord on my favorite guitar. It's the same one I was gifted at graduation from my parents. Everything I've ever written has been on this instrument. I used to call it "lucky strings" in the same way a basketball player might consider a pair of socks after winning a state championship in them. This guitar used to tell *me* what to write. It doesn't feel so lucky anymore.

I tuck a pen between my teeth and play the next few chords. Over and over until five minutes drag into ten, ten into twenty, twenty into an hour. The melody is there but nothing else. Nothing but empty words and blank promises.

I shove the guitar off my lap and chuck the pen across the room. It slaps the wall and topples, end to tip, on the floor.

I'm distracted. It's been three days since meeting with Quinn's teacher. I convinced myself I didn't give a shit how long that business card lived in my car; I was never going to look at it again. That was before doubt sunk in. Fear that they might all be right about her.

I've tried every trick I know to help Quinn communicate—getting her to look at me when I'm speaking, asking her to repeat what she said, attempting to fill in the blanks for sounds she leaves out. I don't know what else to do.

An evaluation feels like the only option.

Most days I've been in such a hurry to get in the studio that today's slow, defeated climb down the stairs has me noticing they don't creak anymore. Next time I see Will, I'll have to thank him for that too. I register I'm heading toward my car before I mentally catch up.

The number of reporters lurking outside the house has died down in the last few days. Must be bored with my new mundane life. I'm still discreet, snatching the business card for the speech therapy clinic from my glove box and stuffing it in my pants pocket before getting out of the car. It's not how I imagined utilizing the soundproof paneling in my new studio, but letting the tabloids catch wind of the phone call I'm about to make is the last thing I need. Whether or not they're legally allowed to write about what happens in the confines of my private property is irrelevant. People talk and word will travel fast.

I rush back inside. *You're just finding out your options,* I remind myself as I prop my feet up on the desk and lean back in the chair. *This doesn't have to be a sure thing.*

An automated voice answers after a single ring. "Hello!

You've reached Words Matter. Press one if you'd like to schedule an appointment. Press two if—"

I punch the number one, and a perky voice answers. "Thank you for calling Words Matter, this is Katie!"

"Hi." The word rushes out of me before I can take it back, hang up, and burn the business card.

"Can I help you?"

"Uh... yeah." I scratch the top of my head and run a palm down the back of my hair, flattening it. "My daughter's teacher recommended your clinic."

"Typically, we take referrals from the child's pediatrician. But if you provide their name, we can reach out and get the information for you. Can I get your daughter's first and last name, please?"

It hits me, the panic...

How much information are these people going to want to know?

"Uh... I was hoping to ask a few more questions first," I answer.

"Of course. How can I help?"

I want to tell her I don't need her *help*, but that's the reality of why I called, isn't it? There's no sense skirting the truth with this woman the same way I did with Caroline, Quinn's teacher, even Summer.

"Who finds out about this evaluation?" I ask.

"It's completely confidential. We encourage you to share the results with your child's pediatrician and teacher so they can be a part of the progress monitoring that's put in place to support your daughter's needs. But if you prefer to keep it private, you can turn down the form."

I add *turn down the form* to the mental pros column.

"And what exactly will we be committing to by having the evaluation done?"

"Nothing yet. The first step is to simply find out if she qualifies for services," she says.

Making this phone call felt like admitting she already needed them. I hadn't considered she might not even qualify. The tension in my neck and shoulders eases with her answer.

"If she does qualify, there are a few things that determine how often she'll be seen here. It will depend on how many visits in a calendar year your insurance covers and the severity the evaluation uncovers. Most of our kiddos come once a week. If you are open to it, I can send you the preliminary paperwork by email to get started while we wait for the referral from her pediatrician. You'll need to fill out the forms to the best of your ability before her evaluation."

"Okay."

"We have some availability next Monday. Would that work for you?"

A week to change my mind about this.

"Yes," I agree.

She asks for my email address. I give her the fake one I use whenever a situation warrants discretion as well as the pediatrician contact information before we end the conversation, and then I pick up an incoming call.

"You'll never guess who came into my office."

I rip up the business card, toss it in the trash, and pick up my guitar.

"Em, I don't exactly have time for gossip right now."

Appearances have always been important to my sister. Not in the same rich-obsessed way as her boyfriend or the having-it-all-together way as me. She cares about being in the know and what people think of her.

"That gal from Quinn's birthday party... Summer? She interviewed with me this weekend."

I sit up taller and abandon my instrument. That was not what I was expecting her to say.

I contemplate a light response. Act interested for her benefit, when in reality, I'm trying to figure out Summer for myself. She's recently divorced, living with a friend, and up until this weekend, was gunning to be my nanny. Now she's working with my sister?

"You're interviewing?" I ask. This is the first I'm hearing about this. I didn't realize Emma's assistant quit. What was her name...? Gloria?

"Yeah. It's been... yeah."

Well, that's a lot to go on.

"How did it go?" Maybe that question will encourage details.

She squeals. "She's so amazing! I hired her in the first five minutes."

I clutch the phone a little too tight. My hand cramps. *I found her first*, the stupid voice in my head argues.

"Like full time or..."

"I mean, you know my hours. They're all over the place. She didn't seem to mind though. I got the impression she could use the work, and I love that I get to help someone who needs the money."

"She needs money?" I ask before thinking. That's why she's been offering to help me.

"Wow. What's with the twenty questions? Are you into this girl or something?"

"You were the one who called me about this. I'm making conversation," I argue.

"You're in your music studio, aren't you?"

"What's that supposed to mean?" I snap.

"I can tell when you're working on music lately. You're tense."

"Gee, thanks."

It's not like she's saying something I don't already know. But she had to point it out?

"You know, Ev, if the label is pressuring you in any sort of way, I can look into your contract."

I don't need my sister meddling in my career.

"Thanks, but no. I should go though."

"Okay, well, if you need any help with Quinn—"

"Em, I've got it," I bark.

Had it, before you went and stole my nanny anyway.

She sighs. "When did we stop relying on each other for things?"

Probably when my problems became a burden to your social life, I want to say but don't. That was a long time ago. We aren't kids anymore.

"I'll call you tomorrow?" she finally offers. As if we'll be ready to have this conversation by then. Something I highly doubt is true after we've managed to dodge it for years. But I want her off the phone, so I agree.

By the time she hangs up, the email from the speech place hits my inbox. The document opens in Adobe Reader. I itch the skin on the back of my hand, reading over the section asking for guardian contact information. The spot I'm tearing into becomes a full welted rash by the time I reach the family history section.

Cursive letters read *confidential* across the bottom. Sure as hell better be as I check the tiny box that feels like a confession of something I haven't had to admit to anyone in a very long time.

I hope I'm not making the biggest mistake.

Summer shows up to preschool drop-off on Tuesday in the brightest red dress I've ever seen. There's not a single person in my sister's office that won't notice how much it hugs every curve on her body. That fact wouldn't bug me if it weren't for everything I know about the head of the firm. I've seen Jason Ford's wandering eye despite the gold band on his ring finger.

She hasn't been a minute late since that first day I ran into her a week ago, but she might be to Emma's with the way she's attempting to run across the parking lot in a pair of stilettos. I'm going to guess this is one of her first times wearing them. Her ankles are rocking to keep herself upright. I really wish I didn't have to talk to her looking like that, but I need to have this conversation.

"You have legal assistant background?" I ask as we meet on the pavement.

"And you have a close relationship with your sister," she replies. An assumption that's not entirely accurate as of late, but I nod anyway.

I'm not surprised my sister hired Summer on the spot. She makes it difficult not to like her. But now I'm left feeling guilty for even considering what I'm about to do next.

"If you're worried about me infiltrating your personal life, don't be. I had no idea it was your sister's law practice until it was too late," she justifies.

"I need some help with Quinn," I rush out.

She pauses. A smirk tugs at the corner of her mouth. My eyes decide to stray way too long on that corner before I scold myself and stuff my hands in my pockets.

She folds her arms. "Wait a minute... is Rhett Dawson asking me for help?"

I grind my molars. Of course she's going to make this as difficult on me as possible. If I have to spell it out for her, she's only going to get a one-word answer from me.

"Yes."

She shrugs. "I'm sorry. I'm already taken." Then she turns away from me. I grab her wrist before she can get any further and twist her around. Her eyes snap to where I'm touching her, the pressure on her skin softening with the ease of my fingertips. I should let go, but I don't.

"Whatever she offered, I'll pay you double."

I don't miss it when her eyes flare. It means she's considering it.

My sister is good at what she does and is compensated as such. There's no doubt she offered Summer a generous hourly wage. But it's not one a billboard-topping artist can't compete with. Even one who is only earning royalties at the moment. I no longer care how desperate it makes me sound.

Summer surprises me when she shakes her head and starts to walk away again, her wrist slipping from my grasp. I follow after her.

"It was your idea to be my nanny," I argue.

"I told you in a roundabout way when we met that I'm impulsive. By definition, it means I don't stick to the things I commit to."

"Does that mean you're going to drop my sister too?"

God, I'm practically poaching Summer from her. I don't really want that for Emma. She seemed genuinely excited about employing her. If Summer could use the money, maybe she can work for both of us.

"Of course not!" she says, sounding offended as her heels *click clack* across the parking lot.

She's almost to her car, and I'm running out of time. "Five weeks. After school until eight and a few hours on Saturdays. It'll give me the time I need to finish the last three songs on my album," I clarify. "What will it take for you to say yes?"

She spins around and folds her arms. "Well, for starters, you haven't said please yet."

I glare at her. Not this again. The thought of me begging her makes me want to die. It's also making my skin hot. I survey the parking lot before I whisper it. "Please."

She cups the shell of her ear. "I'm sorry, did you say something? I think I might hear it better if you were down on one knee."

If reporters caught wind of my morning commute and started following me to Quinn's school, they'd have a heyday with this charade she's putting me through. I don't need them spinning up a false story about my relationship status.

"That's what I thought." Summer's ponytail swishes as she flips around and opens her car door.

Dammit. "Fine!" I shout and drop to a knee. "Will you *please* be Quinn's nanny?"

She looks over her shoulder at me, chewing on her bottom lip.

I am going to hell. This is the worst idea I could have come up with. I should have just let her work for Emma. Because if she does that around my house all the time with me there, I'm going to have a much bigger problem on my hands than trying to juggle Quinn and the record label. I'll be fighting with a tight dress, plump lips, and a walking billboard of red.

"All right." She folds her hands. "I'll do it."

Relief floods my system. I thought for sure she'd say no. I start to stand, and she pushes me down by the shoulder. "But I get to keep my job with your sister while Quinn is at school."

Took the idea right out of my head. I nod.

"And you have to do the spring play," she adds.

This time I stand. "Why do *you* care about the school play?"

"Because I think Quinn would like it," she says.

With the number of hours I'm putting in at the studio right now, it's hard to find time to spend with Quinn. I suppose I can spare an afternoon once a week without it setting me back any more than I already am.

"Okay," I agree.

Her timing could not have been more coincidental as the same guy who asked me to do the play approaches us.

"Hey!" He greets me with another jovial slap to the shoulder I don't appreciate. "How about that school play?"

"I've decided to help out." I keep my eyes on Summer to see how she'll react. "As long as she volunteers too."

"Wh-what?" gusts out of Summer's mouth. I don't miss it when the guy's over-the-top grin falters.

"Summer... that's... yeah. Great! Thank you... both... for your participation." He takes a step back. "See you on Monday at three o'clock." Then he pivots on his heels and beelines for the building.

That was... *weird.* Summer never even got a chance to answer. I'm sure I overstepped by dragging her into this, but it's outside of my comfort zone, and she's good with kids.

There's a bizarre dynamic happening that I can't figure out. I still don't know that guy's name, but with the way Summer's eyes track him all the way down the sidewalk and back into the building, I'm going to bet she does.

"Who is that guy anyway?" I ask her.

She still hasn't looked away from those closed double doors.

"The principal. And my ex-husband."

On my way.

That's what her text said the last time I checked it.

I acted on instinct yesterday. Hired Summer—*officially*—after my sister did. I lay awake all night wrestling with these uncomfortable, *jealous* feelings that fought for more time with her than anyone else gets. I asked her—*begged her*—to be my nanny. Memories of me down on one knee haunt me. Mostly because it felt more right than any other decision I've made since I moved back home.

Then she dropped the bomb on me that the principal is her ex-husband, and I felt bad that I asked her to show up there on my account every day. I picked up Quinn from school on my own. Told her she could finish up at Emma's office before coming over. Now I'm pacing around my living room while Quinn eats her chicken nuggets at the table, awaiting Summer's arrival like a whipped teenager. I can't stop thinking about how, for several hours every evening, she will be roaming my house, playing with my daughter, leaving her lemony scent on my furniture, and taking up even more space in my head than she already does.

And the scary part is, I don't regret it.

A rhythmic pattern rattles the front door. I know it's her before I even answer. A knock like that is a very Summer thing to do.

I swing it open. She's holding a bouquet of un-bloomed flowers—pink peonies, I think—and adorning what's quickly becoming my favorite grin.

"Hi!" she says.

"Hi." I take an intentional step forward, more so to move out of the pathway of the door, but it doesn't hurt when our shoulders brush too.

Earlier, when I grabbed her wrist... I've thought about that touch more than any first kiss I've ever had. She must have thought about it too because her eyes stray to that same place.

"These are..." She extends the bouquet of flowers toward my chest. The pitter patter of small footsteps approaches and she spins, squats, and holds out the bundle to Quinn. "For you! They haven't bloomed yet but just wait until they do. They're my favorite flower."

Quinn beams at her. "Wav? Wav?"

"Wave? Water? Web?" Summer attempts to decipher what Quinn is saying.

She shakes her head at every guess.

"Show me?" Summer asks, and Quinn grabs her hand, dragging her toward the backyard. Before they've even made it outside, Summer spots her cardboard creation. It's sat out there for a week now, Quinn playing in it every evening because I didn't have the heart to throw it away.

"Oh! *Lab?* You want to take the flowers to the lab?"

"Yep!" Quinn says, and Summer looks over her shoulder at me, knocking me out with her dimple.

"How did you do that?" I stare in astonishment at her.

She shrugs.

I may have had my reservations, but I have a feeling Summer is exactly what Quinn needs.

13

SUMMER

A shot of water blasts through the window, dousing our hair, our faces, our clothes.

So much for that after-dinner entertainment.

Quinn's and my shrieks fill the cardboard space as I lift her by the underarms and attempt to squeeze us both through the makeshift door. There are sprinklers shooting from every corner of the yard, drenching any dry spots that were left.

Rhett is jogging across the grass from the garage when I look up. He scoops Quinn from my arms and drags the box fort by the window. When we make it to the patio, we're all staring in a state of shock at what transpired in a matter of seconds.

"I'm so sorry. I had no idea they were going off tonight," he apologizes.

"Da-eee wet!" Quinn complains, peeling her palms from his soaked shirt and shaking them off.

"*You're* wet." He holds up a clump of curls in front of her eyes. She sticks out her tongue and captures the droplets that fall from the ends of her hair. A smile stretches across his face, rivulets running through the maze of tiny crinkles around his eyes. Then he's laughing. He's looking at her as if she holds everything good in the world. Tucking her under his chin and squeezing her tight.

It's a tender moment. One that has me desperately yearning for the same kind of love in my life.

The moment ends when he makes a break for the back door. He stops when Quinn shouts.

"No! Da-eee see?" She points to the crumpling structure that used to be her hideout.

I get the impression from the guilty look on his face that he's never been inside. His eyes drop to the watch on his wrist. The hands are big enough to read from here: seven o'clock. He still has another hour in his studio, and it's Quinn's bedtime.

I hold out my hands. "I can take her in and get her ready."

He shakes his head. "No, it's okay. I'm all done for the night. Besides, I think I have a cool fort to see."

I cringe at the soggy cardboard, one side already collapsing in on itself. "Better take the chance while you still can."

He snorts and sets her on her feet. "Better."

Quinn drags him by the hand through the opening. When I made the door for this thing, I wasn't intending for a grown man to squeeze through it. He chuckles when his shoulders get stuck and tears a section of cardboard away to fit.

"Wow," I hear him exclaim when he makes it inside. "This is cool!"

It's nothing special, especially now. But the way their voices escalate makes me feel more appreciated than I have in a long time. I wait outside the entrance, unsure if I should go in the house and let them have their time together. A shiver passes through me as wet clothes cling to my skin, but I'm too busy listening in on their conversation to care.

Glass clinks, and I know she's showing him her collection of critters now—two ants, a moth, and a praying mantis. The fact that the jars survived the choppy ride across the grass and the collapsing cardboard is a small miracle.

A minute later, she peeks her head out the front door and waves. "Tum in!"

Not only was the door not built for adults but the space inside wasn't made to fit *two* of them. I fight my way through the opening, trip, and land with a plop right on a lap of muscle. I scramble for purchase on something to help me stand, but all I'm doing is ripping holes in the cardboard.

"Relax. I don't bite." His voice is a rumbly sound in my ear, an octave below his usual one.

You sure about that? I want to joke, but it gets lodged in my throat. My pulse hammers across my skin. There's no way he can't feel it with us pressed together. Quinn's jabbering a whole bunch of nonsense, or maybe it's fluent sentences, how the hell am I supposed to know when my attention is glued to the hand that's stroking a circular pattern on my knee. Aside from yesterday when he gripped my wrist, Rhett's never touched me before. I didn't know I'd need a warning if he ever did again—a chance to gather my senses before they all went haywire.

My first day on the job and I've ended up in my boss's lap. This would already be completely unprofessional by any standard, but especially with his daughter right here.

I clear my throat, vaulting myself in an ungraceful exit out the door. "Last one inside is a rotten egg!"

The mention of a game lures Quinn right out and into the house, with Rhett trailing behind her.

He snags a hand towel from the kitchen on the way, mopping up the trail of water we leave behind.

There's technically another forty-five minutes before my nanny hours end, but if he's not going back out to his studio, I imagine he doesn't need me. "I should head out," I alert him as he carries Quinn to the stairs.

He stops on the second step. "You're not driving home like that."

I know he's referring to the clothes that are plastered to my skin. The ones that would soak the seat of my car if I left right now. To show him I don't care, I wave a hand at him. "It's fine, I—"

"You can use the room across the hall from Quinn's. There's a shirt in the top drawer, sweats in the bottom."

He doesn't wait for my response. I stand there for a minute longer after he's already gone.

I shouldn't stay. There's no need to. The problem is... I *want* to.

Another minute passes before curiosity carries me after them. I've never seen this part of the house before. There's a long hallway at the landing with three doors spread out. The farthest one on the right is cracked, showcasing floral wallpaper and a naked toddler fleeing large hands that are threatening to tickle her. I don't know how long Quinn's bedtime routine lasts, so I hustle toward the door he told me to go in.

I flick on the light and am met with rich brown walls and a faded bedspread. The whole room is filled with warmth, but that's not what has me closing my eyes. *It smells like him*—a mix of expensive cologne and Tide laundry detergent.

This is Rhett's room.

I run a hand over an old dresser, stopping at a picture of a decade-younger version of the guy I've been getting to know, his sister I'm now working with, and another boy in a cap and gown. I'm gathering he's a close friend with the way Rhett's arm drapes over his shoulder.

Another shiver wracks my body. One that's difficult to ignore without the distraction of Rhett and Quinn this time. I give in to the dry clothes I was promised, stripping everything off but my underwear.

There are two pairs of gray sweats in the bottom drawer of the dresser. I grab one of them and shimmy them up my legs. It requires cinching the drawstring as tight as it will go to keep them from falling back down to my ankles. Basic tees line the top drawer, and I opt for the black one, hoping like hell it hides the fact that I'm now braless and still freezing.

By the time I slip into the hall, the small sliver of Quinn's room is black. My eyes adjust to the darkness as he tucks the covers up to her chin.

I hear him whisper good night and watch her latch onto the sides of his face with two tiny palms. She pulls him in close and kisses him on the forehead, right above the bridge of his nose and between his eyebrows. I can only make out shadows from here, but I picture his whole face softening like it did on the patio. I'm still staring when he leaves her room and cracks the door.

"Thank you for the clothes," I whisper. That's the real reason I stayed lingering in the hallway. Just to tell him that. *Definitely not* for another chance to talk to him before I have to go home.

He's still soaked, the wet strands of hair sending streaks of water down his cheeks. Without thinking, I reach up and swipe one of them away.

His eyes drop from my face, which is now heating as he takes in his baggy clothes on my frame. "Would you like a drink?"

A drink is exactly what I need with the vigorous cardiac workout my heart is putting me through. Water would probably be best, but who's to say alcohol won't cool my pounding pulse. I'm technically off the clock since Quinn's asleep, so I guess he wouldn't judge me for accepting. He's the one offering.

"Sure."

"I'll just be a minute," he says.

By the time he meets me downstairs, he's wearing the other pair of gray sweatpants I saw in his drawer.

"Thank you... for tonight," he gets out. "She's rarely affectionate with me." It's the most unsteady in his words I've ever heard him. A stark contrast to the calculated commentary he usually hits me with. The astonished look in his eyes also suggests he believes I'm the reason for the affectionate gesture he received from Quinn tonight. I know that's not true.

"She's really great," I say, hoping it conveys how much I liked my time with her. How much I like it *here*.

The living room light is off, the kitchen one spilling in to compensate. Upstairs I could only make out shadows, but down here, I notice details. The faint crease between his brows. The subtle droop of his mouth. The slight downcast of his eyes.

"She always asks for her mom when I put her to bed. She didn't tonight. Do you think that means she's forgetting her?"

It's hard to look at him when I don't know how to answer that heartbreaking question. She *is* little. How long does a child actually remember someone who isn't in their life every day?

"Maybe she didn't feel like she needed her mom tonight. She has you."

He offers me a smile. It's reluctant, but it's there.

He tucks his hands in his pockets. "Listen... about the principal..."

We're standing at the foot of the stairs. We still haven't even made it into the kitchen for that drink, and I could care less. I'd be okay if we spent the rest of the night right here in this magical spot where he's opening up to me.

"Brian," I fill in for him.

"I would have never asked you to do the play if I'd known." His eyes are pleading for forgiveness when they don't need to be. I've managed to dodge Brian every day I've dropped Henry off at school. I wasn't naive enough to believe that would last forever. I'm bound to run into him a time or two, and I need to get used to being around him without it being... weird. After twelve years of living and sleeping in the same bed with someone, all to have it stop overnight, I don't know any other adjective to describe it.

"I know." I drop my head to stare at his carpet as I expel a puff of air from my nose. "It feels unfair that you know something so deeply personal about me."

Besides the comment he made about Quinn's mom and the fact that he's living in his childhood home, all the personal things I know about him I've heard from the news.

When he turns and walks away, I realize why. Rhett holds everything close to his chest. He's a private man despite a very public profession. It's hard not to wonder if there are parts of himself he's hiding. And I thought we were opening up there for a minute, but now I'm afraid I crossed a line—offended him without intending to.

"I promised you a drink," he says, and I relax. Some people use alcohol to open up. Maybe that's what this is.

I follow him into the kitchen. He stops at a cabinet next to the fridge. It's the only one with a glass front displaying various bottles of liquor. I drag out a barstool and sit on top of it while he pulls two copper mugs from the bottom shelf. He adds a small scoop of crushed ice from the freezer, then holds up a bottle of vodka.

"This okay?" he asks.

"Sure."

He twists off the top and pours a couple of ounces, then chases it with ginger beer.

"Where'd you learn how to do that?" I ask as he garnishes the mug with a lime wedge.

He smirks. "Humpin' Hannah's."

I know the place—a popular downtown nightclub with live music. Been there a few times.

"Wasn't always Rhett Dawson," he reminds me.

I try to picture him as a bartender. It's a fuzzy image barricaded by the even bolder and brighter one of him singing on a stage. Makes me realize how very little I know about *Everett* Dawson. The guy I want to know everything about.

He slides the glass across the countertop. It stops mere inches from my hand. I quirk a brow, impressed. Then I sample my drink. The tart of the lime and the sweet of the ginger mix. It tastes as good as it looks.

"Nice to know a mediocre singer has a fallback plan."

He leans a forearm onto the countertop, fixing his eyes on me. It sends the hair on my arms standing at attention, and a tingling sensation skitters down my spine.

"What about you? Always wanted to be a nanny for a famous musician?" He lifts his glass to his tightly pressed lips. The look he's giving me is a dangerous one.

I nod. "One with a big ego too."

His chuckle is deep and throaty.

"I've always wanted to do something that makes me happy. I think being around kids does that," I add. "Did you always live here? Before Nashville, I mean."

He watches the pale amber liquid swirl in his glass with the rotation of his wrist. "The tabloids haven't given that one away yet? Or do you only watch 73 *Questions*?" His expression is blank when he looks up again and waits for my answer.

"I meant here," I say, stretching my arms out toward the walls of this home. I know he's referencing the *Vogue* YouTube series I absolutely did watch before I met him. The fact that I had a maple fritter donut in my car that morning at drop-off was simply a coincidence from that video.

"No. I moved out right after high school."

From the unsettled look on his face, I gather he'd rather not be back. "And you don't like it here?"

"At my parents' house? It's not where I wanted to end up, no. How long have *you* lived here?"

"I moved right after high school too. It's expensive living in California, and I'd never been to Idaho before, so..." I shrug. There wasn't much more to the decision than that. I'm not the five-year plan type of gal.

"Did you meet him here too?"

I nod. "When I was nineteen."

"Nice guy?"

I wouldn't have married him if he wasn't nice, I want to argue. But I know he's just curious like I am about his life.

"Brian grew up in a strict family. A big one too. There were bills to pay and mouths to feed and no excess for any kind of adventure. Education was an expectation not an opportunity, and Brian did what his father had done because he felt obligated to. When I met him, he was knee-deep in his senior year at Boise State—finishing out his last semester of student teaching. I was the girl at his fraternity party ready to show him a good time.

"My life experience far exceeded his in the realm of fun. I'd moved states on my own, visited five different National Parks sleeping in the back of my Honda Civic, and had no intention of settling down. I'd traveled with my parents, sky-dived, swum with sharks. My life excited him at first. But then it became a push and pull of expectations I could never live up to after we got married. He'd press for me to get a new job when the last one didn't work out and then be disappointed when I'd find something in retail, working weekends rather than spending time at home with him on his days off."

I check his face to see if this is too much. He said *Nice guy?*

and I gave him a monologue. Even though all along I know he was asking whether my ex was nice to *me*.

"Well, anyway... things change. It was for the best," I finish.

Doesn't matter *why* Brian ended things. They're over.

"Sounds like you deserve better."

"We were both at fault. I think Brian wanted to be a good husband as much as I wanted to be a good wife. I didn't give him what he needed. Some people aren't the right fit." We didn't bring out the best in each other, no matter how much I hate admitting that. Staying together isn't as simple of a choice as I used to believe it was.

He acknowledges my answer with lingering eye contact before looking away and taking another long pull from his glass. "Quinn has a speech therapy evaluation in a week."

I don't have to guess if this confession has something to do with the teacher's meeting he had the other day. Don't have to ask him if he's worried about it either. I can hear it in his voice.

"You said it was unfair for me to know something so personal about you. Well, there you go," he adds in the wake of my silence.

His words drip with self-consciousness. An unease that's not hard to miss.

Is that why he fought going? Because he's embarrassed?

"You know the results aren't a reflection of you as a parent, right?"

His silence is all the answer I need. He's blaming himself.

"Says the woman who doesn't have any children."

I blanch, then burn inside. Of all the things he could have said, I didn't expect an insult. What stings the most is that he's right. I can't pretend to understand what it must feel like to have a child who is struggling. To have a child at all.

I can brush off most things, but this is the one topic I get the most defensive about, and insecurity spills over into my response. "If it bothers you so much, then why did you hire me to help with Quinn?"

He straightens and holds up his palms. "Shit, Summer, I'm sorry. It doesn't bother me. I'm just tired of everyone knowing more about parenting than I do. Why is this the hardest job I've ever had?" His head collapses into his hands, his walls slipping and his vulnerability showing. "I don't know how to raise a kid. Up until tonight, she's never even asked me to go in that box fort you made her. Never kissed me good night. Never did any of the things she did to show her mom she loved her."

It's clear what I originally said did nothing to make him feel any better. In fact, I think I might have made matters worse. Because now he sounds like he wants my opinion, and I'm in no position to be giving anyone life advice. I've told him as much. It's my turn for another personal truth.

"Last spring I was on a hike by myself, contemplating what to do after my last job didn't work out. Brian seemed supportive enough when I told him the news that morning, but I was still visibly spiraling. I almost stepped on this tabby cat's tail when she came darting out of the sagebrush and batted at my shoelace. She didn't have a collar, so I brought her home with me, and when I walked in the door, Brian took one look at the kitten and said, 'Really, Summer. You can barely take care of yourself.'"

I don't mean to get emotional, but that's exactly what surfaces while dredging up the memory of his words.

Everett circles the counter, stopping right in front of me.

"That's why you pretended Henry was yours." He doesn't ask if it's true. Just says it like the statement it is.

I hug my arms around my torso. I'd rather throw myself in traffic than say this out loud. "Do you know what it's like for a woman in her thirties who looks like a stay-at-home-mom but doesn't have any children? Everywhere I go it's the first question

I'm asked. *There must be something wrong with Summer if she hasn't had a kid by now.* There couldn't possibly be another reason for why someone would *choose* not to have one. So, yes. When you made a comment about Henry being mine, I let you believe it. I didn't want you thinking—"

He wraps his palms around my arms, stroking up and down in a soothing pattern. "The only thing I was thinking was *a woman that confident must make an incredible mom.*"

I shake my head and let the tears that have been pooling in my lash line free. "The old me was confident. Now I can't even go over to the house I shared with him to get a cat he doesn't even want back. I'm too afraid he'll be home and remind me I don't deserve her."

Rhett's hugging me by the time I let all of that out. And I thought I'd stop there, but the warmth of his body seems to be pulling every last admission from me. "I wouldn't have dared bring a child into the world with a man who'd resent me about a *cat*. It wasn't that I didn't want one." My chest lurches against his with an embarrassing hiccup and I pull away, swiping at my eyes.

"I'm so sorry, this was about you. I'm clearly not the right person for advice on this subject. And you have enough going on. You don't need to listen to me blubber on about my tragic past."

"Summer."

I take backward steps, catching my heel on the edge of the living room rug and pinwheeling my arms to keep from tipping backwards. "You know what—"

"Summer," he tries to interrupt again.

I point at him. "Maybe you should ask that mother-in-law of yours. She seems bursting with feedback."

He chuckles as my back connects with the front door. I bend down to slip on my tennis shoes.

"If she said anything offensive to you, I'm sorry. Caroline is insufferable when it comes to Quinn."

"I think all Caroline wants is to be a part of Quinn's day. And I mean, I get why. After spending time with her, *I'm* ready to take your ass to court for custody."

A smile unfurls across his face as he watches me hop on one foot to get my left shoe over my heel.

"You're good with her, ya know."

I choose not to hear the *better than me* I have a feeling he's implying. Secretly, I want him to say *You're good with me too*, but I know he's a stubborn man, and he'd never admit to needing anyone else.

"I should go," I blurt, reaching for the door handle. The distance between us is helping me think more clearly, and I'm sure I've overstayed my welcome.

"Yeah, I guess I better get to bed too. There will be an alarm clock shaped like a toddler starting my day before I know it."

I pull on the handle and a draft of cool night air filters through the opening.

"Thanks again for the clothes."

"You're welcome. Good night, Summer."

"Good night."

He turns around and I slip out the front door. The breeze is a shock to my system, and I realize there's one more thing I never got the chance to say. I hadn't closed the door yet, so I push it back open.

"Everett?"

He turns quickly. "Yeah?"

"You're doing better than you think you are."

14

EVERETT

I know she's here even before I spot her Range Rover by the clubhouse. On Sundays, Caroline plays bunco with a group of ladies from her country club. The draft of chlorine mixed with Lysol dredges up memories with Eliza as we clear the entrance to the building. I wouldn't be here if it weren't for Summer's comment on Tuesday night. Her reminder that all Caroline has ever wanted is to be a part of Quinn's day.

Quinn spots her first, pushed up to a marble-topped table and sipping a margarita. "To-To!"

Caroline's head turns at the sound of Quinn's voice, her eyes widening. She pushes out her chair, anticipating her granddaughter's hug before she's even close enough to receive it.

"My Quinny! What a happy surprise! What are you doing here?"

She's looking up at me. Her question is followed by a series of *awws* from the five other ladies circling the table. They all fuss over the new red Speedo goggles, ladybug swimsuit, and floaties we picked up at the store on our way here. It's been an unusually warm spring, so I imagine the pool is already open. If not, I know they have a year-round hot tub she can swim in. I set Quinn's overnight bag next to Caroline's chair.

"I was wondering if Quinn could spend Sundays here with you after bunco. And if she could spend the night tonight too? I could use the extra time in my studio."

Writing music is not what I intend to do with all of that time, but I don't tell her that. I know Caroline doesn't support my career, and she certainly wouldn't appreciate that I plan to spend my evening with my nanny.

"Of course she can." She scoops Quinn up in her lap, pushes back into the table, and flags the server. "Pierre, could we get a Shirley Temple please?"

He nods.

"I'll come pick her up tomorrow morning before school," I tell her.

"That's not necessary. It's on the way to my gym class. I can drop her off."

"Thanks."

Quinn's busy eating up the attention she's getting that she doesn't even notice when I duck out the door without a good-bye. I send a quick text to Summer from the parking lot and get back the answer I was hoping for before driving home to pay my neighbor a visit.

"Come in," she says when she finds me on her porch.

"Hi, Delilah."

Most neighbors would greet you, hug you, or wave you inside their home. Delilah skips all the formalities when she presses her back to the front door as my cue to enter. It used to confuse me. Sometimes when I'd hang out with Will in high school, she wouldn't even acknowledge that I was over. At first I thought that meant disapproval until I figured out it was just her personality. Now it's what I love most about her. I've never had to act like I owed her anything.

"I'm not catching you in the middle of something, am I?" I ask.

Her house is silent. Eerily so. Evidence of Will's concerns map a path around me. The large clock that used to lean above the fireplace is missing. Same with the TV that sat on the now-empty console table. The dining room is a sea of wood without the rug in my studio breaking up the brown tones. And all that's left of the gold mirror that used to hang in the entryway is the nail that held it up.

"Nope. Just got off the phone with Phillip. I was about to pour myself some brandy. Want some?"

With anyone else I'd check the time, but with Delilah I know that means it's mid-afternoon. She's the five-o'clock-somewhere type. She also goes to bed early.

"I'd better not, but thanks."

"Suit yourself," she says, waddling toward the kitchen. I scrutinize her appearance now that she's facing away. The shuffle is not new. Will told me once she got in a motorcycle accident when she was younger. Shattered her right leg. When in need of a bone graft, she refused that part of the reconstruction process. Stubborn Delilah... would rather live with slightly uneven legs for the rest of her life than be reliant on crutches for a month.

The kitchen is a lot like the view from the entryway, but I'm glad to see it hasn't spilled over into permanent things, like the cabinets still attached to the walls. She opens one of them. It holds the bottle of brandy and is fully stocked with food. The only thing missing is her full-size fridge replaced with one you'd find in a dorm room. I tread lightly.

"So, how have things been?"

"Sounds like I should be asking you that." She barks out a laugh. I listen for signs of sickness, but all I hear are years of smoking. Even though she quit cold turkey when Will moved in, the damage had already settled into her lungs.

I scrub my neck. "I take it you've seen the internet." There's an open laptop on the counter next to me. I guess that explains the lack of TV.

"They lettin' you come back?" she asks.

"Trying to. I have to finish three songs for my album first."

"So, what's the problem?"

She makes it sound so easy.

Well, you see, Delilah, I've got a toddler strapped to my hip, a career that's been put on hold, and an imminent speech evaluation that threatens to upend my life. What isn't the problem?

I'm learning I could use some advice.

"Do you miss him?" I ask.

Delilah lost her husband, Edward, to a heart attack when Will and I were seniors. If there's one person who might understand what it's like when I think about El, it's her.

"Ed would have wanted me to move on," she grunts.

I nod, gathering what she means. Dwelling doesn't help a person move forward. Doesn't mean you forget them either.

She takes a swig of her drink and looks me dead in the eye.

"Do you like her?"

I clear my throat. "I'm sorry?"

"These fences are tall, boy, but that voice is as chipper as they come. Ivy doesn't hide *that* much."

I smirk. I should have known Delilah would notice the extra adult with my parents out of the country. Summer's spent every night since Tuesday hunting for bugs with Quinn in the backyard.

"Have you been spying on me?"

"There's not a lot to do now that you boys are grown."

It's the first time I'm catching any sort of comment tied to Will.

She misses him, that much is obvious. But she's determined to keep the conversation on Summer when she says, "Not easy raising a kid on your own. I'm glad you got yourself some company."

It feels validating having someone comment on the challenges of being a single parent.

"You're a good neighbor, Delilah."

A popping sound chimes from her computer, and a faceless image takes over the screen. Her waddle morphs into a gallop as she rushes to her computer.

"I better get that. It's Phillip," she says.

I stand. "Sure. I won't take any more of your time. But if you need anything—"

She waves me toward the front door. "Tell Will I'm fine and your parents to have a good trip."

I'm already outside by the time the chiming on her computer stops and her voice, full of life now, says hello.

I send a quick text to Will from her porch.

> EVERETT: Visited Delilah. She said to tell you she's fine. 😔 She's been keeping busy with Facebook Phillip?

I feel inspired when I leave Delilah, writing two more melodies in the studio before it gets dark outside. Still no lyrics yet, but I'm reminding myself that I have to start somewhere, and music has always come easier than words ever have.

My evening plans route me three miles away from my parents' house.

The homes in downtown Boise border commercial buildings, with the largest high-rise on Eighth and Main being Zions Bank. Summer lives in a little single-story home with blue shutters. I park like everyone else who visits this part of town—on the street.

Cobblestone steps, uneven with the growth of a giant oak

tree's roots, pave the way to the front door. I knock, and Henry answers it.

"Summer's not here right now." He starts to shut the door in my face when a hand blocks it, and a woman with dark hair piled atop her head pries it back open. She wipes her hands on an apron and holds one out to me.

"I'm so sorry about that. I'm Julia, Henry's mom."

I smile and shake her hand. Despite the drastic difference in hair color, he looks more like her than he ever did Summer.

"Summer is on her way. I was in the middle of making blueberry scones when Henry started begging for a banana, and we were all out. It was this whole thing." She waves her hands in the air before inviting me in.

"It's not a problem. I'm in no rush," I tell her.

Julia's home is boxy like mine, rooms separated by walls but with low ceilings. I don't know if it's the smell of fresh pastries, the lack of difficult memories, or the kind company, but it feels homier somehow. A timer sounds from the kitchen.

"Ope. I've got to get that. Please make yourself at home. Henry, scoot back from the TV."

He wiggles an inch and continues staring at the screen, his head tipped back.

I take a seat on the couch next to him. "I like the hat."

He gives me a look like *You should; it's yours*, before watching the guy on the screen stuff his hand in a glass jar with what looks like a giant wasp. I cringe as the insect creeps closer and closer to his outstretched thumb. Chew on my bottom lip when it finally crawls on his skin.

"Careful, it can smell fear."

I vault to my feet.

Summer folds her arms across her chest, a look of pleasure painted on her face.

"What the hell—o?"

"Hell is a bad word," Henry says.

Summer's still smirking as I scratch my jaw.

"You're right. Sorry," I apologize as Julia joins us in her living room.

Summer hands her a grocery sack, and with the look of gratitude Julia returns, I can tell these two have been close for a long time. My appreciation for Julia only increases when I remember Summer's tale of her shitty ex-husband. I haven't stopped thinking about it since she opened up to me the other night, and I'm glad to know Summer's had support through her divorce.

"Don't apologize. He's heard worse," Julia says.

"My dad says 'fuck' sometimes."

"Henry!" Julia gasps.

Summer and I both fight to hide our smiles as he pulls his attention away from the TV to his mom.

"You said it's good to tell the truth."

"I didn't mean..." She trails off, shaking her head.

"You ready?" I ask Summer.

"You haven't told me where we're going."

I'm sure she found it strange when I texted her on a weekend inviting her to go somewhere with me that didn't involve Quinn, but I wasn't sure how else to swing this. I didn't know if she'd even say yes. She tends to flee when it's just the two of us.

"You'll see."

"Have fun, you two," Julia says as we make our way to the front door.

"It was nice to meet you. Bye, Henry."

He's lasered in on the screen again, and I follow his gaze at the *worst* possible time—right as the wasp buries its bottom in the guy's hand. I'd say the kid had weird taste if my own didn't love bugs so much.

"Henry, say bye," Julia prompts.

He waves his hand over his head without turning around. Julia rolls her eyes before offering her own wave and closing the door.

Everything heightens the moment Summer and I are alone. The dark, the quiet, her proximity. It's been a long time since I picked up a girl—*woman*—from her front door. We're not exactly young enough to be "hanging out" anymore, and I didn't make my intentions for this evening very clear. I'm concerned I should have offered more details. Wondering if she typically brings that larger-than-a-purse bag slung over her shoulder to something that's not a date.

"You look prepared."

She holds out the bag to me. "They're your clothes I borrowed. Julia washed them."

"Oh."

I haven't stopped thinking about how she stripped in my room. That her bare skin touched my shirt. The same one she sure as hell wasn't wearing a bra underneath.

She's smirking when I take the bag from her outstretched hand, and if it wasn't for the vibrating phone in my pocket, I'd be fumbling for more to say than a simple *thanks*.

The welcome distraction is a text message from Will.

WILL: Phillip is news to me. Kind of like the rest of Delilah's life. 😊 Thanks for checking on her.

I send a laughing face emoji back.

"Coming?" she asks, opening her own door and climbing in my front seat.

It's my turn to leave this woman at a loss for words.

"What are we doing here?"

We're parked down the street. Summer's back is glued to her seat, her eyes trained out the window at a modest house on a sprawling property. I'll admit, it's impressive for a principal's salary, even one who works at a private school. The guy clearly knows how to invest his money.

A quick Google search told me where he lived.

A dog barks up the street, sending a crow scampering from the white picket fence out front. I don't answer her as she takes the place in. I want to be the one asking all the questions. "Did you plant those?" I say when the first one comes to mind.

"Yes," she confirms.

She said she wasn't brave enough to come back here, but I know that's not true. I'd never have noticed the pink peonies tucked behind the fence slats if there wasn't a vase of them blooming in my kitchen. I moved them inside after Quinn's box fort fell apart.

"They were my favorite part about this house."

She's more confident than she thinks, and stronger than she knows. Still, I didn't want her to have to do this alone.

Her breath hitches as a flash of orange dashes across the sidewalk and dips under the cracked garage door.

"Do you trust me?"

If she said no I wouldn't blame her. We're both taking a risk by being here.

Her eyes are wide when she looks at me. The woman who has sky-dived and swum with sharks, yet she's afraid to get her cat back. I won't let her live without it.

"Do. You. Trust. Me?" I repeat, waiting for her to answer.

She gives a jerky nod before I slip from the car and jog through the shadows to the garage doors.

It's second nature for me to glance around for security cameras. To my benefit, the only one this home has is by the front door. For whatever reason, the crack under the garage looked a hell of lot larger from across the street. I have to flatten my body against the pavement, skin grating on rough cement, to inch under it.

I'm well aware this is breaking and entering—the last thing I should be doing as a public figure with a career already on the line. Not to mention, I'm putting Summer at risk with her ex. For all those reasons I make quick work of it, scouring the garage. My eyes adjust to the dim light leaking beneath the door when I spot her cat in the corner, lapping at a bowl of water.

She sees me and freezes. I take a careful step closer. She flees behind a cardboard box.

"It's okay," I whisper. "I'm a friend of Summer's."

What the hell am I doing? I'm speaking to a cat as if it knows what I'm saying.

I inch closer until she's cornered. If I can just... reach...

She springs in the air, latching onto the cardboard box, and claws her way up the side. She leaps, nails digging into my shoulder through the sleeve of my shirt and launches off me. I clamp down on my bottom lip to keep from letting out a hiss of pain. A yowl fills the space as she scampers underneath the garage door.

Great. I bring Summer all the way here and I can't even catch this pet. I don't know what I expected—purring maybe?— but I just got taken advantage of by a cat.

Back to an army crawl, I shimmy into the moonlight.

"Who's there," a voice booms from the front door. I don't have time to react when Summer grabs my hand.

"Come on, come on, come on," she chants. The cat is

already clutched in her arms, bobbing up and down as we dash back to the car.

The engine revs—*so much for a subtle exit*—as I start up the vehicle and flip a U-turn.

"Go! Go! Go!" Summer is bouncing up and down in her seat, tapping the dashboard, eyes glued to the rearview mirror. She's still grinning and laughing, and I'm drunk on the sound, barely keeping my eyes on the road. I need to pull over before I hit something. We whip around a corner on a random side street and I park against the curb.

"Did you see that?! Did you hear him?! That was incredible! That was—"

Summer launches herself across the center console and crushes her lips to mine. I hardly register she's kissing me before she pulls away.

Her hand lifts to her mouth. "I'm sorry! I'm so sorry! I shouldn't have done that. I got swept up in the moment and... oh my gosh, Everett, your shirt!"

I'm still trying to figure out what just happened when she draws my attention down to where a jagged stretch of fabric flaps open on my sleeve.

"It's nothing," I tell her.

Well, actually, it was your cat. She's a vicious little thing. Or *was.* Now she's purring and relaxing in Summer's lap.

"It's not *nothing.* Here..."

She reaches into the back seat for the bag she brought and pulls out my T-shirt, but I know it won't make a difference. It's what's underneath that's the problem.

She sucks in a gust of air when she sees my bare shoulder.

"What happened?"

The damage is not as bad as it looks. Three deep scratches lance the skin, but the blood is already dried. "Your cat doesn't like men," I joke, using the ripped shirt to wipe away the burgundy spots. I meant it as a funny statement. She looks anything but amused.

"Is there a first-aid kit in here somewhere?" She bends in half to look under her seat.

"The glovebox."

The compartment falls open when she tugs on the handle. A little white box with a red cross is what she opens, shuffling through the contents and tearing at the packaging of an anti-septic wipe.

"When was your last tetanus shot?"

I hiss when the alcohol-soaked pad comes in contact with my torn flesh.

"They made me update everything before I went on tour." I'm not worried about it.

"I really am sorry," she says, squirting a line of Neosporin over the wounds and covering them with an extra-large Band-Aid.

"Really, it's nothing." I pull the new shirt over my head so she'll stop worrying.

"Okay."

It sounds like she doesn't believe me. The mood in the car is tense for a lot of reasons now. I don't know if she wants to continue talking about everything that transpired in the last ten minutes, or if she'd rather pretend it didn't happen at all. I can't even dissect it in my own head because I'm still reeling. Wishing it hadn't happened so fast. Wondering how she would have tasted if I kissed her back. Disappointed that I might never have the chance again.

While she stows away the emergency kit, I pull onto the road. I hadn't made plans to take her anywhere after this, so I guess we're driving back to Julia's.

I've never seen Summer this quiet. I don't know what to

think or say or *do*. I don't want her to feel uncomfortable now. She's been so good for Quinn, and I can't screw that up.

I park the car and kill the engine in the same spot we were thirty minutes ago. Everything feels different though. For a moment I'm afraid she'll take her cat and I'll never see her again after this.

"Thank you," she says instead. "Getting Millie back was the nicest thing anyone has ever done for me."

"I don't know that I did much more than get in her way."

She giggles when she finally looks up. "I'm sorry again about..."

"Summer, it was nothing. Really. I'm glad you're Quinn's nanny. She really likes you."

It wasn't *nothing*, but her commitment to my daughter feels like the only thing I should be salvaging right now.

I try to read her face. It's impossible with her usual smile plastered across it. "Of course! I'll see you tomorrow!"

I reach into the back seat, dumping my pants out of her bag and handing it to her. She takes it. With her cat cradled in one arm and the empty canvas tote in the other, she struggles with the door handle. I reach across her lap, our arms brushing, and push it open.

Another *thanks* is the last thing she says before she leaves my car for good.

15

SUMMER

"Okay, replay the situation again so I can be sure I heard you correctly. You *kissed* him?" Julia flits around the kitchen, filling a to-go thermos with coffee and stuffing what looks like a stack of handwritten exam notes into her bag. She's much more alive at six on a Monday morning than I'll ever be. I prefer the barstool I'm perched on as I slip Henry's lunchbox in his backpack.

"He *rescued* Millie, Julia. Of course I kissed him. I would have kissed *you* if you had done that for me."

As if she heard me, Millie's paw drags down the sliding glass door next to me.

"Just let her out."

"What if she runs off?" *Or worse—leaves me for Brian's.*

I don't know if I'd recover if she did that. I know she missed me. That much was clear when she slept on my face all night. But not more than she's missing being outside.

"You're right. You should do what you feel comfortable with."

"Thank you," I say, ignoring Millie's desperate attempt to

flee this house. "Speaking of comfortable... what's up with you and Jake?"

I haven't had a chance to ask her about that heated kitchen conversation the other morning and I'm dying for details.

Julia groans. "Nothing. Same as it's always been."

I take a sip of my coffee and drizzle it back into the mug. "Needs more creamer."

Julia pours in a splash, and I give her hand a heavy nudge. I take another sip. *Better.*

"It didn't look like nothing when he was touching your hand and begging you to answer his question."

"Fine. We shared a moment."

Duh is written all over my face followed by *Get to the good part.*

"The day we got back from Everett's concert, Jake kept thanking me for all I do with Henry. How much I've taken on by myself. He apologized for not being there. It was like he finally saw me. And so, when he leaned in, I didn't pull away."

Her eyes cast to the floor. A mixture of bashfulness and shame outweighing the giddiness I saw in that second to last sentence.

He finally saw me. It's plain as day that's what she's wanted from him all this time: not having to explain every decision she's making for herself and for Henry. It's what I've wanted for them too.

"So, what was his question?"

"He wants me to go on a date with him."

"And that's a bad thing because..."

I try putting together a puzzle I don't even have the pieces for. If she didn't pull away when he tried to kiss her, there's clearly still sparks there. And if anyone would make the most sense in Julia's life, it's a guy she's already had a kid with.

"Because I can't trust him." She groans and sinks her head

into her folded arms. "He's always said one thing and done another. His actions have rarely lined up with my expectations, and I'm typically the one who has to pay the consequences. He's still in the same place he was five years ago when Henry was born. Still afraid to spend the night alone with him. Still calls me when he does, wanting a play-by-play of how to take care of his own son. I want more for us. More for *me*. Is that so bad?"

"No," I'm quick to reply. I grab her hand. Julia deserves everything. Henry's diagnosis came with its challenges, but she's never let it hold her back from being the best mom, the best nurse, the best friend she could be. She does more than show up for the people she loves, she takes care of them. Which is more than Jake's done. "Of course not. You deserve it all."

She lifts her head, showing off a sheepish look. "It felt... nice. When he kissed me, ya know? Just because I'm not sure if I want to be doing that with Jake doesn't mean I don't want to be doing that at all. I miss being taken care of."

I gather she doesn't mean taken care of in the financial sense.

"Speaking of dates..."

"Everett asked you out, didn't he?!"

"What? No! Everett's my boss. I think he made that pretty clear last night when he said the kiss meant nothing and he appreciates me helping with Quinn." It's obvious he's not keen on blurring the lines from professional to personal. "Joe the banana guy asked me out."

I study her reaction. She's rightfully shocked. I mentioned nothing to her about him, since Everett was already here by the time I got home from the store.

"*Joe the banana guy*," she repeats at the slowest speed. I hear how ridiculous it sounds coming out of her mouth, but he was hot. Sometimes you don't need any other explanation than that.

"I was into his act. It worked for him." I shrug.

"I'm going to need the whole thing." She spins her finger in a circle and slides off the barstool next to me, taking a seat again.

"'You look like a woman who knows her bananas.'"

"What?" Her brow wrinkles.

"That's what he said to me." I chuckle.

"*That's what he said to you?*"

"Are we going to keep doing the repeating thing?"

"I'm sorry, I just... and that line worked for you?" She squints at me, mouth agape.

She didn't use to be like this—so serious all the time. I think Julia might have lost her playful side.

"You're right. I'm sorry, I'm sorry, I'm sorry." She's waving her hand now. "What did he say next?"

"You aren't going to ask what *I* said?"

She tips forward on her elbows. I've piqued her interest.

"I'm more of a watermelon girl," I say.

Her eyes study the ceiling.

"Stop trying to find some dirty connection with watermelons. I meant it in the most literal sense."

She flushes. "Right. Did he at least ask for your name?"

"Yes, but he didn't believe me after I told him it's Summer. Must have been the watermelon reference." I wiggle my eyebrows, and we both chuckle.

"I can't imagine that. So, did you help the poor guy pick out his bananas?"

"I convinced him to buy the bright yellow bunch. Told him he wouldn't have to wait so long to eat them."

"Summer!" She swats me with a towel. "And you're the one who said to get my mind out of the gutter."

"I had to mess with him a little."

"How do you do that? Flirt with a guy you know nothing about?"

I take another sip of my coffee. The creamer has had a chance to blend in. It's like drinking straight sugar. "I know something about him. He's a veterinarian."

She barks out a laugh. "You made that up."

I was wondering if she'd catch the reference. It was mostly a joke when I said it in Nashville minus needing someone in my life who is the opposite of Brian. Who would love Millie.

"I'm serious."

"And all of that led to a date on a Monday night?"

"It did when I handed him my phone, and he put his contact info inside it."

Honestly, I never intended to text the number, but after the awkward kiss Everett and I shared, I thought it would be best to remove him from that category in my mind. Start something new.

"Wow."

"I told you his act worked."

"No, I mean *wow* as in I'm never going to find someone if that's what it takes."

"That's not true, Julia. A certain tatted motorcyclist comes to mind. You two can even jump past the formalities and skip to the good part."

She rolls her eyes. "Right. So, you'll go nanny for the super-hot country music star and then go out with the sexy veterinarian after?"

"No. Everett doesn't need my help with Quinn today. He already has plans." I don't tell her about the evaluation. He confided in me in private, and I was under the impression he didn't want anyone to know. It's not my news to share.

"It's the start of the school play though, right? You'll see him there?"

While I forced Everett's hand to participate, I stand by my conviction that Quinn will love doing the play with him. The fact that he roped me into it too was not something I expected. Honestly, if it weren't for Brian's involvement at the school, I'd be thrilled to help. I hate that I'll have to see him there every Monday though.

"Don't remind me. Do you think Henry will be okay doing it?"

"He will if you bring him this." She hands me a banana.

We exchange a laugh as I stuff it in the side pocket of his backpack. "Good luck on your exam today."

"Good luck with the play."

He's wearing my favorite jeans and green T-shirt when he walks into the gym holding Quinn's hand. Their presence is a comfort after ending my day at the firm being accosted by my first disgruntled client. For the most part, the people Emma meet with are a delight. They show up on time, exchange polite conversation with me—usually about the weather—and disappear into her office. Not today. A woman barged out of the elevator demanding advice about her upcoming court-ordered mediation—something I'm not allowed to provide—while Emma was occupied with another appointment. I lost track of how long it took to get this woman to agree to a future meeting to discuss her concerns. I'm surprised I beat Everett and Quinn here after that.

A flood of memories and feelings from last night rush through me when our eyes meet. Everett's lost his smile today. Dark circles ring his eyes—a clear indicator he stayed up all night—and the first thing my mind goes to is Quinn's evaluation. It's after play practice, and I can't ask him about it with twenty unsupervised children staring at us.

That's the situation I walked into when I stepped foot in this gym. And you'd think they'd be parkouring off the edge of the stage or participating in a massive game of tag. They're silent.

"Where's the drama lady?" Everett asks, cutting right to the point.

"Broken hip," a familiar voice answers.

I stiffen.

"Mr. Dawson, Quinn, you made it!" Brian acknowledges them. Completely ignores me. I knew he would be difficult. I was hoping he wouldn't be *around*.

"What do you mean a broken hip?" Everett presses.

Mrs. Farris runs these plays. She's in surprisingly good shape for being the oldest teacher at this school. The fact that she's never married and lives alone might explain why she's pushing seventy and still working here.

"Mrs. Farris fell down her stairs and broke her hip last night. She's home with a concussion and awaiting surgery. She'll be out at least two months. I'm trying to find a replacement, but it might be next week before I do. There wasn't a single staff member who could arrange their schedule to accommodate with such short notice. I was hoping you could sing some songs with the kids today until I can figure things out?"

Everett bristles, and I don't blame him. This is the last thing he needs on his plate.

"We've got it covered," I speak for him. I don't want him to have to worry about any of this. In a way, we both roped each other into this situation. But the least I can do is make it a decision he doesn't regret.

When I look up, Brian is acknowledging me with a stare. "Summer, can I speak to you for a second?"

"You okay?" I double-check with Everett first.

He nods, so I follow Brian. My blood pressure rises when he

leads me out of the gym and clear down the hallway to have this conversation.

"Wow. Drop the news on the poor guy and then ditch him in there with a room full of kids. Great plan."

Brian stops and finally faces me. "Millie is gone."

I don't even have to hide my surprise.

"Wh-what do you mean, *gone*?" I hope the first sound I drug out didn't give away that I know exactly where she went. That I drove up after dark and swiped her from the property we used to share.

"I heard something hit the garage door last night, so I went out to check on her and found a clump of hair and some... blood smeared on the driveway."

I try to hold in the sigh that wants to fight its way out of my lungs. He didn't see us. Everett's shoulder must have rubbed against the cement when he rolled underneath the garage door.

Brian is studying my expression just as much as I'm studying his. Mapping out the truth.

If I say *maybe it was a coyote*, it would be an accurate guess. It's not unheard of to have them roaming land that's so close to the foothills. But if it wasn't followed by a flood of tears, he'd know I was making something up. I'm not that great of an actress.

"I hope she's okay" is all I say.

"Me too," he lies. He could care less about that cat. "I just thought you should know."

My eyes narrow. What is his real motivation for bringing me out here? A reminder that he got to keep Millie?

"She's strong," I add. "She'll pull through." What I really mean is *I'm* strong, and *I* pulled through. "Thank you for telling me. I better get back in there."

He nods but snags my hand before I finish turning. "Oh, and Summer?"

The warmth of his skin seeps into my palm, the slope of his smile all too familiar.

"I liked the red dress and heels."

That's the outfit I wore to my second day at Emma's law practice, the one I was wearing when I made Everett drop to his knees and beg me to work for *him* too. Of course Brian liked it. It wasn't something the old me ever used to wear because I never had to look business-professional. He doesn't deserve any details about the situation, but this sick part of me still wants to prove him wrong.

"I'm a legal assistant now. No need for your spousal support anymore."

His eyebrows meet his hairline, proving I was right to say it. His reaction is incredibly satisfying.

I yank my hand from his grasp and disappear through the gym doors.

Everett's done a great job engaging with the kids in a conversation about music since I stepped out. I do a quick sweep of the room, surveying what we have to work with. There is a basket of soccer balls in the corner, basketball hoops on either end of the ceiling, and a stage. None of that feels very play-esque. I'm at a loss for what to do until I land on the instrument strung around Everett's neck.

"Can I borrow that?"

Everett's eyebrow lifts as he transfers the guitar to my outstretched hands.

I play chords E, A, and D in a repetitive pattern, singing "Ninety-Nine Bottles of Beer."

Henry covers his ears.

Everett looks amused. "An alcohol song at an elementary school?"

"A *campfire* song," I correct him, and keep singing.

He chuckles, but it's working. Kids are clapping to the beat.

A couple know the tune and sing along. When I get to the end, I strum up and down for dramatic effect, and they all break out in applause.

"Didn't know you had that in you," Everett says.

I lift the strap off my shoulders and set it back over his head. "I'm full of surprises." *Like the fact that I'm harboring a secret crush on you.*

A throat clears, and I pull my attention back to the kids. "Anyway! I'm Summer and this is—"

"Rhett Dawson," a tall boy with a backward baseball cap shouts between smacks of his gum. Judging by his height and superiority complex, he's the only fifth-grader here.

"You are correct. What's your name?"

"Blake."

"Well, Blake and everyone else, I know you all came for the play, but—"

"Mrs. Farris got an ouchie." An adorable girl with a head full of cornrows wiggles her front tooth.

"That's an understatement," Everett mutters under his breath.

I'm sure Brian's two-month estimate was generous before. A hip replacement at seventy will mean a long road to recovery.

"What's your name?" I ask her. She sucks in a little drool that escapes her mouth when she pulls her fingers from it.

"Etta."

"Hi, Etta. You're right. She got a big ouchie. There's a chance we might have to do this play without her."

"Does that mean we still have to do *The Rainbow Fish?*" asks a boy in a wheelchair wearing a basketball jersey. He's parked at enough of an angle for me to read the name across his upper back—Isaac.

I've come to a few of Mrs. Farris's performances to support Brian. She does a good job. Always picks a story with a moral lesson and a few songs to go with it. But I can tell from the *I don't want to do that one* groans followed by a *Yeah, me neither* and *It's boring* that these kids would rather do anything else.

"Well, what do you all want to do instead?" The room gets eerily quiet. So much so that I wonder if they've ever been asked that before.

It would come as no surprise to me if they haven't. Be the Brave is prided for its academic success and religious beliefs. Their moto is *Believe, become, be the brave,* not *Get creative, think outside the box, and have fun.*

I repeat my question. Everyone's still staring until one brave little hand goes up in the front. It's an Asian boy wearing a lime-green jump rope T-shirt.

"What's your name?"

"Noah. Can it have magic and Pokémon?"

A collective breath is held waiting for my response. I look at the exit—the place where the only person who can stop us is out of view. A giant smile spreads across my face before I feed him the answer that my own heart needs to hear.

"I don't see why not. How about we include everyone's favorite things. Let's do a talent show!"

I'm questioning all of my life decisions when I leave that gym. Agreeing to step foot in that school again? To sing in a talent show with Quinn? To let myself get wrapped up in Summer's world? It's all too much.

I was riding a high last night. For the first time in longer than I can remember, I got to focus on somebody else's problems other than my own. And her face... *her face* when she held that cat? It was like I gave her everything she'd ever needed. I was in freefall watching her run to my car. Unafraid and unaware of what she was doing to me.

Then her ex pulled her into the hallway this afternoon. A web of discomfort spidered through my chest, and all I could think was *why*.

He didn't even acknowledge her existence before that. I barely kept up a conversation with the kids about music after she was gone because I was bloody stuck on what he wanted from her.

I have no claim over Summer other than she's my daughter's nanny. She can do whatever she wants. And I don't know what their relationship was like other than the few things she told me. Am I to take "it was for the best" to mean she'll never want him again?

The most frustrating part is that I can't ask her about it today because we're heading to Quinn's speech evaluation.

Her teacher wasn't kidding when she said this place was across town. As a kid, a drive to the mall would have taken ten minutes. But since 2020, this place has exploded with people. Road infrastructure is only one of the ways it hasn't kept up with the growth.

I navigate a single lane with stoplights spread out a mile apart until I'm finally pulling into the parking lot. Sandwiched in a complex of office buildings is Words Matter. I park in the back next to one of ten Heating and Cooling vehicles dominating the spots. I don't want to risk my Bronco being seen here. It takes careful effort to get Quinn out of her car seat without bashing the door next to me.

"Are you ready?" I set her feet on the pavement and take her hand.

"Mm-hmm," she says back.

I don't know why I asked her that when she doesn't have any idea what we're about to do. Even for me, it's been decades since I stepped foot in a place like this one. I'm sure a lot has changed.

We follow a wall of chipped stone to the front of the building. A woman gets to the door first, and a chime rings out when she opens it. She smiles at her child as he hops on one foot through the entrance. It drops when she spots us. She does a double take to be sure her eyes aren't playing a trick on her. Dread coils in my stomach fast and tight, already proving my worst fear. It's going to be difficult to make this appointment discreet.

I silently plead for her to hurry inside. That's not what happens. She waits. While we're still halfway down the sidewalk. Forces me to hustle Quinn along so I don't have to make her hold the door longer than she has to. Then she stops us when we finally get to her.

"Would you sign my shirt?"

Does this woman think I carry a Sharpie in my pocket? "Uh... I don't have anything on me. I'm sorry."

"I do!" She reaches in her purse, whips out a ballpoint pen, and hands it to me.

Her shirt is tight and ribbed. On so many levels this is a recipe for disaster. I let go of Quinn's hand to uncap the pen. I'm not about to sign this woman's cleavage in front of our children if that's what she thinks, so I step to the side. It's awkward even touching her shoulder. I use as little pressure as possible dragging the dried-up pen meant for paper down her cotton shirtsleeve.

"I don't think it's working."

I hoped she'd say "Thanks anyway." Not step aside when an onlooker offers their child's marker.

Terrific.

I scribble my signature and pass it back.

"Thanks," she finally says. The door collapses with her back no longer pressed to it. I catch it with my palm before it slams into my shoulder.

There isn't anything else that could surprise me about this place after that. Not the neon saturated walls or the toddlers playing with trains in the entryway. Not how the entire city of Boise seems to have a five o'clock appointment here or the speech pathologists who don't look a day over twenty.

It screams of chaos and inexperience, and I come to accept I've made a mistake. One I can't back out of with a front desk lady shoving an iPad against my chest. I barely register the information she's asking for on the screen—our names and Quinn's birthdate maybe?—before someone says, "You must be Quinn."

I look up. An older woman with silver curly hair is bent over at the waist and holding out her hand. "I'm Sue."

"Say hi," I prompt Quinn.

Quinn doesn't look away from the twin boys who are drilling holes in the vinyl tile with a pair of matchbox cars.

"She does better when it's quiet," I tell her.

Sue nods. "Come with me."

It takes a tug of her hand to get Quinn to leave the lobby. Even after that, her attention remains glued over her shoulder the entire way to the exam room.

I was expecting this place to feel older but not small. Sue invites us into a space that's barely larger than a closest, and I must not hide my surprise well.

"I know. It's suffocating." She sighs as she presents us both with chairs that had been previously stacked in the corner. Then she closes the door for privacy.

That's not at all what I was thinking. Refreshing would be more like it. Usually, people roll out the red carpet for me.

"They're wanting to add occupational therapy to the services we offer here, so they had to remodel half the building for it. It will be really nice when it's all done."

"I'm Everett, by the way," I say to change the subject. Now that we're in an enclosed space, I feel comfortable enough to share my name.

She shakes my hand and sits down across from us. "You don't go by 'Quinn's dad' all the time? I swear I didn't have autonomy until my kids were grown."

I go by Rhett Dawson, I think to myself. It's something I've been proud of until this moment.

"I saw on my paperwork that you like bugs." Sue turns her attention to Quinn when I don't acknowledge her comment.

Quinn nods.

"Well, look what I have for you!" She pulls out a wooden bug puzzle and sets it in front of her. "Can I talk to your dad while you play with this?"

"Mhm." Quinn gives her a closed-mouth smile before she takes the puzzle apart.

Sue turns her attention back to me. "She's adorable."

"Thank you," I say.

"I don't know how much was explained to you over the phone, but I'd like to go over the process. Ask you a few questions about Quinn's birth, development, home life, and family history. As her parent, you know her best."

Do I? Two months ago, I would have told this woman, that might be true for most people, but not me. A parent should know their child better than anyone else. It was true for El. But I didn't know Quinn the same way her mom did. Hell, I didn't even know her the same way my parents did when they came and stayed with her after El died. Seeing her a day or two at a time between legs of a tour doesn't give you much of a chance to know that she rubs her right ear when she gets sleepy or prefers Frosted Flakes over Fruit Loops. At least I didn't before.

Everything's changed. Now I know she likes pretending to be a puppy when she eats cereal. How it's best not to argue if she wants to sleep in her rain boots.

A foreign emotion threatens to take over as I realize how little my life has looked the way I thought I wanted it to. It's easier to feel like you know someone when you witness the hurt and the triumph in the little moments of every day. That's what being with Quinn has shown me.

I'm sitting here in front of a woman who has the power to help Quinn. To fill her life with more moments of triumph. How could I deny her that? That's what I can give Quinn by going through with this.

With renewed confidence—something I wasn't sure I'd ever feel walking in here—I say, "I'm ready."

Sue lifts her eyes from the family history form in her hands and studies me through a pair of glasses.

"Okay then. I'd like to talk to you about your auditory processing disorder."

At eight years old, I forgot the correct term the moment it tumbled from the audiologist's lips. All I knew was that I processed sound differently than most people. It meant that I could hear words spoken, but like individuals with dyslexia, they would jumble, sometimes unrecognizably so, before reaching my ears.

It's a struggle that has taken up every ounce of space inside my head for as long as I can remember.

Coming from Sue those three words sound casual and clinical. They don't elicit the same emotional tie for her that they do for me. And I can tell I'm going to be expected to lean into this conversation no matter what feelings it dredges up.

She slides her glasses up the bridge of her nose and drops her eyes back to the documents in her hands. "When did it start manifesting for you?"

The kindergarten portrait frames itself in my mind. A gallery wall of memories that demonstrate my struggle to focus, to follow directions, to comprehend what I was hearing.

I clear my throat. "Five."

I'm sure I don't have to tell this woman that it's like any

other disability. It's vastly different from person to person, and even though I started showing signs of it at that age, it was several years before they put a label on it.

She scribbles something down, then asks, "Did you have any modifications in school?"

Reduce background noise, use pictures for directions, repeat information—just a few of the suggestions the audiologist gave my mom back then after she'd looked into special education services. According to Idaho state law, APD isn't automatically recognized under the umbrella of disabilities that qualify. My parents decided to forego the comprehensive school evaluation and opted for a private therapy route.

I shake my head.

It wasn't from a lack of continued effort. My parents bought an FM system that amplified my teacher's voice through a device on my desk. When I got caught hiding it, I was moved to the front of the classroom instead. That's when I mastered lip reading. I learned if I zoned in on a person's mouth while they were speaking, I didn't need all of those other forms of help the therapists recommended. I'd hide my lack of understanding by mimicking the behavior of other kids around me.

The only thing I admit to Sue is attending speech therapy. That seems embarrassing enough.

Quinn drops one of her puzzle pieces on the floor and reaches for it. The momentary distraction is enough to get my nerves back in check.

"What helped you cope?"

Sue's hand must be cramping from the speed at which she's jotting notes. I'm very aware that everything coming out of my mouth right now is being written down. I choose my next words carefully even if her knowing look gives away that she could have skipped this question.

"Music."

Her pen stops as she waits for me to elaborate. I hadn't planned to tell this woman my entire life story, but I gather that's what she's waiting for. Everything there is to know about me can be found on the internet these days. You can google my address, my family's names, *hell*, even my favorite donut. Between interviews I've done, and articles written about me, it's all there. Everything except this.

"School was difficult for me," I say.

I know Sue meant for the puzzle to entertain Quinn during this conversation, but watching my daughter smile as she fits two pieces together is therapeutic for me to get the rest of this out.

"I struggled with some aspect of every single subject except music. I didn't need to hear it when I could *feel* it... the vibrations through the floor. It made everything else melt away. My mom put me in guitar lessons, and I made sense of my struggles through songwriting."

Sue sets down her pen and leans her back against her chair.

"And what's it like for you now as an adult?"

If any of this information will help Quinn, I need to be honest with her.

"I function just fine until my routines are interrupted or a room is too loud." Those are the two biggest things that make an auditory processing disorder rear its ugly head. The only way I'm able to sing on a stage at all is by controlling the volume. Other than applause, everything loud comes from me.

She chuckles. "So, what you're saying is, since you became a parent?"

I hate admitting that. It sounds like I regret Quinn, which I don't. It doesn't mean it hasn't been hard.

"I appreciate you opening up. I imagine this isn't easy for you to talk about, but I want to reassure you that everything you share with me is confidential. This is a safe space for you and Quinn," she says.

She waits for something—maybe a look to signal that I'm okay?—then she asks a few more questions about Quinn's development since pregnancy. I answer them to the best of my ability.

"The next part of the process is the evaluation. I'm going to check Quinn's receptive language—having her show me where a certain toy is on the table or follow one-to-two step directions. I'll check her expressive language after that. It will give me a better idea at the size of her vocabulary. It should be between one to two thousand words and four-to-six-word sentences at her age. Then I'll test her speech sounds, and we'll finish with her ability to communicate during play. Things like taking turns, greeting each other, and eye contact."

I nod. Mostly because I'm grateful the attention will no longer be on me.

"Okay, Quinn. It's your turn. Are you ready?" Sue asks her.

Quinn gives up her bug puzzle the moment Sue puts a rubber duck, a hairbrush, and a stuffed cat on the table. She starts as promised, having Quinn identify which toy is where. I quickly learn this woman is good at what she does. She redirects Quinn with ease when she gets distracted. Never pushes her so hard that it ends in a meltdown. She makes working with my daughter and understanding her look easy when I know it's not.

As we near the end of the evaluation, I consider what comes next. Answers, I hope, that help us move forward. But I deflate when I ask her as much, and she says it will be a few days before I hear any results.

I realize I walked in today believing an answer might make me feel better. Expecting that assigning a name to Quinn's struggle would help me find hope for growth. Instead, dread is what I'm leaving with.

I thank her for her time, but my feet root to the carpet in her doorway. I'm blocking her exit. The words, glaring and obvious, hang in the air between us. I don't know if I can sleep tonight without asking them. I don't know if I'll ever sleep again when I know the answer. I turn around to face her anyway.

"Do you think..."

My eyes are pleading; I know they are.

From the moment we met, Sue has been stoic. She hasn't allowed emotion to show on her face like she is right now. Regret is all I can see.

"We won't know for sure until Quinn's older. When she is able to repeat numbers, words, and sentences, she can be formally tested by an audiologist like you were. But yes. There's a chance your daughter has an auditory processing disorder."

I don't know how I make it out to the car or how I get Quinn buckled in her seat. I don't know where the lines converge on the street or how many stoplights I have left until we get home. For the first time in my life, I'm thankful I have the drive to Harrison Boulevard memorized.

Tears blur my vision and threaten to fall. I squeeze tighter on the steering wheel, hoping the added pressure quiets the shaking in my hands.

I didn't realize I had a vision for Quinn's future until I saw it tumbling away with the wind.

I wanted her to have an easy time making friends. To hear a story problem in math and not have to look off the kid's paper next to her. I didn't want her to have to ask for directions to be repeated ten times more than everyone else. She'll be different and need help. She'll struggle in all the ways I did and all the ways I still do.

"Daee otay?"

My eyes shoot to the rearview mirror at the sound of Quinn's voice. She's studying my expression like she did on her birthday when I lit that article on fire over the kitchen sink. I clear my throat.

"Yeah, honey. Daddy's okay."

Stuck in a haze, I call Summer.

"Hi!" Her voice is light and happy. Free of burden.

I shouldn't have called. I don't know why I did. I don't have a clue what to say. I wonder if there will ever come a day when our baggage is too much for her to want to stick around.

"Everett, are you there?" she asks.

I swipe at the tears burning my cheeks.

"C-could you watch Quinn tonight?"

Five words. That's all I could get out. I don't think; I just act. Starving for time by myself. Needing to protect Quinn from seeing me like this anymore than she already has.

"Uh…" She hesitates.

I second-guess ever calling her.

"You know what, I'm sure you have plans. I'm sorry. Have a good night, Summer." I hang up.

I'm praying for green lights and cursing at red ones. Everything is against me. The trees, the air, my own breath. Gasping and begging for space, I steer the Bronco down the historic street. Passing Tim's old house—the boy who asked me if I was stupid when he saw my flunked English essay on the bus ride home in sixth grade. I come up on Amy's who turned me down for Senior Prom after she heard I ran out on my date junior year. Moments I've buried are bursting free.

"Summa!" Quinn shouts when she sees her.

She's already in the driveway as I'm pulling in. Her hair is down in long waves, sweeping her exposed back. She's wearing a tight black dress that cuts off mid-thigh with a top that fuses to her skin. Her bare legs are on display. Long, lean lines peeking out from a slit on the side of her thigh. There's only one explanation for that outfit.

"You have a date," I say as I shove against the car door. It shuts harder than I intended it to.

She jumps and then folds her arms across her chest, wrapping her hands around her biceps. "Had."

The second I let Quinn out of the back seat she runs to Summer and jumps in her arms. They both squeeze each other tight.

I'm still staring at her. Trying like hell to remember why I even called her in the first place.

"Are you okay?" she asks, snapping me back to focus.

"I'm fine. I'll be in around ten," I bark.

I abandon them both in the driveway for the only place I've ever felt like me.

18

SUMMER

I fed Quinn some Annie's macaroni and cheese before we turned on *Wish*. It felt very reminiscent of the evening I was planning to have: dinner at an Italian restaurant followed by a movie at The Flicks theatre. Except my intended company was much older.

Joe took it decently well when I called and canceled. Not so well when he asked to reschedule and I turned him down. I don't know what happened to Everett today. I don't know what happened between us the other night. But I do know my priorities lie with him and Quinn. I've never been more sure of anything. Which is strange because three weeks ago I would have jumped at the chance for a free meal and a fun night out with a new guy who had everything going for him.

But beyond this being my job, I care about Everett and Quinn's well-being more. If he needs me, whether or not in the way I was hoping for, I'll be here. Nothing is going to stand in the way of that.

"Okay, Quinn. It's time for bed," I tell her as the credits roll.

She yawns, tucking her small fists beneath her cheek and snuggling into my side.

"I know. I could fall asleep here too. But I've also sat on your bed, and I promise it's cozier."

"Otay," she says.

I pick her up and carry her with her arms draped around my neck. She nods off against my chest, but jostles awake as I swim through a mountain of stuffed animals to get her tucked beneath the covers.

"Bunny?"

I sift through fur and stuffing, hands coming up empty for a bunny. "I don't see it. Where'd you leave it?"

"Da-eee woom." She points across the hall. His door's shut. I've been in there before, but that was when he invited me in. This time it feels like an invasion of privacy.

"Do you think we can get Bunny tomorrow? Look at all of these other cute friends you have... Mr. Chicken, bok, bok." I swing his bird legs so they brush the covers. She giggles. "Or Mrs. Piggy, oink, oink." She scrunches her nose, creating tiny creases on the sides that I lean forward and kiss.

She shakes her head.

"No? It has to be Bunny?"

She nods.

If I wait long enough, she'll probably fall asleep. But I don't want to risk making her cry before that. Grabbing a bunny isn't the end of the world.

"Okay, I'll be right back."

I pad across the hall, which is ridiculous because Everett's out in his soundproof studio. The glass handle turns with the twist of my wrist, and I flick on the light to his room.

It looks the same as the last time I saw it. *Smells* the same too.

I spot the bunny right away, an ear flopped over the edge of the nightstand. When I pull it from the surface, it exposes a notebook, cursive handwriting scrawled in blue ink across the

page. At a quick glance, the only specifics I catch are numbers...
eighty-seven, eighty-eight, eighty-nine.

I peek at it again. They continue on, nearly reaching the
bottom of the page.

I should walk away. I got what I came in here for. But
Everett's so closed off sometimes. So withdrawn. It would be
nice to have some idea of what he's thinking.

One line, I convince myself. That's all I'll read, and then I'll
leave.

87. Don't use the pull tabs when putting on her favorite
pink boots.

I read another.

88. Throw out the pancake batter. Stick to cereal.

What is this? My eyes fuse to the page.

89. Use detangler on her hair when she gets out of the
bath.

90. Don't bathe her before school.

Suddenly I'm picking up the notebook. My fingers are glued
to the pages. *It's a list.*

I'm flipping back to the beginning. Searching for number
one. When I find it, I choke back emotion at what I read next.

Mistakes I Won't Make Twice

1. Hold her when she cries.

2. Read her a bedtime story.

3. Kiss her ouchie when she gets hurt.

4. Tell her mommy's coming home soon, even if she isn't.

5. Sing if she needs you to.

I'm drinking in this list like it's water in the desert sun.
Afraid if I don't finish it, the world as I know it will cease to
exist.

"Summa," Quinn whines from across the hall, and I snap
the journal shut. Fling it on the nightstand and flee the room. I
stall in the hall, swiping at my eyes and hiding the evidence that

I've been crying. Then I pop the bunny's head from beyond the doorframe and hear her giggle.

"Bunny!" she squeals.

Bunny gets tucked under the covers just like Quinn. She snuggles her cheek against its soft fur.

"Da-eee home soon?" she asks.

I have to swallow to keep myself from crying. "Yep. Your daddy is going to finish writing a song for you, and then he's going to come in and give you a kiss, okay?"

A happy little sigh leaves her lips, and a dreamy look paints her face. She's gazing up at me; I'm gazing down at her. I swipe the hair from her eyes. Ones that tell a story of devotion. A look that says I'm beginning to mean as much to her as she is to me.

I want this moment with her to last, so I stay until she's fallen asleep. Maybe even a little while after that. I stare in awe at her perfectly pink cheeks and her dark dancing eyelashes as she dreams. I miss her, and I haven't even left her room yet. *Is this how it feels to love a child so completely?*

Thoughts of Everett are the only things that finally pull me from her room. I pace the hallway for a while, but it's not suppressing the ball of nerves wound up in my stomach. I told him the other night that he's doing better than he thinks. After finding that list, I'm not sure he believes me. I need to see him.

I snag the baby monitor from the kitchen and check the screen. Quinn's still fast asleep, but I should make this quick.

A soft melody floats down the garage steps as I ascend them. The closer I get to the door the more I recognize the song. It's my favorite one he's ever written—words of love and devotion painted in sounds.

The door is cracked. As if he kicked it and it rebounded off the frame. Not open enough to see more than his boot through the slit, so I press on it, and it expands. A *creak* follows and the music stops.

I see him now. The voice was coming from his phone. It's clutched tightly in his hand, and he's crying on the sofa.

"What are you doing out here?" He stuffs his phone in his pocket.

His eyes are stormy and guarded. He looks broken. A bottle of bourbon is clutched in his hands. Shattered fragments of records litter the ground. At one point, he must have launched off the couch and kicked the leg of the coffee table because it's snapped off and the whole thing is collapsed on one side.

"I came to see if you're okay." I step across the threshold, glass crunching beneath my shoes. He hasn't moved from the place he's reclining on the couch. I get close enough to sit beside him, to reach my hand out, and he jerks back like my touch stings.

"Do I look like I'm okay?" he spits. His nostrils flare and his ribs expand with every new puff of air they take in.

No. In fact, he looks terrible. The place reeks of alcohol and sweat. I won't touch him if he doesn't want me to, but I'm staying. I'll sit across the room. That's the most space I'm giving him. I'm not leaving him out here alone. I can tell he needs someone right now, and he's going to have to get used to my being around.

I flick open the kickstand on the back of the baby monitor and rest it on the cracked desk. The chair with the broken wheel beside it tips to the right when I sit down.

Everett is a good listener. I've seen him study my lips. Watched the corners of his eyes squint as he takes in what I'm saying. That's the kind of person *he* needs right now.

"It looks like you could use someone to listen," I offer.

"Is that what you do, Summer? Listen to the men in your life who tell you what they want from you?"

I know he's referencing Brian without saying his name. I can spot jealousy when I see it. I just don't know why he's acting that way when he's made it clear our relationship is strictly Quinn-related. I'm the only other person in this room. An easy target. He's choosing to throw a less-than-subtle jab at me instead of facing whatever it is that's got him worked up.

Based on that video he was watching, he's been out here thinking about Eliza. He wrote that song for her. He's hurting, and hurt people hurt people. But I won't let Everett hurt me.

"No," I say back.

"That's what I thought. So why did you let that prick drag you into the hall?" He has this dangerous smirk on his face now, and I'm getting whiplash from the different versions of Everett that are existing in this room. He's using a cavalier sneer as a weapon to shock me. I won't let it. Another thing I choose to ignore.

"How'd Quinn's evaluation go?"

His head twists to the side. "I don't want to talk about it."

"Why not?" I press.

"Because it doesn't fucking matter, okay? It's too late."

"Too late for what?"

I watch Everett's brick wall crack right in front of me. It starts with his head, tipping forward in his hands. His fingertips grip his hair and pull until his shoulders are shaking. His entire body shudders when the devastation leaves his mouth. A wail swallows the silence in the room until his pain is all I hear. My body is begging for me to cross the space and comfort him.

Normally I'd fill the silence, but not this time. He needs me to wait and listen. To stay put and respect his space. He confirms that was the right decision when he finally whispers, "It's too late to save her from me. I gave her my disability. I gave her APD."

"What does that mean?" I ask. All this time, I sensed that Everett was hiding something. I think this might be it.

He lifts his head, defeat blanketing his features. "It means that when I'm on a stage with thousands of fans screaming my name or I'm stuck in a room with a shrieking toddler, everything I hear sounds butchered and messed up in my head. Nothing makes sense. And no matter what I do to fix it, it's never enough."

I don't think I'll ever be enough.

I haven't said anything at all. Haven't moved in the several minutes he's been talking. Because he hasn't stopped. It's as if this dam has broken and everything it's ever held back is pouring out of him. He tells me how music saved his life. Made him something when he was nothing but a struggling student barely passing high school. He tells me he plays because he's good at it. That the harder he works, the more he forgets. But the part that breaks him the most, what has him crumpled against my chest when I finally give in to the pull of being closer to him, is when he says he's living out his worst fear. That he thinks he's a terrible parent because he gave his daughter the one thing he hates most about himself.

This man is fracturing into thousands of tiny pieces right before my eyes, and I'm terrified I won't have what it takes to put him back together again. I've never second-guessed the words coming out of my mouth more than the ones I'm about to say.

"Everett?"

I need him to hear this. I don't want him to miss anything, so I push him upright. I slide my hands on either side of his face to get him to look at me. I dry his cheeks with the back of my hand, and I wait for him to do that thing he does.

When his eyes pinch at the corners and he studies my mouth, I begin.

"You're enough. You've *always* been enough. For your family, for your fans, for Quinn, for *me*."

I didn't intend to include myself in that list, but I can't help it when it's true.

"Quinn is lucky," I continue. "So, so lucky to have you as her dad."

He tries to remove my hands and look away, but I grip on tighter. "She asked for you! Tonight, at bedtime, she asked for *you*. When I tucked her in she said 'Daddy home soon' and I told her you were out here writing songs for her but that you'd be in to kiss her good night."

Just when I think there can't possibly be anything left, new tears fall down his face.

"So, it's not just her mom she needs, Everett, she needs *you*. She doesn't care if she got your eye color or your hair texture or even your APD. She isn't going to blame you."

I let him turn away this time when he tries. "You don't know that."

I fold my hands in my lap. "You're right; I don't. But I don't blame my parents for the challenges I've had to face in my life. Even the ones they could have prevented or the ones they claim are their fault. She's going to see that you tried to help her. That you took her to speech therapy and taught her everything you know to help her cope. You can give her something no one else can... understanding. You're the only one in her life who knows what it feels like, and she'll have you to lean on when she needs someone. She'll be grateful she doesn't have to do this alone like you did. You don't have to be afraid anymore. You can be yourself, Everett, and the people who love you will stay. The ones who don't were never meant for you."

I can't even look at his face to see if he believes me. If what I said made him feel any better. Because now I'm emotional. That feels like all I can give him for one night. I could pour a million other things from my heart, but they might all be too honest, too vulnerable. More than he can handle right now. Stopping while I'm ahead is for the best.

I stand, grab the baby monitor, and head for the door. I don't make it through the opening before he speaks again.

"Why didn't you go on the date?"

The frustration in his tone is back. The walls are up again.

When I turn, I find him standing too. His arms are folded across his chest in a dare, and I don't know what to do. My feelings for him would be another weight on his plate he doesn't need to bear right now.

He takes a step closer. "Answer me."

This time there's a fire in his eyes that frustrates me. Why does he *care*? Is he looking for a fight?

"*You* called *me*," I remind him.

He takes another step closer. "Summer."

Because I wanted to be here, okay? Because I'd rather be here with you than anywhere else.

That's what I should have said.

"You know why."

He shakes his head. "No. I don't. You're single. You can do whatever you want." He growls. "And you look *fucking* incredible in that dress. You deserve to be *seen* in it."

Suddenly the air is vacuum sealed out of this room. It's hotter. Sweltering. My legs are Jell-O, the door I'm slumped against the only thing holding me upright.

"I am being seen in it," I whisper.

His eyes do a long, appreciative drag across my whole body, lingering in all the places I want him to. All the places that this dress was meant to accentuate for Joe but were always for Everett.

He eats up the rest of the space between us, rasping, "You're about to be seen *out* of it."

From the look in his eyes, I'm expecting his kiss before his mouth is even on me. What I'm not expecting is the searing heat of his palm against the small of my back jerking me flush to him. I'm not expecting the impatient way my nails score his chest through his shirt either. My resolve is slipping with his mouth touching my skin.

"Everett," I pant. "You're drunk and not thinking clearly and I'm—"

Old Summer is desperate to lean into this delicious feeling. New Summer knows this is a bad idea. When his lips fuse to my neck, I finally get a gulp of air. A grip on reality. He might not actually want this—*me*. The heightened emotions and high blood-alcohol level pumping through his veins could be to blame.

I could sleep with him. Shove aside every reason why we shouldn't do this. Remove every piece of clothing that stands between us and get lost in him. But we could both wake up tomorrow and regret it. I want this with Everett, not angry Rhett Dawson.

"I think we should stop," I get out.

As if my words are a bucket of ice water, he rips his lips from my body and stalks away, wiping his mouth with the back of his hand and leaving me plastered against the wall. I gulp down more air. It's not enough to fill my starved lungs.

"What do you want from me, Summer? Why are you here?" he shouts.

"I came to see—"

"If I'm okay. Yeah, you said that already. I mean why are you *here*?" He points to his own head. "Fucking with my head. The only sound I hear." He collapses on the couch again, his breathing ragged for several minutes before sleep takes him.

I retrieve the baby monitor, run inside for a blanket, and come back out to cover him up. He doesn't even stir at the sweep of a broom or snap of the garbage can lid. It's not a deep clean but I make sure there's nothing he can step or fall on that could puncture skin. Then I go back into the house. I plug in the baby monitor by the kitchen sink and lie down on the couch. I google APD and soak up every article the internet has to offer on the subject before I finally close my eyes. I want to be rested if Everett or Quinn need me.

One thing's for sure... there isn't anything I wouldn't do for him and his little girl.

19

EVERETT

I wake sometime in the middle of the night drenched in sweat. My studio looks very different from how I left it before passing out. I know without having to think about it who is responsible for that. Fractured moments from earlier drift in and out of focus. Some of the things I said have bile creeping up my throat. Or maybe that's the empty bottle of alcohol eating at my insides.

It's long past ten o'clock, and the image of Quinn sleeping in the house alone has me bolting from the couch. A weight in my pocket bats against my thigh. I forgot I stuffed my phone in there. My head swims as I bound down the stairs two steps at a time and then across the driveway. I slow when I see Summer's car. Guilt coils through my stomach. No matter how upset I was, I should have never started drinking. Minus the cocktail I shared with her last week, it's been months since I've touched alcohol and for good reason. I have a responsibility that shouldn't be up to the woman who... is asleep on my couch?

She's curled up in the fetal position and—mostly—covered with a blanket. One bare leg has slipped from the fabric and hangs limply over the edge of the sofa. Even sleeping, Summer takes my breath away.

Her skin is still warm minus the exposed limb. She sighs when I slip it beneath the blanket.

She stayed. That's all I can think about when I look at her. Physically, emotionally, in every way, I've been relying on her. I promised myself a long time ago I'd never need anyone. I don't know how not to need Summer.

I check on Quinn next, kneeling by the side of her bed. A soft hum exits her parted lips as I brush a thumb across her cheek.

She asked for you.

Summer's declaration swims in my mind as I look at Quinn. I've never taken the time to sit and marvel at the beautiful little person El and I created together. Marvel and mourn too.

I clutch her hand and whisper against her cheek, "I'm sorry." What I wouldn't give for Quinn to have every part of her mom. Not just her dark eyelashes, wild hair, and heart-stopping smile. "I'm so sorry."

I kiss her cheek just like Summer said I would, making grand promises my heart is desperate to trust. "You're going to be okay. *We're* going to be okay. I won't let you go through this alone."

I choose to believe the twitch of her hand in mine means she heard me. A confirmation that she knows I'll stay as long as she needs. And that's exactly what I do.

The next time I wake it's to the smell of bacon. A groan leaves my lips. Every part of my body aches. I know I can only blame a fraction of that on Quinn's floor. I should shower, but the growl in my stomach leads me to the kitchen instead.

Summer is flitting around in an apron with Emma's handprints on the front pockets. She's bathed in golden light from the window over the sink, and I can't take my eyes off her.

"You're still here."

She startles. "Oh! You're awake. Good morning! How are you feeling? Would you like some coffee?" She volleys at least a half dozen more questions in my direction.

All I manage to get out is, "With a side of Advil, please."

"That good, huh?" She chuckles softly to herself.

Steam curls from the top of the mug she hands me.

"You don't have any creamer," she comments.

I scratch the back of my neck. "Yeah, I like it black. But I think there might be some sugar in the cupboard if you want some."

She flips a piece of bacon on the stove and then turns to face me, a smile unfurling across her lips. "The one with the candles in it or..."

Never going to let me live that one down, I see.

"I thought you were the one with the habit of going through other people's cupboards?" I tease.

"Something you still haven't thanked me for, by the way."

At this point, that's a long list that's only growing. Last night being at the top of it. A subject she seems to be avoiding as her gaze returns to the stove.

She heaps two plates with bacon and strawberry jam–covered toast and sets them in Quinn's and my usual spots at the table.

"You aren't having any?"

"I wanted to make sure you both had breakfast before I left. Your sister asked me to come in to work early, and I need to go home and change first."

The modest apron is doing too good of a job at hiding her black dress from last night.

"Yeah, Emma never has any fun. Doesn't have any friends either from what I can tell."

My sister graduated at the top of her class at Berkeley and

applied to every open law position in the Boise area. I never understood why she wanted to be close to home when it limited her options. Jason Ford, the partner of her boutique family law firm, hired her as his junior associate. It didn't leave much time for anything but assisting with his caseload.

"Sounds like someone else I know."

Touché.

"Well, thank you for breakfast."

"It'll cost you overtime." She winks at me.

I owe her a hell of a lot more than overtime after she stayed the night on my couch. Money won't fix the fact that I'm afraid it could happen again. I won't put her in that position. This is a lot to ask of someone, but there's only one way I can think to prevent it.

"Summer, I—"

A shrill sound rings out. It takes me a couple of seconds to determine that it's coming from my pocket. A squeeze of my temples is doing very little to dull the pounding in my head.

"It's okay, you can answer it," she says.

"Will you please stay until I'm finished with this? If you're late to my sister's office you can blame me." I still haven't asked my question.

Summer has never made me feel self-conscious about my appearance. If anything, it's been the opposite. You don't buy a shirt with a guy's face on it if you're not attracted to him. But that version of me is not this one she sees right now, hungover and unshaven. I suddenly feel self-conscious with her eyes bouncing around my face.

"Yeah. I'll go check on Quinn."

"Thanks," I say, sweeping a hand through my hair for good measure. I doubt it did much. What I need is a shower and a nap.

I answer the call after she's halfway up the stairs. "Hello?"

"You let that woman spend the night?!" Caroline shrieks through the speakerphone.

My brain fights to catch up as I hunt down the button I accidentally pressed when accepting the call. "It's all over the news today" manages to come through too before I silence it.

"What were you thinking dragging Quinn through more drama?"

I pace the kitchen, putting it all together. The reporters must have seen Summer's car parked in my driveway all night. It wouldn't be the first time they made assumptions about my life. I'm sure whatever article they spun up is not surprising. At least not to me.

"I've told you… Summer is Quinn's nanny. I was working late and didn't want to make her drive home in the dark." That's half the truth anyway.

"That's not what it looked like from this photograph they snapped!" Something crinkles on her end.

She printed it?

I don't really care what the reporters think they saw. What I want to know is why *she* does.

"What is it you're worried about exactly? That it looks like I'm moving on from your daughter, or that I'll tarnish your family name with you connected to me?"

"I am protecting—"

"The only person you're protecting here is yourself. And for your information, I accidentally fell asleep in my studio, and Summer stayed on the couch out of the goodness of heart for Quinn. So, Caroline, I'm going to say this, and I'm only going to say it once: What I choose to do with my life is none of your business. I've gathered over the years that I'm not your favorite person and you don't carry a lot of respect for my chosen career. All of that is fine with me. I don't need you to love it. But if you want to have a relationship with Quinn, you need to have a positive one with me. And I need you to stay the hell out of my personal business. We'll see you on Sunday at one."

I hang up while I'm still ahead. Before I can say anything more and potentially regret it. I know I'm throwing myself under the stack of buses weighing down Caroline Blackwood's opinion of me, but it's clear the boundaries need red ink to be visible to her.

The only thing I regret about that conversation is not going into another room with a closed door to have it. Summer is standing at the bottom of the stairs staring at her phone.

20

SUMMER

I've read a lot of Rhett Dawson articles over the years. Some of them surprising, most of them not. The only difference with this one is... my name's attached to it.

The headline on the homepage of *Celeb* reads: "Can Someone Say New Mommy?"

It's followed by: *Lines are blurring, and boundaries are crossed. Rhett Dawson entertains overnight guest in his childhood home on Harrison Boulevard. Summer Rogers, a recently divorced woman he hired to be the nanny of his four-year-old daugh—*

"Don't read that." Everett snatches my phone and marches toward the kitchen.

I follow him. "Excuse me? That article is about me. I think I have every right to see what it says."

He stops and turns, making me rebound off his chest. I stumble before he steadies me.

"They'll stop talking if they see your car here every night."

I squint at his unflinching response. "Wait... you want me to *move in?*"

"Yes," he confirms.

His cool confidence stuns me. I barely think before my biggest concern comes tumbling out of my mouth.

"Me living here won't stop those reporters from assuming we're—"

"It's a tabloid, Summer. All they do is assume."

Right. It's all I do too, I guess. I thought it would bother him more than it seems to be. More than it's bothering *me*. That article stripped me down to nothing more than a floozy sleeping with her boss. It's not the kind of fresh start I was hoping to have post-divorce. It can't be the image he wants tied to his family either.

"Did Caroline put you up to this?" I heard his side of their heated conversation. I can see her suggesting a publicity cover up: Convince Summer to move in to change the narrative.

"What? No. This has nothing to do with her. It's what I was going to ask you before she called."

He pulls out his chair at the kitchen table, sits down, and takes a bite of the breakfast I made him.

"Then *why*? There's only three weeks left of this arrangement," gusts out of my mouth next. *I'm the impulsive one, not you.* Moving in is something I would suggest if he needed more help. *Does he?* Because he won't ask for it if he does.

He sets down his half-eaten slab of bacon, wipes his hand on a napkin, and looks right at me. "I'd like you to move in so that if I end up out in my studio past dark again, you have a comfortable bed and pajamas. Unless you have a habit of sleeping in... *that*."

His subtle joke about my dress does little to hide his nerves when he swallows. This is about last night. He's afraid he put me out when I slept on his couch. The truth is, I'd do it all over again if it meant he'd be okay. I tell him as much by saying, "I slept in something of this nature my entire twenties, and I was fine."

"There's a lot of shit I did in my twenties too. Thirties are for comfort, and the guest bed has one of the best mattresses in this house."

I don't want him choosing this if he feels like he has to. But I'm sleeping in an office right now. It's not hard to compete with that.

"Well... I'm..."

"Is that a yes?" He polishes off the second half of his bacon.

After our heated moment in his studio less than twelve hours ago, sleeping in his guest bed down the hall might not be such a good idea. Doesn't stop me from wanting to though.

"Summer?" he prompts.

I should come up with an excuse. A reason to say no.

So why can't I think of one?

"Thank you so much for coming in early. Jason, the firm's partner, is having knee replacement surgery in a few weeks, and I'll be taking his caseload while he's on medical leave. I need to be ready for this."

His *entire* caseload? I've managed Emma's for two weeks now and she barely has time to pee. No wonder she's stressed.

Her fingernails clack at her keyboard. She acknowledged me with a nod when I got here. But that was ten minutes ago. She hasn't looked up from her computer since.

The coffee maker dings. A bougie blend of vanilla and cinnamon swirls around the room.

"It's no problem," I tell her, filling two ceramic mugs. The rich brown liquid melts to a hazelnut as soon as the creamer touches it.

What I should be saying to her is *thank you*. The move-in

conversation has consumed my every thought this morning. I managed to leave Everett's with an "it's not a no," but I needed some space to make a final decision.

"It's quiet today," I notice. Not the usual chatter from down the hall I've grown accustomed to.

She smirks. "And you wonder why I work most Saturdays. Jason just happens to be at a conference today, so he gave Tara and Jasmine the day off."

I hate that those women bother her so much. It's no wonder Everett thinks she doesn't have any friends. I need to get her away and show her what it's like to have a good time.

"Would you want to grab a bite to eat when we're done here?"

"Yeah. Sure."

I chalk up her unenthusiastic response to the stack of emails in her inbox. Judging by the nervous tick in her knee, her schedule is in immediate need of managing.

"Great!"

I send two quick texts: one to Everett asking for the night off and the other to Julia, asking if Jake could pick Henry up from school and inviting her to dinner. I'll be seeing a lot less of her if I decide to move out.

"I'll be at my desk if you need me," I say, taking a much-needed gulp of coffee.

"How long have you been sleeping with my brother?"

Hot liquid sprays from my mouth and rains on every surface in a three-foot radius from my body. Emma launches from her chair, racing for the stack of dishcloths she uses in lieu of paper towels. She hands me a few.

"I'm so sorry!" I apologize, mopping up my mess.

By some miracle I managed to miss her computer. But the edge of her desk, the chair, the hardwood, *her trousers*, all have sticky brown dots covering them.

"It's fine," she says, twisting off the top of her aluminum water bottle, wetting the tip of a rag, and dabbing it against fabric. I cringe as wet splotches paint her dress pants.

"Who told you that?" My eyes are stuck on the floor. No matter how many times I scrub the same spot, it takes me a solid minute to notice it's clean. What a humiliating conversation to be having with your boss about her brother.

She chuckles. "You just did."

I stumble to my feet. "We just kissed. But there's a *Celeb* article suggesting otherwise."

"I never believe those things." She inspects her chair and sits back down.

Up until this moment, Emma hasn't brought up Everett to me. I think she respected my situation enough not to ask questions. Based on her nonchalance now, I don't think she cares if the article is accurate or not.

I should reciprocate that respect and keep her out of it. He's her family and blending the two could get messy. But after last night, she's the only person I know who can answer some of the questions I still have. Let's hope her lack of concern over tabloids also extends to personal information.

"Can I ask you something?"

"Of course," she says.

She's abandoned her computer and swiveled her chair to face me.

How do I say this? "What was he like... before... you know, when he was just... Everett?"

Her eyebrows shoot up. "He told you."

Not in so many heartbroken words, but yes.

"His trashed music studio after Quinn's evaluation yesterday did."

Surprise leaves Emma's face. It's followed by a lack of fine lines around her eyes and mouth. A blank expression. I'm starving for more of a reaction from her, but all I'm getting is indifference. "Hard to read" runs in the family, I guess.

"He must really like you. Everett doesn't tell anyone about that part of himself."

"Right time; right place." A nervous laugh slips out of my mouth. The truth is, I don't know if Everett would have ever said anything had I stayed inside his house.

"He was hopeful about the future," she answers. "Just as anxious, I think. Less exhausted. But he was more open with me back then. You might know him better than I do now."

I finally get the reaction I was waiting for. It's not the one I expected though. She's hurt.

"I wouldn't say that," I reassure her. I don't like witnessing other people's turmoil when there's nothing I can do about it.

She makes her point by saying, "I didn't know Quinn had an evaluation yesterday."

He didn't tell her. And I overstepped. *Keep* overstepping as I fill in details that should have come from her brother.

"It was for speech therapy. They think Quinn could have APD like him but won't know until she's older."

"That's why he trashed his studio." She connects the dots.

I nod. "Does Caroline know?"

She shakes her head. "No one does."

I assumed as much. Caroline would have a lot more respect for him if she did.

"I'm sorry he didn't tell you himself," I say.

Emma reaches across her desk and grabs my hand. "Don't be. He's lucky to have you, Summer. So am I."

Emotion brims beneath the surface, but I force it down. I don't want to cry in front of her.

"Thank you. But enough about this. It sounds like we have our work cut out for us, and I'm not about to let you give up your bathroom breaks." I hustle for the door.

"What bathroom breaks?" she asks.

"Exactly!"

"Wait... Summer?"

I spin around. "Yeah?"

"I almost forgot to tell you that yesterday was pay day. Should be enough for that down deposit on an apartment you were needing."

Oh is all I can manage for half a second. Especially when a text pops through from Everett at the same time.

> EVERETT: Does this mean you're still thinking about it?

> SUMMER: Still thinking about it.

> EVERETT: Of course you can have the night off.

"Thanks," I reply to Emma and step out into the hall in a daze, selecting the bright green app on my phone instead of responding to that message. A direct deposit of sixteen-hundred dollars stares back at me.

There's the reason I was looking for this morning. This is why I took this job. It's what I've been working toward.

It's just not how I thought I'd feel when I got here.

We finish up for the day around six and meet at Red Feather Lounge—Emma's suggestion, based on its locally sourced ingredients and energy efficiency. I got an earful about their environmental sustainability approach on the elevator ride to the lobby. With the glass bottles in her office mini fridge and her lack of paper towel use, I should have guessed eco-friendly practices are a passion of hers.

A black-clad hostess leads us through an ambient-lit cellar to where Julia's already seated, perusing a menu. The deep crease wedged between her eyebrows is shadowed by a flickering tea light in the middle of the table.

"Your waitress will be right with you," the hostess says.

Julia snaps her menu shut and scoots out of the booth. "You're here!" She hugs me.

"You're early."

"Well, what's new?" She leans past me, holding out her hand. "I'm Julia. You must be Emma."

"Yes. Hi!" Emma returns her handshake.

"I love your outfit. I've always wanted a reason to own a business suit, but a nursing student wasn't exactly the gig for it."

"I miss jeans," Emma confesses. Our combined laugh draws a glare from the couple seated across from us.

I slide in the same side of the booth as Julia. "At least you two know the appropriate attire for a situation. I wore a little black dress to have macaroni and cheese with Quinn last night."

Julia jerks her head in my direction. "I thought you were going on a date with veterinarian Joe?"

I don't know why I look at Emma when she says that—the woman who's more focused on shrugging off her dress coat and draping it on the open seat next to her than judging me.

I haven't had a chance to fill Julia in on all that transpired since I left the house yesterday. Might as well skip to the big part.

"Everett asked me to move in with him."

All eyes remained trained on me despite the interruption of a waitress with the largest hoop earrings I've ever seen dropping three bamboo coasters in the middle of our table.

"Welcome! I'm Maria. I'll be your server tonight. What can I get you ladies to drink?"

Emma looks at her first. "We're gonna need a round of margaritas for this conversation."

Maria chuckles. "Been there! I'll be right back."

"Well, *that* wasn't in the *Celeb* article."

"You did read it!" I gasp at Emma.

"I told you I didn't believe what it said, not that I didn't read it." She unfurls her cloth napkin and cloaks her lap with it.

Julia opens to the homepage of Celeb.com and is skimming the humiliating highlights. If she didn't know what we were talking about before, she's filled in now. When she finally looks up, she's smirking at me.

"What?"

"Nothing. I'm just trying to connect the dots. Sometimes I don't know which one to start with."

I'll give her which one to start with.

"Everett needed my help, so I canceled on Joe."

The prompt arrival of three beverages steals the attention from that sentence.

"You have impressive timing," Emma jokes with our waitress.

"Isn't that my job? Interrupting a juicy conversation?" She arches her back with her laugh.

"Good thing we're just getting started." Julia elbows me in the ribcage.

I'd be panicking a little more if my friends weren't adorning big grins. A sign that they're enjoying our night out, even if it's at my expense. Mission accomplished.

Maria plunks a margarita on each coaster. "Well, let me get right to the point and I'll be out of your hair. Drinks look good?"

Julia takes the first sip. "Amazing!"

"Perfect. Can I get some appetizers started for you? Or are we ready to order dinner?"

"Uh… I think we might need another minute," I pipe in, having yet to open my menu. Which wouldn't be a problem if deciding what to eat at a restaurant for me wasn't akin to making everyone in the world agree on something.

"No problem. I'll be back."

Our waitress makes herself scarce, but instead of studying the options in front of me, I launch back into our conversation.

"I'm looking for advice here, ladies. What am I supposed to do? Is it crazy to move in with someone for three weeks?"

I thought the paycheck I received earlier would be my excuse not to move in. A chance to experience living on my own now that I have the means to do so. Why am I still hesitating?

Julia squeezes the wheel of her lime over her glass. Coarse salt falls from the rim as she samples her drink. "You don't need our advice, Sum."

"I'm afraid I'll repeat the same mistakes. I don't want to rely on another man to take care of me."

"That's not what's happening here," Emma steps in. "It's three weeks. And Everett is relying on *you* to help with Quinn. Not the other way around."

"But what if…" My words burrow beneath a mountain of shame. The number of jobs I've accepted surpasses the fingers on my hands. Every one of them has ended in failure. Who's to say this time will be any different? Especially when the stakes are tied to my solo livelihood. There's no room for error. An insurmountable pressure to swim. If I sink and screw this up, I can say goodbye to both jobs.

Julia reaches for my hand and rearranges the words I was going to say. Fills them in with ones I need to hear. "But what if it works out?"

She's not asking, she's telling me to picture that version of my life. One where I have two successful jobs that I'm loving.

"That!" Emma points at my smile. It's the first time I've heard her shout or get excited about anything. "Right there... that's your answer!"

Julia gives my hand a squeeze. "See. Don't let Brian steal your joy anymore, okay?"

"Yeah." I nod. She's right. I've submitted to him for as long as I can remember. Choosing to follow my heart and trust in a situation that's making me happy feels like a step in the right direction to taking that power back.

"What about you and Henry though?"

It's the only worry left that's keeping me from jumping into this. Julia's learned to rely on me while I've been living with her. I can't leave her high and dry.

"We'll be fine," she contends. "Maybe I'll ask Jake to help out more."

"You will?"

Julia pauses to fill Emma in on all the necessary details to keep up with this conversation, and I take the opportunity to scan the menu.

"I said maybe," she reminds us.

"Does this mean you're considering his date request too?" I ask.

"He asked you out?" Emma swirls her glass and takes a sip.

Naturally she left out that little detail, and pink stains her cheeks.

"We'll see."

I cover her hand. "I love this for you."

She feeds me an appreciative smile. "Thanks. What about you, Emma? Any men in your life?"

Emma lets out an awkward laugh that turns into a hiccup

and smothers it with a long pull of her drink. She wipes her upper lip with her napkin. "It's a complicated story."

"Lucky Henry is with his dad," Julia pipes in.

"And we have all night," I add, planting my elbows on the veneer tabletop.

Her thumb buffs at the stem of her margarita glass. "'Good' is not the word I'd use in this case."

The more I'm getting to know her, the more I'm recognizing her and Everett's similarities. She's difficult to crack open.

Julia sits taller. "Well, now you *have* to tell us."

"It can't be any more embarrassing than finding yourself in a tabloid with Rhett Dawson," I joke.

Emma sighs. "I've been seeing someone on and off since high school. His name is Nathan."

I hold up a hand. "Wait, is that the guy in the graduation picture on Everett's dresser?"

I recall it. Longer, curly hair. Boyish grin. He was cute.

Emma blanches. Julia yanks on my shoulder.

"I'm sorry, *on his dresser?* You sure you don't want to update your little cover story for that article?"

"No! It was a wet clothing situation. That's it."

Her eyebrows shoot up. It's amazing how many years we've been friends, and I still manage to surprise her.

"You know what, we were talking about Emma." I point at her for good measure. "Is this Nathan guy the one from the photo?" I repeat my question.

Emma's cheeks burn a brilliant coral. "No. That's Will Baker."

"Are we ready to order, ladies?" Maria interrupts for the third time.

"Yes," Julia says, rattling off her order without looking at the menu. I'm sure she picked it ten seconds after being seated.

"I'll have the wild Alaskan salmon, please," Emma says next.

"And what about you?"

It's no Cheesecake Factory, but there are still too many options for someone with a severe case of FOMO. I expected to have a minute, not a paperless waitress taking no notes. Damn her for being so good at her job.

I abandon the menu. "What do you recommend?"

"Our most popular are the burrata, crispy calamari, or the lounge burger."

"I'll take all three," I announce, snapping my menu shut and handing it to her.

"Well, okay then! I'll have those out shortly."

My hand is halfway to my drink when I catch Emma and Julia's entertained expressions.

"I'm going to miss living with you," Julia says first.

"And Quinn's going to *love* living with you," Emma says second.

Not everyone finds the kind of friendship where you feel seen and validated exactly as you are. It's a special kind of love. One that I feel lucky to have found in Jules and now Emma.

"You're doing me a big favor, you know." Julia grunts, offloading a gaping box in the back end of Summer's SUV. I give it a shove, wedging it in the tight space before trapping the pile of belongings behind the liftgate.

"Why's that?"

"Do you know how much coffee creamer that woman goes through in a week?" Julia scrubs her palms on her jeans. "The Rhett Dawson franchise might need to take out stock in Dairy Farmers of America."

I chuckle. It takes the edge off the nerves that have been ricocheting around my abdomen for the better part of a week. Apprehension that has nothing to do with Summer moving in and everything to do with the tracks I sent Todd a couple of hours ago.

What will the label think of them?

Will they ask what they're about?

Do I care if they do?

I'm trying not to let those unanswered questions consume my every thought. Instead, I focus on Julia's comment and the note it reminds me of in my phone. The one I titled *Summer's*

Favorite Things. I'm not sure why I made it when I know I won't forget them, even if I wanted to. Hazelnut creamer is at the top followed by pink peonies and candied pecans.

"Anything else I should know?"

"Well, now that you ask..." Julia opens her hand, palm facing up, and keeps tally on her fingers. "She sleeps barefoot, loves music, thinks toxic TV dramas make great Friday night entertainment, has a hundred dreams swirling around her head at any given moment, and she's the best friend I've ever had. Break her heart, and I'll send a fleet of reporters to your doorstep." She nods her head with a closed-mouth smile and folded arms.

"Thanks for the warning," I say, even if that's the least threatening thing anyone has ever thrown my way.

A part of me feels guilty for taking Summer away from her best friend. But not as much as I am relieved that she said yes to this in the first place. I've not had another breakdown in my studio, but it's bringing me so much peace knowing she'll be there for Quinn if I ever do.

"What are you two whispering about out here?" A hot-pink suitcase topples over on the uneven cobblestone walkway behind Summer. She rights it with the kick of her foot, hauling it toward us.

I shove my hands in my pockets, rocking back on my heels. "Julia was just warning me about how you sing my songs in your sleep."

Summer's head snaps in Julia's direction. "You're dead to me. I think I'll save my goodbye for Henry." She jerks her luggage in a clunky one-hundred-and eighty-degree turn back toward the front door.

"Does he know about the shirt though? I might need to add that to the list," Julia teases.

"Dead to me!" Summer hollers over her shoulder.

Henry hands her a pillow—the last item left in the entryway. "Are you going to marry Rhett Dawson?"

"Wh-what?" Summer chokes out a cough.

"Mom says people move in together when they get married. That's why my dad doesn't live here."

"Uh—" Julia hustles over to him and shoos Summer toward her car. "Yeah, that's not... I think they need to get going, buddy. Let's tell them goodbye, okay?"

"Bye," he says, and walks back inside without his answer.

Dammit. I was really wanting to see what Summer would come up with.

"Bye." I wave back, moving closer to my new roommate. "Are you ready?"

"Yes. No!" The handle of Summer's suitcase clanks to the ground as she abandons it and shoves against the door they almost shut on her face.

Okay? Confused, I collect the luggage to stow it in her passenger seat. With the minute alone, my thoughts drift back to the studio.

I never asked Summer if she told Emma about that night. I wouldn't care if she did. But it would explain why I found a new desk chair, coffee table, and vinyl records on the wall the next day. It was like it never happened. A nightmare stripped away with open eyes.

Until the evidence stitched itself into lyrics. Inspired three songs in five days. *I did it.* Whether or not that accomplishment is something to be celebrated remains a mystery.

My phone buzzes against my thigh. I whip it out of my pocket, expecting it to be Todd.

WILL: I see you took my advice 😊

I think it's about time you get laid was his counsel the last time I saw him.

EVERETT: You're next.

I stuff my phone away. When I open the car door, Summer is sailing out of the house again, Millie wrangled in a death grip under her bicep. The cat is clawing at Summer's pillow, wriggling toward her shoulder, and fueling her panic.

I step out of her way as she dashes toward me. Within a couple of feet of the car, she flings the cat in her vehicle and slams the door shut. A cloud of orange fur rains over top of us.

"And I thought it was just men she didn't like."

Summer expels the kind of breath that follows a four-hundred-meter dash. "It is. She could sense you a mile away."

"And my holeless shirt, no doubt," I add.

That gets her to laugh.

"Do you have this under control?" Backward steps carry me toward my own car. She doesn't notice with her focus stuck on mapping her cat's escape route.

I think she responds by the time I'm in my front seat. Wouldn't know when I turn on my vehicle and all sound is drowned out by a phone call connecting to my car speakers.

I jerk the door shut and swallow. My vision narrows to my side mirror. The second there's a gap between two cars I navigate into it, pulling away from Julia's house. Then I answer.

"Dude! I just listened to the demos."

I knew this call was coming. Prepared myself for it the moment I hit send. But I have to fight like hell to keep my voice even as I respond. "And?"

He doesn't even hesitate. "I don't know how you did it, but these songs are your best work."

I didn't expect that. What I sent him were rough takes.

They're not well rehearsed or anywhere near refined. There is no vocal track layering or instrumental arrangement additions yet. They're raw cuts from the only time I haven't cried singing them since I wrote them.

"Seriously, Rhett. I'm blown away over here, man," he adds in my silence. "I can't wait for the label to hear these."

Todd's always been honest with me. I know he wouldn't be saying this if he didn't mean it. After being stuck on melodies for weeks, hope blooms in my chest.

"Thanks. That... really means a lot."

"You're going to get back out on that stage, Rhett. You were born to do this. There's no doubt about it."

His belief in me should be the source of that hope in my chest, not the means of relief that is spreading through my body. I'm grateful he didn't ask about the inspiration behind the lyrics; I don't intend to keep my disability from Todd forever, but I'd like it to be in person when I finally tell him.

"Thanks, man."

"Hey, about that *Celeb* article..."

I still, my hands on ten and two. "What about it?" I have no idea if it dredged up good or bad publicity. If it was the latter, I think I would have heard from him sooner.

"It's no big deal, I just wondered if that was the woman from the concert?"

The way he scrutinized her that night, I'm not surprised he recognized her from a grainy photo snapped at dusk.

"I didn't know she was from my hometown until I moved back and ran into her. She's been helping out with Quinn." *Also, she's the reason why I wrote the songs I sent you. And she's moving into my house.*

"She seems good for you," he says.

"It's not like that." *Yet.*

"Whatever you say, Daddy Dawson. We'll talk soon."

"Let me know what the—" *label says*, I finish, after he's already hung up.

Guess I'll spend the next however many agonizing days waiting for another response. Thankfully, Summer takes my mind off it when her name pops up on the touch display. I spin the volume dial down four notches when aggressive meowing assaults my speakers.

"Millie, quit!" I hear her whisper-scold.

The Bronco jostles with a hop on the curb.

"Worried about how you'll get that cat out of your car?" I pull forward on the driveway, leaving ample room for a straight shot to the front door. I hope she knows I'm joking. That I don't expect her to handle this herself. It's why I'm waiting in the driveway until she gets here.

"It's all I've been thinking about the entire drive over, but that's not why I called." The sentence rushes out of her in a string of words. No pause. No spaces. Tethered together by one breath.

"You mean you weren't going to ask if I had a straitjacket you could borrow?"

"Now that you said something..." She pretends to be thinking about it when in reality, there is a foot-long feline to blame for hijacking her attention.

I draw her back to the conversation with, "If it wasn't why you called, then..."

"Are you worried what Quinn will think of this?"

I'm not. I told Quinn about it earlier today. We were on our drive over to her Sunday date with Coco. I did my best to explain the situation, and all she asked was if Summer could read her a book before bed. I don't think she understands.

"How so?"

"Just... her getting attached," Summer clarifies. There's real fear behind her tone. I don't want to read into what that means when we have three weeks. All I'm leaning into is the fact that this feels like the best decision for everyone involved.

"Well, you'll definitely have to part with Millie when you move out, so better get on board with that now."

"Do you ever take anything seriously?" she mocks, throwing my words from the first night we texted back in my face.

I know that's not what she meant. I also know it's too late to protect any of us.

"She's already attached, Summer," I answer quietly.

"Close your eyes. No peeking!"

Quinn giggles from her twin bed. She's perched atop her comforter, fresh out of a bath, fingers splayed over her eyes.

I point at her. "Hey! I saw that!"

She tucks them in tight and squeals with glee.

"I mean it, young lady."

Summer backs into the room with Millie cradled in her arms. You'd think she gave her a sedative compared to the version I carried in earlier. At least my shirt and shoulder stayed intact this time. She must be warming up to me.

"Okay, here comes the surprise!"

Summer plops her cat in Quinn's lap.

"Titty!" She launches her arms around Millie's neck.

Summer and I fight to contain our smiles.

"We'll work on it," I say. *Tomorrow*, I think.

Quinn's evaluation results came back. I met with Sue on Friday to discuss them—a meeting I thought would be difficult to face—but it wasn't such a shock this time. I felt prepared for the expressive language disorder label they want to use in place of the potential APD one that could come later in her life.

"Might need to start with the letter *k*," Summer jokes.

"Tum see!" Quinn coos as Millie flops on her back and rolls from side to side amongst a pile of stuffed animals.

Summer runs her hand up Millie's tail. "She likes you."

"Show Mommy?"

I freeze. This is the first time Quinn has asked for her in a couple of weeks. I expect Summer to look to me for help, but she confidently answers all on her own.

"Your mommy is right here." She places her palm over Quinn's heart, then presses Bunny against her cheek. "I think she likes Millie too."

There's never a moment when I'm not impressed by Summer. In awe of her ease with Quinn. Like she's done this parent thing before when I know she hasn't. I wish that kind of intuition came easy to me.

Quinn smiles so big I can barely make out her pupils from tiny slits. After months of adding to my journal—hundreds of things I've done wrong as her dad—I finally feel like I did something right today.

Quinn taps on Summer's arm. "Weed?"

This time Summer looks to me for confirmation.

"I did promise you'd read her a book."

Summer tucks her arm around Quinn. "I'd love to."

Quinn wriggles free. She scoots to the edge of the bed and slides off the comforter, racing for the old magazine rack that became a bookshelf when we moved in.

Without her snuggle partner, Millie's enchantment with Quinn's bed ends. She springs from the mattress to the floor, sauntering my way.

"I guess we'll be going now." I watch her tail swish through the exit.

"Don't have too much fun," Summer teases.

"Come on. That's all Millie and I have." I bend down to give Quinn a squeeze, and she drops her books for our nightly ritual —a kiss on the forehead. "Love you."

I don't make it very far when I find myself leaning in the shadow outside the doorway. Summer is sprawled on the bed, Quinn tucked up under her arm beside her. I chuckle at the stack of books ten deep in Summer's lap. Poor thing doesn't know how this game works. If you don't give Quinn a two-book limit, she'll grab the whole shelf.

"Dis one," Quinn says, pulling on the spine of a blue paperback until it frees from the center of the pile.

"Ooo, the fish? Okay."

Quinn leans in closer, snuggling against Summer's chest. The sight makes me feel something I wasn't sure I'd ever feel again. Settled. Like there's nowhere else in the world I'd rather be than right here. A foreign concept I've never felt in my childhood home until now.

The adorable display morphs into pure entertainment the moment Summer begins reading *The Pout-Pout Fish*. Inflection dances in her tone and her face twists into expressions I could never attempt. Quinn is kicking her feet and eating it up.

I've read this book to her before. I know what's coming. But nothing prepares me for the repetitive part when Summer pooches out her lips and her voice drowns to a sad, pathetic tone. She pauses and says, "Hey! This book is about your dad!"

Quinn giggles simply because Summer does. And me? I'm crouched on the floor, my face stuffed in the sleeve of my shirt to drown out my cackle. It's doing a decent job of muffling because neither one of them looks over here.

Somewhere between the last few pages Quinn slumps against Summer's lap. I watch her transfer Quinn's head to her pillow and tuck the covers up around her shoulders. She buries

Bunny by Quinn's neck, turns off her lamp, and tiptoes toward me.

I stand as her proximity backs me farther into the hallway. When she sees me, she worries at her bottom lip. "How much of that did you hear?"

I smirk. "Enough to know you think I'm a pout pout fish."

She snorts. "Well, if the face fits."

"I'll have you know, I'm a lot more self-aware than that grumpy aquatic creature."

"Are you?" she teases, but Summer loses her smile when my gaze lands on her mouth.

"I don't need anyone to come along and tell me what will make me feel better."

Tension coils and crackles in a vortex around us. I know I built a wall of mixed signals. I told her our kiss meant nothing. Made her believe all I cared about was her help with Quinn. My penance for that should be keeping my hands to myself. Too bad there's nothing I want less.

An impulse drives me forward, backing her into the wall. She yelps when her shoulder blades meet the plaster. I smother the sound with my mouth, drawing out the perfect pressure from the push and pull of our lips. Heat trickles in a steady stream down my spine and spreads to every cell in my body. I'm nothing but sensation and want. A need to be as close to her as possible. One hand threads through her hair, the other squeezes her waist. This kiss is everything that I wanted to feel from the first one that was over before it started. The desire to stop hasn't even crossed my mind when she pulls away.

Right, left, right, left, her eyes flit. The longer she studies me, the more I question what she's thinking.

"Feel better?" she whispers.

I press my forehead against hers and shake my head. *More like utterly destroyed.* "Not even close."

She giggles, then clears her throat. "Well, um... I should... probably..."

When I pull back she's pointing at the guest bedroom door. It's only eight o'clock, but with dinner and a game of hide and seek, it didn't leave much time for anything else. I'm sure she was hoping to unpack her things.

"Yeah," I finally get out, dragging a hand through my hair.

"See you in the morning?" She offers me a smile while taking backward steps. I nod, then she dips behind the door.

"The morning," I repeat to the silence. An exhale puffs out my cheeks as I cage both hands behind my neck and tip my head to the ceiling. Since when did kissing a woman have to be followed by a million unknowns? The one I'm stuck on is if she'll always retreat to her room after Quinn goes to sleep. I hadn't thought about this part of the evening until now. I've been perfectly content to watch TV or mess around on my phone by myself most nights, but my desire to be alone has vanished.

An hour goes by flopped on my mattress, then two. Even after removing my shirt and slipping on sweats, I'm still hot, uncomfortable, and restless. Sleep feels miles away at this point, so I give up, grabbing my glasses off the nightstand. I'm tempted to stop at Summer's door, but it's dark when I pass it.

I've acclimated to the creaks and groans of this older home, but not the sound of running water in the middle of the night. It has me rushing down the stairs and startling a very awake Summer making coffee in my kitchen.

"I'm sorry, I didn't know anyone else was up." She tugs at the hem of her T-shirt that's three sizes too big.

I smirk at the outline of my face screen-printed on the front. *She bought it like that on purpose.*

"Nice pajamas."

Summer crosses her arms, bunching the fabric a good couple inches higher. "My Chris Stapleton one was dirty."

The chuckle that works its way up my throat sounds husky. "I'm sure."

My team had to have picked the thinnest possible blend of cotton for that shirt line with the way her panties and lack of bra are showing right through it.

"You wear glasses," she comments.

Moonlight is leaking through the window and causing her lidded gaze to glow. She *likes* them.

"When I have to. Do you always drink caffeine at one in the morning? That would explain the boundless energy."

"It's decaf, smart-ass. Do you want any?"

The coffee machine beeps, and she spins around. All words and their meaning leave me when she opens the cupboard above her head and stands on her tiptoes, causing her shirt to ride a few inches higher than before. The utter definition in her legs punches the air from my lungs. A stiffening cock reminds me how long it's been since I've had this reaction. I almost forgot she asked me a question by the time I'm a foot away from her.

"No, thanks. I'm already hot." *From this room but also that shirt.*

"Sometimes a warm drink helps me sleep," she whispers.

Unless she's giving that sugar from the cupboard a go, there's no way she's drinking that. Creamer is at the top of my grocery list, and I planned to go to the store before anyone woke up.

Has she been up all this time? I can't read her face with her still turned around—not that it's done me a lot of good up to this point. She tips the coffee pot over her mug as I cage her against the counter. A splash misses the rim and puddles on the granite with her gasp.

"Everett, about earlier—"

"Tell me what you want, Summer." I can't stop myself from saying what I'm thinking any longer. Can't deny this chemistry between us. I need to know what she wants from this. From *me*. Because I'll walk out of this kitchen and back up those stairs if it's not us. But if this is about her not trusting her own decisions... if she thinks she needs validation from Julia or anyone else in her life, she's wrong.

Her hands shake as she stuffs the coffee pot away.

"I want you to know... I took this job for Quinn. I like spending my time with her, and I don't want to do anything to ruin that."

"I know. You aren't," I assure her.

"But if this is a game to you—"

"I'm a thirty-three-year-old widower with a toddler, Summer. I don't have time for games." I've thought long and hard about this, is what I'm saying. Leaning into sex just because it feels good is not a luxury I have anymore. I know the ramifications of this dynamic, and I want *her*. "I need to know what you want."

"I just—"

Her sentence cuts off when I run my nose along her shoulder. Her back arches, and the move sticks her ass out. She can't press it against my lap and expect me not to find out what that means. Her head falls back on my shoulder, her perky tits tenting her T-shirt. Swift pants follow the rise and fall of her chest. I'm waiting for her to say it. To break the charged silence.

"I want..."

My breath ghosts against her skin at the base of her throat.

"I need..."

I'm dying here. Desperate for her to finish that sentence.

"... you to touch me." Her voice is barely above a whisper. A soft plea she's afraid to say. This *is* about trust. Summer is scared to ask for what she wants, and I'm going to make her not so afraid anymore.

The pads of my fingertips graze her thighs, coasting up the tense muscles that bunch beneath her skin. She braces herself against the counter, sagging forward at the waist. A quiver follows the path I'm drawing higher and higher. By the time I reach the apex of her outer thighs, there's no doubt she can feel everything she's doing to me. It's as far as I planned to take this without more direction. "Now what?"

She's still trembling. Still hasn't moved or touched me back. I don't want her to. This isn't about me. She has to know how much this is affecting me.

"Higher," she pants more boldly this time.

My fingertips slide under her shirt. Coast over delicate fabric. I squeeze her backside, and she groans, giving in to the pressure of my hands and tipping even further forward. I'm barely holding it together with her bent over like this. Pressure is building, drawing my balls in tight. When my hands slide up her waist, so does her shirt. Fabric drapes so high white lace is on display. I'm already gone, and we've just started. Impulse and need are gnawing at my spine. Temptation is literally in my lap, but I want to prove to Summer that deep down she knows what she wants, and she deserves every bit of it. I'm not going to stop until I convince her otherwise.

She grinds against me and whimpers, "Take off my shirt."

I drag it over her head and toss it on the floor. Two soft breasts fill my hands when she presses them to her chest—helps me squeeze her nipples with our thumbs and pointer fingers entwined. It's erotic watching her take charge of her own body and give herself over to the intoxicating friction. Her hand slips to her waist as she peels her underwear down her legs and kicks them off to the side. Then she finally, *finally* spins to face me.

She grabs my wrist when I touch the rim of my glasses. "Leave them on."

Oh. Then she's kissing me. Tongues, hands, legs, everything's tangling. There's no hesitation left in the way she's grinding against me. I forgot how good this can feel. What it's like to chase a high and race toward a finish line. I need her on this counter. I thread my arm around her waist and then I'm jerking her on top of the surface.

Her lips split into a laugh when her heel bangs into a drawer, metal rattling inside of it.

I have no idea how far to take this. I'm leaning into what she wants, and right now that's my face between her thighs as she pushes on the crown of my head. I rip my glasses off, sliding them toward the sink, and kneel before her. Both her legs wrap my shoulders, and her head knocks against the cabinet behind her.

"Shh," I whisper, blowing a breath right where she wants me. Her hips buck with the swipe of my tongue. So many sounds are tumbling out of her mouth, every one of them coaxing the fire inside that's threatening to burn me alive. She's no longer holding back what she wants.

Faster.

Right there.

Don't stop.

Her muscles tense and release beneath my hands as I hold her steady. I can tell she's close when she clamps down on the two fingers I'm pumping inside her. Spots are popping up in my vision, my world rapidly tipping on its axis.

"Everett..." Her hand sinks in my hair. "If you don't stop..." She rocks against my face. "I'm gonna come..."

"I'm counting on it," I growl as she cries out. I carry her through her release until she slumps, sated, against the cupboard behind her. Only in the silence between the ragged breaths we share do I hear my name being called.

"Da-eee?"

With a sudden rush, I leave Summer, running for the stairs.

23

SUMMER

I open my eyes to a foreign ceiling. It's less textured, more swirled. A sparkly chandelier replaces the dull glow of the boob light I'm used to. This isn't Julia's office.

The sleepy fog lifts and everything from yesterday comes rushing back... the move, his kiss, *the kitchen*. Things that would have never happened if I were anyplace but here. Crisp white sheets cover the shirt he peeled from my body last night. The one I swept off the floor after his daughter called his name.

I got married too young to ever experience a one-night stand. Does a person usually feel anything but confused the next day? I stood in the kitchen for an embarrassing amount of time after he left. He never came back.

We share the same priority, Everett and I. I would never have expected him to return if Quinn needed him.

She has her first speech therapy appointment today, and I intend to expend all of my focus and energy into that. I know deep down her progress is important to him, and once a week with a professional is not very much time to accomplish that. I'll need to glean as much as I can from this session to work with her every other day of the week.

A cool draft of air meets my bare legs with the comforter tossed to the side. I catch a glimpse of my appearance in the ornate mirror suspended above the dresser—disheveled hair, rosy cheeks, swollen lips—all signs of what we did. I could really use a shower. I snag an outfit from the suitcase I never unpacked because I was so busy dissecting our hallway kiss. That warm cup of coffee was a lame excuse for why I was even awake in the first place.

Their rooms are empty when I dash to the bathroom to get ready. The spray of the shower and the drone of the fan block any signs of people being awake. Once they're both turned off and I'm dressed, I hear his voice. It's muted, but I think he's singing in the living room. He sounds *happy*. I let that settle in for a second. At least last night didn't make him spiral.

With the smoky smell of bacon absent from the air, I decide to help with breakfast. I see them before they see me descending the stairs. Everett's still in the same sweats. The sight makes my stomach clench.

Quinn climbs on top of her blanket that's splayed out on the carpet. Everett squats down and bunches each corner into one fist. He lifts her off the floor and swings her like a pendulum. Her head pops through a small opening between the edges.

"Summa! Woot at me! Win-a-wa!"

Everett turns over his shoulder. He's wearing his glasses again and has never looked more handsome to me.

"Good morning," he says between verses of "The Lion Sleeps Tonight." Quinn squeals through her made-up win-a-wa version of the lyrics.

"Good morning," I choke out. Emotion seems to be invading my voice.

This is the happiest I've seen them together since I showed up on their doorstep three weeks ago.

Near the end of the verse, he sends her sliding across the polished wood floor near my feet. She jumps up to hug me.

"You have a fun daddy," I tell her. I'm looking at him; he's looking at me. There's nothing but admiration in his eyes.

"Again! Again!" Quinn shouts.

"We need to finish breakfast. You have school today, and then Summer is picking you up for a fun appointment."

I catch it when he struggles to get out the word *fun*. I know he's doing this for Quinn. Making it sound exciting when I'm sure his memories of it are anything but. He hasn't shared any more about his disability since the night in the studio, but I gathered that "fun" wasn't a word he would ever use to describe it.

"Otay!" She bounds for the table, and he turns to me.

"I sent over a signed form this morning granting you permission to take her to her appointments. If they give you any trouble, you can have them call me."

I nod. "I'm sure it will be fine."

"Would you like some coffee?" he asks. Next to the mug is a bottle of my favorite hazelnut creamer. "I figured, if you're going to be living here, you deserve for it to feel like your home too. Julia told me you like this one."

The confused feelings I woke up with vanish. You don't ask a girl's best friend what her favorite kind of coffee creamer is if you don't like her.

"I'd love some. Thank you."

"About last night," he says, handing me the mug.

I was going to avoid this topic until later when we didn't have a toddler in the same room, but now I have a sudden urge to clear the air.

"Everett, I—"

He grabs my wrist—the same one he touched that first time in the parking lot. It's an intentional gesture. A reminder of the moment we shared.

"I'm sorry for leaving you like that."

He isn't letting go, and I don't want him to.

"Quinn doesn't usually wake up in the middle of the night, let alone in this house. She needed her mo—I slept on her floor."

That's why he never came back. Not for the million other reasons that had me second-guessing my decision to move. I know he's trying to convey that he doesn't regret it. And if his eyes focused on my mouth don't send the message, the distracting stroke of his thumb on my wrist sure does.

"You don't have to apologize."

He leans in close and with a sultry whisper, says, "The only thing I'm apologizing for is not getting to see you wake up in that shirt."

He lets go and brushes by me, leaving the heat of his hand, his mouth, everything behind. I blow out a breath, hoping it expels the warmth from my cheeks with it. If not, I'm going to need a big gulp of this coffee to explain away the flush that has found a home in my face.

"There's always tomorrow."

We exchange a stolen glance.

"I'm counting on it."

"You must be Summer," the speech therapist says, sitting in the chair across from us.

Everett briefed me over breakfast. He wasn't kidding when he said this place is busy, even at 3:00 on a Monday. There was zero chance for introductions in the packed waiting room she retrieved us from.

"Yeah, I'm Quinn's nanny."

Sue is exactly how I pictured the stoic yet inviting person Everett described her to be as she shakes my hand.

"I'm so glad you could come see me again today, Quinn."

We both laugh when she says, "Yeah," instead of *me too*, her attention too enraptured on a family of plastic figurines in front of her to pay us any attention.

"Before we get started, I was hoping I could run something by you." Sue turns toward me.

I sit taller. "Of course."

"I noticed Quinn's dad left this form blank. Do you know if he plans on signing it?"

I briefly scan the document she hands me, plucking out words like *HIPPA*, *school communication*, and *progress monitoring*. All of which tell me Everett would be granting this practice the ability to pass Quinn's confidential target goals and growth over to her teacher.

Would he want this?

"I'm not sure," I reply.

"That's okay. It's optional. Maybe you could take it with you though and double-check?"

"Of course."

"Awesome. Well... your turn, Quinn. Ready?"

"Re-eee," Quinn repeats.

"I see you've found my friends here." Sue holds up a female doll with gray hair. "This is the grandma."

"To-To," Quinn says back.

Sue looks at me.

"Coco is her grandma's name."

"Oh! How cute!"

I smile at her. *Don't say that to Caroline.* I wonder if Everett's told her about any of this. After pushing for speech therapy at the birthday party, I'm sure it would win him some brownie points if she knew he had gotten Quinn the help that she needs.

Sue holds up the female doll with black hair next. "This is the mommy."

"Mommy," Quinn repeats with ease.

Sue jots down a couple of notes, then holds up the matching male doll. "And this is the daddy."

"Da-eee."

"Yes, daddy," Sue says again, only this time she emphasizes the *d* sound in the middle of the word. "You like your daddy, huh?"

Quinn nods.

They practice labeling each figurine before Sue collects the dolls off the table and stows them in a wicker basket near her feet. Without the distraction of the toys, Quinn waits. Sue reaches for a binder on a metal shelf bolted to the wall next to her. The laminated pages fan as she flips to a picture of a girl on a rollercoaster.

"She's going down. Can you say 'down'?"

Quinn nails the word on the first try.

"Good!" She scans for another page. "She's on a ride. Can you say 'ride'?"

A shuffle of feet and a flash of shadows draw Quinn's attention to the door. Sue makes popping sounds with her mouth. It redirects Quinn's eyes to her lips. "Try it," she encourages when it makes Quinn smile.

Quinn mimics the noise.

"That's a fun sound to make, huh?"

"Yeah!" Quinn carries on with the lip-smacking.

"What about this one?" Sue points to her mouth as she shows Quinn how to form the sound for the letter *d*, touching her tongue to her front pallet while bringing her teeth together.

The sound gets easier for her to make the more times Quinn tries it.

"That's it!" I cheer proudly. I wish Everett were here to see how well she's doing.

Sue breaks her focus from Quinn to me. "That's how you can help her at home. The more practice, the better. Talk your way through daily tasks: 'I'm putting on your shirt. Look, it's pink. It has a kitty on it.' It will feel silly since we don't annotate our day like that, but exposure to sounds is what will help her vocabulary grow."

"Okay." I can do that.

At the end of the session, Sue holds out a prize basket. Quinn fishes through Kit Kat bars and stretchy bracelets, pulling out a ladybug sticker.

"I put those in there just for you." Sue winks at her. "I'll see you next week, okay?"

"Otay." Quinn peels off the back and sticks it to her purple shirt.

"It looks great on you!" I tell her as I thank her speech therapist and follow her lead to the front door.

"Show Da-ee?" Quinn asks as we step outside into the sunshine.

"Yes," I say. But what I'm really thinking is, *just wait for the day, little Quinny, when you have even more to show your daddy from this place than a sticker.*

"How'd therapy go?" My thumb peels up the edge of the ladybug sticker stuck to my chest before flattening it for the fifth time. Quinn couldn't wait to show it to me, so they picked me up, and we're carpooling to talent show practice.

"She did amazing!" Summer beams, pulling her eyes briefly from the road.

Grass and sky blur to a smeared shade of seafoam out the window. "That's good."

She clears her throat. "Her therapist wanted me to ask if you'd like to fill out this form?"

A piece of paper flutters from her visor when she opens it and I snag it from midair.

"Sue said it would be helpful for Quinn's teacher."

I glance at it while she's stopped at a stoplight, recalling the release form. I opted not to complete it. That was before I promised myself that Quinn would be okay. That I'd help her in any way that I can. "I'll sign it when we get home."

Summer clings to the steering wheel. "You okay?"

"Yeah." *I thought I was.*

She nods, doing her best not to look obvious that she's trying to read me.

I got the email I've been waiting for. The one from the label executive. They love the new tracks and reinstated my tour. It's everything I've been wanting. All I've been working for. Hours in the studio coming to what should have been a pinnacle of relief. Instead, reality sunk in. The fantasy's been stripped away. I'll be touring with songs too personal to sing without breaking down. How am I supposed to perform without raising speculations? How will I guarantee there's no repeat of last time?

I'm reeling, and that isn't even the worst part. Shortly after the email came through, Todd called to discuss the new contract they drafted. A detailed document spanning dozens of pages laying out my new term length, advance, and breach clause. Stakes so high that career and financial ruin will be what I face if I screw this up again. I'm lucky they didn't sue for lost profit damages when I failed to fulfill my contractual obligations last time. That leniency won't be shown again.

"How was your time in the studio?"

Summer knows by now that opening up has never been easy for me. Doesn't stop her from trying.

"It was fine."

"Fine?" she pries.

"It was stressful, okay?" *Painful too.* My studio used to be the place I'd go and retreat from my problems. Now they fester through music.

"If you need more time..."

"It's not about time!" I snap. "It's about the fifty-million-page contract I just signed. Jonas Records will destroy me if I don't deliver all I've promised them. It's about leaving Quinn who knows where with another family member before I think she's ready. I have no idea how I'll live up to my word when at any second I could lose control again."

There's so much there that Summer could unpack. It's the part I left out that she zeroes in on.

"You wrote the songs."

There's awe in her voice that would be flattering if I weren't freaking out.

"And that's the problem. The lyrics hit too close to home. I can't get through them without getting upset."

She smiles at me. *Smiles.* "Will you play them for me later? Please?"

I just told this woman I wrote music that causes me a great deal of turmoil, and she asks me to play it for her?

Yet something in her voice... It's always her voice that has me breaking down my walls and saying, "Yes."

Cars are spilling out of the parking lot when we arrive at the school. Summer's too focused on finding a spot to witness her ex-husband in an orange vest and tailored suit directing traffic. The guy looks incredibly pompous.

We've had very few interactions. I am no relationship expert. But I can't see him without passing judgement for the way he treated Summer. It took me one week to figure out how lucky I was to have her taking care of Quinn. He threw it all away over a self-righteous comment about her ability to keep a cat. The fact that his words made her doubt herself... I have no room for patience if he ever tries to approach her again.

"Win-a-wa, Da-eee?" Quinn begs when I get her out of her car seat.

"I don't have a blanket."

"Hoe hans?" She reaches her left to me and her right to Summer. Together we count down.

Five.

Four.

Three.

Two.

One.

She sails forward, and the sound of her unrestrained laughter sends a rush of serotonin through my body, easing the stress brought on by today's events.

We repeat the process a dozen more times before Quinn lets go of our hands to help with the door.

Summer flicks her hair over her shoulder and flashes me a flirty grin. "See... all you need is a good win-a-wa to make you feel better."

That's not the only thing that makes me feel better, and she knows it. She yelps when I pat her on the bottom.

Walking into week two, there's still no teacher assigned to this play. I'd be concerned about that fact if it weren't for Summer catapulting herself into the role with zero hesitations, corralling kids in a giant circle in the middle of the gym.

Despite her confidence, I can tell she's running this thing with a don't-ask-apologize-later policy. I'm hoping by the time Mr. Rogers catches wind of her talent show plan, we won't have enough practices left to change course.

"First things first, everyone needs a talent," Summer announces. "Henry, let's start with you. What do you want to do?"

"I don't know." He shrugs, taking the last bite of his peeled banana.

"Well, what do you like to do during recess?" She reframes the question.

Etta pinches her nose. "All he does is talk about stinky reptiles and stuff."

Several kids snicker.

Henry stares at her. "Reptiles don't have sweat glands. You stink more than they do."

Summer appears unfazed by his response.

"Etta has the right to think reptiles aren't the greatest. But thank you for the facts, Henry. You should bring Max in for your talent!"

"Who's Max?" Blake asks, twisting his hat backward.

"My bearded dragon," Henry answers.

"Woah!" Noah gasps. "You have a bearded dragon? You never told us that!"

Henry holds his blank expression. "You never asked."

Summer's eyes brighten. "See, Henry. Bring Max and you could change some people's minds about reptiles. What about you, Etta?"

Etta's sporting a tiny hole in place of the tooth she was wiggling last week. "I like to play hopscotch and jump rope and Simon Says and—"

"We get it." Blake rolls his eyes and crosses his arms.

I'm not sure why he's here if he doesn't want to be.

"I can do both at the same time! Wanna see?" Etta doesn't wait for anyone to answer. Her sneakers light up when she jumps to her feet. An imaginary hopscotch unfolds in front of her as she skips one leg across the gym.

I clap because, for a four-year-old, she has some serious body control.

"Wow, that's impressive, Etta. You should definitely do that!" Summer says.

Etta claps and sends her cornrows in a spin around the back of her neck when she plops back in her spot.

"What about you, Blake?"

"What about me?"

He's refused to sit with the group and is leaning on the wall off to the side of the gym.

"You look like a guy with a lot of talents."

He blows a giant bubble, making a smacking sound when it pops. All he does is stare at her. *Is he always like this?*

"Okay, well... think about it. We'll circle back to you."

He pulls his phone from his pocket as Summer moves on to the boy in the wheelchair.

"Isaac, right?"

"Yeah." He runs his gloved hands over black tires.

"What do you like to do at recess?"

His chin tucks toward his chest. "I like basketball, but I'm not very fast, so I usually look at my basketball card collection and let the other kids play."

Now that he's said something, I spot a stack wedged between his thighs.

"Noah, weren't you saying last week you like Pokémon cards? Maybe the two of you could learn a magic trick or something and use your favorite cards to do it? I bet we could find a YouTube video to learn from."

"Cool!" They exchange a smile.

One of the many adjectives I'd also use to describe Summer. She's beautiful and smart and funny and good at everything she does. These kids have wild imaginations, and she runs with all of their ideas, creating an entire interactive show of everything they're good at. As usual, I'm in awe of her. Barely able to lift my jaw off the ground by the time she says, "Who's ready to make some props?"

Ten minutes later, she's raided the teacher's lounge. How she knew where to find it is a perk of being the principal's ex, I'm sure. I try hard not to think about how much time she's spent in this building with him.

As the fourth and fifth graders, Blake and Isaac are assigned the big jobs. They cut cardboard into playground backdrops like slides and swings and sky. The little ones, Quinn and Etta, color flowers and hopscotch and top hats. Henry and Noah and everyone else use construction paper to make ladybug, wizard, and fairy costumes.

Summer is at the helm of the ship, and I'm assigned the crow's nest. Obligated to look out for anyone who needs help. The irony is not lost on me that she gives me the job where I'm forced to see my least favorite word—help—through a child's eyes. In the light I used to before I made it into something ugly.

"That's grass," Blake mocks.

I look over, and Quinn is coloring the bottom of the backdrop with a purple crayon.

"Are you stupid or something?" he asks, and everyone freezes. No one more than me.

Quinn shrinks in her spot as if his words stung. I know she doesn't know what they mean—not really—but it was his tone and the stunned faces all around us that caused her to react. She knows whatever he said wasn't nice, and she's looking at me for help.

You got an F? Are you stupid?

My hands shake, and my vision blurs. Everyone is staring at me. Waiting for me to do something about this situation. To stand up to this kid and fight for my daughter. And I can't look at him when all I see is Tim from the sixth grade, reducing me to my biggest weakness and flaring my deepest insecurities. I can't look at any of them. I'm desperate to get the hell out of this building. To be anywhere but *here*.

"Blake, this is a talent show to celebrate our differences. We..."

I don't hear the rest of whatever Summer is saying to him because I'm already jogging for the exit in an all-too-familiar escape. Reinforcing a debilitating pattern of self-torture. Sucking in the outside air until my best friend, silence, once again calms me.

25

EVERETT

The parking lot is a stark contrast to the hustle that welcomed us when we got here. In the—almost—hour since we've been inside, every car has left but two.

I've never seen this place so empty, which might be why I hadn't noticed the bright yellow block letters that paint the cement until now. The name *Rogers* stakes claim to the car closest to the building.

Of course he has his own parking spot.

When metal hinges grate behind me, breaking the silence, I'm met face-to-face with the owner of said vehicle.

"Nice vest," I say first.

Brian looks down as if it hadn't crossed his mind he still had it on. "Everyone's trying to use up their PTO days before the end of the school year." He feeds me his lame excuse, pulling at the lining like the lapels of a suit jacket.

"Sounds like something they have a right to do." My response is honest. Something I could have kept to myself maybe, but he's the one who stepped out here when I'm not in the best place for small talk.

Brian folds his arms. A sinister smile slithers across his face. "Having fun pretending?"

My amused gaze drops to his costume. "I'm not the one pretending." Does he really think he's fooling people with this kind crossing guard act?

He strips the vest and tosses it against the closest brick wall, proving me right. He doesn't care about doing good around here. The whole thing is for show. He's a wolf in sheep's clothing.

"This little game of house you're playing with Summer... it won't last, you know."

I've got two guesses where he came up with that. He read the *Celeb* article or saw the three of us walking in here today and assumed. Either way, he's the one who let her go. He has to live with his insecurities over that.

"Why, because yours didn't?"

He rolls his shoulders back and circles me, feeding me his response like a lion stalking their prey, slow until the bite. "No... because she doesn't want to have kids... and judging by the look on your face, you didn't know that."

The only stunned part of my expression is that he never realized she *does*.

He plants his feet in front of me, waiting for me to react. *Good.* I want to look him in the eyes when I say this. "You sure it wasn't that she didn't want to have kids with *you*?"

He barks out a laugh. It comes off a little too strong.

"Keep telling yourself that," he says over his shoulder.

I got under his skin, and he's walking away because of it.

"Stick around long enough and you'll see what I mean," he adds.

I'm counting on it. Because little does he know that Summer already had this conversation, it just wasn't with him.

He swipes the vest off the pavement before he gets blasted by the door of his precious school.

"Watch it," Brian hollers at a kid who barrels out of the building. "No skateboards on school premises."

The kid leans back, front wheels lifting off the ground as the board comes to a stop.

It's a shock he listened after that kind of exit. He tucks his board under his arm, spinning his hat backward.

Blake.

Pain and anger build in equal measure just looking at the back of his head. He walks to the farthest bench from me, sits down, and pulls out his phone.

"Practice is over," he says to the person on the other end of the call he just made. There's a brief pause where he spreads his legs out wide, taking up as much space as he wants. The opposite of how he made Quinn feel minutes ago, shrinking to fit into the insignificant box his label put her in.

"Please, I don't want to walk all that way," he pleads.

We're the only two people out here, and Summer drove. I don't have her keys. Not eavesdropping on this conversation is impossible.

"Come on," he whispers when he pulls his phone away from his mouth. His elbow sinks into his knee as he leans on it, pinching his forehead and temple between his thumb and middle finger.

"Yes, I have my skateboard, but it's... Fine. Got it. Yeah, you too." He hangs up, sighs, and stands.

"Hey," I call out.

I don't have a plan for what I'm going to say, but I'm not letting him leave here without clearing the air. As pissed as I am about his comment, he's a kid who has a lot to learn. I want to make sure it doesn't happen to anyone else.

"Yeah, no skateboards on the premises, I know," he repeats, tucking the board under his arm.

I move closer to him. "That's not what I was going to say."

He waits for me to continue.

"You picked on someone smaller than you in there," I remind him.

A flippant *I'm sorry* follows that statement. "She can color the grass whatever she wants."

"This isn't about what color she chose, Blake. You called her stupid. I know you're the oldest one here, but imagine if you weren't. Pretend you're the youngest one and a bunch of middle school kids embarrassed you in front of everyone. How would that make you feel?"

"I said I was sorry," Blake repeats.

"I'm not the one you need to be apologizing to." Yes, his name-calling dredged up some of my own shit I try to keep buried, but that's not his fault. This is about Quinn.

"I said sorry to her. You weren't in there."

Thank you for the reminder.

"There's a difference between saying it and meaning it. Quinn wants to fit in just as much as you do."

I eye his graffitied skateboard and his backward hat and the wad of bubblegum wedged between his molars. Looking cool matters to him whether he'll admit it or not.

He studies me for a second. Makes me believe my words are sinking in. Then he flips his hat forward, turns, and walks away.

"On the phone... was that your mom?" I stop him.

He glances over his shoulder, the bill of his hat shading his eyes from me. "Kind of nosey, don't you think?"

"I think you sound like a kid who could use a ride. Where do you live?"

"A few miles from here."

I'm inferring based on the limited information I gathered that he has troubles at home. It's no excuse for his behavior, but he deserves someone who will make sure he's okay too. Like I should have done with Quinn.

Were his parents going to let him ride *miles* by himself? In a suburb, *yeah*, I can see it. But this school is touching two of the busiest intersections. Downtown traffic stops for no one. Drivers don't look for pedestrians either. The memory of El strapped to a dozen different tubes keeping her alive invades my thoughts. The odds of this kid making it home are not something I'm willing to risk.

I stall. "You're pretty good on that thing."

Blake smirks, tucking his board closer to his armpit. "You saw me ride two feet."

"Well, I couldn't even make it that far." *That's an understatement.* "Wanna show me a thing or two?" The parking lot is no skate park, but something tells me he doesn't need one to impress me.

His gaze sweeps the school perimeter.

"I won't say anything if you don't."

He shoots me a lopsided grin. "All right." Then he drops the skateboard on its wheels and plants his back foot on the tail, his other foot hanging slightly off the front end. In one swift motion, he leans his weight on his back foot and pops his board in the air. It does a full rotation before he lands on it. I'm intrigued and he hasn't even left the sidewalk yet.

There's a rail touching a ramp for wheelchair access to the bus drop-off lane a few feet away. He rolls over to it. With his hand hanging on to the underside of his board, he jumps up and slides down the metal, shooting off the end and racing in an arc around the concrete lot. He kicks the back end and picks it up, stopping in front of me.

"Impressive. How long have you been skating for?"

"A couple years or something. It's faster to get home that way."

Six cars pile into the pick-up lane. A momentary distraction. By the time I look back at Blake, he's already headed home.

I jog the impressive number of paces he took to catch up to him. "Hold up. Do you ride home a lot?"

He shrugs. "Most days, yeah."

And yet he still called that person for a ride. Something tells me he was hoping he wouldn't have to.

"Does your mom work late or something?"

"My dad does."

"Is that why you did the play?"

"You ask a lot of questions."

I'm just trying to figure this kid out. See if he was forced into being here. Strapping a reason to his behavior. Blaming his actions on resentment rather than bullying. There's no excuse for how he acted. But the first option—indignation—is redeemable in my eyes. I can work with that. His avoidance of my question tells me I'm right.

"I'm kind of nosey like that."

That makes him smile for a second. Then he drops his head to stare at his Vans. "I don't like... being home alone." Vulnerability oozes from that delayed admission. He's about as good at opening up as me.

A blast of chatter bursts through the front doors of the school. Everyone from practice funnels out.

"Come on." I wave him in the opposite direction he's still walking in.

"Why?"

I shuffle backward. "Our ride is here."

I don't wait to see if he follows me. My attention magnetizes to the slumped shoulders of my daughter. She's walking toward the car holding Summer's hand.

She's okay, Summer mouths to me when we make eye contact. This feels anything but. When I get to Quinn, I drop to a squat and squeeze her hands. "I'm so sorry."

Her bottom lip quivers. "Da-eee, stay."

I squeeze my eyes shut. Here I was giving Blake a lecture about how he treated her, and I'm no better. I left her when she needed me.

I brush the hair out of her face. "I know. I'm sorry." *I want to be able to stay for you.*

How do I tell a four-year-old that my own trauma surfaced? That I wasn't going to be able to comfort her until the anxiety attack calmed. She won't understand any of that. All I can do is show her how much she means to me. I wrap my arms around her little body. She melts against my chest, tucking her head under my chin.

"I thought your dad was picking you up early?" Summer asks Blake.

I stand with Quinn in my arms and turn around. Blake dodges eye contact with every parent and kid walking by us who overheard that.

"I—"

"He's riding home with us," I whisper to Summer. "You coming?" I ask Blake.

Without a word, he follows us to Summer's car and climbs into the back seat. After I've buckled Quinn in, she peels the ladybug sticker off my shirt and holds it out to him

"He ya doe!"

"Oh, he gets the lucky sticker now?" I tease.

A hesitant arm reaches for it. He smiles at her. "Cool. Thanks."

She watches him flip his skateboard over and stick it on the veneer artwork sketching the bottom. Then she gives him my favorite closed-lips, you-pleased-me smile. And just like that, she's forgiven him. Why is it never that easy for adults? I ponder that question all forty city blocks it takes to get to the two-story home with navy blue shutters. The driveway is empty. No signs of life in the dark windows either.

"This is it," Blake confirms, shouldering his backpack.

"You good?" I ask, knowing he won't let us stay. Worried how long he'll be alone for.

"Yeah. Thanks again for the sticker, Quinn. I love it."

The best apology if I ever heard one. Maybe he did learn a thing or two. She feeds him another smile.

A gold key glints in the palm of his hand as I watch him round the car. When he summits the final step on his porch, I call out his name through a rolled-down window.

"Yeah?"

"That thing you did on the sidewalk..." I do a little swirl with my pointer finger. "You should do that. For the talent show."

A dimple sinks into his cheek with his tipped-up smile. "It's called a heelflip, Rhett Dawson."

Of course it is. An ego check from a fifth grader. Nothing puts you in your place quite like it.

26

EVERETT

This is by far the worst.

That's the thought running through my head as I add the 312th mistake I've made with Quinn to the open journal in my lap. Sharpie wouldn't make it any more glaring than it already is.

I messed up today. It started when I let the record label's email get to me. I realized that their pressure went beyond having three songs ready and hinges on a successful tour. Something I am seriously doubting I can give them after the school incident.

Every coping strategy I've ever relied on has lost its power, and I'm out of ideas.

Summer offered to read to Quinn at bedtime again, so I came out on the patio to repent for my shortcomings. Also to call the one person who has always offered me advice when I needed it.

"Everett? Is everything all right?" His gravel tone crackles through the speaker when he answers.

I yank the phone from my ear to look at the clock. *The time difference.*

"Dad, hey. Everything's fine. I'm sorry to call so... early? What time is it there?"

"Doesn't matter. Hang on a second," he whispers.

There's a creak, a shuffle, a pause, and a click before he speaks again. "Sorry about that. It's good to hear your voice."

The revelation that we haven't spoken since Quinn's birthday smacks me square in the chest. That was a month ago.

"Yours too. Where are you?"

"In the bathroom."

I chuckle. "I meant in Italy, Dad. What part of Italy?"

"Oh, right." A clear indication that I woke him for this conversation.

They've texted me pictures from Naples, Rome, and Florence since they left the Amalfi Coast. The most I've sent back is a heart. Communication is not my strength when life gets overwhelming. When I moved to Nashville, my parents used to check in with me all the time. They stopped when I got too busy to answer, waiting for me to call them first.

"Well, we made it to Milan yesterday. It's the home of designer purse brands, apparently. I couldn't tell you the names of any of them. Pretty incredible cathedral though."

"Sounds awesome. How's Mom?"

"Had to talk her off a ledge yesterday, but she's good now." A muffled laugh follows his attempt at a joke.

"I'm sorry I haven't called sooner."

I promised them a few days the last time we spoke. She has every right to feel upset over four weeks.

"Taking care of a kid is a lot," he argues.

I appreciate the validation, but it doesn't make me feel any less guilty.

"Speaking of... how's Quinn?"

I pick out shapes in the clouds—a fish, a bear, a tree—to calm me. "She had an evaluation a couple weeks ago and started speech therapy."

A hum slips from his lips. Silent patience follows. My disability may have forced me to excel at lip reading, but being a good listener is a skill I learned from him.

"Can I ask what it was like for you when you found out about my APD?"

It's a question I never thought to pose when I was younger. There are certain things you don't appreciate until you're a parent too.

For ten seconds I think he turned on the bathroom fan. When the whirring stops I realize the sound came from him.

"I started therapy."

Silence—from him—follows that sentence. Surprise follows it for me. Not at the visual of my dad lying flat on a couch talking with a professional about his feelings—he's never been too proud to show vulnerability—but at learning it wasn't my mom on that couch, talking to a professional.

Because it was her who suggested I attend therapy after the concert fallout. She suggested it when Eliza died too.

I wait for him to elaborate before realizing he answered my question already. In as few words as possible, but the meaning behind them is still there—he was struggling and sought help.

"Do you think I could have the number?"

"I'm texting it to you right now. His name is Charlie. I've been seeing him for twenty-five years. Not every therapist is right for everyone, but he's put me back together more times than I can count."

I would have never guessed.

"Thanks. I have a hard time trusting people with this stuff. But I think if I go to someone who already knows about me, I might have an easier time opening up."

No matter my lack of belief in it before, I think this will help me. It's what I need to do.

"He does Zoom calls," my dad adds. "You can speak to him from the privacy of your own home. And he also doesn't pry or push like I plan to about this nanny of yours who's living with you."

I clear my throat. "How did you—"

"Your mom and sister talk over each other when they speak on the phone."

"Just on the phone?"

"Quit dodging the question."

"I suppose you know her name too?"

"What was it... Sutton? Sybil? Sydney?"

"Summer, Dad. Her name is Summer."

"Right."

"I met her at my last concert. She lives... *lived* a few blocks from the house. Her best friend's son is in Quinn's preschool class, and she needed a job."

"And your sister hired her first," he comments.

"How much of this do you already know?"

His tongue clicks while he pretends to think about it. "That's it. Are there any important details I left out?"

Those are the highlights, not the details. If it's specifics he wants...

"She built a box fort in the backyard for Quinn before your sprinklers destroyed it."

"Mom didn't want to burden you with her secret garden," he defends.

"I know."

"What else?"

"She knows my favorite donut. Brings me flowers and pretends they're for Quinn. She made me join the school play and morphed it into a talent show celebrating all the kids' differences. She made up the nanny position in front of Caroline and pushed me to ask for help. She's infuriating and stubborn and beautiful and—" An endless string of adjectives flies out of my mouth. There will never be one word to describe Summer, and there shouldn't be. Layered and nuanced is what drew me to her in the first place. I'll never make her feel like her life was destined to be one thing. Never put her in a box. Not a nanny or a school volunteer or a cat mom or even *mine*. But the reality is that I'm falling for a woman I'm relying on emotionally. I'm afraid if I continue to, a prison is what I'll put her in instead. I won't be any better than Brian.

"I'm scared I need her more than she needs me," I confess to him.

"Well... I obviously haven't met her yet."

I love that he uses the word *yet* as if it's inevitable. I want Summer to be inevitable.

"But from how you've described her, she sounds like the type of girl who wouldn't be there if she didn't want to be. Also, the kind of girl I always imagined for *you*. Ev, only when we're whole can we be there for somebody else."

He's right. It's why I struggled taking care of Quinn on my own. If today taught me anything, I've been pretending to be okay when it's obvious I'm not. There are things I need to work through. I let his words settle into a safe space in my heart.

"Thanks for the number, Dad."

"Thanks for calling, Ev. Night or day," he reminds me.

"I know."

I'm lucky. Knowing he'll answer is something I've never had to doubt.

She's the epitome of devastating next to a golden backdrop—hair a little messy, clothes comfortable. Exactly how I pictured her at night now that she's living here.

Summer has achieved the impossible. Made *here*—Harrison Boulevard and my childhood home—my new favorite place. There's only one thing it's missing.

"Chris Stapleton? Seriously?"

There's a playful flicker in her eyes and a cocky swivel to her hips as she brushes by me in a T-shirt I thought she made up. *Nope.* The smug smirk tells me she knew how much this would affect me.

"We go way back." Her eyes are trained on me as she runs her fingertips over the full blooms of a snowball bush at the edge of the patio.

"Bet he hasn't experienced what Rhett Dawson did last night."

She fights a laugh and sits down in the lounge chair next to mine. "Your mom has impeccable taste."

I track her gaze to the limbs of a tree budding with pink blossoms.

"Her favorite book is *The Secret Garden*. She took her love for it quite literally. Doesn't have any peonies though," I comment.

"So, the woman isn't perfect. There's beauty in flaws."

I don't feel like we're talking about flowers anymore. Especially when her attention abandons the yard to look at me.

"What other wisdom do you have to offer?" *Because I seek advice now, apparently.*

She gathers her hair in a fist and drapes it over one shoulder. "Peonies are usually covered in ants. It helps them fend off other bugs." She looks away and smiles. "Henry taught me that. He has autism and is the smartest person I know."

I wondered. That was a diagnosis my therapists considered

for me before I was old enough to be tested for APD. Sometimes the two have overlapping struggles. I think it's why I like Henry so much. We have things in common I don't share with many people.

"I have a lot to learn from that kid," I say.

"Keep watching *Brave Wilderness* with him, and you'll catch right up."

I scratch the back of my head as if those ants made a nest in my hair. "I'd rather burn in hell."

She snorts.

"Did she go down okay?" I stare beyond the sliding glass door where the baby monitor is perched on the edge of the counter.

"Yeah. But she missed you. Can I ask what happened out there today?"

Shame is the first emotion I feel. Somehow it manages to bring a fresh wave of sadness with it too.

How do I describe a disability to someone who hasn't lived it? Some things you have to experience to know.

It's not like a cold where for two weeks—at most—you deal with the miserable consequences, then life resumes as if you never had it all. There is no break from words processing in a scrambled format. But I try for her, because the way she's looking at me right now, she really wants to understand.

"I've never told anyone I have it. Not my manager, my closest friend, not even El. I've always been embarrassed of it. Tried to hide it. It doesn't mean people are oblivious. When Blake called Quinn stupid today, it brought back all the labels kids used to slap me with. It's the last thing I ever wanted to give her."

Summer reaches for my arm. "You don't know she has it yet. And even if she does, it doesn't mean she got it from you. I read—"

"Wait. You... researched it?"

When? *Why?*

"I wanted to understand."

It's the most intimate thing anyone has ever done for me. Something I've been too afraid to do myself.

"Wh-what did it say?"

"That most of the time, they're unable to identify what caused it. You can't always blame genetics."

All I can do is hum in response.

"It's why you should stop blaming yourself too. You have a right to feel disappointed about the challenges Quinn might face. But the only thing she got from you is her strength. She forgave Blake the second he apologized, and then proceeded to color an entire stretch of cardboard grass purple. And when you saw her sad in the parking lot, it was because we came looking for you and couldn't find you, not because she was upset you didn't stand up for her."

"Oh" is all I manage to say back. I keep drawing parallels between Quinn and me. Unfair comparisons when she's so much younger than I was. I'm also back to dragging Summer down my emotional rabbit hole as I process everything.

"I'm sorry. I keep putting all of this on you."

"You don't think I've leaned on you? You've been there for me too. I've never met someone who listens like you do. It's not a skill all men possess; trust me. I've never felt more heard than when I'm opening up to you."

I swivel my hips to a seated position, grip the edge of her lawn chair, and drag it closer.

"You're easy to listen to, Summer." I brush a thumb over her bottom lip, studying it. "Thank you for standing up for her today and for always making sure I'm okay. I never told you this, but you're the reason I didn't fall apart that first night we met. You have a way of calming me down that no one else has. Even knowing you such a short amount of time, you've managed to make me feel like there's more to me than my disability."

If we kept to the pattern of last night, I'd kiss her right now and we'd part ways. I'd collapse on my bed and torture myself that she's two doors down from me. I don't want to do that tonight.

"You want to—"

"Come with me." Summer stands, holding out her hand.

I was going to say *watch a movie*, but I thread my fingers through hers, letting her guide me through the house. I'd rather see what she has in mind.

My pulse jumps when I realize she's aiming for the wide staircase. Thick carpet erases the combined pad of our feet as we ascend them. When we reach the landing, she drags me into the first bedroom on the right.

I've been in here hundreds of times before. With very little furniture, it always felt like the most spacious room in this house. Now that I'm being backed up to the guest bed, it reduces to nothing. My focus entirely centers on the woman who just used her free hand to close the door behind us and is now dragging her fingertips over my wrist. We both stare at the spot she touches.

"Do you trust me?"

I don't have to think about her question before I answer. "Yes."

Two more steps and my knees buckle against the edge of the mattress.

"Close your eyes then," she says, slipping off my glasses. They fall shut, hypnotized by the way she presses her lips against the shell of my ear. There's something sexy about the edge to her voice. A sign she's drunk on the control she's taking.

Sound heightens with the loss of sight—the chirp of a cricket, the hum of a distant vehicle, and the whir of a sound machine down the hall. Noises I've learned to notice and filter in a controlled environment. But the soft inhale of breath that's dancing next to my ear is impossible to miss. It's all I can focus on.

"Keep your hands on the bed," she instructs, and I lean back on my palms. Two padded circles fit over my ears and the world goes quiet. I can't see or hear her with the headphones on. I don't know what she's doing or where she is. The drum of my pulse keeps time in my chest, accelerating the longer I sit here waiting.

Space, time, breath, everything centers on the first place she touches. A featherlight sensation traces down my forehead and around my eyes. Over my cheeks and across my jaw. Goosebumps pebble my skin with her fingertips working in circles on my scalp and down the back of my neck. I'm barely breathing by the time she cups my face.

I've never been on this end of foreplay before. I'm the one who makes the woman fall apart, not the other way around. But that's exactly what she's doing to me, making me fall. The anticipation is agonizing when her hands leave my body.

I normally seek silence, but I want to *hear* her.

Is she laughing?

Panting?

Is all of this driving her as crazy as it is me?

Her touch returns with the pad of her thumb, skating the bridge of my nose and dropping to my parted lips. I finally get to taste her—a hit of salt and something sweet mixing. She smears the wetness from my tongue, coating my top and bottom lips with it. I want to haul her closer and crush that perfect mouth to mine, and it's as if she knows that. As if she's ten steps ahead of every sensation she's creating, because she's gone again before I can do anything.

I'm dragging in air like the ascent of a mountain climb.

Fighting against nothing but patience and arousal. Anticipation peaking and freefalling when her hands finally ghost beneath the hem of my shirt. My skin is kindling, and her touch is the match. A fire coursing through my veins so hot I'm about to combust.

This is *insane*. It's always been about the explosive finish for me. I've never experienced this kind of torture. I'm painfully aware of how vulnerable I feel. How close she is when I've promised not to touch her. It's all I can do not to arch into her hands as they splay and score down my chest. Seeking more. Seeking *her*.

I gladly help her when she fists the back of my shirt and hauls it over my head. A new wave of goosebumps spreads with the cool draft of the room brushing my exposed skin.

I want her. I've wanted her like I've never wanted anyone or anything else before. I know so much of that has nothing to do with her touch. It's been difficult for me to let people in. To get past ever feeling worthy. She—*this*—makes me feel worthy.

"You're amazing," I say—out loud, I think. Every touch is magnified and I'm drowning in it. Her hands slide through my hair again, tugging at the strands and tipping my head back. I can feel the vibration of the groan that accompanies the other sounds she is pulling from my body. Probably a heavy exhale and a choked version of her name when I discover she's removed her shirt. Her bare breasts press against my chest, and I lose control, wrapping my hand around the small of her back. Fusing us impossibly closer.

She runs her tongue from my clavicle up my neck, and it's my turn to thread my fingers in her hair. I might be abiding by her rules of no looking or listening, but I sure as hell am not keeping my hands to myself anymore. She doesn't stop me either. Even when I use them to guide her face closer until our lips touch. She opens for me, invading my mouth with her tongue and my lap with her hips rocking. A new wave of arousal zips up my spine.

I'd be perfectly content kissing her all night. It doesn't need to go any further than this. But the longer our kiss goes on, the more urgent it becomes. She finally draws the headphones off at the same time I open my eyes. We're inches apart, sharing each other's air, when I finally get to read her face. She's more serious than I thought she'd be.

"Everett," she whispers.

"Yeah?"

"There's so much more to you than how you hear. You deserve not to let that hold you back anymore. You're perfect just the way you are."

27

SUMMER

His lips crash against my mouth the moment I'm finished speaking. They're no longer nipping and teasing, they're hungry for more—a confirmation that he must have liked what I said. That I made him feel seen for who he is. I want him to believe it.

He grips me by the waist and spreads me out on the comforter beneath him. Our hands, our hips, everything is fighting to get closer.

A choked "I don't want to stop" flees his mouth.

"Then don't," I say, pushing on the waistband of his sweats. He's hard as stone above me, and all I want him to do is bury me with it.

He props himself up on his elbows, sweeping away the tangled hair that's fallen in front of my eyes. "I don't have anything."

"You don't?" Not that I care. I don't need him to have a condom when I'm already covered in that area. But I expected a famous musician—even one who lost his fiancée nine months ago—to be prepared. To have a cornucopia of women knocking down his door.

"I'm a single dad with no time. I haven't been with anyone." He creates a little more distance between our bodies. "Have you?"

"No," I'm quick to reply. "Not since Brian. And I'm still on the pill."

"Okay."

"Okay. So, can we please stop the torture now?"

"*You're* tortured? I didn't see you in a pair of headphones." His lips close around the shell of my ear.

"You didn't *see* anything," I tease.

"Exactly" is the last thing he says before he's giving me another heady kiss and stripping off every other layer of clothing left between us.

He climbs on top of me and settles between my thighs. I reach for him, dragging his stiff cock exactly where I want it. My hips buck as it passes over my clit.

A throaty chuckle rumbles in his chest. "I knew you didn't need anyone telling you what you want."

He's right; I know exactly what I want. *Him. On his back with me straddling his waist.* And that's exactly what I do. He rolls with me until I'm above him, lifting up on my knees and sinking down on his length.

"I want *this.*" I clench down around him, and he hisses, eyes going to where we're joined.

"Fuck, you're so tight."

A small part of me registers that those words are coming from *Rhett Dawson.* I'm being intimate with a man who has women shimmying their cleavage in his direction every time he walks by them. He could have anyone. But the greater part of me recognizes he's here with *me,* giving *me* this version of himself very few people know. That's what makes this—him— *more.* More than one night with a famous musician. More than all the words he hears and the ones he won't. He'll always be more to me than five weeks.

Tight bands of muscle tense in my thighs from the endless loop of circles he's been drawing with the pad of his finger. Round and round and round until I wind so tight I'm chanting, "Don't stop." I wanted this to last. Wanted to take my time. To know what else draws out a choked version of my name from his mouth besides my bare chest. I'm not ready for this to be over yet, but my body is screaming to let go.

I grip the headboard for support, knowing I'm about to fall apart. Our eyes lock, and then I'm shattering into a million brilliant pieces, a mirror of ecstasy twisting across his face as he watches. His hips pick up speed, his hands gripping my waist as he chases his own release. A guttural moan flees his mouth as he jerks inside of me, and I collapse against his chest.

"That was so much better than watching a movie," he groans.

I pull back slightly. "That was your plan?"

"It wasn't a good one."

His sculpted chest vibrates with our combined laughter.

A man who can admit his flaws... imagine that.

"Is that what you want to do next... watch a movie?" I tease.

"Absolutely not." He spider-monkeys me with strong thighs and crossed ankles.

I plant a kiss on his mouth before pressing up and cupping between my thighs. "Hold that thought. I'll be right back."

Scampering down this hallway is the only time I've ever thought to myself *I'm glad Quinn is asleep.* Teaching a toddler what a naked dash to the bathroom means is not in my nanny job description. Then again, there's nothing about what's happening here that feels like it's a part of a job at all. Especially in the way I savor my flushed reflection in the bathroom mirror after cleaning myself up. When was the last time I felt like this—completely satisfied and unafraid of consequences? Somewhere along the way I think I stopped leading with my heart and let my head do all the decision-making. I can't help the smile that blooms under the pads of my fingers as they feather swollen lips or the one that follows me back into the guest bedroom where I left him waiting for me.

Everett is reclined on his back in the middle of the bed, arm tucked under his head. I swipe my abandoned shirt from the floor on my way in.

"Please tell me you aren't wearing that to bed."

I toss the Chris Stapleton tee at his face and grab the one he didn't get enough of last night, slipping it over my head.

"I don't make promises I can't keep, cowboy. What about you? Are you going to play me those songs now?"

"For those of you who don't know her, this is—"

"Miss Maimy!" Quinn shouts, cutting off Brian's introduction.

Over the last two weeks, every part of my life has slipped into a steady routine: carpool Quinn and Henry to school, manage Emma's client schedule at the law practice, spend my evenings with Everett and Quinn now that his songs are written, and on Mondays after speech therapy, the two of us lead the talent show practice. It's a shock to see anyone else here.

Quinn rushes for the stage where her teacher is waiting with open arms.

"Quinn! I didn't know you would be here!"

"What's going on?" Everett asks as we approach.

Brian faces us, hands folded, shoulders rolled back. "I was just introducing Mrs. Farris's replacement to the group. Miss Amy has agreed to take over the play."

"It's two weeks until the performance," Everett argues.

"And we're doing a talent show," Blake points out.

I'm at a loss for words. Unable to look anywhere but at Brian.

Irritation plasters his face as he stares at me. "What talent show?"

"Isaac and Noah are doing a magic trick!" Etta claps.

"And Henry's bringing his bearded dragon!" Noah volunteers.

A muscle in Brian's jaw flexes. "Summer, can I speak to you in the hall for a second?"

Everett steps in between us. "I don't think that will be necessary."

Brian folds his arms. "I recall informing both of you week one that I would be finding someone else to help. This shouldn't come as a surprise."

"And it's been a *month* since then. Summer has taken the lead on this for four weeks, and you're just going to come in here and kick her out?"

"Does this mean we have to go back to the play?" Etta's bottom lip wobbles. "There aren't any fairies in *The Rainbow Fish.*"

Brian's gaze tracks to the heap of props beyond the stage curtain he must have missed. He ignores Etta's question and looks at Everett. "Nobody said anything about kicking Summer out, Mr. Dawson. She can stay if she wants to."

"I'd love to see what you all have been working on," Miss Amy says. Her supportive tone adds another voice to an already overwhelming majority on our side.

No matter what, this isn't a conversation Brian's going to win. He knows we're right. There's no time to start over. Props have been made and parts rehearsed. We need all the practice we can get. Memorizing lines takes weeks. These kids would never be ready in time for the play that was planned before.

I touch Everett's arm. "It's okay. I'd like the opportunity to explain."

"I guess you'll be filling her in on this talent show," Brian grumbles to Everett as he steps away from the group.

Be right back, I mouth to everyone before following Brian into the hallway. I wait until the door closes behind us and we're clear down the hallway out of earshot before I start speaking. "I can explain..."

He whips around. "There's nothing *to* explain. Typical Summer, doing whatever she wants."

"This isn't about me," I argue. "These kids want a voice. They had no say in the play before."

"Yet they still chose to show up. It's voluntary."

"Yes, because they're creative and smart and funny and interesting and they wanted to showcase that. Instead of forcing what that looks like, I let *them* take control. Don't you want that for the students at your school?

Didn't you want that for me? The underlying message of that comment hangs in the air between us.

"It wasn't your place to say yes to this!" he chastises.

"I know. I should have run it by you. But this isn't even about the talent show and you know it. This is about control over me!"

He scoffs. "There is no controlling you. That much is obvious. Now, apparently, you've resorted to making stuff up to look successful too. A law firm, Summer? Nice cover-up."

"Excuse me?"

"According to *Celeb Magazine*, you're nothing but a glorified babysitter."

"You don't know what you're talking about," I say, heading for the gymnasium door. This conversation no longer deserves my time.

He snags my wrist. "Did you wear the red dress for him too?"

I jerk my arm away. "That's none of your business."

A chuckle bubbles up from his chest, dark and diabolical. "You think this one will last any longer than every other job you've failed when you're screwing your boss?"

He doesn't see it coming. One second he's smirking at me and the next I've slapped it off his face. A stinging sensation spreads across my palm as he lifts his hand to cover the red welt it left behind.

"What do you want from me, Brian? *You* left *me*!"

"I want you for *once* to have to work for what you have," he spits, dropping his hand.

My mouth falls open. "You're jealous. That's what our divorce was. You've been strapped to a career you detest for years, and you resent me for not experiencing the same thing. Well, guess what, Brian... you chose this life for yourself. I never asked you to follow in your father's footsteps. I would have supported you through anything you wanted to become."

"Support me with what money, Summer? You were never realistic. We would have been broke if it wasn't for me!"

"I wasn't talking about finances. Heaven forbid we have an emotional connection over a fiscal one. I didn't need the house with the land or a title attached to my name. I would have been happy in a shack if it meant we were passionate about each other and pursuing our dreams."

"Not everyone has parents who give them a choice," he argues. "Some people have to work hard regardless of what they want."

I shake my head. "I'm sorry you felt you had to live up to your parents' standards, but you're an adult who hasn't lived under their roof in years. You don't get to do the same to me by tying my worth to your expectations. I refuse to be trapped in a life that doesn't bring me joy. If you ever loved me at all, you would have wanted that for me too. Instead, you threw me out because you couldn't bear to see me happy in moments you weren't. This was the right decision for us. I can't imagine raising children with someone who doesn't love and respect me."

He blanches.

"I hope you got everything you ever wanted—a stable job and a big old 401k to go with it," I finish.

I'm fuming when I leave him. Struggling to settle the feelings I've pushed down in his presence and the conversation we should have had a long time ago. I found more love and respect in the last two months of my life than I was shown for twelve years in the one I shared with him.

I take three deep breaths before I reenter the gym. Everyone's in full costume and spread across the room. Props are placed and a playground from a magical storybook is what their imaginations created onstage.

It never occurred to me that I'd love this—working with kids—as much as I do. I've never understood how anyone is expected to know what they want to do with their life without trying it first. *This fulfills me* is the thought running through my head as I take in all that those four weeks with these talented kids have accomplished.

"You okay?" Everett asks, leaving Quinn's side. Blake is slowly rolling her around the gym floor on his skateboard.

I should be honest with him that I'm anything but. I can't here, though. "I'm fine."

Everett slides his arms around my waist. It's the first time he's touched me in front of Quinn or anyone else. A declaration that I am, in fact, sleeping with my boss, even if I haven't been nannying as much as I was before he finished his songs. Tears are threatening to surface as I pull away from him. I don't want Brian to be right about me, and I can't fall apart in front of everyone.

"You don't have to pretend you're okay with me. You

deserve to be pissed or hurt. The guy tried to bulldoze all of your hard work."

"He brought Miss Amy in here because he thinks I won't see this through. And he was right to worry. I've walked away before when I didn't love something. But that's not what's happening this time. I can't explain why working with these kids and spending time with Quinn makes me happier than anything else has."

He brushes a thumb across my cheek. "If it makes you happy, Summer, it doesn't have to make sense to anyone else."

This time when he tries to hold me I let him. I hug him back, and I don't let go. Because this is what a relationship is supposed to look like—communicating about difficult things rather than skirting them. Showing up for the other person with understanding and support rather than leaving them.

It's how unconditional love is supposed to feel.

"Will you go on a date with me?"

The sidewalk touching Blake's house shrinks in the rearview mirror, along with his skateboard on the porch steps where he abandoned it before heading inside. A warm breeze funnels through my rolled-down window post talent show practice. If my hair wasn't tied back, I'd miss the fine lines that appear around Everett's eyes in my peripheral view.

He's surprised. After everything that went down with Brian at the school, I can't blame him. My sticky cheeks from drying tears are evidence he thought I'd need the night off.

This request is anything but spontaneous. In two days, Everett is leaving on tour. My time with him and Quinn is rapidly ending. Sulking over my failed marriage is not how I plan to spend one of my last nights with them.

"Going out? Like... dinner, movie, and a goodnight kiss?" he clarifies.

He tracks my gaze, eyes still fixed on the suspended mirror between us. Quinn's swinging her feet in the back seat and smiling at a woman bent backward as she clings to a leash attached to her boisterous yellow Lab.

"More like, dinner, dessert, and a bedtime story with Quinn. Considering I'm your babysitter, I was thinking we'd stay in. And I don't kiss on the first date."

He fights amusement. "We'll see about that."

One of the things I love most about Everett's and my connection is how unorthodox it is. We don't play by the traditional rules I did with Brian. He and I both know where this night will end up—in the same place every night this last week has. I still like to mess with him.

"What did you have in mind then?" He reaches across the center console, toying with the frayed hole in my denim shorts.

"I'm still waiting for you to say yes," I remind him.

I suck in a little breath when the warm pad of his finger comes into contact with my inner thigh.

"Yes, Summer. I'd like to go on a date with you. But I have one request."

I finally pull my eyes from the road to look at him. His have warmed to a hypnotizing shade of liquid gold. "Anything."

"Wear the dress."

29

EVERETT

Quinn twirls, sending tulle billowing around her. I admire her smile through the elongated mirror bolted to the closet door. We spent the last hour raiding every drawer and shelf in this house to pull together a decent tablescape—the one thing Summer put us in charge of for the evening—before heading upstairs to change.

"You look like a princess," I tell her.

"I wuv it!" she exclaims, brushing her hands down the sparkly pink bodice and patting them on the skirt of her dress.

"And how do I look?" I stand from bended knee, straightening the braided leather around my neck. Dark denim, boots, and a sport coat were the best I could pull together from the wardrobe I brought home with me.

"Dood!" Quinn clasps her hands in front of her chest and jumps up and down.

"Good, huh?" I swoop her up, spinning her in my arms.

Let's hope Summer thinks so too.

I admit, I'm nervous. I haven't felt this jittery for a date in a long time. I can't separate how much of those feelings are a result of knowing I get to see Summer in that little black dress again or the conversation we need to have later this evening. She knows that I have two days left here before things will change. We haven't talked about what that means for us yet.

"Ready for dinner?"

"Weh-ee!" Quinn replies.

I can't pass the guest bedroom anymore without a giddy feeling taking over my stomach. It's become my favorite room in this house, and I hate knowing it will sit empty soon.

Quinn bounds down the stairs in front of me. Excited is an understatement. Whenever I imagined taking Summer on our first date, I pictured us at a five-star restaurant on a rooftop terrace, alone. Seeing Quinn light up over an invitation to a fancy dinner at home with the two of us replaced that vision with a better one. Knowing it was Summer's idea to include my daughter solidified the question I plan to ask her after Quinn goes to bed.

"Hey, Google, play 'Today's Top Hits' on Spotify." The device on the windowsill repeats my request, and music streams through the speaker. With the table set, I don't know what else to do to keep busy. Every nerve in my body is a live wire, anticipating Summer's entrance with rapt attention.

"Summa, wook!" Quinn capitalizes on her arrival with a pirouette.

The moment she's visible through the opening to the living room, I can't take my eyes off her. The last time she put on that dress, she was thinking of someone else. Tonight she's wearing it for me.

"You look so beautiful!" Summer gasps, holding Quinn's hand to help her twirl a second time.

"Fank you. I wuv yuh dess." Quinn swishes her palm over the tight black fabric stretched across Summer's stomach.

Fuck, I love your dress too. Now I'm secretly wishing this was the first date I had envisioned for us. It's going to be impossible to remain a gentleman while Quinn is around.

"Thank you!" Summer giggles.

"Tum see! Tum see!" Quinn drags her by the hand toward the table where I'm standing—and still staring—waiting for them. When our eyes meet, we share a heated look that's nothing like a first date glance. Maybe because the comfortability feels nothing like a first *anything* with her.

"Wook!" Quinn exclaims, holding up a gold fork we found in my grandmother's china collection.

"Pretty!" Summer's attention bounces from me to the silverware, back to me, and then to the corner of the pale-blue tablecloth that Quinn's now waving around.

"I love it all! You've outdone yourselves." An orange ember glows in her eyes as she praises our candlestick centerpiece. "Now, who's ready for their cooking lesson?"

Quinn jumps up and down with her hand raised. "Me!"

Summer skirts past me for the Target bag on the island. She parachutes the plastic as a resealable pouch lands with a *plop* on the countertop. "In case you ever run out of cereal."

Quinn squeals at the sight of the Krusteaz label.

"Finally. Someone with good taste in pancake brands." As a middle-aged man, I should probably feel embarrassed that she thinks I need to learn how to make them, but all I feel is appreciation. The only mornings Quinn has had hot breakfast, Summer made it. There's a chance it will all be up to me again soon. I try not to think about that as I slip off my sport coat and roll up the sleeves of my dress shirt. "Where do we start?"

Summer rips open the seal and glances behind me with an entertained smirk.

"With that." She points to a yellow bowl being carried by

the teeth of my resourceful toddler. Quinn's scooting a stool with both hands across the hardwood floor at the same time. We jump apart before she can ram it into one of our ankles, and then she climbs on top of it and dumps her contribution on the counter. "Hew ya doe."

"Never a dull moment around here," I say.

Neither is ten seconds later when Quinn knocks over the bag of mix, coating her hair. Flour-like powder wafts through the air and settles against her scalp like dandruff.

"I can't take you anywhere."

"Sowee."

"Here." Summer releases the clasp on her barrette, sending long golden waves tumbling down her back. She gathers Quinn's curls in a fist, twists them up, and fastens them in her sparkly clip. "There. All better."

"I see?" Quinn feels for the barrette.

I pull out my phone and capture a picture of her new updo.

A gasp flees her mouth when I show her the screen.

"I want you to have it," Summer says and a sudden grunt punches from her lungs as Quinn launches at her waist.

"I think she loves it," Summer whispers to me.

"I think she loves *you*," I whisper back, fighting the urge not to say those same words for myself.

Somewhere in the last week I've been teetering on a ledge I never thought I'd get close to again. Wondering if I let myself fall, whether I'd fly or die. I don't get to wonder right now when I startle from her gasp. The intimacy of the moment snaps as the music jumps five notches with her command. The chorus of "Pink Pony Club" by Chappell Roan belts from the speaker, and Summer drags Quinn by the hand to the middle of the room.

I lean against the counter, taking in the entertaining view of shaking hips as Quinn flips around and shows off something closely resembling a twerk.

"Did she learn that from you?" Summer tips her head back with her laugh, and I snap another picture. I want to remember this moment when I'm missing home on tour.

"How do I know she hasn't learned that from *you*? You're the one spending the most time with her."

"Maybe she has." Summer toes me in the shin and feeds me a smile. Then she's grabbing me by my bolo tie and pulling me into the middle of the kitchen with them. "Now, come dance with us."

It's close to eight o'clock by the time I get Quinn to bed. After pancakes for dinner, a dance party, and a bath, reading books was no longer part of our date. She let out a happy little sigh right before passing out on my shoulder as I carried her upstairs. There was a time not long ago when I hoped for a moment like that. A connection with her like her mom had. Now that I do, I can't imagine leaving her.

"You look incredible tonight," I whisper as I sit beside Summer lounging next to the fireplace and press a kiss to her bare shoulder.

Her fingers slip down the corded leather around my neck and clutch the metal clasp. "You look pretty good yourself."

"Good enough for a first date kiss?"

"I think I can make an exception." She tugs me closer and presses her lips to mine. The hesitancy that once lingered between us is gone now, replaced with urgency whenever we're alone. A promise to sink into each other's touch. A sign that I need to pull back if I still want to get this off my chest.

I tip my forehead against hers. "Wait, I need to talk to you about Quinn."

When I pull back, she's cataloguing my body language. Trying to guess what I'm about to say even before I do.

"I'm scared to leave her. She's been through so much change in the last nine months. I don't want to upend her routine. I don't want her to feel alone."

"Quinn's strong. She'll be okay. And she won't be alone. She'll have Caroline, right?"

"I want her to have *you*. To wake up to you like she's used to. Will you stay with her while I'm gone? At least until Sunday after Caroline's bunco?"

I can tell by the look on her face she imagined tomorrow to be her last day with us. She didn't expect this. Maybe she didn't want it either when the first word out of her mouth isn't yes.

"I don't know if I'm the best choi—"

"I trust you," I cut her off. If this is about what she said at the school earlier, I'm not worried about her failing to show up. She may have walked away from obligations in her past, but she hasn't once done that with us. Summer stays for the people she cares about. She'll stay for Quinn because she loves her. I saw it in her eyes when she gave away her barrette tonight.

It takes a minute for the crease between her eyebrows to soften. "Are you sure?"

"Yes."

"Okay," she says.

A rush of relief follows her answer. *Okay*. Now for the hard part of the conversation. I reach for her hands, as if touching her will make this easier to get out.

"Summer... when I get back we're—"

"I know." She forces a weak smile. "It was always the plan, right? Five weeks and then move back to Nashville?"

"Yes, but—"

"You don't need to worry about me. I'm going to be fine."

After struggling to trust herself, I should be proud of her confidence. Instead, it stings to hear her sound so sure of herself. It reiterates my worst fear where she's concerned: I need her more than she needs me. Vulnerability is still so new to me, but I won't hold back if it means I might lose her.

"*I'm* not going to be fine," I admit. "I can't picture our days without you in them. I don't want to. I want you to come with us."

I'm asking for a lot here—a cross-country move away from the people she cares about, and a life she may not have imagined for herself. It's selfish, I know, but what else am I supposed to do when I can't be the one to stay here. My career won't allow it.

Tears spring to her eyes as she presses a kiss to my mouth. "I can't. But I want you to know that spending time with you and Quinn has been the best job I've ever had. The very best."

Pain twists the muscles in my forehead. "Is that all this was then? A job?" *Because it's meant everything to me.*

"Of course not! That night in your studio when you asked me why I didn't go on the date... it was because I wanted to be here more than anywhere else." She presses her palm to my chest. "But if I were to move with you right now, I'd be back to relying on another man to take care of me. I need to know I can take care of myself first."

"You don't have to live with us," I'm quick to add. "You can have your own place there." It's an empty argument though if it means she's still nannying Quinn. When she said she didn't want to rely on a man, I have a feeling she meant she doesn't want her income coming from me.

"Emma needs me at the law firm for a little while longer. So does my résumé. And Julia is in the middle of her nursing program. She's been so good to me. I owe her this—to stay and help with Henry."

I want so badly to tell her *I'm* the one who needs her. That I want her to be mine. But I promised myself I wouldn't put her in a box. And even now, after I've already decided it's what's best for me, it's hard admitting the truth. That I need time on my own just as much as she does. To start therapy and heal from my past.

When she grips my neck and kisses me again, I let her, even though it wrecks me. My head screams for distance, but my heart wants *her*. Patience is all I have.

"Then I'll wait for you. You go be the badass, independent woman that you are, and I'll wait."

"I'll be dreaming about that day," she says through her tears.

Me too, I think, but it hurts too much to say out loud. All I can do is hold her while a long silence draws out between us.

"It feels unfair that you know something so personal about me," she finally jokes.

A choked laugh tumbles from my lips with that familiar phrase. I know she said it to break the tension, and because I didn't say anything back, so I lean into her lighthearted tone. I ease her against the carpet until her hair is fanning around her shoulders, a smile dancing in those big blue eyes. "You're killing me in this dress, you know that, right?" I trace the neckline with my pointer finger.

"Well..." Her top teeth snag her bottom lip. "You said I should be seen in it."

I shake my head, inching closer to her mouth. Mint and chocolate from the Andes brownies we had after dinner swirl in the breath I pull from her exhale. "I think I said you're about to be seen out of it."

Her eyes heat. "So, see me out of it."

Before my mouth closes over hers the words are right there... on the tip of my tongue... on the edge of that cliff. I jump off and let them consume me.

"I love you, Summer."

Thursday morning comes faster than I hoped it would. I could barely bring myself to leave the bed this morning with Summer in it, let alone stand here on the front steps preparing for the goodbye I've been dreading.

I squat to be eye level with Quinn, grabbing her hands. "I'll be back in a few days, okay?"

Her bottom lip wobbles despite her efforts to be brave, and she nods when I know she wants to cry instead. I wrap her in my arms, letting her cling to my neck as long as she needs to. A wave of emotion surfaces when she pulls away to plant her lips on my forehead.

"Otay."

I stand and hold out Todd's business card to Summer. "I need to turn off my phone tomorrow in preparation for the concert. My best chance of this going well is not to have any distractions. If there's an emergency or you need anything at all, you can call my manager. He'll get the message to me."

Summer slips the card from my fingertips. "I will."

I tug her toward my chest, filling my lungs with the citrusy scent of her hair. "Thank you for taking care of her."

"There's nowhere else I'd rather be," she says.

I take a step back and offer them both a weak smile, and then do what I have to do and turn for the Uber.

I'm ten steps away when Quinn cries out.

"Daddy! Don't doe!"

I freeze, and time stills.

She said my name. All five letters of it, clear as day.

She said my name.

So many seemingly insignificant tries have all stacked up to meet this hard-earned milestone.

I wasn't prepared for the gravity of it. Didn't anticipate the pounding in my chest. The weight it would free. The walls that would tumble in its wake. The space it would unlock. All of it belonging to her.

For the first time I see myself as more than a son, a brother, a friend, a lover. More than an auditory processing disorder or even a country music star. I'm her *dad*, and there's nothing I want more than that.

I turn around to her bottom lip bubbled out, her eyes glassy. She's squeezing Summer's thigh in a tight embrace as if she has to tether herself to something to keep from running to me. The moment I hold out my arms she's clomping over in her rain boots and tumbling into them.

I stroke her hair and squeeze her tight. "Quinn, I'll never leave you. I'll be back, I promise. I love you so much."

Before now she had her mom, and then my parents. She didn't need me. Now I'm leaving a giant portion of my heart here with her. When she loosens her tight grip around my neck, tears form in my own eyes. She lets go and bravely holds Summer's hand.

I stand once more. "Are you sure I'm doing the right thing?"

Summer cups my cheek. "Touch the world with your music, Rhett Dawson. We'll be here waiting for you when you get back."

All I can muster is a nod.

"Wuv you, Daddy."

"I love you too."

This time I give her a quick wave before I turn away so that the tear can slide down my cheek without her seeing it. *I'm doing this for us* is something I find myself repeating for the next hour and a half until we land on Colorado soil. Warm sun, bright lights—the idea of touring again feels so much less like home than it did before.

For the first time in my life, I miss Harrison Boulevard.

30

SUMMER

"How's that cereal?"

Quinn's lost in the opening credits of her show. A soggy swamp of Cheerios float in the bowl in front of her.

"Do you want pancakes?" I offer instead. She ate fine for me after Everett left yesterday, but I don't want her to go to school hungry this morning.

When she ignores my second attempt, her speech therapist's voice bounces around in my head. *It helps to have her looking at you before you begin speaking.*

I grab two new options and tap her on the shoulder.

"Pancakes or oatmeal?" I hold up both boxes.

"I all done." She pushes away from the table, carrying her bunny by the ear to the couch.

Well, this isn't going as planned. My first full day of being entrusted with Quinn while Everett is out of town, and she won't eat anything. I grab a granola bar from the cupboard and stuff it in her backpack for snack time. Tack on ten more minutes of a show and the five it takes her to get from the couch to car at the slow amble she is walking and I'm even more concerned than when she slept in.

"Are you okay?" I ask.

She nods. With flushed cheeks and slightly red eyes, I think she's about to cry. She missed him at bedtime. Cried herself to sleep, actually. After getting used to having her dad around, maybe she misses him. I can't blame her. I miss him too.

"There's a snack in your backpack," I tell her as I walk Quinn and Henry to their classroom.

"Otay," Quinn replies.

"See you after school, okay?"

I can't count the number of times I've said the word *okay* this morning. Nothing feels okay. But maybe it's me and the pressure my nerves are causing. Another rung on the dependable ladder I'm desperate to conquer. Even Quinn's leg hug and Henry's thumbs-up were more of a confidence boost of an average morning than the one I'm attempting to give myself on my commute to Ford Law. *Just an average morning. No emergency.*

Everett's event is tonight. The last thing I want to do is derail the concert he's worked so hard for. I'm still deep in deliberation of whether or not to call him when a voice pulls me from my thoughts.

"Is it true you're sleeping with Rhett Dawson?"

The doors of the elevator sail back open as Tara and Jasmine shove their way through them. Every morning for the last two weeks they've beat me to work. On opposite sides of the building, we rarely cross paths during the day. I select the fifth-floor button again and the doors zip shut. I'm not in the mood for their judgement or drama.

"Yes, Jasmine. Would you like to know his dick size too?"

That shuts her right up. A charged silence shadows us to our top floor destination until we part ways.

Emma's the one who greets me today with a piping cup of creamer-loaded coffee. She knows me so well.

"The gossip train has landed," I warn with an eye roll.

"Let's get busy then." Emma hands me a stack of new case files and disappears into her office.

Aside from the usual sorting documents and relaying messages about upcoming cases, my work hours are spent contemplating what's next for me. I've been stockpiling the money I've made knowing the day I'd need my own place was fast approaching. Just because I'm fiscally prepared doesn't mean I'm emotionally ready. The thought of a permanent move for all of us has a crater the size of Mars forming in my heart.

Normally work is a great distraction. Not with Everett out of town. I refuse to be late picking Quinn up from school and exit at a prompt 3:10 with Emma following me to the elevator bank.

"Look at you leaving before nine o'clock at night." I nudge her as the doors slide wide.

A bald gentleman sporting an expensive-looking gold watch and a tailored suit stands in the opening. He lifts his gaze from the phone clutched in his palm. "Hi, Emma."

Emma acknowledges him with a nod. "Mr. Ford."

Her formal greeting surprises me. Emma has mentioned she's almost made partner. I assumed that meant these two were on fairly even playing fields.

His eyes bounce from her to me. He does a sweep of my body, stopping at the rhinestone cowgirl boots manacled to my feet.

"Who's this?"

"This is my new assistant, Summer Rogers. Summer, this is Jason Ford, partner of the firm."

His lips press into a fine line as we exchange a stiff handshake. "Welcome to Ford Law."

It strikes me as odd that I've worked in his practice for over a month, and we haven't met yet. Probably a good thing, considering the disdainful way he's appraising my footwear, he's making his disapproval of Emma's hiring decision clear.

"Are you both headed out for the day?" He covers the slat, stopping the doors from closing as we trade him spots.

"Yes. Work-life balance," Emma responds.

A low rumble of amusement follows his smirk like he doesn't believe she's capable of that. "See you tomorrow then."

He disappears down the right hallway, and I stare after him. Emma leans across me, punching the bottom elevator button. The button for the ground floor illuminates as the doors snap me back to reality.

"He seems—" *Judgmental.*

I could balance a teacup on Emma's poised shoulders, so I decide not to comment.

"You know what, never mind. If you're looking for a Friday night recommendation, *Tell Me Lies* on Hulu and popcorn for dinner are a go-to." That's the one thing I do miss—my Friday nights with Jules. Something I'll be able to resume when Everett and Quinn move. A bright spot I'll hang on to on the hard days I know are ahead of me.

She relaxes. A smile curls the corners of her mouth. "That actually sounds perfect! What are you up to this evening?"

"I've got Quinn while Everett's at his Denver show. I'm going to let her pick."

A *ding* precedes our exit on the bottom floor.

"You'll make the best mom, Summer," she says, stepping out of the elevator while I stare at her, stunned by her compliment.

I don't know what she means by that. I'll make the best mom in general or for Quinn? I'm processing and overanalyzing when she notices that the only sound bouncing off the lobby tile are her stilettos. She looks over her shoulder and chuckles. "Are you coming?"

"Yeah!" I scurry toward her, grateful I gave up on heels after my first day. The blisters and toe rubbing weren't worth it.

Emma is the first one out the door, greeting someone on the other side. "Can I help you?"

I glance to my right to see who she's talking to. My ex-husband was the last person on the list of potential people I pictured.

"What are you doing here?" I demand.

"I came to talk to you," he says, stepping around Emma.

I fold my arms. "I think we said everything there was left to say the last time we spoke."

A hand rests on my shoulder—a gesture of support. I've told Emma I'm divorced before. Considering I don't ward off men at work on a frequent basis, I'm sure she'll put the two together. "I'll see you on Monday" is how I tell her I'm fine. She nods and walks to her car.

"So, you *do* work at a law firm," he continues.

"I told you I did. You're the one who chose not to believe me."

"Well, how am I supposed to believe a woman who's never worked the same job more than two months in a row?"

I'm *so* tired of my job history being the only topic we ever discuss. He shouldn't *care* anymore. As soon as he accepts that, the better off we'll both be.

He happens to be blocking the side of the parking lot my car is on—probably on purpose—so I have to brush into his shoulder to get by him. "I don't have time for this. I'm late to pick up Quinn and Henry."

"Her grandmother already picked her up earlier this afternoon," he says to my back.

I stop and turn around. "What are you talking about?"

Outside of their Sunday routine at the country club, Everett never mentioned Caroline being involved while he's out of town. I must be failing at hiding my confusion based on his malevolent smile.

"Quinn came down to the office sick, and the nurse tried to call her dad. When he didn't answer, she called the emergency contact we have on file in her records."

The skipping breakfast, the slow to move, the pink cheeks and bloodshot eyes. Quinn wasn't missing her dad this morning; *she's sick.* That's something I should have realized. I should have never sent her to school. This is all my fault.

"I need to go!" I sprint to my car.

Brian beats me there, pressing on the door with his palm before I can get it open.

"What are you doing?"

"How long does he plan to keep his secret for?"

"What?" I say, but there's only one secret Everett has, and Brian can't possibly know what that is unless... "You read her evaluation records."

The blood in my veins turns to ice. *He knows.* When he looked up Quinn's emergency contact he must have read her entire file. It's written all over his face.

"Those were confidential! You had no right—"

"I have *every* right to know about the students attending my school."

It's my turn to press in closer to him. If he wants to have this conversation chest to chest like two gorillas, he picked the right contender.

"Did you come here to provoke me about Everett?" The red dress comment, the jab about him being my boss the last time we talked... "You can't stand to see me move on with someone else, can you?"

"*Psh.*" He blows out a smug breath. "You think I'm jealous of a disabled guy?"

Anger boils like hot acid to the surface of my skin. It takes a true coward to insult someone behind their back. I know Everett doesn't need me to defend him, but I can't help it. I'm protective because... *I love him.*

"Don't you *ever* say that about someone again. You lead a school with a special education program. You should be ashamed of yourself! Not only is Everett smart and talented but he's supportive of me and a better partner than you ever were."

Brian scowls as he starts to walk away. "We'll let the world decide once they know the truth."

I straighten. "Is that a threat?"

Would he take something like that to the tabloids?

The answer to my question is written all over his face. A version of him far gone from the guy I once married.

"I don't know who you are anymore," I whisper.

He used to hold open every door I walked through. Planned FaceTime calls when he could tell I was missing my parents. Brought home all three flavors of ice cream when I couldn't choose one. He used to be thoughtful and charming, but his actions are proving he's capable of ruining every good moment we've ever shared.

Right now, my priority is Quinn. I need to get to the school. He could be lying about her getting picked up. She could still be waiting for me, and this was his plan all along—to make me late and look bad to Everett or Caroline. To look like the flaky fool he chose to divorce instead of the confident woman who fights for the people she loves. Well, to hell with that.

I jump in the front seat and slam the door in his face. Luckily I don't pass any cops on the way to the school pushing fifteen over the speed limit. I'm breathless by the time I'm crossing the parking lot. Hopeless by the time I'm facing Quinn's teacher.

"Summer, hi!"

I grab Henry's hand. "Where's Quinn?"

"Oh, I'm sorry, I thought you knew... her grandmother picked her up earlier today. Poor thing could barely keep her head off the table."

My heart plummets. "Miss Amy, I'm... I'm so sorry. I should have known she was sick. I should have never sent her to school and—"

She places her hand on my arm. "Do you know how many times I dropped my kid off and got that phone call? It happens to everyone." *Even moms* is what she's trying to convey. Even moms could send their child to school sick. But moms would also be the emergency contact, and I'm not either of those things.

"Thank you," I say back. In five seconds flat an entire plan arranges itself in my brain, and it starts here. "Miss Amy, I might not be able to make it to the talent show practice on Monday. Would you run through everyone's parts onstage if I'm not there? It's our last rehearsal before the program next weekend, and I want them to feel confident."

A nervous giggle escapes her lips. "I won't be nearly as good at it as you are, but of course! Is everything okay?"

I give her a shaky nod because I *hope* it is. "Thank you."

We lose eye contact when she waves at the next guardian. I try to make conversation with Henry on the way to the car, but my mind is already spinning a web ten paces in front of me. Mapping out what to do next, where to go, who to call. I don't have to scroll very far into my contacts for the next person on that list. I text Julia once we make it to the car, but by the time I'm dropping Henry off at home it's Jake who greets us.

"Hey. Julia couldn't get out of class."

"Thanks for coming," I say.

"Hi, Henry." They exchange a—awkward by Jake, normal by Henry—greeting with their eyes. No high fives, hugs, or handshakes. At least he knows his son doesn't like to be touched.

"Thanks for giving me the opportunity," he says before I wave goodbye to both of them. I know Julia has struggled to give Jake much of a chance lately, but maybe he wants to be a bigger part of Henry's life now. I don't wait to make sure they make it in okay. Based on the morning Jake let himself in the front door, Julia has given him a key.

Evidence of Everett's absence hits me the second I follow the empty median that centers Harrison Boulevard. Reporters no longer camp in the middle of the street with him gone.

Trapped butterflies take flight in my stomach at the first sign of Caroline's Land Rover in the driveway. She could have taken Quinn to her own house after picking her up from school, but my instincts told me she would bring her here to the comfort of her bed. For the first time in a long time, I trusted myself, and I was right.

I waltz through the towering front door like I own the place and cause the semi-circular transom window above it to rattle when it closes. A savory aroma of herbs and broth wafts down the hallway where Caroline stands, trapping me in her stare. Blocked by wainscoted walls, I can't see where Quinn is resting.

"Is she okay?" I ask.

In the few interactions Caroline and I have shared, she's tried to ignore me or put me in my place. The current shrewd look tells me this one will be the latter.

"She's sleeping."

I nod. "Caroline, I—"

"She shouldn't have gone to school," she barks.

"I know; I'm sor—"

"She shouldn't have been left behind for another concert either."

She's upset and blaming both of us. Frustrated over how this situation transpired. It's obvious she believes this all could have been avoided with better decision-making. I admire that she wants what's best for Quinn, but I need her to see that Everett does too. I wait until it's clear she's gotten everything off her chest before defending him.

"He's trying to support her in the best way he knows how."

If she would have witnessed the turmoil he faced leaving Quinn, I'm confident she'd understand that salvaging his career isn't a selfish pursuit. Maybe it was before he lost Eliza, but not anymore.

"He's not perfect," she says as if I have the naive notion that he is. I'm not some girl swept away in the fantasy of dating a famous musician. But at this point, Caroline doesn't know my intentions. In fact, she knows very little about me if she assumes I'm looking for perfection.

"Have you ever made a mistake?" I ask her. It doesn't faze me when she remains silent. It was more of a rhetorical question anyway. "I've made my fair share of them. I was married for twelve years before I met Everett. My ex and I had our good times, but we both avoided self-reflection. We struggled to communicate and grew apart because of it. Everett is a man who keeps a list of every mistake he's ever made as Quinn's dad in his bedside drawer. That list is long, but he writes them down, so he doesn't repeat them. I think it's honorable when a person intro-spects like that. Recognizes the ways they could improve before placing blame on anyone else. So, you're right; Everett isn't a perfect person. But he's perfect for Quinn because he wakes up every day aspiring to be a better parent than the day before. As her grandmother, I think that's all you can hope for."

It wasn't my place to tell her about Everett's private journal. Especially when he still doesn't know I even read it. I just wanted her to see a side of him she doesn't get to. She has yet to say anything, but that's probably for the best. I have somewhere I need to be, and I shouldn't prolong this conversation more than I need to.

"I don't want to leave Quinn, but something urgent came up since I left work. There's a chance I need to jump on a flight and might be out of town for a day or two. Can she stay with you?"

I'm not going anywhere is written on her face.

"Right. Thanks. I'll just"—I point toward the staircase—"grab my things."

Before I reach the dark-stained handrail, I turn around.

"For the record, Caroline, I know I've made a lot of mistakes in my life, but loving Everett and Quinn is not one of them. No matter what, they're the best thing that's ever happened to me."

My time with them has been challenging and beautiful and not nearly long enough, and at the end of the day, it's made up of a million moments she'll never see. But I hope what she has seen conveys the biggest theme of all—they're the place I call home.

31

SUMMER

Come on, come on, come on. Pick up.

There's an erratic bounce to my knee that keeps knocking into the steering wheel while I drive. Why isn't he answering?

I didn't debate calling. In my mind, this constitutes an emergency.

"Hello?" a voice finally shouts through the speaker.

I hold the phone closer to my face. *Why?* Because I'm no longer thinking rationally.

"Todd? It's Summer, Everett's—" Would he want me to say girlfriend? He did tell me he loves me right before he left. Minutes after I told him I wouldn't move with him though. "—nanny," I finish, to be safe.

"Oh, hey, Summer!"

"Hi! Yeah. I was wondering if I could speak to Everett. It's kind of an emergency."

"Sorry, he's in sound check right now. There's a lot of moving parts in tonight's production, and we haven't had a lot of time to rehearse the set. But I could have him call you after the show?"

"NO! I mean, no. That's okay."

Shit. I switch to Plan B with new information.

I stop at the red light and drop the phone back to eye level to type *Delta* into the web browser. Ten seconds later I'm thumbing through flights.

"Actually, could you do me a favor? I need a ticket to tonight's show."

"Refresh it again," Julia says.

I tap the blue *go* button and the information on the page repopulates. The same political updates as before load on the screen, but nothing about Rhett Dawson.

"Again."

I glance at the driver's seat. She's smirking at the line of cars in the departure lane. "What? Something might have popped up in the last three seconds."

"You're not helping my anxiety."

I've told myself at least a dozen different stories on our drive to the airport. The one where Brian shares Everett's private diagnosis with a tabloid is right up there with *What if I'm too late?* and *What if Everett hates me after this?* Both of which I must have muttered out loud because Julia responds.

"He told you he loved you. He won't hate you."

I hope she's right. She's basing all her validation on my distracted rant of the last forty-eight hours while I simultaneously purchased a one-way ticket on a five o'clock flight. Excuse me if I don't hang my hat on the three words the man said long before hearing how my vindictive ex-husband could wreak havoc on his life. I could be too late by the time I get there. I spam the web browser again. Nothing. *Yet.*

Julia parks against the curb, and I hand her one of two envelopes I acquired on my way over to her house. I keep the one for unexpected tips tucked in my purse. Old me would have never stopped at a bank after making this plan. I would have decided with a credit card in hand and left, to hell with the consequences. Now I think about the impact my decisions have on others. I wouldn't be doing this if I had any other way to warn Everett.

"What's this for?"

"For a place to stay when I needed one."

She flips up the flap on the back, exposing the cash inside, and shakes her head. Then she slides it in the side pocket of my bag. "My home is your home. You know that."

I pull it out again and shove it in her glove box.

She rolls her eyes. "If you need a place to stay when you get back—"

I stop her with a hand on her thigh and squeeze. "No matter what, I have enough to get my own place now. But thank you. I couldn't have survived without your support."

She leans across the seat, wrapping her arms around me. "You never needed me. I needed you. That's who you are, Sum. Someone the people you love can count on."

Between the thirty-minute layover for maintenance repairs and Denver traffic to Empower Field at Mile High, I'm cutting it close. I called Everett's manager again, warning him of my arrival time. Blabbing on about surprising my boss thanks to those glasses of wine on the flight instead of the emergent situation I intend to discuss with the guy I love.

Todd doesn't know about Everett's disability. If he did, I

wouldn't be waltzing up to an outdoor stadium in a different state when I could have warned his manager about Brian's tabloid threat over the phone.

Todd meets me at an unmarked service entrance I located from the map he texted. "It's good to see you again."

Winded from my sprint, I pant, "Thanks... for doing... this."

I breeze past him as he leans against the metal door.

"You should know, he doesn't have a lot of time."

"I'll make it quick," I say, keeping up with his swift strides until we reach a white door.

I skip tapping on it and push it open. Everett's dressing room is three times the size of the ones I've seen in the movies. He's turned away from me, reclined in a chair in front of a mirror. I stand there for a moment, admiring the way his shirt stretches tightly across the broad expanse of his shoulders. It's short-sleeved, the temperature so much different than the last time he played a concert.

The room is empty and silent, nothing around to distract him but me as I choke out his name. "Everett?"

He jolts out of his chair and spins around. "Summer? What are you doing here? Where's Quinn?"

"She's okay. She's with Caroline." I leave out the part where she's sick. If seeing me has him this rattled, knowing that information would only serve to worry him more.

He eats up the space between us, grabbing my forearms. "What's going on?"

"I just—" I blow out a breath, wishing he wasn't touching me so I could stuff my hands in the back pockets of my jeans to give them something to do other than shake in his grasp. "I needed to talk to you."

"It couldn't wait? I told you that you could reach me through Todd. You didn't have to fly to another state to do it."

"I know. I wouldn't have if..." I should have prepared something more to say. Getting this out is harder than I imagined. "Todd doesn't know about this though, and it wasn't my place to tell him."

"He doesn't know about *what*?"

"Brian. He..."

"What did he do to you?" He brushes the hair out of my face and examines the forehead it was hiding. My arms, my chest, any exposed skin he can find he checks.

"No. He didn't do anything to me. He... *knows*, Everett. He saw it in Quinn's file at school, and he threatened to tell the tabloids. I didn't know what else to do."

His hands lift to thread through his hair, and he turns his back to me. He marches away so quickly that when I reach for him, my hands touch empty air. I twist them in front of my lap.

Desperation forces me to take a step forward. "I didn't want you to be blindsided if he did anything."

He flips around. "So, you ambushed me yourself right before I'm about to go on stage? Summer, you couldn't have picked a worse time!"

He's pacing now, fists clenched at his sides. I knew there was a chance I'd regret coming here. That I was acting on impulse. I didn't ask Julia's advice this time. I felt confident Everett would want to control this narrative. Now I'm not so sure about any of it.

"You're right. I... I should have waited. I'm—"

A *boom* vibrates through the walls and rattles the door. Everett palms his hat off the counter. He fits it to the crown of his head before looking at me. I can't tell what he's thinking, or if he's going to be okay.

"We'll talk about this after the show. I've gotta go."

I reach for his hand when he brushes by me. Our fingers touch but never tangle. By the time I turn around, I'm whispering to an empty room, "... so sorry."

Denial. Anger. Bargaining. Depression. Acceptance.

I thought I'd experienced every stage of grief.

That was five minutes ago.

Before everything fell apart.

I picture Brian's face stuffed through the sound hole of my guitar. Calluses rubbing off my fingertips with the pressure I'm strumming the strings. Pretending to punch the guy when I had my chance earlier this week.

That bastard threatened her because of me.

Anger and speed—a volatile combination—build in equal measure.

"Take five," Steven says, halfway through the first verse.

Drums, bass guitar, piano all fade from the background.

No. No. No. Why are they stopping?

I lift an index finger, rotating it in an aggressive fashion above my right shoulder. *I got caught up in the moment; I'm fine,* the gesture says.

Prolonged silence follows.

Denial.

"Rh-e-tt." My one-syllable name chops through my IEM in three.

I toggle on the talkback switch of my beltpack to respond. "Play it again!" My music director gets a warning through gritted teeth.

The audience gets a smile. They hear nothing.

Anger.

Millions of dollars in funding. Months boiled down to this moment. I'm not spoiling it on another false entrance.

I cross the stage in confident strides. Make it look intentional when my purpose is to confront Casey whose drumsticks are frozen in his lap. He's thinking the same thing I'm sure every other person in the crowd is—*What is going on right now?*

He knows the drums open this song. He's the one I need to make listen to me.

"Play it again, and I'll give you a solo at the end of the set," I barter.

Casey is cocky. I put up with his ego because he's the most talented drummer I've ever come across. A guy who would jump at the chance to perform in the spotlight for a crowd this size.

Bargaining.

A whisper breaks out and carries in a wave across the U-shaped stadium.

Casey's still staring at me. Challenging me with a look that says he's not going to do this. He doesn't care about a solo. His reputation is already on the line with the spectacle this long pause is causing.

Reality sinks in.

This is it.

This is over.

This is the end of Rhett Dawson.

The pressure in my chest is so tight now there's nowhere

else for it to go but up. Up, up, up. Until it's stinging my lower lash line. Pain choking every last shred of hope I had left.

I'll never do this again.

I wasn't enough.

Depression.

I turn and face the crowd one more time. The rush of euphoria, the sound of their praise, all gone.

My steps slow as I leave Casey's side, weighed down by defeat and loneliness. I don't know where I'm walking. I don't know what to do now.

Before I realize it, I've crossed half the stage. Settled on a barstool that wobbles when I sit. It feels fitting to end this concert in the same place it was supposed to start—under a bright light and a sky full of stars.

I glance to my right. A ways off the stage, I spot Todd. He's clutching his headset, one foot in front of the other like he's waiting for the call from the MD to end this whole thing. I nod at him. *It's okay.*

It's time. I can't hide anymore.

The standing microphone is a few feet from where the stool ended up. I drag it closer. With zero thought or preparation, I do what I should have done a long time ago.

"Twenty-seven years ago, I fell in love with country music. Right about the same time I was diagnosed with an auditory processing disorder. As a child with a disability, I was called every name you can think of—stupid, worthless, insignificant. Unless I was singing, I was struggling. I hid behind my talent and learned to be someone who was liked for the one thing they could do well instead of everything they couldn't. Someone I love recently said: Be yourself and the people who love you will stay, the ones who don't were never meant for you. She tried to make me see my disability in a new light. Teach me that it's okay to be different. I owe all of you an apology. I'm sorry for not being honest. For being afraid to show who I really am. The thought of losing this career I love was not something I wanted to face. But there's a little girl waiting for me at home who deserves a dad who can be proud of who he is. So, no matter what happens tonight, if this is the last song I ever play on a stage, this one's for Summer and Quinn."

I prop my foot on the rung of the stool and seat the waist of the guitar against my thigh. One strum and the soulful chord rings out in the nighttime air. One by one, thousands of flickering dots fill the stadium as the lights dim. A hush spreads as I start to sing.

Used to dream about being somebody else
Changing my name and zip code
Used to worry 'bout everyone finding out
Hiding through a microphone
But the moment we met, I just cared less and less
'Bout keeping everything inside
What kind of harm would it do
If everybody always knew
'Bout the struggles I was trying to hide

It's easy to show the kind of things we share
Like who we love and how much we care
My favorite car and your favorite flowers
You and I, we can talk for hours
But you're never gonna open up
If scars aren't something you're proud of
The thing about sharing hearts the right way
Be yourself and the good ones will stay

I can hear the words getting all jumbled up
    Scared I'm gonna let it all show
    Not making sense in my head or my heart
    When I'm worried somebody will know
    But my time spent with you
    Fills my world with something new
    A sound I can't seem to ignore
    And the louder it gets I listen to it
    Not afraid of showing up anymore

It's easy to show the kind of things we share
    Like who we love and how much we care
    My favorite car and your favorite flowers
    You and I, we can talk for hours
    But you're never gonna open up
    If scars aren't something you're proud of
    The thing about sharing hearts the right way
    Be yourself and the good ones will stay

The final chord wanes as my right hand stills. I stare out at a silent crowd, dusky light illuminating thousands of hands in the air. I don't know who started it or at what point everyone else caught on, but their wrists are waving—an action in American Sign Language for applause.

They care.

Relief. That's what blooms in the space where tension and fear once existed inside of me. I did it. I made it through the song without falling apart.

A few months ago, I wasn't sure I'd ever perform again, let alone like this. It's proof those lyrics aren't some fantasy.

Before this moment, I believed acceptance was coping with the necessary evils of APD. I was wrong.

It's found in facing the great unknown with valor and embracing what comes because of it.

Acceptance.

The next two hours I deliver my best performance yet with the weight off my shoulders. When I give my final wave, it's Todd who's the first to find me offstage.

"Wallace scheduled an emergency meeting. We have a Zoom call with the label in thirty minutes."

"Okay, I'll be right there," I tell him, eyes on Summer. She approaches me slowly, uncertainty warring in her eyes.

"Hi."

"Hi," I reply.

"You were amazing out there." She points to the stage I left before she's back to twisting her hands like she was doing in my dressing room.

What is she thinking? Is there more she has to say? Would she be okay if I reached for her? are all questions I'm ruminating on. "Thanks" is what I actually say.

"I'm sorry if you felt pressured to do that."

I stop thinking and grab her hand, clutching it between my palms and looking deep into her eyes. "I should have done that a long time ago."

This isn't her fault. Brian did me a favor.

"You're meeting with the label? I overheard."

I glance over my shoulder to find Todd giving us space but waiting for me. I don't even try to hide my concern from her over the conversation I'm about to have with them. I have no idea how it will turn out. The show didn't exactly go off without a hitch. "Yeah. I have to go."

This wasn't the lengthy explanation I'd hoped to give, but I plan to give her more time.

"Okay," she says, sounding disappointed.

"I'm staying at the Four Seasons. The spare hotel key is in my jacket pocket in my dressing room. 304. Wait for me?"

She smiles. "Of course. I'll be there. Good luck."

When I lean in to kiss her, I expect it to be tentative. There's tension between us that won't unravel without a deeper conversation. But the longer I linger, the more she starts to melt into me, and the harder it becomes to pull away. It's reassurance for the both of us that we're going to be okay.

"I'll see you soon," I say, before a group of security guards escorts me away from her and out of a discreet service entrance to a black SUV. When I duck inside, Todd is already in the vehicle.

We apologize at the exact same time.

"No, I should have seen it." Todd stares at the roof of the car, shaking his head. "Every time I'd talk to you, and you'd ask me to repeat what I said. The quiet dressing room request. The stage."

"No. Come on, man. You couldn't have known. This is on me. I should have trusted you with the information. I've put everyone through a lot in the last few months. All I can do now is be honest and see where things land."

He barks out a laugh. "That's your big plan with the label? No wonder you hired me."

"I hired you to stand by my side at this meeting as a middleman for my career. But I want you there as my friend. I couldn't have done any part of this without you, and I don't want to start now. Don't give up on me, okay?"

"You think I'd walk away? I'm your biggest advocate. You know that, right?"

I nod.

"Okay, here's what we're going to do. You're going to start by explaining to me what you need from them. And then, you're going to leave the talking part up to me."

I cringe, knowing this request is a lot to ask after already signing a new contract. If I'm going to move forward, I need them to understand my daughter takes priority over my music.

"First, I need to be flown back to Idaho after next Friday's tour date. Quinn has a talent show, and I've agreed to sing with her at it. I imagine the school would be open to having our performance filmed if that sways the label toward good publicity."

He only responds with one question. "Can I come?"

I give him my answer in the form of a smile.

"What else?" he asks.

We spend the rest of the drive prepping a list of important rider requests moving forward. Most of the time, that consists of me explaining why I need what I do. When we're in the silence of the hotel's conference room, Todd launches the video call.

A group of label executives seated at a rectangular table are projected on an empty wall. Wallace, the executive head of the label, starts the conversation. "Gentlemen, thanks for meeting with us on such short notice. Rhett, it's good to have you back."

The positive lilt to his voice is a good start. I try not to roll back my shoulders to appear put together. There's no pretending. The line between Rhett and Everett has merged. I'm an imperfect person who will need all the help I can get moving forward.

"You can call me Everett, and thank you. It's good to be back."

"Listen, Everett, it's about time we address the elephant in the room. We're here to back you as an artist, and I'm sorry if you haven't felt that from the beginning, but we just have one question."

I swallow. "I figured."

"How can we support you?"

Todd and I share a look of surprise before he screen-shares the new rider with the group. I'll either fly or die with this list of demands. But this time, I'll do it as me.

It's past midnight before I make it up to my hotel room. Summer's asleep in the king-sized bed, sprawled out like a starfish in a pair of shorts and a tank top. I don't want to wake her, but I can't stand being away from her another minute either. Not touching her and making sure she's real and still here. I strip down to my boxers and pull the covers over us. She stirs with the dip of the mattress and scrunches into the fetal position. I slip an arm around her waist, spooning her. She lets out a sigh but doesn't wake. My world feels right again.

Fatigue seeps into my limbs but evades my mind. That part of me is racing with thoughts of everything that transpired today.

I did it. After years of hiding and coping and struggling and trying... I accepted it. In front of an arena full of people, I learned that APD doesn't define me.

33

SUMMER

I wake to the stir of Everett's arm leaving my chest.

"I fell asleep," I say, disappointment leaking into that admission.

My intentions were noble—wait for Everett to get back to the room and finish the apology I started—but my anxiety-high must have plummeted post-concert and emotional exhaustion took me under before he got back.

"I didn't want to wake you." The warmth of his breath skitters across the exposed skin on my neck. I didn't fully realize how attached I've grown to that sensation until I began counting how many opportunities I had left to feel it. The final grains of sand in the hourglass of five weeks together. A sudden ache develops at the thought of this being the last time.

With the room cloaked in blackness from the curtains, I have no idea what time it is. I'm going to guess early by the morning wood that is pressed to my backside. Now that I'm more alert, I recognize our legs are also tangled. His hand is splayed on my bare stomach, and fingertips skate across the smooth surface. A shiver passes through me.

"You cold?" He reaches for the covers that we seemed to

have kicked halfway down the bed while sleeping. Despite my bare feet, with the human furnace next to me, I didn't miss them. He drapes the thin sheet over my shoulders anyway before his hand returns to its spot, drawing circles that are scooting dangerously close to the waistband of my pajama shorts.

I lose all reason when his hand dips beneath the thin cotton. Forget all we had to discuss as it travels further south. This isn't why I came here, but I can't expect to carry on a conversation with the back-and-forth glide of his finger. My hips rise off the bed to meet his movements, my grip twisting the edge of a pillowcase, eyes pinching shut. Heat coils exactly where I need it to.

"You're sooo good at this," I draw out, then turn to kiss him. I'm soaking his hand, my pajamas, the sheets, his thigh as he wedges it between my legs. I may be sorry for the panic I caused him last night, but I can't apologize for *this*. For coming here when I'm so glad I did. For stealing more time with him. I wasn't sure I'd get the chance to tell him how I feel. That I'm going to miss him more than I can imagine.

"I'm not ready for this to be over," I say, clinging to his body.

He pauses. Knows what I mean. Confirms it when he rests our foreheads together and grips the back of my neck. "I can't tell you how much I needed to hear you say that."

"It's not going to be easy." *Has he thought about that? What waiting for us will look like?*

Torture is all I can imagine.

"I meant what I said, Summer. I'll wait as long as you need. I'm in this. It's only you for me."

"It's only you for me," I repeat back, losing myself in his kiss, drowning beneath the pressure of my arms pinned above my head. He threads our fingers together before towing his mouth down my neck and dragging his tongue over the inked heart on my chest.

"Fuck, this tattoo is sexy," he says. His voice sounds rough like the scrape of sandpaper. I've never had to explain its meaning to him. Even now, he doesn't ask. A part of me wishes he would. The word in the middle of that heart is all I want to utter.

Stay.

Stay.

Stay.

We're living in a fantasy world, pretending we never have to leave this room. Never have to stop touching and tasting and exploring each other. Memorizing the way we fit together.

"I need you," I beg as he hooks a finger under the thin strap of my tank top. It drops off my shoulder and exposes my right breast. I expect him to linger and watch in the same way he has every other time he's touched a part of my body this morning. Not this time.

Impatient fingers, calloused from years of rubbing against guitar strings, scrape up my sides and tear off my shirt. It flies and falls somewhere on the hotel floor. His boxers get kicked off next, my sleep shorts too. Then there's nothing but perfect stretch as he buries his cock inside me.

"Look at you, taking what you need." He watches proudly as I meet every one of his thrusts. He sweeps the hair that's fallen in front of my eyes so he can get a good look at the picture of pleasure that's undoubtedly painted across my face.

What I needed to see is if everything that transpired in the last twelve hours would be a deal breaker for him. If our conversation would derail everything we built. He said he was okay after the concert, but I'm not sure I believed it yet. Words don't hold a lot of meaning without action, and his actions tell me we're going to be just fine. I believe if we can make it through this—the threat of an ex and his secret exposed—we can make it through anything

In one swift motion, he drags me to the edge of the bed and hooks my legs over his shoulders. He enters me once more. It's everything I need, his hands squeezing my breasts and my own drawing out the aroused state of my clit. Muscle tension builds and builds for several minutes until finally combusting. A volcanic rush surging through my system and melting us both into the mattress. We stay that way, spent, for a long time. Only parting for a minute or two to clean up and return right back to bed.

"I'm glad you came." He sighs.

I'm glad I came too.

When I wake a second time, Everett's shadow flickers in and out of the strip of bathroom light reflected on the opposite wall. I don't mean to eavesdrop, but the room's not huge, and he didn't shut the door.

"Yes, Can I please get a dozen roses? Harrison Boulevard. Thank you."

I lean back, tucking my legs to my chest. He approaches the bed in my favorite glasses with his hand tethered behind his back.

"What are you up to?"

He plops on the mattress next to me, holding out the largest bag of candied pecans one can buy at a concert. "They're not peonies, but I had to work with what I had."

"Mmm... is this the kind of thank-you a woman can expect after sleeping with you?"

He scrunches his nose and shakes his head. "Happy Mother's Day, Summer."

I stare at the nuts but envision a calendar. May. Sunday. *Is that what today is?* "But I'm not a..."

He leans in, resting his palm right by my thigh. I can feel the heat of his hand as he brushes our noses together. "You take care of the people around you better than anyone I know. You don't have to be the world's definition of a mom to deserve to be celebrated."

It's late evening when we land in Boise. I texted Caroline our arrival time so she'd know when to expect us home and got a one-word response—*okay*. I've never tried to dissect four letters more in my life.

"She'll get past it." Summer plants a warm hand on my knee as I stare at my phone screen.

Our Uber driver's GPS announces a left turn onto Harrison Boulevard, and my stomach clenches. Managing to come up with something to say on the spot to an arena of strangers feels far less intimidating than the handful of important people I kept my disability from. I wanted to wait to have this conversation. Explain where I was coming from when I could speak to my in-laws in person. It's what my therapist recommended. Now that it's here I'm nervous.

"I know," I reply. I glance out the window, counting the illuminated lampposts that stamp my childhood street. Deep down I believe Caroline won't hate me forever. But I'm disappointed at the notion that we may have taken a step back after the slight progress we've made.

When we pull up to the sidewalk, I'm too busy gathering

luggage and thanking our driver to notice the missing black vehicle in the driveway. Anxious to see Quinn, I blow through the front door and dump our bags in the entryway. I holler her name and turn the corner to find her snuggled up on the couch between the last two people I expected to see.

"Daddy!" Quinn squeals, scooting off the edge of the sofa and sprinting for my open arms.

I catch her, tucking my face in the handful of curls clutched in my palm. The familiar citrusy scent of her detangler slowly dissolves the ache I've been carrying around with her absence. "I missed you so much."

"Me too," Quinn says, letting go and running to Summer.

My mom pulls me in for a hug. "Surprised?"

"So surprised. What about Paris? London? The rest of the summer?"

"We have the rest of our lives to travel. We couldn't miss this talent show we've been hearing so much about," she says, letting go so my dad can take a turn.

"Is there any topic you and Emma don't cover during those phone calls of yours?" I smirk at her over his shoulder.

"Actually, Quinn told Caroline. Caroline told me," she clarifies.

I crane my neck toward the kitchen, then the back patio. "Where are they?"

"They left after dinner. Both were pretty tired. Quinn couldn't keep anything down last night."

"What?" I drop to squat, testing Quinn's forehead. Why does something happen every time I'm away? I relax when the back of my hand is met with an average temperature and a lack of clammy skin. No fever.

"I'm sorry I didn't tell you she was sick. I didn't want you to worry," Summer says.

"I fine," Quinn pipes in before running back to her spot on the couch to finish her *Spidey* episode.

When I stand and face Summer, she's biting her lip and squeezing her thumb joint. Putting herself through another round of self-deprecating silence I experienced in my Denver dressing room. Choosing to leave Quinn to protect me is not something I'm holding against her. I part her hands, clasping our fingers together. "It's okay. Caroline and Wade were here for her."

A hand is thrust between us. "You must be Sybil."

"Adam!" Mom swats his forearm, scolding under her breath.

"Just lightening the mood." He winks. "Nice to finally meet you, Summer."

She laughs. "You too. You have a beautiful yard, Mrs. Dawson."

"Call me Jane," Mom says. "And thank you! Your cat sure likes it."

Summer's eyes dart toward the backyard. Her pupils dilate, entranced by the multi-pane glass windows that stretch along the back of the house. The view is cloaked by the inky night sky, and it's impossible to make out anything but shadows.

"Millie's outside?"

"She's been out there all day, brushing up against the lilies. Good thing her fur is already orange, or she'd have pollen stripes."

Summer drifts toward the door.

My mom covers half her face, cringing as she looks at me. "I'm sorry. Were we not supposed to let her out?"

Summer slips outside.

"You're fine. She was worried Millie wouldn't find her way back if she got out, but that cat was desperate to be outside. Trust me, you saved yourself a shirt," I reassure her.

"Now that sounds like a story. Come sit." Dad pats the spot

next to Quinn on the sofa before kicking up his feet on the ottoman and crossing his ankles. I settle beside him in the corner of the L-shaped couch, my mom on the opposite end.

With the newfound silence, I ask what's been on my mind since I found out Caroline left.

"How did she seem? Caroline, I mean."

Quinn nestles into the crook of my arm when I drape it around her shoulders.

"She seemed like any good mother-in-law would—worried about you."

"Really?" I thought she'd be mad.

"Well, Wade did have to ask her if she was okay at dinner six times because she wasn't talking much," she admits.

I knew it would bother her. It's unlike Caroline not to have a say in everything.

"Do you think I should call her?"

"No." My dad is quick to speak first. "You did the right thing."

"Wade was encouraging her to go on a girls' trip to McCall for the week with her bunco ladies now that we are back to help you. I think she just needs a break. She'll be at the talent show on Saturday. You can talk to her then."

"Yeah. Okay," I say, but really I'm clinging to the advice my new therapist offered me during my emergency first session with him in my hotel bathroom while Summer was still sleeping. When I expressed my fear over Caroline's emotions in this situation. *Let others acknowledge and process their feelings without allowing yourself to carry the weight,* he said. *Their expectations are on them. Your boundaries are on you. You get to decide how much you let them in and what you're willing to share. There's strength in knowing you define your own happiness.*

That reminder helps ease the worries I can't control, and I

hold tight to the little person slumped against my side. In the few minutes since I sat, Quinn has fallen asleep.

"I should get her to—"

"She didn't leave!" Summer bursts through the back door with Millie curled in her arms. "And she likes it here!" Her smile widens as a gust of astonishment and contentment exits her lungs.

"What's not to like?" I look at my parents—the two people who raised me in the house I used to resent. If time and memories can heal those deep-seated wounds, there's no relationship in my life that can't be mended by them too.

Mom jumps to her feet. "You two must be starving. Can we get you something to eat? There's leftover pot roast in the fridge."

"Actually, I'm feeling pretty worn out. But thank you for offering," Summer says.

"And I should get Quinn to bed."

"Of course! I'm sure you're both exhausted. We'll catch up more tomorrow." Mom pulls Dad from the couch, dragging him toward their bedroom.

"Good night," Summer and I say in unison before she beelines for the front door.

"Where are you going?" I scoop Quinn up and stand.

The handle slides out of the top of Summer's carry-on as she tugs on it. "I'm going to head out. I can stay at Julia's..." Her sentence fades away as she studies a spot where the carpet meets the hardwood floor. "Now that I'm thinking about it..." She looks up at me, sighing. "My car is at her house. Is the guest bedroom still available?"

"Summer, my parents aren't under any illusion that we aren't sleeping together. You're staying with me."

It's not up for debate, and thankfully, she doesn't argue. I want her here. Just like I have every other night since she moved in.

After I tuck Quinn in bed and haul our luggage upstairs, I unpack my phone charger, plugging it in behind the rickety nightstand. I'd have missed her message if the device didn't buzz.

> CAROLINE: Thank you for the roses.

Words of encouragement from my dad run through my head. *You did the right thing.*

I let that be enough for now, climbing under the covers and turning off the light.

I hear her before I see her. She's walking Henry through his part, her hair tucked back in a clip. Reminding Isaac where he exits the stage with a ramp. Helping Etta fit her light-up sneakers on.

She's a natural at this.

She moves from one child to the next fixing costumes, reassuring fears, and making everyone smile. I'd spend the entire talent show in the shadows of the audience just to watch her if I could.

"Aren't you performing?"

Caroline's voice startles me. I haven't seen her or heard from her since her text about the Mother's Day flowers last Sunday. Everything about my APD has been swirling social media, and I'm not sure how she's taking it. I know I should have been the one to tell her. I never wanted to add to the list of reasons why she wishes she wasn't tied to me. But now I know I should have trusted her with the truth regardless.

"Uh, yeah. Just taking it in from here. I never get to be in the audience."

"A talented performer never should be," she says.

It's the first time Caroline has ever complimented my career, and I don't know what to do with that.

"Caroline, I—"

"Let me start," she interrupts. "I'm sorry for the way I've handled things since..."

She lets that last part fade away. I don't blame her for struggling to utter the words of El's passing. Most days I keep it tucked inside a box so I don't have to think about it either.

"A part of me envies you." She's staring at the stage as she says it. Avoiding eye contact with me. I never realized it before, but I think struggling to open up is something Caroline and I have in common. "You get to keep the only part of her that I have left."

We watch Quinn pretend to fly in a pair of red construction paper wings. Laughter bubbles up from both of us when she almost trips and says, "Oopsie."

"There's so much of El in her," I say.

"I think she has a lot of you too. She's stubborn, for one."

I snort. I had that coming.

"And thoughtful."

"She also might have my disability," I interject. "I had her tested for speech therapy." Acknowledging it out loud to the one person who saw it even before I did feels utterly devastating all over again.

Caroline grasps my forearm. "She has your *strength*. That will carry her through anything, just like it's done for you."

A vulnerable and shaky *thank you* follows her compliment.

Caroline releases my arm as the raw moment fades, drawing her attention back to the stage where Summer adjusts a central microphone.

"She didn't need to tell me about the journal to know what an exceptional father you are, Everett."

For a moment I'm confused. Wondering if I should ask

Caroline to elaborate. Summer told me they shared a tense conversation before she left, but she didn't say exactly what they discussed. I gather she's referring to *my* journal. The one I've never been very cautious about tucking away. Summer must have seen it open on my nightstand and read it at some point. I wouldn't be mad at her if she did. There's nothing in there everyone doesn't already know about me.

"I couldn't have done the last couple of months without her," I say, my breath catching when Summer scurries across the stage herding kids to one side of it.

"I know."

You either is right on the tip of my tongue.

I shove my hands in my pockets. "The label reinstated my tour. They let me come home between legs of the tour for the talent show, but I'll have to go back. We're leaving tomorrow."

Caroline nods as if she saw this coming, and dread coils in my stomach. I never wanted to take Quinn from her.

"Do you think..." Caroline clasps her hands, fiddling with her thumbs. She studies them as they circle round and round each other. "... Wade and I could come to a couple of your shows?"

Her support is all I've ever wanted.

"Of course. I'll make sure the box office has two tickets on reserve under your name."

"Thanks," she says.

I turn toward her. "But Caroline... I could really use some support with Quinn. She won't want to leave you. I don't want to ask you to pick up your life and move for us, but it would be nice to have you and Wade closer."

She finally looks at me, *really looks at me*, her eyes brimming with emotion I've only seen at a funeral. "We want to be where you both are."

It's exactly what I was hoping to hear.

"I know I live this unconventional lifestyle for a child," I explain. "Especially one needing speech therapy. But I promise I'm getting Quinn the help she needs now, and as she grows, that will continue no matter where we are. I'm going to show her that accepting help is her greatest strength."

"You already are." She looks at Summer—*admires* Summer as the fine lines around her eyes soften.

"I asked her to come with us too," I admit. "She's not ready yet, but I hope one day she will be." I want Caroline to know everything. It's important she understands, no matter how hard it might be to hear.

"Okay, everyone, the show will be starting in five minutes! Please take your seats." Summer's voice echoes through the surround sound.

I take a deep breath. *One, two, three, four, five.*

"That's my cue," I whisper.

Caroline snags my wrist before I can walk away. "In case I never find the right moment to ask you this... why didn't you marry my daughter? You were engaged to her for three years. She wanted to be your wife."

Sometimes you lose someone without a goodbye, and they leave you behind with a heap of regret. I think of all the things I wish I could have said if I had more time. Not a day passes when this isn't at the top of that list.

"I never told El about my disability. I wanted to get there. I *tried* so many times. She deserved someone who could fully open up to her, and I believe one day I would have. I know you probably feel like I moved on quickly with Summer, but I promise you I'll never stop loving El. I miss her so much. I just   "

"Love Summer too," she finishes for me.

I nod.

"Eliza would like her," Caroline says.

It's my turn to look away, because the tears are threatening to fall, and I need to be on the stage in a minute. I don't need to be explaining why I'm crying to everyone else.

There's no timeline for when you're ready to start over after your life has fallen apart. No guidelines for when you're prepared to share it with someone new. For me it happened swiftly, like the eye of a hurricane in a desert storm. Sweeping me away to a place more chaotic but equally vibrant than the one I left. So much of that I owe to Summer. She's made room for El to exist in all of our lives while she filled the gaps of longing and craters of emptiness that I thought would always be a part of Quinn and me.

I squeeze Caroline's hand. "Thanks," I say before I head toward the stage. Ready to step into a life no longer as a solo act. I've got an entire village by my side now. I don't have to do it alone anymore.

"Daddy!" Quinn squeals when she sees me, running into my arms.

I scoop her up and spin her around, careful not to bend her wings.

"You look amazing," I tell her.

"It's ah-most ow tun," Quinn says before letting go and running to catch up with Henry.

"You look amazing too," I say to Summer as she approaches me.

"I mean, it's no concert tee, but there are also no mediocre performers here, so..."

"Funny."

She wraps her arms around my neck. "Hi."

"Hi." I pull back, staring into her eyes. That two-letter word holds so much meaning... I missed you; I need you; I *love* you.

I still haven't wrapped my head around how much we'll be apart starting tomorrow. We spent last Sunday night together before I had to head back to Nashville for the week. While I was gone, Summer signed a six-month lease on an apartment of her own. Julia helped her move into her new place, and my parents watched Quinn.

"You made it," she says, sounding relieved.

"I put it in my rider."

She leans back, arms straightening and linking at the wrists. "I didn't know you could do such a thing."

I kiss her, taking my time to savor it. It's been a long week apart with far too many more ahead than I care to acknowledge.

"Can you put that in your rider too?" she whispers against my lips.

I shake my head. It might not be our time to move in together, but it doesn't mean I can't ask for this. "Won't need to."

"And why is that?"

"I'm hoping my girlfriend will come visit me on tour."

She leans her head to the side. "Your girlfriend, huh? Do people in their thirties still call it that?"

I draw her in by the waist so she's flush against my body. "I sure hope so. I like it."

I want to be calling her more than that, but I can't get ahead of myself. She might not know it yet, but Summer and I are inevitable.

I'm not expecting it when her playful smirk softens to a serious expression.

"I love you, Everett."

Words I've been *waiting* to hear.

"I think I've known it for a while now, but I've been too scared to admit it to myself. In part, because falling for someone in a matter of weeks didn't work out well for me in the past. But mostly, because I knew once I acknowledged my feelings for you, I'd have an even harder time letting you go. I hate the thought of you and Quinn living miles away from me."

"Good," I interrupt.

"That's... good?"

I nod. "We'll hate it too."

She laughs. "You know I'll be there to watch you sing onstage whenever I can. I intend to spend this next chapter, however long it might be, loving you and Quinn every chance I get."

"Damn, I like the sound of that," I say, finally showing her how much her words mean to me with my lips. Maybe a little too intimately with the sound of a throat clearing beside us.

Miss Amy is blushing and doing her best to avert her eyes when we look at her. "I'm sorry to interrupt."

"Everything okay?" Summer asks.

"Not exactly. Henry's freaking out and Blake is nowhere to be found, and I don't know what to do!"

I was so wrapped up in this moment I hadn't asked how I could help.

"I'll find Blake," I tell them both as Summer leaves my side for a hand-flapping Henry who is repeating *I can't do it* over and over again. If there's anyone who can calm him down, it's her.

I don't have to look far. A rhythmic hum of rolling wheels leads me right to Blake. His back is pressed against the brick exterior of the school, the heel of his Vans creating the repetitive motion of a bent, then straightened knee.

"Is everything okay?" I sit beside him.

"Yeah. It's fine."

It's not fine. His phone is trapping his attention in his lap. Even though it's a weekend, I should have never assumed he wouldn't need a ride.

"Come on, Blake. You wouldn't be out here if everything was fine. What's going on?"

There's a rattle to his sigh that suggests he's more hurt than angry. "He said he would be here."

Dammit. I want to make promises for a guy I've never even met. Wishing I could tell Blake his dad is just running late. I want to say that sometimes our parents are trying to do what they think is best for us. Maybe for him that means making it possible for his son to go to this school or own a cool skateboard. The man might believe working and providing is enough to show that he cares. But the truth is, I have no idea if his father meant it when he said he'd be here. All I have to offer is my truth and hope it helps him feel seen.

"Can I tell you a secret that I've never told anyone else before?"

That gets him to look at me.

"Sometimes I resent music. I wish I didn't need to be great at it for people to notice me."

Permission. That's what my words offer as he sends his skateboard sailing across the sidewalk. It tips off the curb, stopping at an angle.

"I want you to know that there are people out there who will show up for you no matter what. Whether you're a great skateboarder with cool shoes or an awesome friend. I'm lucky to know you, Blake."

Seconds later, Quinn proves my point. She runs up to him with Summer trailing behind her and tugs on the sleeve of his black sweatshirt. "Tum on, Bwake. Let's doe!"

"Duty calls," I whisper to him and wink.

"Thanks," I hear him say before he takes Quinn's hand and retrieves his skateboard. A small ray of light bounces off a tiny ladybug sticker on the bottom of his board as they disappear inside the school.

The house lights dim. The buzz of noise settles. A small hand slips into mine.

The final act.

"Are you ready?" I whisper.

She answers with the confident clomp of rain boots as she leads me on the stage, black glitter flakes off and sparkles in a trail from the dots on her wings. She sits on the short stool beside mine, her grin the first thing I see when the stage lights beam. Whoops and whistles draw our attention to the first two rows. Mom and Dad, Caroline and Wade, Emma and Nathan, Julia and Jake, Todd... they're all there. I know Will would have been too had I told him about this. Not spending more time with him is my one regret from the last five weeks.

I look at my little girl as she looks up at me. She hums along as I start to sing.

Little girl, head of curls
  Beneath the big blue sky
  Imagine things and spread your wings
  I know that you will fly

A long long way from home, is where you belong,
  Finding yourself and being strong on your own
  But if you ever missin' home, or feeling alone
  You always have me, together we'll be, family

Little girl, stand and twirl
  On the open stage
  Be free, fly and see
  Alone you are so brave

A long long way from home, is where you belong
  Finding yourself and being strong on your own
  But if you're ever missin' home, or feeling alone
  You'll always have me, forever we'll be
  Together you'll see, family

The crowd erupts in applause, Todd the loudest, as Quinn pretends to fly with her ladybug wings around the stage. She circles my stool and runs into my arms.

Who knew that on a tiny stage, in my childhood school, with my daughter, would be my all-time favorite performance.

36

SUMMER

I'm a total mess by the time Quinn and Everett take a bow. I've gotten to hear parts of their song as Everett wrote it, but this was the first time I've witnessed the full thing. He made her shine up there, and if I didn't already love them, their adorable performance would have done it.

I'm so busy hugging them that I don't see Brian pass us and replace their spot in front of the crowd.

"Thank you everyone for coming to Be the Brave's first talent show. As principal, the play has always been my favorite event of the year. Watching the adept staff and students showcase the heart of this school is an honor."

I bristle at his boast. After his freak-out over the content change and his crude disability comment, I'm having a difficult time trusting he has respect for anyone who performed.

Everett cups my shoulder to get my attention. "I'm going to take Quinn to say hi to everyone."

I cover his hand with my own. "Okay, I'll meet you out there."

He winks at me, and I almost miss it when Brian says,

"While I hope this is the beginning of a new tradition for Be the Brave, it will be the last event I attend as acting principal."

Frozen on the side of the stage, I let his words sink. *He's leaving.*

"I've decided to pursue other opportunities next year. The Board of Directors are in the process of looking for the school's next principal."

A collective gasp followed by murmuring floats through the audience.

"It's been a privilege spending the last several years serving this community. I know whoever comes next will be the perfect fit to carry on the legacy of success this school thrives upon. I'd like to thank the faculty, parents, and students for your support. Rhett Dawson for the special privilege it was to have his talent on our stage. Our very own Miss Amy for stepping in last minute for Mrs. Farris. And for Summer Rogers, who volunteered the last six weeks of her time to make this night the ultimate success it was. Wishing you all a great summer break! Thank you."

Another round of applause breaks out as Brian exits the performance area. A wide swath of amber light blocks his vision of me beyond the curtains. His smile collapses the moment I materialize from the shadows.

"Summer."

"You announced your resignation."

"I think it's about time I moved on from this place."

His tone lacks the same melancholy sentiment he offered the crowd seconds ago. I should have expected none of our conversations to sink in. With an exaggerated huff, I shake my head and turn away.

"Summer, wait."

He respects my space and doesn't touch me this time. The fact that this could be the last conversation we ever have is the only motivation for turning around. I'd rather finish what I intended to do and have nothing left unsaid.

"You were right, okay? I'm jealous of you." He grips the back of his neck, eyes cast to the floor. "I envy the freedom your parents fostered and the lack of fear you have surrounding money. I was taught to believe it's a finite resource that only a stable income can provide. Whenever you walked away from a job, it triggered a form of trauma in me I was never prepared to face. It wasn't fair to put that burden on you, and I'm sorry."

I find myself nodding along. We've uncovered more realizations in our relationships in the last few weeks than we have in years. "We didn't take the time to ask the hard questions," I say. It set us up for failure from the start. "And I don't fault you for needing something different in a partner. I just wish we hadn't wasted so many years stuck in the same pattern of hurting each other before realizing that."

"I know. Me too."

I dip into my pocket, pinching the gold band with the cushion cut diamond between my fingers. "Here," I say, holding it out to him. We both stare at it, the only symbol left of our broken union. I brought it tonight knowing it was my last opportunity to give it back.

"You should keep it. I gave it to you," he says, refusing to take it from me.

But I open his palm and drop the band in the center, releasing myself from everything it tethered me to. "I don't need it anymore."

I don't need *him* anymore.

He seems to get the sentiment. His jaw slackens and his shoulders slump forward. It's funny... Brian was the one who initiated our divorce, but I think he might be the last one to realize its finality. The one who is having the hardest time accepting it.

"I want to find something I'm passionate about. The way you have with helping these kids express themselves. I meant it up there. You did an amazing job with this talent show."

His praise isn't needed in my life anymore. Doesn't mean the compliment doesn't feel good.

"Thank you. What will you do now?"

"I've lined up a few job shadowing opportunities while I'm off for the summer. It feels scary not knowing what comes next, but exciting at the same time."

"I'm happy for you," I tell him. Despite everything, I still want what's best for him. I loved him. In some ways, we're in the same spot, him and I. We both settled down before getting a chance to figure out who we were on our own. What we wanted out of life.

"I'm happy for you too. And I'm sorry," he says one final time.

It's not the apology that brings me peace. It's walking away knowing we both get a second chance at happiness that does.

I know I'm well on my way to that happiness by the found family that's waiting for me in the hallway.

"I have the most kick-ass friend!" Julia shouts when she sees me.

"Ass is a bad word," Henry says.

Julia blushes, and Jake looks at her like he's never been more proud, or turned on.

"Nice one," I tease as Emma hugs me.

I spot Everett shaking the hand of a gentleman in a suit. They're both standing next to a smiling Blake. *His dad came.*

It's all I can focus on until Emma lets go and a broad-shouldered guy reaches for her hand.

"You must be Nathan."

His eyebrows pinch, and he points at me. "I remember you. You were the nanny at the party."

I chuckle. "Something like that. It's nice to meet you."

"You were a natural out there," Everett's dad butts in.

I nudge his shoulder. "Well, I'm no Rhett Dawson."

Everyone chuckles. Even the woman who's taking a step forward and holding out a rectangular package wrapped in brown paper and tied with a cream-colored ribbon toward me. A rare smile warms the apples of Caroline's cheeks.

"This is for you."

She got me a gift?

I'm a little taken aback. The last conversation we shared was mostly one-sided. I haven't even had a chance to thank her for staying with Quinn on my behalf. If anyone should be offering up their gratitude, it should be me.

Julia elbows me when my lingering pause airs on the side of uncomfortable.

"Oh!" I gasp—from the blunt force to my ribcage or embarrassment, I'm not sure which. "Thank you!" I collect the box from her outstretched hand.

Quinn tugs on the hem of my sarong skirt. "Help you?"

"Sure." I hand her the present, and she unwraps it in less than twenty seconds. Julia gathers the discarded scraps of wrapping paper from the linoleum floor as Quinn helps pull back on the top of a box. A curtain of tissue paper lifts with the lid, unveiling a leather notebook nested inside. My fingertips trace the gold letters of my first name embossed across the front. "It's beautiful," I whisper.

I can't stop staring at it. Admiring the hand-stitched edging, but mostly the pre-meditated gesture. In the days since I last saw Caroline, she thought of me and cared enough to show it.

"A wise woman once told me it takes an honorable person to self-reflect on the ways they can better themselves. You deserve a fresh start."

We deserve a fresh start, her gesture seems to be saying. I think back to our conversation in the entryway when I told her about how my marriage ended. I know I don't need Caroline's permission to have a place in Everett and Quinn's life or feel worthy enough for them, but I didn't realize how much I wanted her encouragement.

"I love it. Thank you," I say.

"Is it time for my treat now?" Henry asks.

Post-show dessert is what I promised him in my moment of crisis. He was refusing to go onstage, so I did what I had to. I really need to get some better tips from Julia for helping him cope with his nerves.

"How about chocolate chip cookies?" Jane offers. "What do you say we all go back to our house? I think a little going-away party is in order."

A going-away party. I don't love the sound of that.

My goal today was to get so swept up in the talent show that I wouldn't have to think about Everett and Quinn leaving tomorrow. Now that it's over, I don't have the distraction anymore. This might be the hardest gathering I ever attend.

Facing the symmetrical architecture of my childhood home, I take in the pitched roofline littered with leftover leaves from the fall. Black shutters frame the window of my bedroom— the only place I ever used to be me.

Everyone's already gone inside, and I'm preparing myself for the onslaught of noise when I finally follow them.

The wind flutters the tulips tucked up close to where the siding meets the foundation. My mom's hard work is blooming into season. A reminder that it's almost summer and time to leave this place.

"Hey, man," a hesitant voice calls, pausing my walk down memory lane.

Will is unloading groceries from the back end of Delilah's Prius. When I make eye contact with him, he sets the paper sacks on the sidewalk and approaches me.

"Hey." Compunction robs the joy from my voice. It's the first time I've seen him since the day he finished my studio, and the final person on the list of people I owe an explanation to.

"I saw the news." He stops a few feet from me and tucks his hands in his Carhartts.

"I'm sorry I didn't tell you."

"I don't care about that. Honestly, it explains a lot. I just want to make sure you're okay. Are you?"

Looking back, I think I've always known he'd handle it this way. I could trust Will. Seems silly why I didn't tell him in the first place.

"I am now."

"We should go out for a drink and catch up when you're not busy."

"My parents are throwing this farewell thing... Quinn and I are headed back to Nashville tomorrow. Want to come inside?"

He grips the back of his neck. "Oh, uh... I better check in with Delilah first. But I'll try to swing by in a bit. I'd also love to come see you in Nashville if you're ever up for it?"

"Yeah, man. Anytime. Let Delilah know she's invited tonight too."

"I will," he says before turning and walking away.

I glance at Will's house—the place I used to spend a lot of my time growing up—and then look at my own—the one I've spent all of my time in lately.

Harrison Boulevard is different now. A *good* different. Filled with new memories I'll always hold on to. Like the place I parked my car on the cement driveway when I fell for Summer in a little black dress. Or the loft above the garage that Will transformed into my music studio where I nursed my talent back into existence. And the room inside this house that is full of people who helped me navigate every stage of grief I needed to experience on my road to feeling whole again.

I'm leaving. Not for good, but for a while. This time when I think of Harrison Boulevard, I'll only feel love. "Boise's Historic District" is where I found *me... Everett Dawson.*

It'll always be home.

"There you are!" Emma yanks me by a fistful of my shirt into a corner of the dining room the moment I walk through the front door. Judging by her flushed cheeks and quick breaths, something's got her stressed.

"What's wrong?"

Her hand drops to her side. "Well, for one, Caroline is still calling me Emily."

I snort. Good to know I'm not the only one who lets Caroline get under their skin. Which is why I'm more surprised than her by my response. "The woman's done a lot of changing lately. Let's cut her a break."

She swipes a strand of hair out of her face. "Actually, Caroline's the *least* of my concerns right now."

"What's up then?"

In the foot of space she's left herself between the dining room chair and the wall she's blocked me against, Emma's pacing in quick strides and talking with her hands. "I'm taking over for Jason. It's just for the next couple months. He's going out on medical leave for surgery, so he sent over his caseload this morning." She freezes, staring at me.

"Okay?" Am I supposed to be following?

"One of them is Will," she blurts.

"Will? As in, Will Baker? The guy I just talked to outside?"

"What other Will do we know? Yes, Will Baker!"

"Well, what's it about?"

"How the hell am I supposed to know? I haven't met with him yet. All it said was that he wanted to set up a meeting for some legal advice on a family matter."

I scratch the back of my neck, studying the floor.

"What aren't you telling me?" Emma pries.

I'm wondering if this has anything to do with his grand-mother's health concerns. I lift my gaze to hers. "He's been worried about Delilah the last couple of months."

"What?" Her voice cracks.

"He thinks she's sick," I clarify.

"Why didn't you tell me about this?"

"I don't know. I didn't realize you were interested."

"You have to know if I'm interested to say something? He's my friend too!"

"I'm sorry."

She sighs. "I don't want to go into this meeting flat-footed when he clearly didn't want my legal advice. He didn't come to me."

"You can always ask him about it today. I invited him over."

"You did?"

"It's my last night here. I wanted to hang out before I have to leave."

"Right. Yeah. I'm sure it's nothing."

For someone so worked up seconds before, she manages to brush off the conversation for a different subject.

"We haven't gotten a chance to talk since your show. You okay?"

"Yeah." I nod. And for the first time, I mean it. "I finally am."

"Ev, I'm sorry for that day senior year." Her throat bobs with her swallow.

I kind of thought we'd dance around this subject forever at this point. She's referencing prom, and the day I found out graduation was on the line. I was flunking out of English class, and our parents were consumed with helping me. Emma was going through something too, and it was obviously overshadowing that when she yelled in front of the entire prom "It's always about you!" I never realized how much my disability affected her life until that moment.

I shake my head. "Don't worry about it. I know what it's like to want to fit in, Em. Why do you think I never told anyone?"

"I know. But you needed me. I got caught up in my own drama and wasn't there for you."

"It wasn't your job to be there for me. I was the older brother. You were the little sister. And you've been here for me now. Thank you for fixing up my music studio when I needed it."

She blows right past acknowledging it. "If I could go back, I would have done a lot of things differently," she whispers.

So would I. She's not the only one with regrets.

I wrap an arm around her shoulders. "We can do things differently now, starting with dinner. We never had enough of those together."

"That's because you were always hiding in your room with that guitar." She shoots me an exaggerated eye roll.

"Like I said, *differently*." I twist her by the shoulders and lead her into the kitchen where everyone is gathered around the island munching on cookies and sipping drinks.

In the sea of people, I search for Summer. Her hip is tipped against the counter, her foot planted in the crook of her knee, laughing at something Henry just said. *Damn*, she's beautiful when she laughs. I physically ache to be closer to her. Other than the kiss we shared before the talent show, it's been days since I've gotten to touch her. I sneak up behind her and whisper, "You want to go somewhere?"

She scrunches her shoulder to her ear, goosebumps breaking out on her skin.

"Yeah." She already sounds breathless, and it sends my heart on a rollercoaster ride.

I grab her by the hand and lead her out the back door. She

giggles behind me as we climb the steps to the studio. I pull her inside like a teenager sneaking around with his girlfriend at his parents' house and kick the door shut. I thread my fingers in her hair and back her up against it. When she's flush to the wood, I kiss her in the way I wanted to earlier when I had to hold myself back. Every part of me hums with our lips pressed together. She opens for me when my tongue traces the seam. I rake my hands up and down her sides. Tear my mouth away and kiss down the column of her neck.

She pants into the collar of my shirt, "Play me something."

I pause my pursuit. "Our first time alone all week and you want me to play you something?"

Her *yes* comes out sounding broken as I resume the path toward her collarbone.

"What do you want me to play?"

I stop at her tattoo, pressing a kiss over the top of it. I've told her I think it's sexy before, but I never asked her what it means.

She pulls back to study my eyes and picks the song. "Meant to Stay."

Stay. I brush a thumb over that exact word in the center of an inked heart.

I shift all of my weight into the arm that's leaning above her head, wondering why, out of anything she could have chosen, she picked the song I wrote for El. Why she has a tattoo commemorating it on her chest.

"I fell in love with that song before I met you. It gave me hope. That love like that was still possible for me after Brian left. I traveled all the way to your Nashville show to hear it. I obviously never got the chance."

I haven't played it since before El died. I haven't wanted to. But Summer makes me feel like I can do a lot of things I didn't think I could before. She makes me believe a love like that is not only possible, but that it's happening with her.

"Okay."

"Yeah?"

"Yeah," I agree.

The guitar is the only piece of equipment in this brightly lit studio that's been touched in days. It feels like the last time I'll ever play in this space. The end of an era. Better make it memorable.

Summer curls up on the sofa, resting her head on one of the plaid pillows. She tucks her feet beneath my thigh as I prop the guitar on it. A few twists of the tuning pegs and plucks of the strings, and I launch right into it, not giving myself the chance to change my mind.

We didn't carve our names in that old oak tree
    I hadn't met you yet when you were Homecoming Queen
    It wasn't young love sneaking out in the back of my Jeep
    I wasn't looking for love when you said take a seat

But I found it anyway
    I know you were meant to stay
    Until we're old and gray
    I'll love you forever, babe

Everything in my life wasn't all in a row
    Still, you asked me to stay, and I couldn't say no
    One conversation and it started to grow
    I wasn't looking for love at the end of the show

But I found it anyway

I know you're meant to stay
Until we're old and gray
I'll love you forever, babe
'Til my last day

The song I wrote symbolizes time, I realize. That love finds you when you least expect it. All the little moments of life that lead you to the person you're meant to be with. That's what I want with Summer—more time—and I know we'll have it. I believe it with all that I am.

When I look over at her, she's still humming the tune with her eyes closed. The picture of perfection next to me.

It's her voice—the calming, reassuring, happy cadence.

It's always been the sound of Summer that saved me.

EPILOGUE
SUMMER

One year later...

"Mommy! Mommy! Wake up!" Quinn bounces at the foot of the bed.

A groggy memory from a sunny playground two months ago plays in my mind.

Push me higher, Mommy, Quinn squealed as her feet sailed toward the clouds.

Here we go, I said as I pressed against her back and ran under the swing. Smiling on the outside while harboring guilt on the inside over stepping into a role that wasn't mine to fill.

A week later, I found a box in the corner of the garage with a wooden frame inside of it. A picture of Eliza pushing a tiny Quinn on her first swing rested in the center. I stared through the glass at the frozen memory of her mom's smile. I couldn't help but think of all the moments that amazing woman would miss.

Swing rides and first days of school. New friends and first loves. Graduation and a wedding day.

Quinn has so much life yet to live, and my perception of

what that could look like with me in it changed as I admired that photo. The mom looking back at me would want someone to love her daughter through everything that comes next. She'd hope for someone to be there if she couldn't. I know that to be true because that's what mine has done for me. Loved me through a move and a divorce. On my best days and my worst ones too.

It's what I promise to do for the little girl Eliza had to leave behind.

"We're supposed to be letting her sleep in. That's what you do on Mother's Day." Everett's voice pulls me from the memory. He drags Quinn off the comforter as she claws to stay put.

"Come see!" Quinn demands.

Sorry, Everett mouths as I rub the sleep from my eyes.

Our new king-sized mattress dips when I sit up, and a smile stretches across his face with the press of a button. A gentle *hum* signals the retraction of roman shades, allowing light to filter into our bedroom.

He sighs. "That will never get old." One of the many features Everett loves about this house.

We made it—barely—until my six-month lease was up before I gave my notice to Emma and finished out the last leg of Everett's US and England tours with him and Quinn. Wade and Caroline came along too. They've been there for every one of Everett's shows, all of Quinn's speech therapy appointments, and the day I moved my things into this house. They've become like a second set of parents to me now that mine live across the country.

"Okay, I'm coming!" I tell Quinn, draping a robe around my nightgown as she drags me by the hand to the sliding glass door. I stop before I even make it outside, cupping my mouth. Quinn bounds through the opening, spreading her arms out wide at the display of three dozen pink peony plants bunched on the patio.

"I had a little more to work with this year," Everett says, tucking his hands in his sweatpants pockets.

My favorite flowers.

"That's not it!" Quinn stomps her rain boot impatiently. "Come see!"

"Oh, sorry!" I stumble out the door as she tugs me down to her level. She points to a petal that's starting to bud as a dot of red scurries across the blush-colored flower.

"There! See it?"

I do. A tiny ladybug with one black spot on its back.

I believe in signs from the universe. This one came from her mom.

"Ladybugs symbolize love and luck, you know," I say to Quinn, helping hold her hand steady as she tries to encourage tiny legs to climb on her finger.

"Did Henry teach you that?" Everett teases behind me.

I smirk over my shoulder. "Maybe."

A flash of orange dives in front of us and pounces on the flower, sending petals scattering and a pair of wings flying.

"No, Millie! No! No!" Quinn scolds. She sighs as the ladybug soars toward the clouds.

Our happy kitty waltzes back and forth, rubbing against my fuzzy robe and smothering it in fur. "Oh, Millie, what are we going to do with you?"

"She's naughty," Quinn says.

"Hey, good job on that *t* sound. Naughty is a tricky word to say! Especially with a missing top tooth." I nudge her.

She grins, showing off an adorable gap in her smile. Quinn had her one-year evaluation for speech therapy the other day. A test that showed tremendous progress since she first started. We still have several years before any kind of auditory processing evaluation, but I know when it's time, we'll tackle that in the same way we have this—together.

Her growth has been healing for Everett. Where he once used to avoid her sessions, he makes a point to attend them whenever he can now. His desire to learn and be the best communicator as a dad and a significant other has inspired me to do the same. Empowered me to explain why it was important that I have my own career after I moved here.

It's more than wanting to take care of myself. I'm no longer afraid of relying on another man to support me when I know I can do it on my own. This is about needing something for me. Something that provides purpose and meaning in my life outside of the people that I love.

I have an interview next week with the Boys & Girls Club as their Youth Development Associate. I loved my time with Emma at her law firm, but nothing compared to the talent show experience at Be the Brave. This job would be an opportunity to lead a group of youth again. To plan creative activities and encourage their personal growth. I'm excited and hopeful for what this position might look like. Crossing my fingers that they'll overlook the one to two years of experience they were asking for in a candidate with the letter of recommendation I acquired.

I still can't believe that Brian wrote it.

To Whom It May Concern,
I'm writing to wholeheartedly recommend Summer Rogers for the position of Youth Development Associate at your Boys & Girls Club. As the former principal of six years at Be the Brave Elementary, I had the pleasure of having Summer Rogers volunteer as the director of our school's spring play. She stepped in last-minute for a

faculty member who was unable to complete the assignment and went above and beyond in making the production a success for both students and community alike.

In five short weeks, she created an entire interactive talent show to showcase the strengths of the children under her care. She was praised by both parents and staff alike for her positive influence and the self-confidence she developed in the children she worked with. She is enthusiastic, creative, encouraging, talented, and would make an incredible asset to any part of your program.

Hiring her would be the best thing you could do for your youth.

If you have any additional questions, please feel free to contact me. Thank you for your time.

Sincerely,

Brian Rogers

College Admissions Advisor - Boise State University

"Let's plant them!" Quinn says, dragging the closest plastic pot toward the grass. I dismiss the mental distraction of Brian's letter like it's a hat I can shake off.

"Let's do it!" I tighten the crisscrossed lapels of my robe where they gaped open and stand up. My hand meets something in my pocket when I tuck it inside.

I'm busy fishing out an envelope when Everett says, "Why

don't we let Mommy open her last present and get dressed while we start digging some holes."

I lift the flap on the manilla pouch I pulled out and unearth two ticket stubs with barcodes on one end.

"All-American Road Show, backstage pass to... CHRIS STAPLETON?!" I gape at a backward-stepping Everett carrying two peony plants as he winks at me.

"We go way back too, baby."

"We're here!"

The sound of Caroline's voice carries up the staircase as I slick a coat of lip gloss on. She's gotten much better at respecting boundaries now that I've moved in. But she still waltzes through the front door without a knock when she arrives.

"Coming!"

I pull on my rhinestone cowgirl boots and swipe a gift bag off the dresser. Quinn's already dragging her grandparents into the backyard to show off her hard work by the time I make it downstairs.

"What beautiful flowers!" Caroline gushes.

"I know, right? I'm so lucky to have this little gardener here." I knock into Quinn's hip with my knee, but she's too busy stalking a certain ball of orange fur dashing around the backyard.

"I got my eye on you, Millie." Quinn shakes her finger at our cat.

"I take it she's been naughty today," Wade says.

"Always," I joke as I hold out the gold foil, flower-covered bag to Caroline. "Happy Mother's Day."

"You didn't need to get me anything." She looks guilty that she showed up empty-handed.

"It's from Quinn." I wink at her.

Quinn grabs at the tissue paper. "I help you."

"This feels familiar." Caroline chuckles.

"Careful," I say to Quinn as she gets to the fragile part of the gift.

Caroline assists with delicate hands, helping Quinn unfold the edges, revealing the frame on the inside.

"I thought it would look perfect on that entry table you bought on our shopping trip the other day."

Rare emotion brims in Caroline's eyes as she studies the picture of her daughter pushing Quinn on a swing. She kisses the top of Quinn's head before looking at me. "Thank you."

I knew the one I found deserved a spot on Quinn's dresser, but I made a copy of it so Caroline could have one too. No parent should have to lose their child in their lifetime. I can't imagine how this day must feel for her.

The sound of the doorbell startles us all as it echoes through the house.

"I'll get that!" I say, giving Caroline a moment alone with Wade and Quinn to collect herself before Everett gets back. He left to pick up a pizza down the road and should be home any minute.

When I swing the oak door wide, a bouquet of freshly cut pink peonies hides his face.

That's not why my eyes widen though. It's not what I'm staring at.

"What are you *wearing*?" I gasp as Everett shifts the flowers to the side, granting me a full view of his outfit.

"I bought a shirt with your face on it."

A giant, screen-printed outline of my head tipped back in a laugh decorates his chest from a picture he took on our first date.

"I see that."

"Just making sure Chris Stapleton knows who you're going home with tonight."

I chuckle, dragging him across the threshold with a fistful of his new T-shirt. "Come here." Lip gloss smears across his lips when I kiss him.

He picks me up and drapes my legs around his waist. Petals from the flowers he picked in our yard crush against my hip and fall around our feet.

"Careful, Rhett Dawson," I whisper against his mouth. "I just might decide to marry you one day."

"I'm counting on it."

THE END

ALSO BY MEAGAN WILLIAMSON

Remember Me Duet

If I Never Remember

Where the Black Line Ends

THE SOUND OF SUMMER
PLAYLIST

Ease My Mind | Ben Platt
Sun to Me | MGK
Bigger Houses | Dan & Shay
Cowboy Take Me Away | The Chicks
Keep Me Crazy | Sheppard
Dress | Taylor Swift
Shut Up and Dance | Walk the Moon
A Cure for Minds Unwell | Lewis Capaldi
Messy | Lola Young
Love You for a Long Time | Maggie Rogers
Friend | Benson Boone
Landslide | Fleetwood Mac
Somebody Like You | Keith Urban
Growin' Up Raising You | Gabby Barrett
Joy of My Life | Chris Stapleton
Anywhere But Here | Safetysuit

ACKNOWLEDGMENTS

Every book I've written has stretched me in ways I hadn't anticipated. When I sat down to write this story, I didn't realize how much I was working through at the time and how healing of an experience it would be for me.

As a mother of children who have struggled with speech delays, I felt those moments of self doubt and inadequacy that Everett navigates with Quinn throughout this story. There's a lot of unintentional pressure we place on ourselves as parents if our children aren't meeting certain benchmarks or milestones at the same rate as other kids their age. I've learned when I'm feeling the weight of that, it's important to lean on the village around me. That's exactly what this group of people has become—my "writing village."

Britt, you combed through this manuscript with an eye for sensitivity, and I can't think you enough for that. You always transform my words into something better, and your feedback is invaluable.

Cait, thank you for taking on this project and for sharing your grammatical talent with me. Every one of your comments made me smile!

To the graphic design team at Books and Moods, boy did you deliver with this cover. Bookshelves and coffee tables everywhere thank you for these stunning pink peonies. It turned out even better than I dreamt.

My "Creatives Who Cry," you are the best group of writing/reading/therapy gals a girl could ask for. I look forward to our monthly chats on Google Meet.

Kiersten, I'm so glad I sent that Instagram DM after finishing *Safe Harbor*. I had no idea at the time how much you and I would have in common and how quickly we'd become friends. There isn't anyone I'd rather do this writing journey with than you.

Abigail, it was just about a year ago that you told me the story of your hockey moment over Marco Polo—you know the one—and I spouted back this random book idea. Who knew it would land and see the light of day?! It took on a mind of its own and became something slightly different, but the heart of the idea remained. It makes me smile knowing it came from a piece of someone who has become one of my closest friends.

Alyssa, who knew that two people from across the country in very different stages of life could meet on the internet and become fast friends. Thank you for jumping out on a limb with this book and beta reading for the first time. I knew you'd be great at it!

Emelie, Emma Dawson wouldn't be who she is without your law knowledge. Catch me in your DM's as I dive into her story next.

Mom, you've always been my pillar of strength and an example of the best single parent there ever was. I found myself thinking about all of the times that must have been difficult for you while I was growing up while writing a single parent main character, and it's made me appreciate your sacrifices even more than I already do. Love you!

To Nic and my adorable children for putting up with me when I'm mentally somewhere else during the drafting stage and physically behind a desk during the editing one. Your belief in me keeps me going, and I love you with all that I am.

My early ARC readers—Al, Jess, Kinsley, Amanda, Nora—

thanks for being my extra set of eyes on this book, but also, for supporting my work since the very beginning.

And finally, to my readers. *Thank you* for allowing me to do what I love. I wake up every day excited to share these stories and characters with you. I'm always amazed at the number of people they reach, and I know that's because you're passing them along to your family and friends. None of this would be possible without you!

ABOUT THE AUTHOR

MEAGAN WILLIAMSON lives in Meridian, Idaho with her husband and three children. As a former teacher turned romance author, she spends her days writing and dreaming of sharing the kind of love stories that stay with you long after the last page. When she's not chasing small children, you can find her reading, planning the next holiday, or jamming out to country music.

You can find more information about her at www.authormeagan williamson.com